DEATHWISH

Deathwish

JUSTIN RICHMAN

Justin Richman

DEATHWISH

Deathwish
April, 2022
First Printing, 2022

ISBN-979-8-9850601-4-0

Cover Design by Thea Magerand
www.ikaruna.eu/

Dedicated to my son, Declan the Destroyer,
who has broken far more toys than I can count.

| 1 |

"Please state your name for the record."

I looked at the three police officers standing at the other side of the table. "Seriously? When did you guys learn manners? We're saying 'please' now?" The three officers remained motionless, staring blankly at me, waiting for my response. I tilted my head backwards. "Fine. Adam."

"And your last name?" the officer on the right said.

"Come on, guys. I've been here how many times? Eight? Nine?"

"Fifteen," the officer on the left said.

"Okay, *fifteen* times. Do you guys still not understand I don't have a last name?"

"Everyone has a last name," the same officer said.

"I'm like Cher, or Adele, or Madonna. They all basically have one name."

"So you're like a woman with one name?" he sarcastically asked.

I rolled my eyes and shook my head. "Would you have preferred Bono, or Sting, or Prince? How about Slash? Look, for the *fifteenth* time, I moved around a lot as a child. I don't know who my actual parents are. I was adopted and then given up. I was in and out of multiple foster homes until I was old enough to get my own place. You want a last name? How about Daniels? That was the last name of my foster parents when I was eleven. What about Anderson? It was the last name of my foster parents when I was fourteen. And by far the worst name I had was when I was nine—Krochtangle. Try getting through school with that kind of butchered last name. Adam Krochtangle. The kids were really nice to me if you could imagine."

The officer on the right slammed his hands on the table and stared at me. "You've been here fifteen times in just over four months. I don't care about your life story. I care about the safety of the people in Mapleton." Little droplets of spit expelled from his mouth as he yelled at me.

I wiped my face on my sleeve. "Say it, don't spray it."

His face turned a darker shade of red. He leaned in closer, and his voice grew louder. "You are involved in a local fight club. It's an illegal activity. We could throw you in jail for a long time—"

I leaned forward and interrupted his power trip. "No, you can't. First of all, your intimidation tactics don't intimidate me. You remember this is my *fifteenth* visit here, as your fellow officer over there so nicely pointed out earlier. And second, I'm not a part of any fight club. I actually have no idea what you're talking about."

I was telling the truth. This time, at least. I wasn't a part of any fight club. I just fought for money. It wasn't a club, though. Clubs involve badges, members, people sitting around campfires telling stories or singing songs. This was more like a hobby or an activity I took part in. Word had got around that I was indestructible. I'm not exactly sure what it was or how it happened. Something about something weird with my DNA. I can't explain the science crap behind it. Honestly, I don't even understand it. Nor do I care at this point. All I can say is I'm indestructible. I heal incredibly quickly. Almost instantly. So I'm kind of hard to beat in a fight. I never lose. I always get back up after a hit.

Yes, I bleed.

And yes, I still feel pain. But the healing takes the pain away as quickly as it heals me physically.

I first realized I had this ability when I was around five or six. I was riding my bike and my foster parents at the time, the Parkers, were watching me ride up and down their driveway. Then, as most kids do, I fell.

I remember the pain, then looking down at my hand and seeing my fingers bent backwards, obviously broken. But to the Parkers' surprise as they helped me up, my fingers began bending back to normal.

I remember the look on their faces. Imagine you're on a plane and the pilot comes on the speaker and tells you the plane is going down. What's your reaction to hearing that news? Fear? Disbelief? You probably get that *oh my God* expression where your mouth drops and your eyes open wide.

After taking me inside and cleaning the blood off my scraped hands and arms, they each made that face. I looked at them, wondering what the hell was going on. The bones in my fingers had healed and were good as new. They were supposed to bend back to normal immediately after an injury, right? My scrapes were completely healed too, showing no signs of any wounds.

Needless to say, I didn't last long at that household. I scared them off. Something about being a "monster" or "the Devil." That was the end of the Parkers.

There's a local bar I frequent, The Stout House. People started placing bets on these fights. It started when someone picked a fight with me because he thought I was cheating in pool. I was, but that's not the point. Anyway, I won that fight easily. The following day, he came back with a friend. I took them both down. People started placing bets on when I would lose. I was like the Goldberg of fight cl—I mean fight *activity*. "Who's next?"

I started making around $40 per fight off these bets. It soon jumped to $50. Then $100. Word spread and people from other bars started making their way over to The Stout House either to place bets and watch the fights or to participate in the fights themselves. The pot had now jumped up to close to $500 per fight. Because of its popularity, it has unfortunately caused some police attention. They typically show up after the fight has ended and after I've collected my money. They really have nothing on me, because no one ever presses charges. It's become such a popular event at the bar that if I end up getting arrested and can't take part anymore, the person who sold me out will have a lot of angry people after them.

Tonight's pot was worth $613. I won, obviously. I put the cash in my pocket and minutes later, the police showed up. Everyone booed as they placed handcuffs on me and put me in the back of their police cruiser.

I sat in their interrogation room while Lunatic Larry tried his best to intimidate me. I called him that because he flares up and acts like a crazed psycho when I get under his skin, which is quite easy to do.

Larry had a buzz cut with a neatly trimmed beard to match the short hair on his head. He was the guy on the right of the table who slammed his hands down. He had a short fuse. His full name was Larry Jenkinson.

The guy on the left, I called him Obvious O'Brian. His red hair was short with a messy look. He stood a little shorter than Larry. Just under six feet, maybe?

O'Brian liked to state the obvious. For example, a few weeks ago, he arrested me after one of my bar fights. During the interrogation, he pointed out the dried blood on my knuckles and asked if it came from the fight. *No—I was painting a mural of the devil and you caught me red-handed.* I think he may be a rookie. His name was James O'Brian, but he annoyed me. I hate stupid people.

Finally, the quiet guy in the middle; his name was Shane Cranston, the lieutenant of these two knuckleheads and nine other men on the force. He seemed only a little older than me. His hair was short and pushed off to one side. I've seen him wear glasses before, but he didn't currently have them on. He may be a contacts kind of guy.

I liked him, so I didn't have an obnoxious name for him. He's the one who has looked out for me and has always gotten me out of trouble. Unfortunately, he's also usually the one who arrests me. He's always telling me he's "looking out for my best interests" but we agree to disagree about that.

"I oughta come around this table and beat you myself," Lunatic Larry screamed from across the table. "Maybe that'll give you something to think about. Perhaps a loss to end that undefeated streak will surely put a damper on your day, wouldn't it?"

"So you'll want to claim a victory over a guy who's handcuffed to a table, unable to defend himself?" I responded, shrugging my shoulders. "Seems like that would be cheating, wouldn't you think? But, if that's how you want to win." I was just toying with him at this point. I knew I was annoying him.

"I'm going to kill this kid!" he screamed as he tried to leap across the table and grab me. Shane grabbed him and pulled him back.

"Get lost," Shane told Lunatic Larry, and pointed to the door. "Now!"

Larry turned to glare at Shane. I thought he was about to throw a punch at him. Finally, after the short stare down between the two men, Lunatic Larry stormed out of the room, slamming the door shut behind him.

"O'Brian, go calm your partner down. And knock some freakin' sense into him," Shane said.

"Yes, sir," Obvious O'Brian replied, before following Lunatic Larry out of the room.

The door slammed shut again, and I turned to Shane. "I think he's really starting to like me. Do you think I have a shot?"

"What are you doing?" Shane asked me, shaking his head in frustration.

"What do you mean? I thought we had a connection."

"Drop the wise-ass remarks. You know what I mean. Why do you start with him?"

"Because he's an idiot. He thinks he's some tough guy who can boss everyone around. I just like to let him know he can't."

"Well, one of these days, you're going to regret it."

"Thanks for the heads up." I lifted my hands from the table by a few inches, which was all the slack that the cuffs would give me. "Think we can get a move on? I'm pretty sure this is the longest you guys have kept me here. You've got nothing on me, so you have to let me go." I knew they would. I was just trying to make this process go quicker. I also really had to pee.

"Come on." Shane reached across the table and unlocked my handcuffs. I stood up and rubbed my wrists. Those things aren't comfortable to wear for long periods of time.

Shane opened the door to the hallway. Lunatic Larry was sitting on the bench with Obvious O'Brian.

"You're letting him go? Again!" Larry leaped up from his seat, furious.

Shane moved quickly to stand between us. "Jenkinson, sit back down, calm down, and shut up." The two officers shared another glare, and then Lunatic Larry sat back down.

Shane continued to escort me out of the police station. "Go home Adam. Please stop getting yourself into trouble."

"I'm only in trouble because you guys keep arresting me."

"Look, one of these days I may not be around to help you," Shane said. "You're making it harder and harder for me to continue bailing you out. I'm trying to help you. If you don't get your act together, you'll find yourself in jail for a long time—or worse, dead."

"Thanks for the pep talk, *Dad*. I appreciate your concern and all of your help, but this is *my* life. Everyone who said they wanted to help has abandoned me. I'm sure you can understand if I don't believe you either."

"I understand," he said, nodding. He opened the front door to the police station and held it open for me. "You're free to go. I suggest you go home and get some sleep."

"Why? Are you guys planning a party for my sweet sixteenth?"

"If you don't leave, I'll have Officer Jenkinson come out here and release some of that anger in your direction."

"The lunatic doesn't have a shot. I can take him."

Shane turned back around and yelled inside. "Officer Jenkinson?"

"Okay, okay. I get your point. I'm leaving." I hurried through the front door and down the steps. I could easily fight and beat Lunatic Larry, but I wasn't in the mood to have the entire police force breathing down my neck for beating up one of their own. Plus, they'd have something to arrest me for: assaulting a police officer. I didn't want to deal with that kind of charge. I'd never get preferential treatment from Shane ever again. It was time to go home and call it a night.

| 2 |

Martha carried her eight-month-old baby boy in her arms through Confetti Park. It was a beautiful, sunny afternoon, a few days into the spring season, and the buds on the trees had just started forming. The flowers were sprouting. Nature's beautiful colors lit up the park.

Martha sat down on a bench across from a playground and placed her son on the grass beside her feet. She took off her backpack and unzipped it. She reached inside to retrieve a stuffed toy tiger, the boy's favorite toy. When Martha showed her baby the tiger, his eyes lit up and his mouth opened wide. He was smiling from ear to ear. He reached up for the stuffed animal and Martha leaned down to hand it to him. He grabbed his favorite toy and immediately stuffed its leg in his mouth.

"Adam," she said, pulling the leg free. "You don't eat that."

The baby immediately placed the leg back in his mouth as if nothing had happened.

"Already learning from your father to be stubborn and not listen to Mommy, huh?"

The baby gave an awkward but cute smile, exposing his two lower front teeth.

Martha reached into her backpack again and pulled out a large play mat. She unfolded it and laid it out on the grass. She picked up her son and placed him on the mat. Numbers and friendly zoo animals took up most of the square boxes on the mat. Adam looked down at the animals, then took the stuffed tiger's leg out of his mouth and dropped the toy. He rolled onto his stomach and began swatting at the animals beneath him, babbling as he did so.

This activity gave Martha a chance to pull out her crossword puzzle book and finish the puzzle she had been working on earlier while Adam had taken his morning nap.

Unbeknown to Martha, Adam, and the rest of the public inhabiting Confetti Park that day, space debris entered the Earth's atmosphere. A few seconds passed before someone pointed up towards the sky asking, 'What *is* that?' People stopped what they were doing and looked up. Martha put down her crossword puzzle book and joined in. A light as bright as the sun had captured everyone's attention.

The light became bigger and brighter. Some parents yanked their kids off the playground and headed for safety. Martha sat there, watching intently as whatever was falling from the sky suddenly exploded and broke apart into many fireballs, all heading towards the Earth's surface.

A loud whizzing sound came from the sky. One of the broken pieces of the space rock struck a building across the street from the park. This startled the crowd. Instantly, panic erupted. People began running in all directions. Martha went to stand up and was instantly knocked down by somebody running for cover.

A small fragment of rock, about the size of a football, came crashing down into the sand-box, about thirty feet from Martha.

Three more pieces crashed into the woods in the distance. Most pieces seemed to have broken up before making it through the atmosphere, but the rest came down as little rocks and pebbles. Hundreds of them fell all over the park and surrounding areas, leaving small imprints on impact.

It ended as quickly as it had started. Martha sat up and looked around. A few people were lying on the ground, clearly injured. Whether it was a result of the instant panic and chaos, or from the falling space rocks, she didn't know, nor did she care. She stood up and brushed herself off as people around her did the same thing.

"Oh my god... *Adam!*" She had forgotten about her eight-month-old son playing on the mat by the bench. Instantly, she turned to see him still lying on the mat where she had left him. Relief flashed through her. How could she have forgotten about him during this dangerous incident? She hated herself, but was thankful he was okay.

Adam rolled onto his back, and Martha saw he held something in his hand. She rushed towards her son.

"What do you have there?"

He didn't even acknowledge her, but put the object into his mouth like he had done with his stuffed animal.

"No!" Martha screamed as she grabbed his hand and pulled it out of his mouth.

He had nothing in his hand. The moment Martha and her son locked eyes with one another, her heart dropped. Adam titled his head back and swallowed. Martha grabbed her son's mouth and pried open his lips. Adam twisted and turned, flailing his body and trying to escape. He started to fuss as his mother held his mouth open, searching inside. All she saw were his two white teeth protruding from his lower gum.

Martha's heart began pumping faster.

How could I have been so stupid to leave him unattended? What has he just swallowed?

She looked around the mat and saw a small imprint about two feet from her son. She placed her hand on it and saw the mat was ripped. She imagined the hundreds of small rocks and pebbles falling from the sky. Could Adam have just swallowed one of them?

She didn't even care anymore that something had just fallen from the sky. She was focused on only her son and his safety. She packed her bag, picked Adam up, and rushed back to her car to take her son to the hospital.

| 3 |

Present Day

After a long and exhausting day at work, it was time to head over to The Stout House. I worked at The Discount Factory, a department store. I used to work in the back doing shipments, but I was placed in the front doing checkout and stocking shelves—for whatever reason, I'll never know.

I'm not the best people person. For example, earlier this evening a customer walked in and asked if I worked there. First of all, what did he not understand about my shirt that clearly stated *The Discount Factory* in big, bold letters? Second, he asked if we had more of a specific size of pants in the back. I hate when customers do this. Do they think that in an effort to avoid making more money, we would keep products away from them?

I ended up being sarcastic with him. He cursed at me and left the store. I hate working in retail, but it's the only job I really know how to do.

Dealing with customers all day definitely made me want to not be around people, but making a few hundred bucks in a matter of minutes always persuaded me otherwise. I needed the cash to pay rent for my apartment. Working in retail didn't make me enough to get by. But winning a pot of money always helped. It wasn't all about the money. I had fun. I really enjoyed winning at something.

Now that the pot of money was getting larger, I had started buying a round for everyone, just to show my sportsmanship and appreciation for them giving me their hard-earned cash. I wasn't trying to buy friends; I was just trying to be friendly. I also wanted to make sure everyone enjoyed themselves, so the event wouldn't get shut down. Yes, the police came from time to time, but no one ever pressed charges or sold anyone out, so we all just continued doing what we did.

As I walked into The Stout House, Chuck began pouring me a beer. I made my way over to the bar and he handed me my glass. "On the house, buddy."

I took a big gulp. "Thanks," I said, wiping the foam from my mouth.

Chuck Bassman owned The Stout House. He and I went to high school together and he's the only person who knows about my healing ability.

In the tenth grade, Chuck and I were working backstage at one of the school's plays. We built stage props and scenery. I accidentally cut my finger with a box cutter and it bled—a lot. Chuck saw what happened and went running for help. To avoid everyone else from knowing my secret, I quickly called him back and told him not to worry about it. He immediately questioned me and was confused why I didn't want any help. He freaked out once I showed him that my wound was healed. He nicknamed me Indestructible, but dropped it once he realized my nickname had more syllables than my actual name.

The big difference between us was that I never went to college, but he did. He got a degree in business management. During his time in school, he started experimenting, brewing his own beers. He invited me over to his apartment constantly to try his experiments.

He had an instant hit with each beer he crafted. All the students at his parties were always drunk. Unfortunately, I can't get drunk. It comes with the territory of this crazy healing ability. Alcohol, prescription medications, and other drugs have no effect on me. Believe me, I've tried. All alcohol does is make me have to pee. If I drink a lot on certain nights, I have to pretend to be drunk. No one else knows about my healing ability, so I'll slur my words on purpose, I'll fall down, I'll get really loud for no reason. It's actually pretty easy to act like that when everyone around you is acting the same way. No one ever notices. On the plus side, I've never had a hangover or gotten sick.

Once Chuck had graduated from college, his father helped him buy the building by giving him $25,000 to help with a down payment. It wasn't close to the $700,000 price tag when Chuck bought it, but with his work ethic and determination, he managed to secure a loan to afford this place. He had seemed to do pretty well with it thus far. It always seemed packed. Even more so now that I had become a key attraction.

"Any takers for tonight?" I asked, taking another sip.

Chuck leaned over the bar and pointed behind me, towards the dining area. "That big guy with the baseball hat."

I turned around and looked in the direction he was pointing. "Him again?"

"Yup. Back for round two."

The big guy with the baseball hat had been here about a month ago. He'd probably been my toughest competition yet. His name was Owen. The last time we battled, I left covered in blood. So did he, though. He was tough to take down.

These fights do a number on me. I still hurt with each punch and hit I take, but the pain eventually goes away. Everyone probably thought I was severely injured that night. I'm pretty sure he broke my arm twice. I had to take a few days off to play the part of an injured soul, but then I came back looking for my next victim.

"What's the pot up to?" I asked Chuck.

"I just counted it about a half hour ago. It was just over eight hundred bucks, but there's been a few additions since then. You could be looking at close to a thousand dollars tonight."

I couldn't believe it. A thousand dollars? I could pay my rent and utilities just from tonight's fight. "That's incredible!"

Suddenly, Chuck put his hands down on the bar in front of me. He had a serious look about him. "Adam, I wanted to talk to you tonight before anything happened. I think this is getting too big. I don't want to put my bar at risk of being shut down. I also don't want you getting in trouble. We've done pretty well so far. Let's just walk away while we still can."

"Seriously? You're quitting on me? Alright, look, I'll up your take to twenty-five percent. How about that?"

"It's not about the money anymore."

"Thirty-five percent?"

"I just think we've done enough already."

"How about forty-five percent?"

"You're undefeated. Don't you want to end your streak on a high note?"

"Will you take fifty-five?"

"Are you even listening to me?"

"What about fifty?"

"Now you're going in the opposite direction. Do you even know how to negotiate?"

"Come on Chuck. I need this. I make just under two thousand dollars a month at my job right now, after taxes. I can make almost half of what I make all month in one night here. You've got to let me have this. Please?"

"I don't know. Look, if you need financial help, I can lend you some money. I can even let you bar-tend at night to make some extra cash."

It wasn't so much about the financial help as it was about the excitement. Yeah, I was definitely in a rough spot financially. I had a little studio apartment that was falling apart, a car that was on its last legs, absolutely no savings, and a job that helped me live from paycheck to paycheck—barely.

"You're going to make me beg, aren't ya?" I placed both of my hands together in a prayer posture. "Please? Please?"

"Don't do that."

I leaned in closer to him and got more annoying by begging. "Please? Please? Please? Pretty please?"

Chuck sighed and rolled his eyes. "Alright, fine."

"Yay!" I tried to climb over the bar but landed flat on my stomach on its surface. I reached out and wrapped my arms around Chuck. "Thank you, buddy."

"Seriously?" He grabbed my hands and detached my grip, then threw my hands back towards me and placed his palm on my forehead. He pushed me back from the bar counter. Clearly, I'd embarrassed him. I landed on my feet and fixed my shirt by tugging it down around the bottom.

"Let's get this party started." I brought both of my hands together and rubbed them back and forth. My hands were clammy. My sweat and whatever wet substance I had touched on the bar made for a disgusting rub down as I made my way over to my competition.

Having faced Owen before, I knew what I was up against. He was a few inches over six feet and probably weighed about two-forty or two-fifty. He was a tough guy. He also outweighed me by at least sixty or seventy pounds. I had some muscle on me, but that was from when I actually used to exercise. Owen didn't look like he had any muscle at all. He looked like a giant linebacker. They don't look strong under all that fat, but they could certainly run you over.

I walked over to his table, stood next to him, and tapped him on his bulky shoulder. "Hey beautiful, remember me?"

Owen quickly spun around in his chair and looked at me. The two friends sitting with him turned in my direction as well. Owen pushed out his chair from under the table and stood up—*way* up. I had to look up just to keep eye contact. I liked to show I wasn't afraid, and even though some of these guys were larger than me, I could still stand up to them. Figuratively speaking.

He stared down at me. "You really better watch the next words that come out of your mouth, boy."

Boy? Really? Was he really trying to threaten me? I believe I won last time.

"I have a question for you before we get started here." I tried to watch the words leaving my mouth. My eyes followed the air into the distance, but the joke clearly went over his head.

"I've been wondering something about tall people." I looked down at his over-sized shoes. "You know that saying about big feet?"

Owen stared blankly at me.

"I was wondering if that were true? Because I always thought it was the size of your brain. And we all know you've only got a monkey up there, rattling a few coconuts together, so it can't be—"

Before I could finish my sentence, Owen threw a quick right punch at my face. He certainly had a lot of strength behind that fist of his. It floored me, and pain instantly exploded throughout my face.

"You were saying?" he said as I rose to my knees slowly.

I shook off the pain and looked up at him. He was rubbing the knuckle he had just used to hit me.

"What I was trying to say, before I was so *rudely* interrupted, was that you hit like a girl." I smiled and winked at him, which I know must have made him even angrier.

He pulled back his right arm to hit me again.

"Wait! Wait!" I yelled, sticking both hands up. I turned a little to the left, still on my knees. "Okay, go ahead." I dropped my hands. "I just wanted to have an equal amount of pain distributed on both sides of my face before we got started."

Owen didn't even flinch as his second strike came down. At this point, people had made their way over and started watching. We usually held these fights outside, in the alley behind the bar, but tonight it looked like this guy wanted to get started immediately.

Suddenly, his two friends stood up from the table and grabbed their chairs. They held them over their heads and came hurrying over to me while I was still lying on the ground.

The guy on the right had on a white T-shirt and jeans. I remembered him from before. He acted tough, but was all bark and no bite, so, his attempt to attack me was a different experience than the last one.

As he was about to smash his chair over me, I kicked him in the kneecap. His knee may have bent backwards—I wasn't sure as my vision was still a little blurry from the two massive strikes to my face. The guy went down to the ground, screaming. He dropped the chair behind him and it fell onto the table, breaking glasses, spilling beer, and knocking food all over the floor. The other guy dropped his own chair to tend to his injured friend.

This distracted Owen. I jumped to my feet and speared him into the table behind him. We both went crashing through it. Splinters and pieces of wood scattered around the floor. This was exactly why we usually did this outside rather than in the bar. Now I'd have to replace and help repair the damage we'd caused.

I climbed on top of my challenger and grabbed a plate off the floor. I held it over my head, ready to smash it against his head.

"Adam! Stop!"

The familiar voice stopped me in my tracks. I kept the plate above my head and turned to see where it was coming from. A badge made its way through the crowd of people.

"Police! Everybody get out of the way."

People scattered as if they were in trouble. Shane made his way through the crowd and put his badge back in his jacket pocket.

"What are you doing here?" I asked him.

"Preventing you from doing anything stupid," he replied.

I slammed the plate down over Owen's head, then shrugged my shoulders. "I dropped it."

"Get up," Shane told me.

I couldn't believe he would show up and ruin my fun *again*. Especially the day after we had our last run-in. He usually gave me a few days at least before I saw him here again. I had about a thousand dollars on the line, and he had to go and ruin everything. I stood up and stepped over Owen, who was bleeding on the ground.

"What's your problem?" I asked.

"Me? My problem? I should ask you that. I told you to stop getting yourself in trouble and look where I find you."

"I had it under control. I don't need your help."

"I'm calling this in Adam."

"Seriously? Why can't you leave me alone?" As much as I knew Shane was looking out for me, he was really beginning to annoy me. I couldn't have any fun without him interrupting.

Shane pulled out his handcuffs, leaned down, and turned Owen onto his stomach. He pulled the guy's arms behind his back and locked the cuffs in place, then helped him to his feet and placed him in a chair. He reached into his pocket for his phone and began making a call. "This is Shane Cranston, badge number zero-one-nine-seven-nine-five. I need emergency assistance at The Stout House."

I opened my mouth to speak, but he stuck his index finger up to silence me. "Yes. I have three injured here. One with a serious knee injury." He paused, listening to the voice at the other end of the line. "Okay, I'll be here." He hung up and put the phone back in his pocket.

"I'm not injured," I told him.

"I saw what happened. You took two big punches to the face. I'm going to have the paramedics take a look at you to make sure you don't have a concussion."

"No, I'm not having anyone look at me. I'm leaving." I started to walk away.

"Adam, get back here."

"If you saw what happened, then you know he threw the first punch. He was the instigator. I was simply defending myself. Once again, you've got nothing."

I was sure he could get me on public disturbance or some other fighting charge, but he hadn't yet, so I knew he wouldn't start now. I turned my back on him and continued walking out of the bar.

| 4 |

"Adam! In my office. Now!"

I turned around and saw that my boss, Mr. Benson was standing behind me.

"What's this about?" I asked him.

"We will talk about it in my office. Let's go."

This must be serious. Then again, with him, everything was. He wasn't someone who liked to joke. He barely cracked a smile and it was business all the time.

I followed him into his office. The back of his brown toupee flapped with every step he took. We all knew he wore one; it was obvious. But he acted as if no one knew.

He walked behind his desk and gestured to the seat across from his desk. I sat down and watched him as he plopped his fat ass onto a small swivel chair behind the desk. He sank a few inches upon sitting, the springs in his seat praying for mercy.

"You want to explain to me what happened last night?"

"What happened last night?" I asked.

Did he know about the bar? Did he know I was basically in my own personal fight cl—activity thingy? Did he know about my secret ability?

"I received a phone call from a customer this morning about one of my employees. Before he even told me what happened, I knew it must have been you." He squinted at me.

"I'm honored, sir."

He pointed his index finger at me. "Shut up. You're causing too many problems for us. I'm getting too many customer complaints about you. Last night, you became sarcastic and hostile to a customer who only asked if you had a specific size of an article of clothing. I don't know what to say or do about this. The district manager wants me to fire you."

"And?" I said, leaning forward in anticipation. I'm not sure whether I was excited to be fired or excited to hear my story again.

"Do you even care?"

"Of course I care. I care enough to make sure that idiot doesn't shop here again."

Mr. Benson shook his head. "I can't do this, Adam. Our store is struggling. We need customers. We need sales. Online shopping is killing us. And your reckless attitude is driving people away from our store." He rubbed his hands over his face and then they made their way along the side of his head, through what was left of his natural hair. He sighed and dropped his hands back onto his desk. "Even with as much pressure as I'm getting from my superiors, I'm not going to fire you. You're a tough employee. You work hard—harder than most employees here."

I could chalk that up to that crazy healing ability I have. My muscles never ache or get tired after standing, lifting, or moving around all day. I'll get physically tired when it's time for bed, but if I'm doing strenuous work during the day, as long as I'm strong enough to handle the weight, I can keep going.

"I can't afford to get rid of one of my hardest-working employees. So I've decided to place you in a different role—a role that takes you out of the spotlight and puts you behind the scenes. Technically, you won't even be working inside our store." Mr. Benson started moving papers around on his desk. He finally tugged a piece of paper from underneath a book. "Corporate is opening up a new store in Decker City. It's located inside that new entertainment complex that millionaire—" He waved his hand in a circle. "Something Quinn. I forget the guy's name, but the store is going inside that building. Anyway, corporate began shipping supplies to our warehouse behind the store. What I need you to do is take that stuff over to the new store in Decker City. You'll be away from people so hopefully you won't get into any more trouble."

"One can only hope."

He shook his head again. "Please, Adam, stay out of trouble. I'm begging you."

"Alright, I will. I'm just joking around. Don't worry."

"Good. You can start tonight if you're available. You just have to use your own car. And don't worry, we will reimburse you for driving expenses. And you'll get time and a half pay."

I kind of liked the idea of this job, especially the extra pay. It would also let me get away from people and do my own thing. I wouldn't have to deal with anyone. All I had to do was drop off supplies. Sounded easy enough.

"I like it. I'm in."

"Great." He opened his desk drawer in front of him and pulled out a key. He reached across the desk and handed it to me. "That will unlock our warehouse in the back where all the boxes you need to bring over will be. Just remember to lock it when you leave."

"I can handle that."

I couldn't believe they were trusting me with this job. I was always causing trouble around here. I definitely wasn't the best employee. My ability gave me an advantage, but that didn't mean I wasn't slacking off any chance I got. Every day, I hid in a bathroom stall for an hour or so to play games on my phone. Some ideal employee I was.

I stood up and went to leave, but then Mr. Benson said, "Hey Adam." I turned back towards him. "Maybe you'll get to see the vigilante while in Decker City. The Gray Hood, or whatever they're calling him."

"Who?" I asked.

"You haven't heard of this guy?" I must have had a blank look on my face because Mr. Benson called me back over to his desk as he began typing furiously on his keyboard. I walked over and stood behind his desk. He opened up a new window on his computer. He did a quick search and pulled up a news article. He moved the cursor to the play button of a video and clicked it.

It was footage from a convenience store. It looked like it was from a security camera. Most people had those now in Decker City, considering the crime rate had skyrocketed. I leaned over Mr. Benson's shoulder for a closer look at the computer screen. Suddenly, a man came into focus, holding a gun at the cashier.

"What am I watching? A robbery?" I asked.

"Shhh," Mr. Benson said. "Just watch."

A few seconds went by as the cashier passed money across the counter, then suddenly the guy with the gun turned to his right. He aimed in that direction but as quickly as he did so, the gun flew out of his hand.

Wait, how did that just happen?

Before I could even ponder that thought, someone wearing a hood over their head came running across the screen, knocking down the man who held the gun. Instantly, the footage cut to another angle from a corner of the store. The two guys went crashing into a display of boxes. The criminal then knocked down guy in the hood. He went running for his gun, but the vigilante moved his hands and the gun slid across the floor.

"This is fake. No one can do that," I said.

"Just keep watching," he told me. I shook my head, but kept watching. The vigilante moved both arms across his body and the criminal went crashing into the shelves next to him. It was as if the guy in the hood had thrown him into it—from ten feet away.

This was impossible. He never even touched him.

The vigilante walked over to the criminal but got knocked down as the criminal jumped up and ran for his gun again. The guy in the hood reached forward and the gun slid across the floor and into his hand.

This footage was clearly fake. No one could do that. It was impossible. It had to have been special effects of some sort.

The footage ended with both of them running out of the store.

"Fake," I said.

"It's not fake," Mr. Benson replied.

"How do you know?"

"Do you even watch the news? He's been sighted all across Decker City over the past few months doing things like this. People claim he has magic powers."

This guy had no idea what magic was. He should try having bones popping out of his skin only for them to suddenly pull back inside and reattach to other bones. No scars and no lasting damage, either. Now that I thought of it, maybe impossible was the wrong word. If I could heal, why couldn't this guy be able to move things without touching them? I was still skeptical. It seemed too easy to fake.

"He doesn't have magic powers. There's no such thing as magic," I said, playing devil's advocate.

Mr. Benson didn't take his eyes off the screen. "I don't know—seems like magic to me."

I walked around from behind his desk and headed towards his office door. "If I see this hooded freak during my time in Decker City tonight, I'll tell him his biggest fan says hi."

| 5 |

26 years ago

Martha came storming through the front doors of the hospital, clutching her son in her arms. "Help! I need help!"

A doctor rushed to her aid, asking what was wrong. Martha started rubbing Adam's head, explaining that he had ingested something he shouldn't have.

"Do you know what it was?" asked the doctor.

"No, but it may have been dangerous," Martha said.

"Follow me," the doctor told her. They both strode towards the emergency wing. As she walked down the hallway holding her baby boy, Martha glanced at all the people in the emergency room. Some people were lying on hospital beds with IVs hooked up to them. Some had ice packs on their wounds. Many were just standing around injured, still waiting to be seen. Martha almost felt guilty just walking in immediately, but the guilt faded quickly. It was her son who could possibly be injured or poisoned. He was a baby. He deserved immediate attention. She wouldn't let her guilt stand in her way of making sure her son was alright.

What was it that fell from the sky? Where did it come from? Was it dangerous?

These questions plagued her mind as she followed the doctor into an empty room. She walked over to the bed and sat Adam down. "I'll get a pediatrician for you," the doctor said. He grabbed a clipboard from the table and handed it to Martha. "Fill this out. We'll need it for insurance purposes."

"Thanks," Martha said. She sat down next to her son and began filling out the paperwork. She took her son's favorite stuffed animal tiger from her purse and handed to him. His eyes lit up, and he reached out for it. The arm of the tiger made it into his mouth first. Martha just smiled and went back to her paperwork.

At least he seems to be okay.

As she filled out as much of the information as she could, she kept looking back at her son. He seemed content, just sitting there waving the tiger around like a flag blowing in the wind. He was smiling and laughing. Her son seemed perfectly normal.

Just as she put down the clipboard, a doctor removed the curtain and approached them. "Hi, my name is Dr. Holden." He extended his hand for a friendly handshake, then turned and closed the curtain surrounding the bed. He turned his attention to the baby sitting next to Martha. "And who do we have here?"

"My son, Adam," Martha replied.

"Well, hello there, Adam," Dr. Holden said as he crouched down to the baby's eye level. "What are you playing with?"

"That's his little tiger. It's his favorite," Martha said.

The doctor smiled at Adam and then stood up straight and took the clipboard from the bed. He skimmed through the details, speaking to himself quickly and quietly under his breath.

The doctor finally looked at Martha and said, "So it says here he ate something poisonous?"

"Yes," Martha answered. "Well, I don't know."

"What do you mean, you don't know? What did he swallow?"

"I don't know."

"Miss, I can't help your child if I don't know what he swallowed. You obviously have an idea, since you brought him here. Did he get into detergents, or soaps, or any medications? I need something to go on."

"He..."

"Look, there are a lot of other people here who need medical attention. If you can't cooperate with me, I'm going to have to ask you to leave."

"He swallowed a piece of that thing that fell from the sky!" she exclaimed.

The doctor studied her son. Adam was looking at his mother when she raised her voice. Then he continued waving the tiger around, smiling.

Dr. Holden turned his attention back to Martha. "Let's start with some blood work first, and depending on how that goes, we may have to get an x-ray of his stomach to see what we're looking at here. If it were poisonous, he would have been affected by now. It's been about an hour since that fireball came crashing down."

"Does anyone know what happened or what it was?"

Dr. Holden shook his head. "We've been busy with patient's injuries caused by either the fireball or the associated panic. I just get little bits of the story here and there. You'll probably find out what's going on before I do. But anyway, let me go get something to take his blood. I'll be right back." With that, Dr. Holden left the area, pulling the curtain closed behind him.

Adam accidentally dropped the tiger on the floor and started fussing. Martha leaned over, picked him up off the bed, and placed him on her lap. He leaned forward, trying to grab the tiger off the floor, but Martha kept holding him back. He started to wiggle around and whine in her arms. She leaned over and picked the tiger off the floor and placed it back in her purse. "No, Adam. It's dirty.

You can't have it now." It didn't stop him from fussing and trying to grab her purse.

Dr. Holden pulled the curtain open again and approached them. He smiled at Adam and rubbed his index finger down Adam's arm. "What's wrong, little guy?"

Adam became distracted and quietened down, his attention now on Dr. Holden.

The doctor displayed a plastic bag, which he tore open. He placed the contents on a little table in front of him and wheeled it towards the bedside. He grabbed a needle and held it up. "Miss, I want you to hold your son still. This will be over before he even knows what's going on."

| 6 |

Present Day

It was a little after midnight, and I was on my third delivery of the night. I had started around seven o'clock and just kept going. It took about forty-five minutes to drive to Decker City and another forty-five to get back home to Mapleton. Basically, all I was doing was filling up my car with as many boxes and bags as I could and then dropping them off in this new building complex in Decker City.

I was surprised upon arriving at the place. It was huge! The pathway alone suggested I was walking into a high-end facility. I didn't know why our discount store was going to be making an appearance here. It would look out of place with other stores taking most of the available spots.

I made my way out of our empty store and closed the glass doors behind me. Every time I had walked out of here tonight, I'd noticed the door across the walkway from our store. It was bothering me because it seemed random and out of place. After walking by twice and ignoring it, I decided to check it out. Maybe it was my curiosity that got the better of me, but I wanted to know what was behind that door. It would probably just be a bunch of offices or something. I walked up to it and grabbed the handle. It was locked.

"Hey! You!"

I spun in the direction of the noise. A man was standing a few storefronts away, staring at me. Of course—I'm trying to be on my best behavior and the second I do something I probably shouldn't, someone sees me.

"Me?" I asked.

"Yeah, you. What are you doing?"

What was I going to say? I was hoping there was a grand prize behind door number one? Maybe a car? We could always make a deal.

"I'm looking for the bathroom," I lied.

He walked closer. He was tall, a few inches taller than me. He wore a suit and horn-rimmed glasses. Who would wear a suit in this place at almost midnight? His scruffy beard made it seem like he hadn't seen a razor in a day or two. This guy seemed out of place, but then again, so did I.

"There's no bathroom here. You'll have to find somewhere else to go. Also, this is a closed facility. What are you doing here?"

The man placed his right hand on his hip. Did he have a gun? Did he think I was trespassing?

I put my hands up to my chest.

"Whoa there, Rambo. I don't know if you're reaching for a gun or not, but all I'm doing is delivering supplies to my store over there." I pointed behind me at the glass doors. "My boss told me I can start dropping off boxes of stuff tonight since this place would be open for employees to set up their areas."

The man nodded and looked me up and down. "This door is private and for staff only. Your job is to deliver your products, not snoop around. Do you understand?"

"Got it," I replied.

What was with this guy? Was he security? Maybe he was that Quinn guy Mr. Benson was talking about. I'd never seen him before, so I didn't even know what he looked like.

"If I catch you doing something other than what you're supposed to be doing, I'll make sure you won't be allowed back." The man pulled out a key and unlocked the private door. He opened it and slid inside, giving me one last look before closing it.

What a weirdo. I was already in the doghouse with Mr. Benson, and I didn't need to cause anymore trouble, so I let it alone and made my way out of the facility.

Once I got in my crappy car, all I could think about was that jerk who'd threatened me. I wanted to go back inside and slap that smug look off his face. However, I couldn't risk it right now. As much as I hated my job, I needed it. I put my key in the ignition and started the car.

* * *

I took 11th Street towards the bridge connecting Decker City to Mapleton. I kept playing with the radio in my car, trying to find something good to listen to. My crappy car didn't have Bluetooth or satellite radio, so I was left with boring AM and FM radio. This city sucked when it came to rock music stations. There was only one decent station at this time of night, but the DJ talked more than he played music. I hated that. I just wanted to listen to—

P-TAFF!

The noise echoed in the distance and startled me as I was changing stations. What the hell was that?

P-TAFF! P-TAFF! P-TAFF!

Were those gunshots? I slowed the car and listened closely.

Another crack of gunfire, this time closer. It sounded like I was right next to it. I put my car in park, got out, and walked along the sidewalk towards the closest street corner, which was where the noise seemed to be coming from. Slowly, I peeked around the corner and two men stood behind a blue truck, shooting at a police car. I kept low and as hidden as possible, watching from a distance. A police officer stuck his head above the car and began to open fire at the two men, who ducked back behind the blue van.

Suddenly, a hooded figure came running across the street and slid behind the police car. Who was that? Wait, was that the vigilante Mr. Benson was talking about—the Gray Hood, or whatever his name was?

The two men behind the van reloaded their guns and returned fire. The officer ducked back down behind his vehicle. One man became pretty daring and walked out from behind the van, continuing to fire towards the officer. Suddenly, the man's gun flew into the air and landed on the ground. His head flipped back slightly as the gun left his grip.

Had the gun just hit him in the face?

He put both hands to his face as if he was crying or blowing his nose. The other criminal stood up behind the van and aimed his gun at the police car.

As he made his move, so did the vigilante. He threw his hands to either side and the man's gun flew onto the sidewalk, a few feet from the criminal. I shook my head, wondering if I was dreaming because there seemed to be no way someone should be able to do this. I guess the video Mr. Benson showed me was true.

The guy with his hands on his face finally removed them and reached down for his gun. I was about to yell, but before I could even open my mouth, the officer took two shots at him. The criminal fell to the ground, screaming in pain. I'd never imagined I'd see someone being shot. In the movies, it never affected me because

I knew it was fake. But watching that guy go down like that, it was real and yet I honestly felt no different from watching it in a movie. Maybe it was because he was shooting at the police officer. I watched everything play out and I couldn't help but root for the good guys.

I watched the vigilante reach out and then the gun dragged along the ground toward him. I had no idea how he did that, but I was certainly intrigued. This vigilante was taking down these criminals like it was nothing. It was really exciting to witness him in action—until the remaining criminal saw me and came towards me. Now my excitement turned to fear. I knew I could regenerate my body at an extraordinary rate, but when I'd just watched this guy open fire on a police officer, my ability never entered my head. I'd never been shot, or even shot *at*, and I didn't plan on sticking around to find out what it as like.

I turned the corner quickly and ran towards my car. Deep down, I was screaming at myself to stay and help. I knew I could take the criminal out. But after what I had just seen, my first instinct was to get the hell out of there.

I made it to my car and slammed the door shut. I went to put the car in drive, but immediately a hand came through the open window. The criminal grabbed my shirt with one hand and opened the door with the other.

I was in complete shock, and I couldn't even tell my body to fight back. As I was being pulled from my vehicle, all I could think to do was slam on the horn.

The criminal tossed me onto the side of the road and got into the driver's seat. He slammed on the gas and the tires screeched on the pavement. I watched from a sitting position as he drove onto the sidewalk to run over the vigilante as he turned the corner. Luckily, the vigilante dove out of the way just in time to prevent himself from becoming a splattered bug on my windshield.

My car leapt off the sidewalk and bounced for a moment as it hit the street again, trying to control itself. But it didn't last long. Suddenly, the police cruiser made an appearance, flying into the intersection and slamming into the driver's side of my car. I watched in horror as the only car I'd ever owned flipped over and rolled into a building across the street. Bricks, cement and glass scattered all over the street and on top of my car. The police car had stopped in the middle of the intersection with a smashed front end and bullet holes littered all over it. The area looked like a war zone.

I sat motionless, and everything else seemed to have come to a standstill, too. My car lay upside down against a building. The police car, riddled with bullet holes, sat in the middle of the inter-section. The only movement came from the vigilante, who ran over to the police vehicle. As he did so, I saw the police officer begin to climb out of the window of the car. I looked over at my car and saw the criminal slowly crawl out of the passenger-side window. Once the officer had emerged from his vehicle, he limped over to the criminal, pulled both of his hands behind his back, and hand-cuffed him.

"Sir," the officer yelled from across the street. "Sir? Are you okay?"

Was he talking to me? He looked in my direction and I pointed at my chest, in a silent question.

"Yes, you," he said.

"Yeah," I managed to say finally. "I'm okay."

"Good." He brought the criminal to his feet and started to walk back to the police car. "Stay there. I'll be right back." He opened the back door, placed the criminal inside, and shut the door. It seemed more like a holding cell than anything, since that police car wasn't moving anywhere anytime soon. As the officer walked along the intersecting street, I heard sirens in the distance.

What the hell just happened here? It all had happened so fast. I knew that I'd seen the guy in the hood, the vigilante, the Gray Hood, in action, and that I had been carjacked. Now I had no car. How was I going to get back home? How was I supposed to continue delivering supplies to the new store? That clearly wasn't happening anymore. My car was smashed and lying upside down in the front entrance of a building. How was I going to explain this to Mr. Benson?

A moment later, multiple police cars with flashing lights and loud sirens came swarming in from all streets. Just like in the movies, backup *always* knew how to show up *after* the action had already taken place.

| **7** |

"What was he like?"

"What was who like?" I asked.

The officer seemed like a little kid excited about his favorite celebrity. "You know, the guy in the hood. I never saw him before, so I just wanna know."

"Know what?" This guy was getting on my nerves. Did he think I'd hung out with the vigilante?

"What he's like?"

"What he's like? You think I had time to talk to him while I was being pulled out of my car by some guy with a gun? Or maybe that I could get a word in while I watched my car become a permanent fixture of that building back there?"

His excitement faded. "I'm sorry, sir. I didn't realize your situation. My apologies."

Crap, now I'd upset him. Were people always this sensitive? If he had seen the situation I was just in, he wouldn't have been asking me these questions. He wouldn't have been as excited as he was. But he wasn't there. He didn't know what had happened. His job was only to take me home. I guess he was just trying to make conversation. Dammit, now I felt bad.

"He was exciting to watch, when the danger didn't involve me," I told him, trying to lighten the mood.

The officer perked up again. "Really?"

"Yeah. He could do things I've never seen before—moving things without touching them."

"It's incredible, isn't it? There are all these videos online about the vigilante sightings. People record them on their phones, so the quality isn't the best, but they're really cool to watch."

I zoned him out as he kept talking. I guess I'd made him feel better after all. All I wanted to do was get home, but I had to listen to this officer talk nonstop about the hooded guy. As much as I didn't want to admit it, especially to the officer, the vigilante in Decker City was pretty cool. Watching him tonight was unbelievable. I had no idea how he could do what he did. Obviously, no one else did either. The more I heard about him, the more of a mystery he seemed. After that adrenalin kick about an hour ago, I was wide awake. I wouldn't be able to sleep when I got home. How could I, after what I had just witnessed?

"And then there was this time—"

Oh my God, the officer was still talking. I stared out the passenger-side window and saw The Stout House's sign lighting up the street.

"Pull over here," I interrupted the police officer.

"—how he could have—" The officer stopped speaking. "Here? Why? Your place is another few blocks away."

"My friend owns that place," I told him, pointing at the bar. "I'm going to go in and say hi. I can walk home from here. Thanks for the ride."

"No problem," the officer said.

I stepped out of the police car and walked inside the bar. The place was emptier than usual, but that could be because it was almost closing time. I wandered over to the bar and sat on a stool. Chuck grabbed a glass and filled a beer from under the tap, then placed it in front of me.

"You're here late this evening," he said.

"I had an interesting evening. I may get fired," I told him.

"Oh. Well then." Chuck turned back towards the bar for another glass and filled it. He spun around and placed it next to my first glass. "You'll probably be needing this."

I laughed, getting the attention of the few drunks lingering in the bar. "Thanks. You're probably right."

"Tell me what happened."

I told him about my deliveries, which led me to finding the confrontation between those shooters and the police officer. Then I brought up the vigilante, what he had done and how he could move things without touching them. He had saved that officer's life.

Now I sounded like that officer who drove me home. Unbelievable.

"How does this lead you to getting fired?" Chuck asked.

"Oh yeah." I took another swig of my beer before continuing. "My car ended up in the front end up a building."

"Your car ended up—how?"

"I was thrown out of my car and—"

Chuck interrupted me. "You were thrown out of your car?"

"Yeah, by one of the men shooting at the police officer."

"You didn't tell me that. Why didn't you tell me that? You made it seem like you just witnessed the events, not that you were a part of them."

"My bad. I was carjacked and then, as the guy drove away with my car, the police officer sped down the road and slammed into it. It flipped and rolled into a building. Now the place has a nice crappy car monument at its front entrance. Oh, and a cute girl interviewed me. I forget her name, though. She spoke to me for like ten seconds."

"A cute girl talks to you and you forget her name?"

"I'm sorry. I kind of went through a bizarre situation, what with the guns and the destruction of my car. A date wasn't necessarily the first thing on my mind."

"Well, you always seem to find where the action is. Your life can be pretty exciting sometimes."

"Exciting? I was ripped from my car. Now it's destroyed and I may not have a job after tonight. I wouldn't necessarily call that an exciting life."

My life was boring. I worked in a boring retail store, doing boring and laborious work, driving around in a boring car—which was now totaled—and I lived in a boring little apartment. I'm not sure how he thought my life was 'exciting.'

"You have a unique talent that no one else has. An ability. That makes you special. That makes you exciting. Think back to all those fights you won. I'm not proud of them, but I know you are. And you have this wittiness about you. You can talk yourself out of any problem. That's a gift. You have talents you're not utilizing."

"Yeah, but how does that help me with my car?"

"Who cares about your car? That's replaceable. Your job? Replaceable. Get over it. Why don't you use your ability for good instead of a cool bar trick? Obviously that vigilante has some kind of ability, too, and he's using it to help people. Why don't you?"

"Why don't I what? You want me to dress up and go fight crime? Are you looking to be my sidekick? You can throw beers at criminals while I beat them up. We can be called the Drunken Duo. Oh, I know, how about the Double Shots?"

"Stop acting like this is a joke, Adam. I'm being serious. You can do some real good with your ability."

I was about to open my mouth to reply, but for some reason, I stopped myself. It doesn't happen all that much. I'm kind of a jerk like that, where I just don't care what I say.

I picked up my beer and finished it. I knew Chuck was right. I was taking this whole thing as a joke. I guess I could blame it on the night I'd had. I didn't have a car and I still had to let my boss know what happened, and then I probably wouldn't have a job either. It was time to get serious. I reached for my second glass of beer and took a sip. Then I said, "You're right."

"Whoa wait—what?" Chuck backed up and raised his hands. "Did you just say I was right?" He reached for my empty glass and examined it. "What kind of beer did I just give you?"

"Don't make me come across this bar," I said.

"I'm just surprised. I believe that's the first time you've ever said I was right."

"And it'll be the last time, too."

But Chuck was right. I needed to do something with myself. I could use my ability for good. All this time, I'd been using it to make money, which had been great. Maybe it was really time for a change, though. Maybe I needed to be more like that vigilante in Decker City. I just couldn't see myself running around and doing what he did. He seemed heroic. I was just some plain, boring loser from Mapleton.

I took another gulp of beer, and then it hit me. "Shane!"

"What?" Chuck asked.

"Shane, the officer at the police department. Maybe I can talk to him. He always seems to want to help me. Maybe I can work with him."

"You mean the one that arrests you all the time?"

"And lets me go all the time," I said with a smile on my face. I definitely had it easy with that guy. He always let me off the hook.

Chuck pounded on the bar three times and then cupped his hands to his mouth. "Closing time people. Finish up and get the hell outta here."

Within seconds, people began making their way to the doors. I quickly downed my second beer and placed the glass on the bar. I stood up from my bar stool, but Chuck said, "Not you. You can hang out here a bit longer."

"Nah, it's okay. Thanks for the beers. I'll pay you back, eventually."

"With the tab you have, eventually will be a long time from now."

* * *

When I reached my apartment, I picked up my laptop and started looking up articles about the vigilante of Decker City. A bunch of links cascaded down the screen. I clicked on the top one which led me to a story about his different sightings. I went back and clicked on the next link. This was about all the various criminal activities going on in Decker City, and how the vigilante was making a difference. The article mentioned a few robberies and deaths as a result of the criminal activity. It was awful what was going on there. I had no idea how much violence there was in Decker City. The article also stated the police disapproved of him, but the public seemed to be fascinated by him. They obviously hadn't spoken with the officer who drove me home.

But why would the police be against him? He was helping them.

I clicked back and went to the next article. This one was about the convenience store robbery Mr. Benson told me about. I skimmed through the page and noticed that a video accompanied the article. I clicked on it, and found that it was the surveillance video I'd already seen. I watched it again, noting how quickly the vigilante moved and how confident he was when fighting criminals. When he moved his hands, the gun slid out of the way. He also pushed the guy from across the store into a display area, without having touched him. I restarted the video, and then watched him push the guy from across the store again. It was incredible. I watched the whole video three times before I clicked back and moved on to the next article.

Having watched the vigilante in action tonight, and now having researched him a little bit, I realized I wanted to be like that too. I wanted to be the hero he was. I wanted to go to Decker City and help him. I wished I could move like he could and take down criminals as easily. I already knew I could fight and win. How much harder could it be?

After clicking through a few more articles, I closed my laptop and decided to get some sleep. Tomorrow—actually, *today*—I was going to be a new me.

| 8 |

"You're fired!"

"You can't fire me over this. It wasn't even my fault." I knew I was fired. I was just trying to play it off like I cared when I really didn't.

I called Mr. Benson when I woke up and told him what happened last night and that I could only get three deliveries done before I ran into trouble. He was not happy. He yelled all kinds of profanities at me. I just let him get his anger out. No need to make things worse. Although, how much worse could it really get? My plan was to get fired, and hearing him now, I realized I didn't have to push him too hard. After last night, I didn't want that job anymore, anyway. I had a new line of work in my sights.

"Yes, I can," Mr. Benson said. "You have shown a systematic tendency of causing problems and getting in trouble. I have multiple customer and employee complaints about you during your employment here. You may be a hard worker, but I can't do this anymore."

I gave in at this point—there was no sense in acting anymore. I didn't want him to actually change his mind. "Fine. But what about my car?"

"Insurance will cover the damage. You were on company time so we'll pay for it."

"Damage? What do you mean by damage? The car is totaled," I told him.

"Then you'll be getting a check. Once the insurance company assesses the damage and cost of the vehicle, you'll get a check in the mail. As of now, you are done with the Discount Pavilion. Please delete my number and do not contact me again." And then he hung up. Nice way to say goodbye. At least I was done with that place. Now on to bigger and better things: being a hero.

***

"You want to do *what?*" Shane asked.

"I want to join the police force with you."

After my phone call with Mr. Benson, I made my way down to the police station. Luckily, Shane was there. I was too excited to about this. I wanted to have this conversation and make this change now. But after all the times I'd sat here in this seat while in trouble, I thought he'd be happy that I wanted to change. Instead, he cocked his head a little to the left and looked at me as if I was crazy. But I wasn't crazy. I knew what I was doing.

"I'm sorry. I need to come to terms with what you're actually asking me. I'm not quite sure I understand," Shane said, still sounding confused.

"I," I pointed to myself, "want to team up with you." I pointed across the desk at him. "It's really that simple. I'm not sure how you got this far here if you don't understand this. Use those detective skills of yours."

"No, no. I get it. But I just don't *get* it." He squinted and shook his head slightly.

"Get what? Okay, now you're confusing me. See what you're doing here?"

"Let's start from the beginning. Why do you want to join the police?"

"I was watching one of the *Lethal Weapon* movies last night, and it seemed like it would be fun. Big explosions." I raised my hands above my head in fists, then I opened them up quickly and brought them down to my sides, imitating an explosion. "Car chases." I put my hands on an imaginary steering wheel in front of me. "Conspiracies and—" I leaned in closer to his desk. I looked around the room and then whispered, "—finding out who the deep cover mole is."

"Let me stop you right there," Shane said, raising a hand. "First of all, there's no mole in this office. You watch too many movies. And there won't be any explosions or car chases. That stuff doesn't happen around here."

"It does in Decker City," I said, referring to the bombing at the building a few months ago.

"That's Decker City, not here. You can't compare the chaos going on over there to the calm here. The police are investigating the bombing that took place. Secondly, you can't join the police just like that. You have to work for it, earn it by taking many tests and physical exams. Once you're done with those, and if you actually pass, then you can apply."

This seemed like too much work. Maybe I could just become a vigilante like that guy in the hood in Decker City. That would bypass all these boring tests. But I needed a job, and more importantly, money. At least working with Shane would provide an income *and* I could use my ability for a good cause.

"But most people won't just get hired immediately. Many departments look for experience. For example, I had to work for the local prison for three years before I worked here. And what happened to your job, anyway?"

"I was fired."

"You were?" His shocked expression turned to worrisome. His eyes opened wider, his head tilted. He looked generally concerned for me. "What happened?"

I told him about my night and how my car had ended up in a building after the vigilante came to the rescue.

Shane shook his head. "That damn vigilante in Decker City is causing all kinds of problems up there."

Was he a hater too? Why were the police so against him?

"Wait—so you don't like him?" I asked.

"No, I don't like him. He's a menace and is taking the law into his own hands. Vigilantism is illegal. Plus, he's making the police look bad by doing their jobs for them."

Maybe it was a bad idea to bypass the tests and the time it would take to become a police officer, to become a vigilante like the guy in Decker City. Shane was already after me when I got into trouble. How would I stay out of his cross hairs if I was doing what the guy in the hood in Decker City was doing?

In my head, this conversation had gone very differently. Shane had welcomed me with open arms. I would have been one of the guys. We would have had a beer to celebrate my new employment and I would be out saving lives and catching bad guys by the end of the night. It didn't seem like any of that was going to happen.

"But the vigilante is catching bad guys. He's making a difference," I said, trying to stick up for him.

"Exactly. He's making a difference. He's making it so more people like him get the same idiotic idea to go out there, dress up, and risk their lives to do what we are trained to do. The vigilante in Decker City is just that: a vigilante. He doesn't have magic powers. He's not a superhero. He's got some fighting skills and does some things I can't explain—maybe a trick of some kind, or it's staged. Either way, it doesn't mean he should be out there doing what he does.

Ultimately, he just gets in our way and is a danger to the public and to us. In all honesty, he's just going to get himself killed."

This really wasn't going well. I liked the idea of becoming a vigilante. I liked what the Gray Hood was doing in Decker City, even though Shane didn't. All I really wanted to do was go out and do what the vigilante was doing to help take down bad guys. Maybe I had gotten too far ahead of myself. I thought maybe by joining the police, I could use my ability, arrest the bad guys, and never get hurt. And I could get paid for it, which would be nice since I currently didn't have a job. It would be nice to make some honest money doing something I might enjoy for a change.

"Anyway," Shane continued, "we're getting off topic here. Let's get back to the original point. You want to join me. Why? What made you suddenly want this change?"

"To be honest, it was because of last night—the vigilante."

Shane rolled his head back. "Ugh. Really?"

"I don't know if you've ever seen him in action before, but he really has magic powers, or something. He's—"

"Stop." Shane put his hands up. He dropped his left hand onto his desk and rubbed his head with his right one. "There's no such thing as magic, or people having super powers. It's not real."

"Yes, it is. I saw—"

"Stop," Shane said, interrupting me again. "It's nonsense. I've seen videos of him before. It's fake. It's not real. This magic or super power stuff, it doesn't exist."

If he only knew what I could do.

"This is stuff you read about in comic books or see in the movies. This is stuff reporters make up to sell magazines or newspapers, or to scare or excite people into watching the news." He shook his head in frustration. "Look, if you promise me not to follow in the footsteps of that idiot in Decker City, I'll take you out on a ride-along."

"What's a ride-along?" I asked.

"You'll be riding in the cop car with me while I drive around, patrolling the city. I have to pull a double shift tonight because an officer called out this evening. So, if you're available, you can come. But beware, you'll be in for some boredom. The stuff you read about Decker City doesn't happen around here."

It sounded like a good idea. It might actually help decide whether this would work out for me. I guess it would be interesting to see from the officer's perspective. I'm just usually the one seeing it from the other side. "Sounds good. I'm in."

"Good. Meet me back here around eight o'clock." Shane went back to his paperwork on his desk.

"Okay, thanks." I stood up and walked towards the door. "Oh, I have a question, though." Shane looked up. "What should I wear tonight? Should I look like a criminal since I'll be riding in the car with you?"

"No. Wear your normal clothes. You don't need to get dressed up," Shane said, frustrated.

"Don't dress like a clown, then? Got it."

"Why would you dress like a clown?"

"First of all, it would throw people off. And second, I heard cannibals don't eat clowns because they taste funny."

Shane cracked a smile. "You're an idiot. We won't be running into cannibals out there tonight. And if you dressed like a clown, you might end up scaring people half to death."

"What happens when you get scared half to death twice?" I replied instantly.

Shane shook his head and pointed to the door. "Get out."

| **9** |

I spent the rest of the day looking online for a job. I knew Shane wouldn't help me, so I had to take matters into my own hands to make some money. It was amazing what jobs were out there and what people would pay others to do. If I had a car, I may have just signed up for Uber and acted as my own personal taxi. I could have just driven around the city all day and made a lot of cash. Unfortunately, my car was totaled, and I didn't have the money to buy a new one.

I thought about opening an online store on eBay and other auction sites and using a drop-shipper or wholesaler. Upon further research, I decided against it. There was already an over saturation of those kinds of things out there. Plus, I needed money to make money.

The only available positions were entry-level, low-paying jobs; retail and fast food. I was sick of that. I wanted to get out of this hellhole apartment I couldn't even afford anymore. I was at a dead end. I might have to take up Chuck's offer of some borrowed cash. I hated asking for money. Maybe he'd give me that bar tending job instead. I had no idea how to make a drink, but I knew how to drink them. That must count for something.

The alarm on my phone went off. It was 7:15 pm. It was my reminder that it was time to head to the station to go on that ride-along. I was pretty excited, and looking forward to learning about what the police did out there and what dangers they faced.

* * *

Being without a car was very frustrating. It wasn't that I minded walking; driving was just more convenient.

I arrived at the police station around 8:20 pm. Shane was waiting by his car, leaning against the driver's side door. "You're late," he said.

"Well, it's a pleasure to see you too," I replied.

A bullet-proof vest hung from Shane's right hand. He tossed it to me.

I examined the police logo on the back. "A gift? On our first date? You shouldn't have."

"Put it on."

I slid it on over my T-shirt. "I thought you said nothing happens around here?"

"It's for your protection. Just in case. And you'll be in the car for the duration tonight, so it's a very teeny-tiny, almost non-existent 'just in case.' The police department of Mapleton and our insurance company requires all ride-a-long passengers to wear one."

"I think you could have made a better argument if you opened up with the requirement part."

He closed his eyes and rubbed his face. "This is going to be a long night, isn't it?"

"Well, each night has a certain amount of minutes and hours, so depending on when you classify when night begins and when it ends, and also factoring what season we're in and location of the Earth to the Sun—"

"Just get in the car, smart-ass," he interrupted. He opened the front door and got in. I walked to the passenger side door and got in as the engine roared to life. "Seat belts," he said, just before he hit the gas and turned onto the streets.

I clicked my seatbelt into place and fidgeted with the buttons on the console between us. "What's this do?" I asked as I pushed a square, white button. A flashing light appeared outside the vehicle, followed by a short siren burst.

"Stop that." Shane reached over and pushed the button to turn it off. "Look, if you're going to come along tonight, I need you to behave. Touch nothing in the car. This is police property, and I don't want you messing with anything, or worse, breaking it."

"Sorry," I said. I wanted to be there, so I didn't want to do anything to make him kick me out tonight. I wanted to learn what went on behind the scenes.

"I'm going to start off tonight by showing you our territory. I'll drive you around to the edge of the area we enforce."

"That's it? That's all we're doing? I thought you were going to take me out tonight and show me all the crime in our city?"

"Adam, I told you, crime here just isn't the same as what you read about in Decker City. I'm expecting a quiet night, as it usually is. If something comes up, yes, we will respond and you'll get to see what happens."

Suddenly, static came through the radio. "479, we have a reckless driver, driving a black Honda Civic. Was seen driving around with their doors open and headlights off."

"Oh! That's something! Let's go!" I exclaimed.

"That's not for us," Shane told me.

"What do you mean? There's a reckless driver out there. What if they cause an accident? Someone might get hurt. Isn't that something to respond to?"

"You're right, but our number is 472. 479 is Forest Hills district. Mapleton, Forest Hills, Danielsville and Paradise Grove all use the same radio frequency. Decker City used to be a part of it as well, but with the rise in crime, they became too busy and needed their own frequency."

"We're basically going to ignore the call?"

"We aren't necessarily ignoring it. It's just not in our district, so we don't need to respond to it, unless someone calls for assistance. It's Forest Hills' call to respond to. It's in their area."

I felt a rush of disappointment. I was excited to get a call, and now Shane was telling me we couldn't even go to it. I wanted to see some action, to be involved in something. I didn't want to drive around all night in a car with nothing to do.

"If we get a call, can I push the button?"

Shane let out a sigh. "Fine. You can push the button."

"Thanks, Shane. I need some excitement. You can't let me sit here all night with nothing to do. Is it always this boring?"

"There can be times where we sit here with nothing to do. Especially in the snow or rain, we can just sit here and listen to the windshield wipers swipe back and forth. Back and forth."

"Wow. The excitement is just radiating from you. If you're trying to get me excited about wanting to help or join you guys, you're not doing a good job."

We drove around for about an hour with no other calls. Shane showed me Mapleton's territory and we drove around some parks and down some back roads I never would have driven down. But this wasn't what I'd signed up for. It didn't seem like the ride-along I'd expected. I wanted to see the kind of crime the Gray Hood was getting involved in. *He* had exciting nights. *I* was stuck in a car, driving around, with nothing to do. Although, Shane told me not to expect it to be what it's like in Decker City—and he was right. I was just hoping he'd be wrong.

Static came through the radio. "472, we have a possible robbery in progress. Electronic Depot. 5th and National Drive."

Shane picked up his radio and responded. "Understood, 472 responding. ETA about five minutes." He placed the radio back in its position, dangling from the center console.

"A deal's a deal," Shane said. "Push the button."

"Yes!" I yelled as I slammed down on the button. But nothing happened. I slammed down on it again, almost punching it.

"Dude, just push it. No need to be aggressive."

"Sorry," I said, and gently pushed the white button. The flashing lights popped on and the siren burst screamed from outside our vehicle. Shane spun the car around and sped back in the opposite direction.

"It looks like you might see some action tonight," he said. "When we get there, you stay in the car. Understand?"

"Why?"

"It's for your own safety."

"Why?"

"I don't want you getting injur—" Shane glanced over towards me. His eyes squinted in anger. "I know what you're doing. You're like a five-year-old. Just shut up and just stay in the vehicle. Okay?

"Okay, okay. I get it," I told him.

* * *

Shane reached over and pushed another button on the console. The siren shut off but the lights continued to flash. It was an adrenaline rush, speeding around in a police car. Shane was driving in and out of traffic and blowing every red light. This was the fun I was looking for!

Shane pulled onto National Drive and flipped a switch. The lights shut off. He turned down an alley and parked the car. He pushed the button on his radio and said, "472 on the scene. Approaching the building."

The voice on the other end of the radio confirmed his status and told him to proceed with caution.

Shane quickly unbuckled his seatbelt and reached for the door handle. "Adam, I've never been more serious with you than I am right now. Stay in the car, please. *Do not* get out."

Before I could even respond, he opened the door and got out. Shane closed the door gently and crept slowly towards the end of the alley towards the front of the building. He unbuckled his gun from his holster and grabbed it. He switched on his flashlight and turned the corner. Shane was now out of sight.

I was alone.

Silence.

Nothing happened for what seemed like a few minutes. It may have been only a minute, but I wasn't counting. Waiting for something to happen just made the seconds seem to tick by very slowly.

What if Shane needed backup? There was no one here but me.

Should I go in? Should I call for backup?

Shane had told me to stay here.

What if he was in trouble? I should at least see what was going on. It wouldn't hurt to do that. Every officer had a partner. They always had backup. I just wanted to look, anyway. No harm could come from that.

I opened the car door and stepped into the alley. Cautiously, I took one step forward, stepping on my toes to avoid making any sound and—

POP!

What was that? A gunshot?

POP! POP! POP! POP!

Definitely gun shots. But from who? Shane? The guys robbing the store?

I ducked down, as if ducking would help me dodge the bullets not even coming towards me.

Adrenaline pumped through me. I felt the excitement of being near the action. But there was another feeling, not something I've felt all that much. I shook a little bit, but I wasn't cold. My heart was throbbing in my chest. It was beating furiously. I wanted to move but I was stuck. My brain wouldn't communicate with my body.

Was I scared?

I took a deep breath to calm myself.

POP! POP!

More gunshots.

I couldn't believe myself. I was motionless. This was fear. I wasn't accustomed to feeling this all too much. I knew I could heal. I knew I couldn't get hurt. Well, not get *too* hurt. Having to deal with bullets flying at me was a completely unfamiliar situation. I'd only ever dealt with my own personal injuries and those sustained during my fights. Guns typically meant death. I was all about testing my abilities, but going from hand-to-hand combat to suddenly dealing with guns seemed too much of a leap for me at this time. Could I even survive a gunshot?

POP! POP! POP!

My natural reflexes made me duck with each shot I heard. I had no idea what was happening in there. After the shots, I found the courage to jump to my feet and reach for the car.

I opened the passenger door as someone came running around the corner and down the alley. It wasn't Shane. I didn't even have a moment to get inside the car.

The stranger was on me in seconds. He grabbed me, wrapped his left arm around my neck, and pulled me into his chest, then held onto me tight. He used his right arm to extend his gun towards the entrance of the alley, in the direction where he came from.

I don't know what came over me, but I yelled, "Shane, watch out!"

The guy turned his gun on me and snapped, "Shut up!"

Shane made his way slowly around the corner, and the guy holding me pointed the gun back in his direction.

"You okay?" Shane said.

"Me or him?" I asked.

"I said shut up!" the criminal holding the gun said.

"Yes, you, moron," Shane responded.

I nodded with what little room I had to move my head.

"Let him go," Shane said.

The criminal kept taking steps backwards, quickly. He was looking around for an escape. "Drop your gun!"

"I can't do that. You have a hostage. I don't know what your intentions are with him. Before you make this worse, you need to let him go."

A hostage? Me?

No.

Wait—hold on.

I was supposed to be the confident one. The one who couldn't get hurt. The one who could talk his way out of any situation.

What was I thinking? How had I allowed myself to fall into this mess?

Courage flooded within me. I felt confident and relaxed again. I knew I could get out of this situation. I was calming down. And then my mouth started.

"I'll give you five bucks if you let me go," I told the criminal.

"Are you serious?" he said.

"Absolutely. I have it in my pocket. If you just let me get—"

He stopped me abruptly by slamming the butt of the gun down on my shoulder. "Shut up!" he yelled.

My shoulder ached and a pain ran down my right arm.

Shane used the distraction. He fired his gun, missing me, hopefully on purpose. The criminal behind me ducked slightly and released his grip. I threw my left arm up and my elbow caught him on the side of his face. I moved out of his reach in a split second, but apparently not quickly enough. I turned to see that he had his gun aiming at me.

POP!

Shane fired and took out the guy's leg. As the bullet hit him, the criminal pulled the trigger of his own gun. He fell to the ground and winced in pain.

If I ever wanted to know what it felt like to be shot, this was it. It hurt. A lot. The bullet must have hit my right arm. I flinched in pain when the bullet hit me.

Wow, my arm really hurt. The pain radiated throughout my entire arm. It was a sharp pain that I wish would have gone away quicker than it had lasted.

Shane ran over to the criminal on the ground and snatched the gun out of his hand. "Are you okay?" he asked me.

I clenched my teeth in pain, but as quickly as I did so, the pain had started to calm. I took a breath and the pain began to subside. Was I healing already? Was I immune to bullets, too? I looked down at my arm. I could move it just fine. The pain was barely noticeable now.

"I think so. I don't think he hit me," I lied. I didn't want Shane to know what I could do. And now that I knew I could heal after being shot, this made for a more interesting situation.

"I saw you flinch. Are you sure he didn't hit you?" Shane stood up after handcuffing the criminal and approached me.

He held my arm and inspected it. "You're not in any pain?"

"No," I replied. At least I was being honest about that. I literally had no pain anymore. "Wait a minute. You shot at me! What the hell was that about?"

"I missed, didn't I?" Shane responded, rolling his eyes.

"Hopefully on purpose."

Shane shrugged his shoulders and continued inspecting my arm. "What's this?" He pulled up my sleeve to reveal a bullet hole in it. "You sure you're okay?"

I looked down as if surprised to see the hole in my shirt. "Oh yeah, look at that."

"This is serious, Adam."

"I know. I'm not hurt. It must have just missed me."

Shane looked behind me and felt around the brick wall behind me. He took out his flashlight again and shone it onto the wall. He pointed to a spot and tapped it. "There's the bullet." He shone the flashlight on the ground at my feet and then again and my arm. "You have blood on you, too. Are you sure you're not hit?"

"Yeah. It must be his blood." I could see from Shane's face that he wasn't buying it. He looked completely lost.

"Whatever—at least you're okay," he said finally. He walked away to his car, reached inside, and took his walkie talkie off of the dashboard. "Gunshots fired at 5th and National. Two victims. One deceased and one needing medical attention with a gunshot to the leg." He threw the walkie talkie back in his car and picked up the criminal off the ground. He opened the back door of the police car and carefully placed him inside.

Shane turned to me and said, "I thought I instructed you to stay in the car?"

"You can't get mad at me. I helped you stop him."

"How? You were caught. You were his hostage."

"I was a distraction."

"A distraction that got shot."

I stuck my index finger up at him. "*Almost* shot," I reminded him.

He rolled his eyes. "If you're going to be out here with me, you need to listen to me. This isn't a game." He walked back towards his car to answer his walkie talkie.

He was right, this wasn't a game. I needed to listen to Shane. I had learned something tonight, after all. Bullets hurt, but I could still heal after being shot.

| 10 |

We arrived back at the police station after a quiet car ride. I wanted to experiment more with my ability. The thrill of healing from a bullet wound had my adrenalin pumping. Could I heal from multiple bullets?

I knew I could heal from fights, but I'd never experimented with more aggressive acts of violence, such as guns. I'd never even held a gun before. Maybe a nerf gun when I was a kid, but not a real gun.

The idea of healing from a bullet wound also frightened me. I needed to know more about this healing ability of mine. I needed to know my limitations. I needed to know how far I could push myself.

What more was there, if I could heal from a bullet wound?

What if I could heal from everything?

What if I couldn't die?

That was a scary thought. *Immortality.*

I could definitely use that to my advantage, but who wanted to stay alive forever? There had to be some disadvantage to this ability.

I had a gift. Or a curse. And I wasn't sure where it came from. All I knew is that I was stuck with it and I had to make the best of it. Maybe it was time to use this ability for something other than a trick.

"Come on, knucklehead. Let's go," Shane said as he exited the vehicle. I unbuckled my seatbelt and followed him inside the police station. He continued, "We need to write up a report about tonight, so now you'll get to see the real boring part about the job: the paperwork."

That did sound boring. Didn't they have interns or low-level rookies to do this stuff for them? I guess I was pretty clueless when it came to police work. I didn't want to do paperwork. I wanted to go fight bad guys and let others clean up my mess. Wasn't that how it was supposed to be? Movies and TV shows made it seem like that. Who wanted to do paperwork, anyway?

"What'd he do now?" Jenkinson shouted from across the lobby.

"Hey buddy!" I responded. I raised my arms in the air to show that there were no handcuffs this time. "I wanted to come surprise you and say hi to my best friend!"

Jenkinson looked at Shane. "You're kidding me, right? Is he with you?"

"I took him on a ride-along," Shane said.

Jenkinson's face turned a shade of red. "Are you crazy? Why would you bring *him* with you? He's the kind of person we want behind bars, not riding around with us. Don't encourage him!"

"Calm down, psycho. I actually made an arrest tonight," I told him.

"Okay, hold on," Shane interrupted, holding up his hands. "You didn't technically make an arrest. I did."

"Well, I assisted," I told him.

"No, you didn't," Shane said.

"Yes, I did."

"Adam, shut up. No, you didn't."

"Did I distract him so you could shoot him? Did I help you take him into custody? Should I get some kind of reward, perhaps a badge of some sort? Did they land on the moon for the first time in 1492? I believe the answer to all those questions is clearly *yes.*"

"They landed on the moon in 1969," Shane said.

"Then what was 1492?"

Jenkinson jumped in. "Columbus, you moron."

"Adam, you were a distraction," Shane said. "Not an assist. Didn't you become a hostage tonight?"

"Irrelevant," I said.

"Wait, they took Adam hostage?" Jenkinson shouted. "Oh man, I wish I could have seen that!"

"Shut up," I said. It's more than you did tonight. At least I made an arrest."

"At least I wasn't taken hostage."

"Okay, enough you two," Shane interjected. "Knock it off, Larry." He turned and pointed at me. "You, come with me. We have paperwork to do."

I followed him into his office and he shut the door behind me. He sat down in his chair, tapped his keyboard, and the computer screen lit up.

"What do we do now?" I asked.

"We write about what happened." Shane moved his mouse around and clicked. Behind him, the printer sprung to action and started spooling paper. Shane organized the papers and placed them on his desk. "What do you remember about tonight?" he asked me while clicking his pen.

"You left me in the car listening to Barry Manilow. I wanted to kill myself."

"Seriously, Adam."

"Okay, okay. You told me to wait in the car while you investigated a crime." Shane started writing.

"What else? What were you doing while you waited?"

"I sat in the car and waited. I got bored, so I got out and I heard a gunshot. I thought you may have been in danger, so I wanted to check it out." What more did he want from me? Did we really have to go through this? I thought we just went out and stopped criminals, and that was it.

We went through our account for the next few minutes. Shane asked me multiple questions, and wrote everything down. He finally looked up at me.

"Okay, I honestly don't believe you about the gunshot in your arm. I saw you flinch. I saw the blood. As part of my, and the department's, investigation, I am going to test the blood I found at the scene. I don't know how it was that I didn't see any marks or injuries on you, I don't understand what I saw at all—nor am I convinced by your explanation."

I didn't know how to answer. Was he going to find out it was my blood? I was pretty sure it took a few days for the blood analysis to be processed, so I knew I had time to come up with some kind of explanation.

Shane continued, "But tonight was a rarity. I can count on both hands how many times I've had to fire my weapon, ever. It's not something that happens around here. *But*, because there was a discharge of my firearm and a death, there will be an investigation. This means I need you to be available. Do *not* disappear on me. The department may contact you for further questioning. Don't worry, you're not in any trouble, but I don't need you to make matters worse by being a smart-ass if they call you in for an interview. So please just be on your best behavior and be honest if they bring you in."

That was going to be hard. Honesty wasn't something I did very well. I'd had to hide and lie about my ability all my life. Hopefully, I wouldn't get called into this "questioning" by Shane's department.

I wondered if I could ask someone to go on my behalf so I didn't have to go.

"As for now, it's time for you to go home. It's getting late. Get some rest. I still have some paperwork to do, so it'll be a while before I leave."

I stood up. "Thanks for letting me come out with you tonight. It was… interesting. But I definitely learned a lot, like which buttons turn on the sirens and how boring it can be in the rain."

Shane shook his head and smiled. "I appreciate your humor and stupidity sometimes. Now get out of my office."

I went to his door, but then turned as Shane called out my name.

"Thank you for tonight. Don't tell your lunatic friend out there, but yes, you assisted in the arrest tonight. And I'll make sure to put that in the report. You were an idiot, and you definitely got yourself in a lot of danger. But if you hadn't put yourself out there like that, I probably wouldn't have caught that guy. Thank you."

I couldn't believe it. Shane just gave me a compliment. *And* admitted that I had helped him.

"You're welcome. And don't worry, I'll make sure this stays between us." I turned and opened the door, walked out and yelled across the floor to Lunatic Larry, "I made an arrest. Shane said so! Suck it, Larry!" I crossed both arms to make an X shape, and motioned them down towards my waist, a move started by a WWF group called De-Generation X back in the late 90s. I probably shouldn't have done that, after what had seemed like a very sentimental moment between Shane and myself, but I couldn't help it. I didn't like Lunatic Larry, and it was a goal of mine to constantly get inside his head.

He quickly stood up and yelled something, but I quickly made a bee-line for the front door and headed home.

| 11 |

26 years ago

Martha sat in the waiting room, waiting for the doctor to come back and tell her something—*anything*. She had been sitting there for over an hour. Luckily, after all the excitement, Adam had fallen asleep in her arms. She stared at him, loving every moment with him. Holding her cute, little, sleeping baby in her arms was the best feeling in the world. She was terrified of what the doctor would say. She knew something had to be wrong. Her baby had eaten a space rock. It had to be bad, right?

Why did babies have to put everything in their mouth?

A nurse stood up behind the counter. "Martha and Adam?"

Martha perked up and raised her hand.

"Would you follow me, please?" the nurse said.

Martha stood up slowly, still holding her sleeping baby and making sure not to wake him. She followed the nurse into a room and closed the door behind her. Again, she was left to wait and contemplate the possible results of her son's exam. She was half-tempted to just walk out and pretend nothing had ever happened. But she had made it this far. She had to know. It would eat away at her if she ignored it.

Maybe it will be nothing.

Maybe it will be something.

Something bad.

Her thoughts came to a grinding halt as the door opened and the doctor walked in with his clipboard in hand. Martha's heart began thumping twice as fast. She was finally going to know what happened to Adam, if anything had even happened at all.

The doctor took a seat opposite Martha. "I see your little boy is worn out, huh?"

Martha looked down at her sleeping baby in her arms. "Yes, I think it's been a little bit of an overwhelming day for him. Excuse me for cutting to the chase, but can we discuss his results, please?"

"My apologies, ma'am. I'll get right down to it." The doctor looked down at his clipboard. "I'm not really sure where to start with all of this. And I'm not sure what exactly is going on with your son. I know these aren't the answers you're looking for, but based on the tests we have done, I can't reach any conclusion."

Martha's eye squinted. She frowned as she tilted her head to the side. "What does that mean? Is Adam going to be okay?"

"I honestly don't know. As of now, he seems fine."

"What do you mean 'seems fine?' Is there something wrong with him?"

The doctor shook his head. "It's kind of complicated. Let's put it this way—we all have good and bad bacteria in our bodies. Obviously, we want to rid our bodies of the bad and keep the good. The bad bacteria are the ones that make us sick. They can multiply in our bodies and even trick our bodies to fight alongside bad bacteria. The good bacteria are known as probiotics. They are used to fight back and protect us against infections. In Adam's case, when we tested his blood, we found no bad bacteria. Everything came back perfect. It's as if your boy has perfect health."

"So that's good, right? He's okay, then?" she asked, still very confused.

"Well, yes, I presume so. But what stumped me was the incredible rate at which his blood fought any antibacterial medicines we introduced. We tested his blood for any infections and any bacteria leading to negative effects on his vital organs. We found nothing, except that his body fought back immediately against anything we did."

Martha gazed at the doctor and pondered his statement. What was going on with her son? Was Adam okay? What was all this bacteria nonsense? She didn't understand any of it. She was stumped. She just wanted her baby boy to be healthy.

"What does this mean for Adam?" she asked.

"I don't know, really. Think of it like the skin, and its regenerative ability. Your son's body fought back against bacteria the same way, but at alarming rates. It's something I've never seen before. Your son seems fine right now. I think whatever he ingested may have had something to do with this phenomenon, but without further testing, I can't be sure."

Suddenly, Adam began fidgeting. His eyes sprung open, and he looked up at his mother. He gave a small smile that suggested comfort and love. Martha looked back at him not knowing what to think about her son's diagnosis. She just wanted a healthy baby boy, but now she was scared about what would happen to him given everything going on in his body. What would it do to him? Would he get sick later on? Would he develop cancer? Or was he really 'fine,' as the doctor had told her?

The doctor smiled and continued, "I would like you to see your pediatrician as soon as possible, so we can monitor this. I don't know what tomorrow will bring, but as of right now, your son seems fine. Take him home and get some rest. You've both had a long and exhausting day." The doctor stood up and opened the door. "Take your time. And if you have any questions, please don't hesitate to reach out to us."

The doctor left the office, closing the door behind him, leaving Martha alone with Adam.

Adam was babbling and was clearly getting antsy, kicking his legs and trying to get down. He seemed normal. Martha stood and repositioned him in her arms. She reached over, grabbed her bag, and walked out of the office.

Questions began to fill her head about the wellbeing of her son.

What if he's sick?

Is he going to die?

What is happening to him?

Is it contagious?

She couldn't shake the flood of questions and thoughts constantly racing through her mind. But despite her worry, the only thing she could do was what the doctor said: take him home and take care of him. And that was exactly what she was going to do.

| 12 |

Present Day

It was 2:45 am, but I couldn't sleep now. Not only had I had an hour of walking to energize me, but the events of the night had my mind racing. I knew I could heal from a bullet wound—it wasn't like I was in any rush to try it again, but it was exciting knowing my lack of limitations. Come to think of it, I'd never really tested my limitations before. I'd only ever found myself in hand-to-hand combat at bars.

Well, that was an enormous leap. Hand-to-hand all the way to guns.

I sat down at my kitchen table, opened up my laptop and googled some keywords about the incident tonight. An entire article popped up, written by Kate Phillips. It had happened only a few hours ago, and she already had an article online. It mentioned Shane, but there was no mention of me.

Oh wait, there I was.

"...civilian taken hostage during the exchange. The criminal was shot once in the leg and taken into custody. The hostage was not injured."

I shook my head. That stupid hostage thing was going to haunt me.

The author's name sounded familiar, though, *Kate Phillips*. Then it hit me. She had written the article about the Gray Hood and interviewed me about my car ending up as a new feature of that building. I put her name into the search engine and it pulled up a few other articles she'd written. Lately she'd been writing a lot about the vigilante in Decker City. As I scrolled down the page, I realized she'd written about him *a lot,* as well as the violence hitting the city.

I clicked on an earlier article she had written about the sports teams in Decker City, and there was a picture of her with the Decker City Devils. She was cute as a blonde. When she'd spoken briefly to me, she was a brunette. She looked tall, even standing next to those athletes. She must be 5'8" or 5'9". She must have been wearing heels, as she hadn't seemed that tall when I met her. Where was she tonight, after Shane and I arrested that guy? She couldn't have come while we were there at the scene.

I was getting distracted. I closed my laptop. My aim was to figure out what I was capable of. I looked to my left to see a kitchen knife sitting on my counter. I reached over and grabbed it. The coldness of the handle made my heart pump fast. I knew what I had to do. But I was afraid. I'd never purposely caused myself pain. I'd never thought of doing that.

I just needed to make a minor cut. That's all. Just something small. I didn't want to overdo it. I put the blade against my hand. It was scary. I knew I would heal, but the anticipation of it just made it worse. I went to drag the blade across my hand, but my hand didn't move. I was so nervous that I couldn't even move my hand. I couldn't hurt myself. This wasn't starting out well.

I put the knife down and stood up, pacing back and forth and trying to psych myself into doing it. Maybe it was the pain I was afraid of? Maybe causing myself pain was what was making me hesitate? If I wanted to be like this vigilante in Decker City, I couldn't figure it out on the streets. I needed to be prepared.

I shook it off and reached for the knife again. It was like pulling off a Band-Aid: you had to do it in one motion. I held out my hand, put the blade against my palm, and pulled it towards me.

Instantly, I dropped the knife. A warm and sharp pain overtook my hand. But as quickly as the pain came, it soon subsided. I looked at my hand and saw that the slight cut I had just made was already healing. I used a towel to wipe the blood off my hand. There was no trace of any cut.

This was unbelievable. I was immune to knives as well.

What if I cut deeper?

No.

I couldn't do that. I mean, technically I could. The only thing stopping me was *me*. I was already testing this knife stuff out. I might as well keep going.

I took a deep breath and held out my hand again. This time, I pushed the blade much harder, and pulled it towards me.

Ouch! Ouch!

This really hurt. I dropped the knife and held the wound. The pain was deeper this time and more severe. Within a few seconds, the pain calmed and then disappeared. I released my grip and looked at my hand. I reached for the towel and wiped away the blood again. There was no trace of any cut. And more importantly, there was no lingering pain. I truly was immune to injury.

Then the thought of taking it further hit me. What about a stabbing wound? My excitement faded away. If I was scared before, I was terrified now. I kept telling myself I would heal and it would be fine, but being stabbed wasn't an experience I'd ever thought I'd have. And now here I was, sitting here contemplating the idea of stabbing *myself*. I had to know. I was terrified, but my curiosity was getting the better of me. I had already made it this far. I had to keep going.

I kept placing my hand in different positions on the table, trying to figure out which method would be best. Finally, I decided to just place the backside of my hand on the table, palm facing upwards. I picked up the knife in my right hand and held it over my left palm.

Was I really going to go through with this?

Just rip it off like a Band-Aid.

I lifted up my arm and brought the knife down, fast. I stopped just before hitting my hand. I should have just followed through. I would have been over it by now. I couldn't help it, though. Who wants to stab themselves? Certainly not me. It's freaking scary, even if you know you'll heal from it. Hopefully. Otherwise, I'd have an interesting trip to the hospital and one hell of a story for the paramedics. I pulled my phone out of my pocket and dialed 9-1-1. I didn't hit the call button yet. It was more of a just-in-case scenario, allowing quick and easy access to help.

I placed the phone next to me and held the knife again. I took a deep breath, inhaling through the nose, exhaling through the mouth. I tried to slow my heart rate down. I did that three more times before I lifted the knife above my hand again.

Here goes nothing!

I slammed the knife down on my hand. I blinked. That wasn't so bad.

I'd spoken way too soon. Pain erupted throughout my hand and spread into my wrist. Oh man, did this hurt. I had to get this knife out of my hand to allow the healing to begin. I reached for the handle and pulled at the knife.

You've got to be kidding me!

The knife was stuck. I had brought it down so hard that the tip went through my hand and all the way into the table. Maybe pre-dialing 9-1-1 wasn't such a bad idea.

The pain kept coming, pumping through my hand. I pulled harder on the knife handle, but it was still stuck.

I wanted to scream out in pain, but I didn't need others to hear me through the paper-thin walls of my apartment. The pain was becoming unbearable. Earlier that night, at least the bullet went straight through and everything healed up pretty quickly. I still had a knife sticking out of my hand, and I couldn't heal. The pain kept sticking around. I had to get this knife out.

I wrapped my hand around the handle again and gave it one last pull. It finally released from the table and flew from my hand. I went falling backwards in my chair. I crashed onto the floor. I rolled over, sat up and wrapped the already bloody towel around my bleeding hand, holding onto it to stop the bleeding. The pain was still there. I hoped I hadn't done this for nothing. I hoped I hadn't permanently damaged my hand.

A few seconds passed and the pain began to subside. It was still there but slowly going away. It was like the feeling of blood rushing back into your hand as if it had fallen asleep.

Slowly, I unwrapped the towel. It was covered in blood, but I couldn't find a wound. I stood up, went to my sink, and washed the blood off my hands. I couldn't find any markings. There was no wound. It was as if the last five minutes had never happened. This was crazy! I was definitely immune to knife injuries. It wasn't like I was planning on going out and getting stabbed every night, but at least it was good to know.

Now that I knew I was invincible, it gave me much more confidence about going out and acting like the Gray Hood from Decker City. He may have been able to move things without touching them, but he had nothing on me. I could heal from anything.

I noticed the clock and realized how late it was. I was supposed to be searching for a job in the morning. I needed to get some rest. I looked at the bloody mess I'd made in my kitchen and just waved my hands at it. *I'll do it later.*

I walked into my bedroom, changed, and got into bed. I was going to test these abilities tomorrow night. I was confident I could handle myself out there. The excitement kept me from closing my eyes. Tomorrow night was going to be an exciting new time for me!

Swing and a miss. I'd struck out at all eight places I went to today. Of course, it was all retail work, which was exactly what I didn't want to do, but I had no idea how to do anything else. It was simple work, but it didn't pay all that well. I was getting close to being in financial trouble, so I needed to find a job quickly. Rent day was approaching rapidly and, without a job, it was going to be difficult to pay.

After walking around for a few hours, filling out applications and getting on-the-spot interviews, I wound up at Chuck's bar. Unfortunately for me, there would be no fight tonight. No extra money coming in. Chuck had put a stop to that after the last incident. He had let me have my fun, and now I had to respect his wishes. It was his bar, after all, and I didn't want to jeopardize anything.

"Did you talk to Shane?" Chuck asked as I sat down.

"Yeah, he took me on a ride-along last night. It was awesome! I got shot."

He looked at me, puzzled. "You don't typically hear 'It was awesome' and 'I got shot' together like that."

I laughed. "What I meant was the ride-along was awesome. I got to see a robbery. I helped arrest a guy… who also shot me."

"I'm assuming that since you're here right now and not in a hospital, you can heal from that too?" he asked, not seeming *that* concerned about the fact I'd been shot.

"Yes!" I replied. "It's incredible. It hurt a lot, but the pain went away pretty quickly."

"You're literally a superhero. I can't believe you can heal from bullet wounds as well. *And* you also helped arrest someone?"

"Yeah. Well, he took me hostage first. That's how I got shot."

"Hold on. Back up. You were taken hostage? How did this happen? Wait, you know what? Just start from the beginning of this whole ride-along story. Tell me everything."

Luckily, it was early in the evening and the bar was fairly empty, so Chuck could hang out with me and not be interrupted. I told him everything from the ride-along, to the robbery, to the hostage situation, and the gunshot.

He was still in shock about the gun. "I still can't believe you were shot. There isn't a bullet hole or anything? You're one hundred percent healed?"

"Yeah, as far as I'm aware." I rolled up my sleeve, showed him my arm, and pointed to the spot where I was shot. "Right there. There's nothing left. No scar. No signs that anything even happened."

"That's insane! You're indestructible. What did Shane say when he found out?"

"He didn't. I told him the blood belonged to the criminal. He looked at my arm but since there was nothing there, he couldn't keep questioning me."

"Did he believe you?"

I laughed. "Absolutely not. He's a smart guy. Being as young as he is, in the position he's in, he must have worked damn hard to get there, and probably outsmarted everyone else. He said there's going to be an investigation into the shooting, so my secret may come out if they find my blood at the scene. How can I explain that?"

Chuck shook his head. "I don't know—maybe just tell them the truth? You're superhuman and can heal from any wound."

"Oh yeah, I'll tell the police department I can magically heal. Imagine the reaction that'll get. Either they'll think I'm crazy or they'll quarantine me to run an insane number of tests to find out why I can do what I can do."

"Haven't you ever wanted to know where this ability comes from? Don't you want to know why you're able to heal?" Shane asked.

"No. Look where it got me. I was in and out of adopted families and foster homes all my childhood. This... ability, or whatever it is, has only caused problems. You're the only one who has ever accepted it. Everyone else ran away screaming, or kicked me out. I have a long history of not being understood by others, so forgive me if I don't share your enthusiasm about telling everyone. No one would accept it, anyway. I'm different, and that'll just scare everyone, just like it has in my past."

"Why won't people accept your ability?" Chuck asked. "We have someone in Decker City who can magically move things without touching them. Maybe this ability of yours isn't so far-fetched anymore. Maybe people will be willing to accept it now, after what they've been seeing."

He was kind of right. People were warming up to the idea of that vigilante having magical powers. I'd read a bunch of articles about the Gray Hood, and the public seemed to be fascinated with him. Maybe it wouldn't be so bad if people knew what I could do.

I told Chuck, "If I went around and did what the Gray Hood is doing, I would probably have to hide my identity. You have a costume lying in the back of your bar somewhere?"

"No one knows you. Who would you have to hide from? From the few people at the police station who know you? From me?" Chuck responded.

"Well, what would happen if someone saw me and they traced me back here to this bar? Then they'd go after you."

Chuck's eyes flicked down towards the bar momentarily, as he thought about it.

"See? I'm right, aren't I?"

"Okay, yes, you do have a point. What are you going to do? Put on a hood like the Gray Hood? Probably can't be gray. Need to pick a different color."

Chuck's sunglasses were behind him by the beer tap. I asked for them, and reached behind him and then handed them to me. I put on the sunglasses and looked at Chuck, who had a confused look on his face.

"Can you recognize me?" I asked him.

He squinted his eyes and tilted his head. "Yeah? Is that your idea of a disguise?"

I took off the sunglasses. "I don't know. I swore I read about a superhero in a comic who put on glasses and no one could tell who he really was. It seemed to work for him."

"You mean Superman? That *disguise* definitely doesn't work for you. It's petty easy to tell who you are."

"Crap, okay." I handed the glasses back to Chuck. "Well, it's time to get going. Tomorrow I have another long day of looking for a job, and probably not finding anything." I went to leave.

"Hey, Adam, wait," Chuck said, and I turned to face him again. "If you need a job, or even just some money to get by, I'm here to help. There's always an opening for you here."

"I appreciate that, but I don't need handouts. I need to go find my own job."

"I get that, but don't let your ego get in the way. This isn't a handout. Let me help you."

I really needed a job, and Chuck was offering me an easy way out of my predicament. I wanted to say yes, but I just felt like he was feeling sorry for me and I didn't want it to be like that. Maybe it was something to consider, but for now, I had to focus on finding my own job, on my own.

"Thank you, Chuck. I'll let you know how tomorrow turns out."

I hoped I could find something the following day. I didn't want to come back empty-handed and then have him offer me a job again.

We said our goodbyes, and I walked outside. Tonight I was going to walk the streets and test out my new ability. I wanted to see how I could handle situations like that vigilante did.

* * *

I wandered the streets of Mapleton for over two hours. There was literally no crime. Shane was right, it didn't really happen around here like it did in Decker City, or even like last night. That's what I wanted, though. I wanted something to happen so I could practice taking on criminals. I wanted to continue building on this ability and seeing what I could do.

It was getting boring. I wondered how the Gray Hood found all the crime in Decker City. Did he just walk around like I was doing? Did he drive or have a ride? Was he working with the police? Did he have a partner?

Maybe I should head over to Decker City instead. I was sure I'd find something to get involved in. I'd spent one night over there and found trouble, so I was sure I could easily find it again. I guess I couldn't really complain, though. The fact that there was no crime was actually a good thing. People were safe here in Mapleton for the most part. But it wasn't helping me test my ability against criminals.

Feeling discouraged, I walked in the direction of the police station, hoping to find Shane there. Maybe I'd just talk to him about this ability. There was no sense in hiding it from him if the investigation would uncover it eventually. Plus, Chuck had a point. People were accepting of the Gray Hood at this point—except the police, obviously. It was nice knowing there was someone else out there like me.

The police station was about twenty blocks away. Maybe I'd be lucky enough to find some crime along the way.

I didn't.

When I got there, I walked up the stairs feeling disappointed. I had this ability, but I couldn't even use it. I'd pushed myself so much yesterday that I wanted to keep pushing today, but tonight I was left with absolutely nothing to do. Maybe Shane would bring me out with him again.

I walked into the station. The atmosphere was an immediate change from what I was used to seeing. Everyone was running around in a panic. I stood and watched for a moment as an officer ran into an office, and another one ran past me, barging into my shoulder. He seemed too much in a rush to even say 'excuse me.' A third officer was on the phone, looking panicked. What was happening here? Nothing I'd seen on my way here could explain this kind of behavior.

I looked around for Shane and saw him hurry out of his office. "Shane!" I yelled. He turned and gave me a confused look.

"What are you doing here?" he asked as he walked quickly towards me.

"I was in the area. I wanted to stop by... and..." I became distracted by the commotion again that I had trailed off from finishing my thought.

"Adam, I don't have time for this. Is your reason for being here important, or can it wait?"

I shook my head and focused on Shane again. "Sorry. What's going on here?"

"A lot is happening in Decker City right now. We got a call about two cars traveling at dangerous speeds on the freeway. Some sort of car chase. We think it's the vigilante and the individual behind everything happening over there. There were also shots fired at a warehouse by the docks a little while ago. Something big is happening, and Decker City police have requested help from surrounding districts. I'm heading out there in a minute. I've been trying to get hold of Jenkinson since he was supposed to be here for his shift an hour ago, but he hasn't been answering his phone."

"Forget him! Let's go to Decker City!"

"Not happening, Adam. You're not coming. It's too dangerous." Shane started to walk away.

I followed him. "No way. You are *not* sidelining me on this."

"Adam, I said no." He seemed pretty stern about it, but I wasn't about to be left behind.

"Look," I began, still following him back to his office. "After what I experienced last night, and yes, after being held hostage, I think I learned my lesson. I'll stay in the car. Pinky swear."

Shane grabbed his phone off his desk and looked at its screen. "Dammit, Jenkinson, where are you?" He slid the phone into his pocket, moved past me quickly and started for the front door. I continued to follow him.

"I'll make you a deal," I began. Shane didn't seem to listen as he walked outside and towards the parking lot. "If I step outside of the car, you can arrest me for... I don't know — whatever reason you can think of."

Shane rolled his head back. "Adam, I don't want to arrest you. I'm trying to help you. This is dangerous, and I don't want you getting hurt."

"Shane, I have nothing right now. I don't have a job. I've been job hunting all day and I didn't get anywhere. I have almost no money. This seems exciting, and I *need* this. *Please.* Let me have this. I promise I'll stay in the car."

He paused for a moment—a moment he probably couldn't spare. He pursed his lips and shook his head. "Dammit. Adam, get in the car. Don't make me regret this."

"Yes! Thank you!" I swung myself into the passenger seat. That moment alone was the most exciting thing that had happened to me all day.

| 14 |

There was no time to mess around during the journey. The moment I got in the car, and before I could even put on my seatbelt, Shane had the lights and sirens going.

We sped through Mapleton and across the bridge to Decker City. I loved how traffic just moved out of the way for us. It was so easy to get through cities like this. I wished I could do it all the time. It was fun.

Once we made it to Decker City, we passed the spot where my car had ended up as a welcoming statue for the building it had crashed into. The car was gone now, but the area was covered with tarps, obviously under construction. How long would it take to repair the area? Did this sort of thing happen a lot over here? Was the vigilante always involved?

Shane quickly made his way to an entrance ramp and onto another highway. Immediately, I noticed a car flipped over on the other side of the highway. Shane slowed down and pulled up to the median. People were wandering around in different directions, and cars had stopped as people tried to figure out what was happening. Shane rolled down his window to speak to the crowd.

"Everyone okay?" he asked.

Most nodded, and a few mumbled some things I couldn't make out, until I overheard a mention of the Gray Hood. I leaned over the car console towards the driver's side to hear more, but only caught bits and pieces.

"—drove off that way." A man pointed in the direction of Mapleton, where we had just come from. "He took my car and... after... back there..."

"Okay, thank you for your help, sir. Officers and paramedics are on the way if anyone needs assistance," Shane told the man. He rolled up his window and continued driving onwards.

"What was that about?" I asked.

"Apparently, this is where the end of the car chase occurred. The vigilante was chasing someone, and they got into an accident. That car you saw upside down was the car the vigilante was driving."

"Is he okay?"

"I guess so. He got out and stole the car belonging to that gentleman I was speaking to."

A loud siren passed us on the other side of the road. I turned in my seat and watched an ambulance come closer. Two police cars followed behind it.

"This is why I'm against this guy doing what he's doing," Shane said. "Do you see this mayhem? He could have been killed in that accident. Look at that." He pointed out a car with its front end smashed into the median. "See? It's dangerous work. Even for us. He takes the law into his own hands, and look at the destruction that follows. He could have gotten himself, or someone else, killed, the way he crashed his car, and in all likelihood the way he was driving it, too."

"But he's been saving people," I responded. I was just going off what I'd read on the internet. I mean, it must have been true, right? It was on the internet, after all...

"Technically, yes. But he's causing more destruction doing it this way. Did you see that car with its front end in the median back there? Did he protect and save those people? There are ways to go about our work and avoid all this unnecessary damage. We are all trained professionals, police officers, and he's just running around doing whatever he wants. It's dangerous, and it impedes us from doing our jobs correctly and safely. He just stole someone's car. Does that sound like a hero to you?"

"Don't the good guys in TV shows and movies do that too?"

"Adam, this isn't a TV show or a movie. We don't just take people's cars. That's called theft."

"What if he needed it? Isn't there a rule that you guys can take someone's vehicle if you need it?"

Shane exhaled forcefully, so loudly that I could hear the frustration building up within him. I could see his face begin to flush red with anger.

"Adam. Stop. You're defending a criminal. Just stop."

I wasn't going to win this battle. Shane had already made up his mind about the Gray Hood. Maybe if he'd seen him in action like I had, he would change his mind. Seeing him that night had made me a believer. Yeah, he broke some laws and caused some damage, but at least he got the job done. He was helping. And people *liked* him. Well, except Shane. He obviously didn't like him. But Shane was just being stubborn.

"Wait a second. Didn't that guy back there say they went that way?" I said, pointing back where we came from. "Why are we going this way?"

"We're heading to the docks, where everything seems to have started. The DC police are heading towards all the activity right now. It's their jurisdiction. We're just assisting so they can follow the trail and put a stop to everything."

Well, that was disappointing. I'd wanted to go to where the action was happening. Apparently, Shane hadn't thought to let me in on that little detail about tonight. Another police car stormed past us on the other side of the highway and my disappointment set in deeper.

Shane was hitting keys in the middle of the console. The screen was flashing different prompts.

"What are you doing?" I asked.

"Another part of the job. While we were stopped and I was talking to that gentleman, back at the scene of the accident, did you notice anything? Gather any information during that time?"

"I didn't know I was supposed to. You kind of forgot to tell me that too, along with the boring ride you were taking me on."

He ignored the second part of my comment and continued. "The license plate of the vehicle that was overturned."

I had no idea what he was talking about. "What about it?"

"Information gathering. I memorized the license plate and I'm plugging it into our database to see who it's registered to. Maybe whoever it is registered to can help us. Maybe they're helping the vigilante. Why did he have their car in the first place?"

This was why Shane was in the position he was in. I would have never thought about that.

The screen lit up again, now filled with information. Shane started scrolling through it.

"What did you find?" I asked.

"The car is registered to an Andrew Kane." He kept glancing back at the screen as he drove, and rattled off stats about the man. "Forty-seven years old. Lives here in Decker City. Looks like he's a doctor at the city hospital."

"Does any of that mean anything?"

"Not sure. But I now know who to start with when I'm questioning people, starting with: why did the vigilante of Decker City have his car?"

He pulled off the next exit and turned right. Within a minute, we arrived at the docks. Vehicles flooded the area. Not only were there a ton of police and emergency vehicles, but reporter's vans were scattered around the area as well. People had their cell phones out, taking videos and pictures. This was a mob scene.

Shane pulled up to an officer protecting the area. The officer waved us through and moved an orange traffic cone out of the way. Shane proceeded into the dock that was coned and taped off. He parked in front of the large double doors of the warehouse, which were open wide. I could see officers walking around inside, and a paramedic pushed a gurney through the doors with a man lying on it. A white sheet covered most of his body, but his head was exposed. Dried blood was smeared across his face. His nose looked a little bent, probably broken. What had happened in there?

"Remember your deal. You stay in the car, right?" Shane said.

Reluctantly, I replied, "Yes. I won't get out." But a wave of disappointment washed over me. Everything was happening right in front of me. I wanted to walk around that warehouse and see everything inside.

"Good." Shane unbuckled his seatbelt and got out. He looked around and then started walking towards the warehouse, then disappeared into the crowd of people inside.

I kept a close eye on the doors of the warehouse, watching to see what was going on. At least, I was pretending I knew what I was looking at. Officers walked around and talked with other officers. Some were looking around and making notes. Others took pictures. Everyone seemed to have a job in there. Of course, my job was to stay put in this stupid car. Why did I come up with this highly intelligent idea? Worst. Deal. Ever.

A tap at my passenger window startled me. I turned to see a girl crouched next to my door.

Wait. Not just any girl. I recognized her. She was that reporter. Kate something.

I rolled down my window. "Hey," she said in a quiet voice. "What are you being detained for?"

"Me?" I asked.

She rolled her eyes. "You're the only person in the car, so… yes, you."

Did she think I was a criminal? I was in the passenger seat. She wasn't much of a reporter if she couldn't figure that out.

"Wait—I'm not being arrested. I'm not even a part of this. I'm here with someone, an officer who's in there right now." I pointed to the warehouse.

She started typing on her phone. "Okay, and what's his name? What is he doing in there? Do you have any information about what happened?"

She was rattling off questions quicker than I could comprehend and answer them. "Hold on, you're that reporter, Kate-something, right?"

"Kate Phillips. Yes, that's me." Then she stared at me. "I know you…"

"You interviewed me about my car ending up in front of that building during that shootout with the police, the vigilante, and the guy who stole my car."

She nodded. "Yes, I remember now. Kind of a weird coincidence finding you in another police car now. Anyway, can you answer my questions? I don't have a lot of time before they find me here."

"They?" I asked.

She shook her head, clearly frustrated that I wasn't answering her questions. "The authorities. I'm supposed to be behind that yellow tape over there." She pointed to where Shane and I had been let through by the officer guarding the area. I guessed he wasn't doing a good job of that. "I snuck over here without them finding me. Happy now? Can you please answer my questions?"

"Sure, after you answer one of mine."

"I already did. Your turn," she retorted.

"Fine. The officer's name is Shane Cranston. We're from Mapleton. Apparently, so much has happened over here that the DC police called the Mapleton police for backup. That's all I know."

She typed what I just said into her phone quickly. "You said you're from Mapleton?"

"My turn," I reminded her.

She looked around and stood up a little to see over the hood of the vehicle. "Hurry up. What?" she said, waving a hand.

"You're very attractive. Can I take you out for a drink sometime?" I asked. What's the worst that could happen? She'd say no?

"No," she replied immediately.

"Why not?"

"My turn," she shot back. "You said you're from Mapleton?"

"Yes."

"There's a man who—"

I interrupted her. "That's a question! Now it's my turn. Why not?"

She shook her head. "You're very difficult, you know that, right?"

"Is that your question?" I asked.

"Is that yours?" she replied.

"Touché." She was good. "Okay, my question. Why not go out for a drink with me?"

"No offense, but you're sitting in a police car. I don't know exactly why you're here, apart from what you told me. And how do I know if you're telling me the truth or not? Also, I don't know you. What's your name again, anyway?"

"Adam."

"Adam what?"

"My turn," I said. "You started saying something about a man, before I interrupted you."

"Rudely, I might add," she said, but now there was a smirk on her face. Was she enjoying this? "Yes, there's a man we're trying to track. Have you seen him?" She tapped on her phone and pictures appeared. She swiped a few times and then held the phone in front of me.

The picture showed a man, his body half turned to the left, but he was facing the camera with a stone-cold look. There was a gun dangling in his right hand, and it looked as if he had a scar down the left side of his face. A scary looking dude.

"Probably not the face you want on your children's cereal boxes. What'd he do?" I asked.

"We're trying to track him down. We think he's behind a lot of what's been happening here in Decker City," Kate replied.

"Who's we?" I asked.

"Me and a guy I'm working with."

"Would he happen to be your boyfriend?" I had to ask.

She swiped the picture away and pulled up her notes again. "No. But I wouldn't cross him."

I almost laughed. "I think I can hold my own."

She leaned closer towards the window and peeked into the car, looking me over. She smiled at me. "*Sure* you can."

"What? Are you being sarcastic?"

"Sarcastic. Having the character of sarcasm. That's very profound of you to point that out. Your partner must be the intelligent one." She rolled her eyes again.

I liked her even more now. She was quick, too. "He's not my partner. He's some guy who's driving me around."

Suddenly, the driver's side door opened. Shane climbed back into the car. "Who are you talking to, Adam?" he asked.

I turned back to my window, to see Kate sneaking away. She turned around and waved to me. She then pointed to her eyes with her index and middle finger, then pointed towards the car. What the hell was she doing? It looked like she was signaling *I see you*. She kept doing it, too. Adam leaned over me and saw her. Once Kate saw him, she turned and moved out of sight.

"Who was that?" he asked.

"Umm…" I decided to tell him her first name and leave it at that. Like he would know who she was, anyway. "Kate."

"Phillips? That damn reporter? What did you tell her?"

"Whoa there, Negative Nancy. She was nice. And how did you know it was her? All I said was her first name."

"I assumed it was her, and you gave it away. She's all over the place in Decker City. I heard she's working with some ex-Special Forces guy. She's trouble. Plus, she's a reporter. Stay away from her."

He turned the ignition and put on his seatbelt.

"So what happened in there?" I asked him.

He turned to face me. "A violent battle. That's what happened in there. Apparently, Mitchell Quinn is behind the crime that has taken place in Decker City."

"That rich dude?"

"Yes, Adam. *That rich dude.* He kidnapped a girl and held her hostage in that warehouse. I saw her and, surprisingly, our doctor, Andrew Kane."

"He was in there?"

"Yes. I only spoke to him briefly. I told him I would be following up with him once everything calms down. I'll swing by his office tomorrow morning for a more in-depth chat."

He edged the car forward. The officer handling the entrance was letting a taxi through as we were leaving. I turned around in the police car and looked out the back window to see a girl walk out of the warehouse with a blanket over her shoulders. The taxi parked, and a man got out. The girl ran over to him and wrapped her arms around his neck. Shane pulled the car onto the street, and I lost sight of the pair.

I turned around. "Can I come with you tomorrow when you talk to the doctor?"

For a few seconds, Shane didn't answer. I could tell he was thinking.

"Look, I listened to you," I said. "I didn't get out of the car. I was good tonight. Come on. Give me that."

He nodded. "You're right. You behaved. Okay, look, keep up the good behavior and you can keep tagging along. Deal?"

"Yes! Deal!" I couldn't believe Shane was allowing me to come along with him.

I started to wonder what Kate was talking about. Who was that guy she showed me on her phone? And why had she seemed concerned when I mentioned I was from Mapleton? Was he in Mapleton? Now I wished I'd had more time to talk to her. Shane had to come back to the car and ruin it. I was having fun with her, too. A few more minutes and I would have had her agreeing to have drinks with me.

Maybe.

During the drive back to Mapleton, Shane told me what had happened inside the warehouse. There had been more reports of the vigilante moving things without touching them. Even the criminals the police had detained had acknowledged it. Even so, Shane still didn't believe it, saying there had to be some other explanation. His most frequently used word during the drive home was "impossible."

"Here we are, right?" Shane asked.

I was surprised when he pulled up to my apartment at a little after 1 am. He had never driven me home before. I was surprised he even knew where I lived.

"Yeah. Thanks. You didn't have to do this, though. I could have walked home," I said.

"Your walk would have been close to an hour. It's the middle of the night. Get out and go get some sleep. I'll be coming to pick you up around ten o'clock. You better be outside waiting or I'm leaving without you."

I believed that. He wouldn't wait for me. I had to make sure I was ready by then. Maybe it was a good idea he'd driven me home, then.

"Got it. Thanks, Shane."

I stepped out of the car. I went to push the door closed, but then I saw something written in chalk, or some kind of faint white ink, on the police car.

"Everything okay?" Shane asked, rolling down the passenger window.

I closed the door. "I think so." I bent down to get a closer look at the writing. There were numbers written on the car. Ten digits. A phone number? Was it Kate's? Was that what she was pointing at while she was driving away? I memorized the numbers, saying them in my head repeatedly. Then I wiped away the writing with my sleeve. "It looked like there was a dent on your car. It was just dirt," I lied.

"Probably from that damn reporter," Shane said. "Anyway, go get some rest. I'll see you in the morning." He rolled up the window and drove away.

I pulled out my phone and dialed the number I'd memorized, repeating the digits as I typed them in.

After the first ring, a female voice answered.

"Hello?"

"Hey, it's Adam. Is this Kate?"

"Look at those detective skills being put to the test," she replied.

"I guess you wanted that drink, since you gave me your number. I didn't even have to ask for it."

"And now we're right back to me thinking your partner is the intelligent one. Can we meet?"

"For a drink?"

"Would you stop asking... You know what? A drink would be nice. You said you're buying, right?"

I knew the perfect place. "Sure. There's a place not far from where I am. I'll text you the address."

"Okay, thanks." She hung up.

I sent her the address of Chuck's bar. I knew this wasn't anything, but it was fun to mess with her. Any tiredness I had felt was washing away in my excitement to meet up with her. According to Shane, she was working with some ex-Special Forces guy, trying to track down this guy with the scar. Maybe my ability would come in handy now.

I started walking towards Chuck's bar, excited to find out why Kate wanted to meet me.

| 15 |

I walked into The Stout House a little after 1:30 am. Chuck was at the bar, pouring a beer for a customer. As he turned to pass the drink to the customer, he gave a slight nod of the head to acknowledge my presence. I walked over to the bar and sat down.

"To what do I owe the honor, with thirty minutes to closing time?" he asked.

"I'm meeting someone here in a few minutes," I replied.

"Kind of late for a date, don't you think? You did just hear me say thirty minutes to close, right?"

"Dude, I've had quite the night. Well, it actually started off kind of boring. Anyway, do you know what's going on in Decker City tonight?"

Chuck shrugged his shoulders. "A giant party? I really don't know. I've been here all night," he said, waving to indicate the bar. "I don't really get out much or know what's happening outside of here while I'm working."

"You have televisions. Put the news on or something," I told him.

"Oh, yeah... because that'll go over really well with the drunks here. Let's take sports off the TVs and put on the news."

"Alright, alright. I get it. Do you know who Mitchell Quinn is? I think that's his name..."

"Yes, he's that rich entrepreneur building the humongous building in Decker City, right?" Chuck asked.

"Yup. Apparently, he kidnapped this girl and got in a car chase with the vigilante. I was out with Shane again tonight and he took me out to Decker City to investigate everything."

"You're out playing police and I'm stuck in this bar..." Chuck responded, shaking his head. He reached for the remote and turned one of the TVs onto a local news channel. It had to have been the story of the night, because the reporters were talking about it at this moment. Someone was talking to the camera in front of the new entertainment center in Decker City. Chuck turned up the volume.

"—ended at this facility behind me. This violence has caused a trail of destruction throughout the city over the last few months, but hopefully it has been put to an end with the death of Mitchell Quinn."

"Whoa, what?" I exclaimed. Shane had only moments ago told me Quinn was behind everything and now he was dead?

Chuck waved his hand for me to be quiet.

"Thank you for that report, David. Hopefully, the city can rest easy now. If you're just joining us, the top story tonight is the death of Mitchell Quinn and his alleged complicity with the attacks within Decker City over the last few months. Hours ago, he was shot and killed by local authorities. He was pronounced dead at the scene. There's a lot of work to be done to clean up the destruction left behind after the events of tonight, beginning with the shootout at the docks and multiple car accidents caused by a high-speed pursuit. We will bring you more information as it becomes available throughout the night."

"Wow. I can't believe this," I said.

"Yeah, it's pretty unreal," a voice next to me said.

I jumped, as this new voice was completely unexpected. Kate was standing next to me. "You scared the hell out of me. Where did you come from?"

"My mom and the authorities are still trying to figure that out," she replied. She sat on the seat next to mine. "So, it looks like you're all caught up now." She motioned towards the TV, then looked around the bar, and finally at Chuck. "Nice place. Can I get a glass of red wine? Do you have Malbec?"

"You know, we're closing in a few minutes," Chuck replied.

"She's with me. This is Kate." I motioned to Chuck. "Kate, this is Chuck. He owns the place."

"Nice to meet you," she said offering her hand.

Chuck smiled and shook her hand. "Glass of wine, coming up."

I turned back to Kate. "What's going on out there? Why is all of this happening?"

"I don't have an exact answer for you yet. But what you just heard on the news pretty much sums it up. Mitchell was a part of the violence in Decker City. But he's not the only one. Actually, Mitchell was only a pawn. He was a nobody."

"A nobody? What about the bomb? The drugs? The criminals taking over? Everything that happened tonight?" I asked her.

"He wasn't behind any of that. Well, I mean he was a part of it, but he wasn't the mastermind behind it." She pulled out her phone and opened up the photo app again, then swiped back to the photo she had showed me earlier. "This is the guy we're after. This is the really dangerous one."

"And how do you know this?" Chuck asked as he brought over a glass of wine.

She turned to him. "I'm a reporter. I have my ways of finding things out."

"Does it have anything to do with this ex-Special Force boyfriend of yours?" I asked.

She rolled her eyes. "Not a boyfriend. And where did you hear that?"

"The officer I was with told me."

"Well, you can go tell your officer that he is mistaken. He's not ex-Special Forces."

"What is he then?"

"Guys," Chuck said, interrupting us. "Back on topic, please." He turned his attention to Kate. "How do you know this other guy that you mentioned is behind everything?"

"Yeah!" I added. "You asked me here. Start talking, missy!"

Kate shook her head. I could tell she regretted coming here. But she continued with her story. "During my investigations around Decker City, I've been hearing rumblings about this other guy, their boss. Someone who's not Mitchell. So I dug a little deeper and with the help of another *individual*," she emphasized the word, looking at me, "I was able to uncover someone else that was involved. And much *more* involved than Mitchell was. The picture I showed you, the man with the scar, that's him. That's who we're looking for."

"Do the police know about him?" Chuck asked.

"Kind of. It's a little complicated."

"How?" I asked. "Can't you just show the police his picture and they post it all over TV?" Obviously, I knew nothing about police work but it had to work somehow like that.

"Not exactly. What do you want me to do? Walk into the police station and say 'Here! This is the guy you want!' and show them a picture on my phone and call it a day?"

"Well, when you put it that way, it sounds kind of ridiculous. A simple 'no' would have sufficed."

She ignored me. "Everything leading to this guy with the scar stems from another police district and someone else who has a history with him."

"The guy you're working with, I assume?" Chuck said.

She nodded. "He was tasked to work in Decker City after the bombing, and he found evidence of the presence of the man with the scar. Everything has escalated, especially after tonight. His front man, Mitchell, has died. That's going to bring this guy more out in the open. Which leads me to why I wanted to talk with you tonight," she said, turning to me. "The man I'm working with, he has tracked the man with the scar to Mapleton. But we need help. You're here in Mapleton and working with the police..."

Chuck chuckled and interrupted her. "I'm sorry. Go ahead."

She looked confused. "What?"

"I'll let Adam take this one."

"Thanks, *Chuck*..." he was ruining this for me. "I don't actually work with the police. I'm just going on ride-alongs."

Kate still looked confused. "What do you do, then?"

This wasn't heading in the right direction. I let out a sigh. "I'm... umm... kind of in between work right now."

"You're unemployed?"

Chuck stepped up to save me. "No. He's working here until he can find something more permanent and suited for his... *abilities.*"

Kate took a deep breath and seemed to ponder her next move.

"And with that awkward silence, it's closing time." Chuck cupped his hands together. "Okay guys! Closing time. You don't have to go home, but you can't stay here."

"Good song," Kate complimented.

"I enjoy my nineties music," Chuck said.

"Look," I said. "I'm working with Shane right now at the Mapleton police department. Not actually 'working'—but I'm going out and learning things. He's picking me up in a few hours to start an investigation. I want to help. I *can* help."

"How?"

"I'll be on the lookout for that man with the scar. I'll be driving around with Shane. I can let him know about it too."

She shook her head. "I'm sorry. It was a mistake coming here." She grabbed her glass of wine and gulped it down. "Thanks for the drink Adam, but I don't think we can help each other."

No.

This was my opportunity to finally make a difference. There were people out there actively going up against these bad guys, and I wanted to be one of them. I had an opportunity to find a way in with this reporter, but she was pushing me aside. I needed to make her believe in me. And there was only one way to make that happen.

As she stood and turned away from the bar, I yelled, "No! Wait!" She turned around, and I reached over the bar and grabbed a knife.

"Adam, what are you doing?" Chuck asked nervously.

I placed the knife against my arm and sliced.

"What the hell are you doing?" Kate was wide-eyed, her hands on her head.

The pain was intense, but I could handle it. Knowing it was only temporary made it easier to manage and control. Blood began to slide down my arm once I pulled the blade away from the skin.

"What is the matter with you?" Kate yelled.

Just wait for it.

I put the knife back on the bar. Chuck handed me a towel from behind the bar. I could see the disappointment on his face when I took it from him. I guess he hadn't wanted me to show her. But I didn't have a choice. If I wanted to help find the guy with the scar, I had to show Kate my special ability that could assist in helping capture the man with the scar. It was kind of exciting, showing it to someone else. Kate's expression was priceless. Her eyes were still wide open and her mouth had dropped slightly, covered with her hands.

I covered my arm with the towel and said, "Watch this."

She dropped her hands from her mouth. "Watch what?" she said. "You're a psycho! Who cuts themselves?"

The pain disappeared. I wiped the wound clean and removed the towel. "Look." I moved my arm forward for her to see. "No cut."

"What?" She walked towards me, grabbed my arm and examined it, touching the area where I had cut myself. "This is a trick, right?" She reached for the knife and picked it up. It was covered it blood. "It's a fake knife, one of those prop knives that leaks liquid that resembles blood. Right?"

"I can heal. I can't get hurt. I've broken bones, gotten beat up and cut up, I've been stabbed…"

"When were you stabbed?" Chuck chimed in.

"After I last saw you. I went home after being shot and wanted to test my ability."

"You were shot?" Kate asked.

"Oh, yeah. And shot. Everything heals within seconds."

It was clear she couldn't comprehend what was going on. She had a look of complete bewilderment on her face. I guess I could understand. She had just seen something which she probably assumed was impossible.

"I don't… How… What?" Kate stammered.

"Look, I don't understand it either. It's just something I've always been able to do ever since I was a little kid."

"But I don't understand. How is this possible?" she said.

"It's as possible as that vigilante out in Decker City that can move things without touching them," Chuck added.

She turned to Chuck, then back to me. "The difference is I've never witnessed him do that. They're only stories I report about *other* people who saw it happen. This, I just saw in person, as creepy as it was." She tried to shake off the confusion. "Okay. You have now creeped me out and confused the hell out of me. I need to process this." She turned to Chuck. "What did you put in my wine? Did you know about this *ability* of his?"

Chuck nodded.

She looked back at me. "I'm going to go now. I think I need to get some sleep after all of this." She started walking towards the door.

"Kate," I said, stopping her. She turned back to look at me. "No one knows about this, other than who's in this room right now. And for now, I'd prefer to keep it that way. I know you're a reporter and all, but I want to ask for your discretion, please."

"Adam, I don't even believe what I just saw. It's not leaving my lips. You have my word."

"Thank you," I said.

She turned and left the bar. I wasn't sure if I had made the right move, showing her my ability, but what else was I supposed to do? This was my way into this investigation, and I had to do it. I wasn't sure I trusted her with the knowledge of what I could do, though. I mean, I had only just met her a few hours ago—and she was a reporter. She'd probably pay for a story like this.

"I can't believe you showed her," Chuck said. "I wouldn't have, but you gotta run with it now."

"I actually feel relieved that someone else knows, that I could show someone. I may have scared her big time, but given what the vigilante can do, maybe it won't be that bad now that I know someone else is able to do something special too."

"I guess you're right. Just be careful, Adam. You don't really know what you're capable of yet and running around hunting bad guys…? Are you really prepared for that?"

I wasn't, especially after my two recent encounters. When I was pulled from my car, I froze up. Then I was attacked and held hostage by another criminal. Wow, I sucked. I really wasn't ready for any of this.

"Yup," I lied, obviously. I couldn't let Chuck know I was nervous and having doubts. I knew I could heal and protect myself that way, but I didn't know what to expect when I was out there on my own. I wondered how the Gray Hood had started? Was he operating by himself, or did he have someone else with him?

Chuck smiled and shook his head. "You're a terrible liar, but you're the most qualified person I know to handle themselves. I watched every one of your fights. This time, you won't have to pretend. You can actually go out there and be yourself. No hiding your ability. Just go be you."

He was right. When I fought here at the bar, I had to act like I was getting injured normally to hide my ability. Now, I wouldn't have to hold back anymore.

"You should probably go home and get some sleep. You have a long day tomorrow," Chuck added.

"Yeah, I know. Shane's going to be picking me up in a few hours," I said.

"And you start your first day tomorrow."

"What? Here?"

"Yes. I told that reporter you worked here, so you're going to work here. You need a job and I won't take 'no' for an answer anymore."

"How about nope?"

"Adam, come on. You start tomorrow. Just come by after you're done with Shane, and I'll show you some things."

I couldn't argue with him anymore. I needed a job, and I'd failed at getting one over the last few days. At this point, it was my only option. It looked like I finally had a job again.

| 16 |

A blaring noise kept repeating. I opened my eyes slowly. Everything was blurry. I reached over and turned the alarm off on my phone.

It was 9:35 am. I was exhausted. I wished my ability could prevent me from feeling this tired. Once I got home last night, I went online, looking up article after article about Mitchell Quinn and what had happened last night. There were a ton of reports about the shootout, the car chase, and the showdown at the entertainment center. Even Kate's article was up already. Thankfully, there was no mention of me. She had kept her word.

I rolled out of bed and began getting myself ready. I didn't require coffee or any kind of energy boost in the morning to get started; although sometimes it helped, I wasn't someone that absolutely *had* to have it. Once I got up and started moving around, I felt awake within a few minutes.

I went into my kitchen and searched for something to eat. I took out a bowl and a reached for a cereal box on top of the fridge. It was empty. Of course it was.

I found some bread and stuck it in the toaster, then, when it was done, and I grabbed the two slices and left my apartment. I had three minutes to spare.

I got downstairs to find Shane already waiting. I swear this guy didn't sleep. I knew he hadn't gone home after he dropped me off last night. He probably had a late night too, and yet he was able to get ready, go to the police station *and* get here before I was ready?

"Good morning, Adam," he said. "On time too. I like it."

"Makes it easier when I get door-to-door service like this," I told him. "You spoil me."

He put his hand on his forehead. "I don't know why I put up with you. Just get in the car, you moron."

He opened the driver's side door, and I got in at the passenger side. "Are we paying the doctor a visit this morning?" I asked.

"Yes. We're starting at Dr. Andrew Kane's office. He gave me his address last night, so that's our first stop."

"First stop? Where else are we going?"

"We are going to examine the evidence from the warehouse last night. We have a ton of pictures to sort through. You said you wanted to be a part of this and learn what we do. Well, here you go."

Great. More paperwork. I guessed it would be kind of cool to be a part of this, but what I wanted to do was go after criminals. I had a new opportunity to work with Kate, trying to find this guy with the scar. Did she really expect me to just find him walking down the street in Mapleton? I wanted to impress her and help find the guy but I had no idea where to start.

We crossed the bridge into Decker City. Barricades had been set up to direct traffic away from the areas of destruction and to maintain the crime scenes while the police finished their investigation. Being in a police car, we could ignore the barricades and just drive through them. We pulled off the highway and started making our way along the city streets, and then the buildings began spreading out, as we made our way into the suburbs.

Shane listened to his GPS as it directed him into what looked like a residential area. We were about a block away. When we pulled up, the place looked like just a house. This was the doctor's office? I had been expecting a more commercial area, whereas this seemed as if he took a house and made it an office.

There was a taxi parked outside. I watched as two people got inside. The vehicle drove away as we pulled up. Shane gave it a quick look and then pulled into the driveway of the house.

"We're here," he said. I unbuckled my seatbelt, and Shane said, "When we get inside, you let me do the talking. You are here to observe, and observe only. Don't touch anything. Don't speak. Don't get in my way. Understand?"

Once again, I was being sidelined. Well, kind of. I was able to join him inside this time, but unable to actively participate. I couldn't really complain, though. He could have easily left me out of everything today, or told me to stay in the car again. He was taking me with him today, and I had to at least be grateful for that.

"Got it, boss!" I replied as I opened the door.

Shane stood out front and looked the house up and down, then approached the front door. I looked up at the house too, but couldn't figure out what the hell he was looking at. I joined Shane as he knocked loudly four times on the door.

A few seconds went by and there was no answer. I looked at Shane as he continued peering up at the house. "Do you think he's home?"

Shane leaned towards the window on the right. "That's what I'm trying to find out."

"Do you think that was him in the taxi that left when we got here?" I asked.

He pulled away from the window and looked at me. "Adam, I don't know." He knocked four more times on the door, with more intensity this time.

A faint noise came from inside. Did someone say something?

"Did you hear that?" I asked.

"Yes, he said 'coming.'" Geez, the guy had the hearing of a bat. He could hear the faintest of sounds.

The locks started coming undone, and the door swung open. "Officer, I'm sorry. I was sleeping. It was kind of a long night."

Dr. Kane's eyes looked heavy. His messy pepper hair was sticking up in some places.

"It's okay, I understand. May we come in?" Shane asked.

"Absolutely." He pulled the door open and welcomed us inside.

"Dr. Kane, this is Adam. He's going to be joining me today. He's an intern, and they have tasked me with showing him the job we do at the Mapleton police station. Is it okay if he joins us?"

He was good. I even believed him, he was so confident in his lie. It made me wonder what else he had lied about, especially to me.

Dr. Kane nodded. "Of course."

He led us past a room that looked recently used. Tools were laid out on a dressing table and towels were laid next to them. They looked like they had blood on them. I knew that if I'd noticed them, Shane had definitely noticed them.

Dr. Kane guided us into a sitting room. We all sat down and Shane immediately began, "Thank you for allowing me to stop by today. After our brief conversation yesterday, you said you were taken by the vigilante to the docks. How did that happen?"

Dr. Kane nodded. "That's correct. I was getting ready to leave here yesterday when he jumped in my car and told me to drive him to this club in the city. And I did. I didn't know who he was at first, but when some guy hops in your car wearing a hoodie and dictating directions, you kind of freeze up and listen. I didn't know if he had a weapon. I just did what he asked."

Shane pulled out a pad of paper and began writing notes. "Why did he come here?"

Dr. Kane shook his head. "I have no idea. Maybe he was in the area? I didn't ask."

Shane continued writing. "Why did he want you to take him to this club? And what was the name of it?"

"Umm… I think it was called The Prime Time. He told me he was looking for someone, and couldn't go in there otherwise he'd be seen."

"But if he had a hood on, who would recognize him?"

"I don't know. I think he was after this guy—Patrick, I think that's his name." Shane immediately wrote it down. "He made me go into the club. I saw Patrick, and he was talking to this other guy. A big guy."

"Do you know who the other guy was?" Shane asked.

"No, sorry."

"Do you know what these two guys did in the club? Did this other guy have any distinguishing features? Any information will help us out."

"I saw a suitcase being given to Patrick, and they ate. That's really it. Oh! And the other guy had a scar down his face."

A scar? Was this the guy Kate was talking about? I hoped Shane would keep questioning Dr. Kane about this man with the scar, but it seemed like he was going easy on this doctor.

I couldn't help myself. "Do you know what side of the face his scar was on?" I asked.

I could feel Shane's eyes glare at me. He had told me not to say anything and I'd just broken my promise. But what if this was the guy Kate was looking for? I was only trying to help.

Dr. Kane touched his face. "It was his on his left side. Yes, that's right. Left side."

It was him! Although this was exciting, I had no idea what to do with this knowledge. I knew he was at this club in Decker City last night. Okay, now what? My excitement faded quickly.

Shane kept taking his notes. "What did the scar look like?"

"It went down his face. From above his eye to… maybe his upper lip?"

"In your medical opinion, could you speculate what may have caused the scar?" Shane asked. "A birth defect? Or do you think something caused it? Maybe an injury?"

"I didn't get a good look at it, since it was kind of dark in the club," Dr. Kane replied. "But I don't believe it was a birth defect. Looked like a nasty cut that may have healed into a noticeable scar. I couldn't be sure without examining him."

Shane continued to write. "One last question, and then we'll let you get on with your day. Do you think what this vigilante can do is real? And do you know who he is?"

"That's two questions," Dr. Kane replied.

"It's a two-parter," Shane said, squinting his eyes, slightly.

"Well, I have seen some bizarre things during my thirty years or so as a doctor—and this is definitely the craziest. I've seen him in action and I can say that, yes, I believe what he does is real. And to answer your second part—no, I don't know who he is. I wish I did, though, so I could learn from him and figure out this ability of his. It's truly an incredible thing that he can do."

Shane wrote some final words, then put his notepad back in his jacket pocket. He stood up and Dr. Kane followed suit. They shook hands and thanked each other for their time.

That was it? I thought Shane would have asked the doctor more questions. He certainly liked to question me for longer periods of time.

As we walked out, Shane pointed to the room I'd noticed when we came in. "What happened in there?"

"Oh, there?" Dr. Kane turned and looked at the things left on the table and in sight. "I was, uh… attending to a patient's injuries. She stayed here last night."

"Was it the girl I saw you around last night?"

Dr. Kane nodded.

"What about the guy I saw her with?" Shane asked.

"Oh, yeah. He was here too. That's her boyfriend. He rushed over to the warehouse when he found out what happened. He stayed with her here to make sure she was okay."

Shane nodded. "Okay. Thank you for your hospitality. You were helpful. If I have any further questions, would I be able to contact you?"

"Absolutely, officer. Anything I can do to help, just let me know." Dr. Kane leaned over and took a business card from the table in the lobby and handed it to Shane, who took it and put it in his pocket. He Dr. Kane and we walked outside.

As we got back in the car, Shane asked me, "So, what did you think?"

"About what?"

"Did you believe him?"

"I think so. He seemed pretty helpful."

Shane shook his head. "You'd make for a pretty bad detective if you believed everyone just like that."

"What? Why? You think he was lying?"

Shane pulled out his cell phone and dialed a number. "Absolutely, he's lying." He put the phone to his ear.

"How do you know?" I asked.

"He gave no information when I asked about the vigilante. Not a single description. When he described that man with the scar for the first time…" He stopped, holding up a finger. "Yes, hi. I'm Officer Shane Cranston and I work with the Mapleton police department." There was a slight pause. "No, ma'am, you're not in any trouble. I'm actually calling to get your help. I'm looking for the whereabouts of a taxi. Can you help me with that?" Another pause. "Yes, I have the number. It's 8291. Yes, I can hold."

He looked at me again, still holding the phone to his ear. "When Dr. Kane described the man with the scar, he called him a big guy. He could describe the scar. Speaking of, how did you know about that?"

"Don't be mad," I told him.

"Things always go great when someone starts a sentence with those words," Shane replied.

"Kate told me about him last night. She showed me a picture of him. She was looking for him in Mapleton. She said that's where he is."

"Leave the police work to the police and let her run around and do her reporting, or whatever she wants to call what she does. But back to Dr. Kane. He could describe that man with the scar, but when I asked about the vigilante, not one single description."

"Well, didn't he say he was wearing a hood? Maybe he couldn't see him," I said, playing devil's advocate.

Shane laughed. "Speaking of a hood, the person I spoke with on the highway last night told me the vigilante was wearing a hat, not his typical hood."

"So he's lying then," I said.

"I would say so. Look, he couldn't even describe the guy, either. How about his size? How tall was he? Did he have a deep voice? Any features about his clothing that stood out? What else was he wearing? I mean, he gave us nothing. Why didn't he just leave when the vigilante dropped him off at the club? Why did he help him? He's holding something back. Hold on. Yes ma'am, I'm here." He paused again, listening to the woman on the other end of the line. "Thank you so much. I appreciate your help. Have a good day." He hung up and put his phone back in his pocket.

"What was that about?" I asked.

"The taxi that was here when we arrived. I got the number and called their dispatch office to find out where it stopped this morning. She gave me a few locations. The first was at 10 am, at a restaurant downtown. That obviously wasn't it. The next was to this address, where we are currently. The stop after here was Decker City Hospital."

"Then whoever was in the taxi went to Decker City Hospital?"

Shane smacked his forehead. "Are you really this dumb, or are you just messing with me?"

I had no idea what he was talking about. I thought I had asked a serious question, looking for a serious response. Definitely not the response I'd been expecting.

"Okay, I'm dumb. I get it. I suck at this. You know more than I do and I could never do this."

"Adam, I'm pointing these things out so you learn. But sometimes I feel like I'm talking to a five-year-old. Dr. Kane literally said 'his patient' and her boyfriend were here this morning. Don't you think it was probably them who left in the taxi when we got there? I mean, just by process of elimination, I'm almost one hundred percent certain that's who we will find when we get to the hospital."

I was dumb. Dr. Kane did say they were here this morning. I guess Shane was trying to help me out. I needed to prove to him I could do this. I needed to be more focused next time.

"So, off to the hospital, I guess?" I asked.

"Yup. I have a few questions for this *patient* of Dr. Kane's and her boyfriend. Like—why there was all that blood on the towels in that room, and why it looked like such a mess. Because when I saw her last night at the warehouse, she seemed pretty unharmed."

"Who was injured, then?"

Shane started the car and backed out of Dr. Kane's driveway, "That's what we're going to find out."

| 17 |

25 years ago

"Honey, it's going to be okay." Steve, Martha's husband, said.

"How is it going to be okay? He's… he's… changed. Something is wrong with him. I just want my little boy to be okay," Martha wept.

They stood over the crib and watched their baby boy sleep peacefully. They had discussed what the doctor had said a few months ago and tried to figure out how to cope with the new changes the doctor had told Martha about her son.

"Come on, let him sleep," Steve said, trying to drag his wife out of her son's bedroom. Martha leaned down and gave her son a kiss on his forehead. Adam twitched and fell still again, sound asleep.

Over the last few months, Adam had had a few injuries, as most babies do. A few bumps on the head from the coffee table. A fall here and there. One time he even cut himself on a can Martha had left out. Adam reached for it and Martha immediately ripped it from his grip, cutting his fingers in the process. This was the first moment she had noticed a major change in Adam. She had thought little of the fact he never got bumps and bruises, or even the slightest bit injured from falling. She just thought he wouldn't easily bruise and her little boy was just a tough kid. But he didn't even get sick. It all just seemed too disturbing to Martha.

When Martha ripped the can from Adam, his fingers immediately bled. Adam became hysterical. He screamed and cried. Martha quickly grabbed a towel, picked up Adam, and wrapped the towel around his hand. She was terrified, thinking he would need stitches, and it was all her fault.

She rushed him into the bathroom and started running the water, then removed the towel and placed her son's hand under the running water. Adam started to calm down as Martha washed away the blood from his hand. She placed some soap on her hands and used it to clean Adam's hands. When she pulled his hands from the water, she expected to see blood flowing from his little fingers, but there was nothing. She took a clean towel and dried her hands and her son's. To her amazement, there was no blood. There wasn't even a cut, or even any mark. She examined his hand closely, flipping it and analyzing the back, thinking maybe the injury had been to the back of his hand. There was nothing. She didn't understand. She knew his hand had been bleeding pretty badly at first. The bloody towel proved that. Why had it suddenly stopped? What had caused him to heal so quickly?

Since then, she had been extremely worried about Adam, becoming distant and scared of him. Martha didn't understand what had happened to her son, and it was scaring her. She loved Adam so much. She wanted the best for her son and for him to be perfect. Whatever was happening to him had put a giant blemish on all of this.

Steve held Martha in his arms. "It's going to be okay," he said again. "Whatever you decide, I'll support your decision."

"It's just hard. You're always working to provide for us, and I do appreciate that, so much. But if Adam needs help—medical help—

we can't afford it. Money comes in and goes right back out. I can't provide the help he needs. I feel like this is all my fault."

She took complete blame for Adam's changes. She had been supposed to watch him at the park, and she had left him. It had only been for a moment, but it was a moment she would never get back, and she took responsibility for that. Adam would never be the same, because of her.

Steve always tried to do his best to help calm his wife. He was a chef at a small restaurant, and worked long hours to provide for his family. He was the only one in the household who worked. They didn't have much, but they were able to get by. Unfortunately, they couldn't be able to give Adam the help he needed. The word 'adoption' had kept popping up in their conversations over the last few weeks. It broke both of their hearts to think like that, but they didn't have a choice. Whatever was happening to Adam was scaring them, and he needed medical attention—a lot of it. Martha and Steve didn't have the time or money for that.

They discussed adoption again that night. Steve told Martha he had had a conversation with the doctor before he went to work. There was a family who was ready to adopt Adam, if they were ready to move forward with it.

A creak came from the top of the stairs. Steve walked around the corner and looked at the top of the stairs.

"Son, please go back to bed," Steve said.

"But Daddy…"

"Now," he said sternly.

His son ducked away from the stairs, and Steve heard footsteps as he went back into his room.

"Do you think he heard us?" Martha asked.

"I don't know. He's going to be devastated, though. But we can't take care of Adam the way he needs," Steve replied.

He wrapped his arms around her. "I'll call the doctor in the morning and maybe we'll be able to meet the family first. We'll make sure he's going to be okay."

He felt Martha nod against his chest. This was the most difficult decision he had ever had to make.

| **18** |

Present Day

"Teach me. What should I be looking for during this conversation?" I asked Shane on our drive to Decker City Hospital.

"Look at everything. Surroundings. Take notice of everything you can. You never know what information you'll need. Listen to what they say and especially to what they *don't* say," Shane replied.

"What do you mean by that?"

We approached a red light, and Shane stopped the car and turned to face me. "What I mean is listen to what they don't say. Facial expressions can tell a lot. Like how I could tell our doctor back there was holding back information about the vigilante. He spoke about this other guy but had nothing to say about the vigilante." He turned back to the road. "I don't believe him for a second. He knows something." The light turned green, and the car moved forward.

"Why didn't you ask him about it, then? Why not call him out on his lies?" I asked.

"I don't know for sure they're lies. I'd rather let him believe he's not in any trouble and that everything is fine. Maybe that way he'll slip up. If I'd pressed him harder, he may have closed up and not given us anything."

Shane was always one step ahead. I had a lot to learn from him. I hoped he wasn't pulling this tactic on me. Was he?

We turned the corner and I saw the hospital was up ahead.

"Same business in here," Shane said. "You are here to observe. Don't touch anything and don't speak, which you failed at last time."

"Hey, I got him to talk about the man with the scar. Now you know he's involved."

"And where does that get us? It gets me a person of interest. I don't know that guy. I don't know this 'man with the scar', what he's done or how he's involved, if even at all."

"But Kate said he—" I began.

Shane cut me off.

"Adam, I don't care what she said. Ignore her. She's not a part of this investigation. Whatever she does in her own personal time or work is her business. Leave the police work to me."

This was where we'd have to agree to disagree. I knew I wouldn't win this battle, so I knew to just shut up about it. Shane would just keep telling me I was wrong. I had proved we needed to know more about the man with the scar, but I was only coming to him with information from a reporter. Shane was better than that. I'd been around him long enough to know that if I wanted to push for something, I needed evidence. He wouldn't budge otherwise.

We pulled up to the hospital and Shane parked in the garage.

"Why are we parking here?" I asked. "Can't we just pull up out front?"

"This isn't an emergency. I can't just park my police car wherever I want," Shane replied.

"Why?" I asked.

Shane pulled into a parking spot. "You want me to abuse the power I have as an officer and park in an emergency lane in front of the hospital, because you're too lazy and don't want to walk a few extra steps?" He unbuckled his seatbelt and got out of the car.

I sat there, stunned. "Well, you didn't have to put it that way," I said to myself, rolling my eyes despite being alone in the car. Then I said louder, so he would hear me, "You know, you don't always have to be a smart-ass when you answer my questions." I opened the door and stepped outside.

"This, coming from the guy who is a *constant* smart-ass?" Shane said.

"Since when did you become the quick-witted police officer?"

"When I started spending so much time with you. Now come on. We have a lot to do today."

We headed to the entrance of the hospital and walked through the sliding doors into a large, two-story lobby with a fountain in the middle. I wondered how many people had fallen into that while looking down at their phones.

Shane walked up to the front desk. "Hello, I'm Officer Cranston and I'm looking for a couple who were dropped off in a taxi recently. It would have been a guy and a girl. Twenty-somethings."

The two women at the desk thought for a moment. One said, "Yeah, I think there was a couple who came in, maybe twenty minutes ago?"

The other one chimed in, "Are they in any trouble?"

"No, they are not. They're part of the incident that happened last night, and I just have some questions for them," Shane said.

"Oh, does it have to do with that Quinn person?" the first woman asked.

"I can't really discuss that, but would you happen to know where they are?" Shane asked.

"I'm trying to remember their names," the woman said. "Started with an 'S', I think. Sharp something? Ship..." She trailed off as she tried to remember it.

The other woman was typing something into the computer. "Got it. Shephard. Fourth floor, room 413. They're checked in as Devin Shephard and Lara Scarlett.

"Thank you," Shane said. He turned and walked towards the elevators without even waiting for me. If I was distracted or busy doing something else, he probably wouldn't have even noticed if I didn't follow.

The elevator arrived and we stepped inside. Shane pushed the button for the fourth floor and the doors shut.

"Remember, I do the talking," he reminded me.

I nodded.

He turned to face me. "Did you hear me?"

"Yeah," I nodded. "You told me not to talk once we got here. I was following *your* directions."

"Yeah, I meant when we… You know what, never mind. Say nothing. That's exactly what I want."

"Nothing."

"What?"

"You said 'say nothing.'"

Shane closed his eyes and took a deep breath. The elevator doors opened. "Adam, I hate you." He walked out.

"Does that mean we aren't partners anymore?" I yelled as I followed him off the elevator. He ignored me as we approached the doors with the room numbers we were looking for.

A girl was standing outside room 413 looking through the glass window of the door. She looked visibly upset, her face wet with tears. She was sniffling as we approached her.

Wait, this was the girl I saw last night.

"Hi, miss?" Shane said.

She turned, startled. "I'm sorry, you scared me." She looked Shane up and down. "I already spoke to the police last night. What is this about?"

"Are you Lara Scarlett?" Shane asked.

"Yes," she said with a tremor in her voice.

"Do you mind if I ask you a couple of questions about last night? I know you spoke with the local police, but I'm from the Mapleton police department. I'm assisting the Decker City police in their investigation, but you know how departments work. They don't like to share things sometimes, and don't like to work together."

"Umm..." she began, then looked back through the window. "Now isn't really the best time."

"This will only take a minute. I promise to be quick," Shane said.

"Well, my boyfriend's grandfather literally just passed away minutes ago. He was very close to him and, well, he's kind of devastated right now. He's sitting in there with the doctors," she said, nodding towards the door.

Shane peeked in. I leaned over to see, too. There was a guy sitting on a chair, with a doctor opposite him. I didn't see a body in the room. They must have taken his grandfather out already.

"I'm sorry for your loss. I can understand how difficult this must be for him," Shane said, in a consoling tone.

"Thank you. Okay, you said it would only be a minute. I'll give you that. What can I help you with?"

"Why did Mitchell kidnap you? Was there a reason for it?" he asked.

She shook her head. "I don't know. I told the officers yesterday that I was at Tommy's apartment, and..."

Shane interrupted her. "Who's Tommy?"

"He's a friend from work. We work at TruGuard—it's a financial company. Anyway, I helped take him home since the three of us, my boyfriend Devin as well, were out drinking. Tommy got a little too drunk, and I went with Tommy to make sure he got home okay."

"Why didn't your boyfriend go with you or take him home himself?"

"He got a phone call about his grandfather being shot. We all rushed here to see him first. When we got here, the doctors told Devin that he was in surgery and wouldn't be out for a few hours. He wanted to stay here, but I told him to go home, that I would take Tommy home and then come see him. That obviously never happened."

Shane took out his notepad and started writing. "Were you with Tommy when you were taken?"

"Yes. He was passed out, though. I kept screaming for him, but he was so drunk, he never heard a thing. He's probably still sleeping off a horrible hangover. He's going to hear it from me when I talk to him again!"

Shane nodded. "He'd better be careful next time he sees you, then. I would give him hell, too. Why do you think they didn't take your friend Tommy as well?"

Lara shrugged her shoulders. "I don't know. Maybe... maybe he was too drunk?"

She kept peeking back into the room, looking at her boyfriend. Was this the sort of sign I was supposed to be looking out for? Shane had told me to watch more carefully.

Shane continued to write. "If your friend Tommy was too drunk and was passed out, wouldn't he have been the better target, any-way? He wouldn't have fought back, as I assume you did."

Lara shrugged her shoulders again. "I really don't know. I tried to scream for him, but he was out of it. He didn't even flinch. A few guys grabbed me. I kicked some things around, trying to escape, and that was it."

The door opened, and a doctor came out, excusing himself as he passed between us. Devin followed behind him, limping slightly. His eyes were a little reddish, as if he had just been crying. I didn't really have any family, so I couldn't understand what he must have been going through, losing someone that close to him. Lara reached out and gave him a hug.

"What's going on here?" Devin asked.

Shane spoke up immediately. "I'm Officer Cranston. I was just asking your girlfriend a few questions. I understand you lost your grandfather moments ago, and I'm deeply sorry for your loss. I don't want to take up your time."

Devin nodded. "It's fine. It's not like I have anywhere to be, anyway." He sounded monotonous, as if his world had just collapsed.

Shane pressed on. "What happened to your leg? I noticed you were limping."

Devin looked at his leg, then back at Shane. "I, uh, my grandfather bought a motorcycle a little while ago. He had me try it and I fell off. My leg has still been hurting now and then."

Shane nodded. "A motorcycle, huh? A dangerous mode of transportation. I'm glad that's all that happened when you fell off. What was your grandfather's name?"

"Paul."

Shane jotted it down. "Lara told me your grandfather was shot. I know it's probably a tough question to answer right now, but if you don't mind, could you tell me how it happened?"

Devin stared at Shane blankly, as if someone had just hit a pause button. He blinked and finally spoke. "Someone broke into his house. I think my grandfather startled them and they shot him."

"Do you know who it was?"

Devin shook his head.

Shane made a note and continued, "Seems like a lot of this focus has been on you. Mitchell Quinn takes your girlfriend and your grandfather ends up in the hospital after being shot. Did you think Mr. Quinn is behind your grandfather's death?"

Devin's face twitched slightly. I wouldn't have noticed it if Shane hadn't told me to focus and watch everything. Devin looked up at Shane and said, "I don't know. Look, officer. Could we continue this another time? I just lost my grandfather. I don't think I can answer your questions the way you want me to right now."

Shane nodded. "Of course. I understand." He put his notepad away. "Again, I'm sorry for your loss." He started to walk away, but then he turned back towards the couple. "One last question. When did you find out Lara was kidnapped?"

Devin took a deep breath. "Umm… when she called me last night after everything happened. I came rushing over."

"Okay. Thank you." Shane turned and walked towards the elevators. I had to do a double take to realize he had walked away without me.

I caught up to him and we stepped into the elevator.

"Let me guess," I said. "You don't believe them either."

Shane nodded. "Yup."

The elevator dinged and the doors slid open. We stepped off and walked through the lobby and outside to the police car. When we got in, Shane started the engine but didn't drive away.

"Something is clearly going on here," he said.

"Why do you say that?" I asked.

He shook his head. "It's nothing. Let's go to the station so we can catch up on all this evidence and add it to what we found out today."

"Oh no. No, you don't. Don't you tell me 'it's nothing' and expect me to just let it go. You better start talking, mister!"

Shane smirked. "Mitchell Quinn went after Devin. At least that's what it seems. I don't exactly know why, but I bet you my paycheck that Mitchell Quinn is either the responsible shooter or he's involved somehow in Devin's grandfather's shooting."

"How do you figure that out after asking those people a couple of questions?"

Shane put the car in reverse. "I'm good. That's how."

I smiled at his cockiness. I liked this side to Shane. It was something I wasn't used to seeing. I was learning a lot during these trips. I hoped to learn a lot more when we finished up at the police station.

"You didn't ask about the blood you saw at Dr. Kane's office, though," I told Shane.

"Yes, I did," he replied.

I was confused. Did I miss a part of the conversation again? I swore I'd listened to everything and paid very close attention.

Shane continued, "Did you notice if Lara had any injury? Anything that may have looked like it would have used those cloths to clean up?"

I thought back, picturing Lara standing there, but I didn't remember seeing anything wrong. She looked normal.

"No, I don't think so."

"Right. She looked fine. But who didn't?"

Then it hit me. "Devin."

Shane shook his head. "His leg. Now why would the *good* doctor lie about something like that?"

"I don't know." I said.

"Me neither. But it's what I intend to find out. Hopefully something back at the station can shine some light onto all of this."

We drove back to the station almost in silence. I was excited to see what else we would find. This was already turning out to be more fun and interesting than I had expected.

We arrived at the police station and walked into the lobby. It was quieter than it had been the night before. Everything looked to be back to normal.

I followed Shane into his office as he sat behind his desk and I sat down opposite him.

He flipped around his second computer monitor. "I'm going to load up the database of photos from the warehouse yesterday. You're going to look at everything I'm looking at. The monitor in front of you will mirror everything on my screen."

"Should I be looking for anything in particular?" I asked.

"Just look. Anything out of place, out of the ordinary, something that shouldn't be there, just anything at all, that's what you look for."

"I'll do my best, I guess," I told him.

"Don't worry. I'll be doing it, anyway. When I find something, I'll show you and try to teach you how I found it and how you can do it on your own. This will be another learning experience for you."

At least he was trying to help me. It would be interesting seeing all the photos from the warehouse yesterday, considering I wasn't able to go inside and we never made it to the entertainment center.

He pulled up the database and started clicking quickly through multiple tabs. The screen brought up a prompt for him to enter his username and password. He input it quickly and moved to a folder titled *Decker City Warehouse*. He opened the folder and little square images filled the screen. He clicked on the first one at the top left-hand side of the screen and it filled the screen. It showed the walkway as you entered the warehouse. Boxes were scattered around and there were trails of blood on the floor. Shane tapped a key and a new image appeared, of a staircase. At the bottom of the stairs was a dried-up pool of blood. This was messier than I had imagined.

"The vigilante did this?" I asked.

"Kind of," Shane said. "He was a part of it."

This definitely shone a new light into what I was getting myself into. I didn't know things got *this* violent. I thought it was as simple as catching some bad guys. This changed my perspective.

The photo remained on the screen as Shane inspected it. He had a notepad in front of him, and jotted notes before moving on to the next photo. It was a similar picture, but at a different angle. He looked closely at it and then tapped his keyboard. This next three images also showed the same scene, but from different angle.

A new photo appeared on the screen—a room, with a chair near the wall, next to a glass window. Ropes lay on the ground beside the chair legs.

"Is this where that girl, Lara, was held?" I asked.

Shane wrote something on his notepad. "It looks like it." He tapped a key to show the rest of the room. It looked empty.

I got to see everything I missed from the warehouse, but it didn't seem like much. Shane scrolled through all the photos and got to the end of the folder. It just looked like a mess. Boxes were broken and scattered everywhere. There was blood on the floor. Guns lay on the ground. Outlines of bodies, made with string, surrounded some areas. I couldn't gather anything from those photos. I was nowhere closer to understanding what had happened there.

"Did you find anything from looking at those photos?" I asked Shane.

"Yeah. I got a better idea of what happened," he said.

"What? How could you tell by looking at string and blood?"

He looked at his notes and pulled up a photo. "You see here? There's a pool of blood on the ground. But look at the stairs, too. It looks like whoever this was, they fell down the stairs. The post is a little bent here..." he pointing to my screen, "and here. I'd be looking for someone who has bruises to match these posts on the stairs." He looked at his notes and double clicked on another photo. "And here, there's a pool of blood on the ground, too. But there's a broken pair of glasses there as well. This person probably wore glasses. So once I get an updated list of mugshots, I can probably determine who this person was and work out who to question at the hospital."

I just shook my head. None of that had even occurred to me. I had just been looking at the pictures the same way someone looks through vacation photos by quickly flipping through them.

Shane pulled up a different folder labeled *Entertainment Center*, and then the door opened.

"Hey, sorry about last night."

It was Lunatic Larry. And he was apologizing?

He continued, "I got really sick with something. I was in the bathroom most of the night and just fell asleep on the floor. I didn't even remember closing my eyes."

"Officer Jenkinson," Shane said. "If you disappear again like that without so much as a warning, you will be relieved of your duties as a Mapleton police officer. Is that understood?"

"Yes, sir," Jenkinson said. "I'm truly sorry. It won't happen again. I really don't know what came over me. I'm still not feeling great right now."

I waved my hand at him, wafting the air. "Then don't breathe that rancid breath over here. I don't want what you had."

Jenkinson blew air in my direction. "I hope you get what I had, you obnoxious piece of crap. I don't even know why you're here, anyway."

"Doing your job for you," I replied. "And better, too."

"Both of you. Stop. Now!" Shane interjected. "You guys are like children. Jenkinson, go assist O'Brian. He's in the conference room labeling the evidence that was collected last night. Go get acquainted with what happened and catch up."

Jenkinson turned and left the office. He apologized? I would never in a million years have expected him to apologize. That didn't seem like him. He disappeared last night and now he'd come back acting different, although, he did still seem to hate me, so all was not lost.

Shane shook his head. "I'm telling you, one of these days, he's going to clock you. And I won't be able to stop him."

"But isn't it your job to protect the public from aggressive police brutality?"

"You've egged him on for so long, one day, he'll snap. Like I said, I may not be there to protect you. I suggest being nice to him. Maybe he'll surprise you and be nice in return."

"Oh, he has surprised me. He apologized to you. *Apologized.*"

"Yeah, well, if he wanted to keep his job, he damn well better apologize," Shane replied. I figured he was right, as usual. "I called him all night and didn't get a response until just now. He is a part of this team and he was MIA last night. I'll be writing him up for that, and it will be reviewed by my superiors. It'll be up to them whether or not to take action. I can't have someone on my team who I can't depend on and trust."

Note to self, don't get on Shane's bad side.

Shane went back to the computer screen and opened up the first photo from the entertainment center folder. It cut right to the chase. It was the body of Mitchell Quinn, face down on the floor. A gun lay a few feet from his right hand. The back of his jacket was a little red, but it was the small pool of blood he was lying in that really caught my eye. I didn't know this guy and from what I'd been hearing, he sounded like a bad person. But it was kind of disturbing seeing someone in this state, and people taking photos of him.

"Do you always take photos of dead people like this?" I asked.

"We have to. We take as many as we can, to preserve evidence to review later. For health reasons, we can't leave the body there for the entire length of our investigation," Shane replied.

He clicked through a few more pictures of Mitchell's lifeless body at different angles. Some were close shots and some had been taken from far away. Next were scenic shots of broken doors and debris around the facility.

"Hey! Those are the boxes I put there the other night," I said, noticing a photo of broken boxes and taped-off areas where The Discount Pavilion, the old store I worked for, was going to be.

Shane didn't acknowledge my comment as he continued scrolling through the photos. My phone buzzed in my pocket, distracting me. I took it out and saw a text from Chuck. He was reminding me about starting work at the bar tonight.

I typed, *New phone... who dis?*

A text came back immediately. *UR Funny... C U tonite.*

Ugh. People who used abbreviations in texts. I hated it. He knew that, too.

"Hey, Adam," Shane said. "You're not paying attention." He'd noticed my phone was out.

"Sorry. Chuck was texting me."

He ignored my excuse. "Are you seeing what I'm seeing?"

I put the phone back in my pocket and looked at the computer screen. I knew instantly what he was looking at. It was a photo of some debris laying on the ground, but in the background was a man wearing a Mapleton police uniform and holding a knife, placing it in a sealed evidence bag. Except Shane and I knew for a fact this man wasn't a police officer. His head was slightly turned, but I could see that he had a scar down his face. I recognized him from the photo Kate had showed me.

"Is this the guy?" Shane asked.

I nodded. "That's him! That's who Kate showed me! What's he doing there?"

"I have no idea." Shane clicked quickly through the rest of the photos. He wasn't in any of the others. He had only been caught in one photo. He had to have been there for longer than a few seconds —how had he only managed to be in one picture?

"A better question might be: how did he manage to get one of our uniforms?"

"I told you!"

Shane looked confused for a moment. "What are you talking about?"

"The mole in the office, like I told you the other day."

"You were referencing TV shows and movies when you brought that up. I hate to say this, because I know you're going to take it the wrong way... but I think you may be right."

"I'm right? I mean, yeah, I'm right. I knew it!"

"And this is why I knew you'd take it the wrong way. You need to shut up and calm down. I don't know what's going on right now. Everything happening in Decker City. Then this reporter tells you about a guy with a scar, and now he's showing up in photos at the crime scene, wearing one of my station's uniforms. I already thought I was going to be busy trying to figure out what the doctor, Lara, and Devin were hiding, but this is clearly more important. I need to know who this guy is and why he's wearing a Mapleton police uniform."

"Duh. He's wearing the uniform to blend in," I said, smiling.

Shane didn't flinch, staring at me with a cold, hard expression.

"Wrong time for a joke? Sorry."

"If Larry doesn't hit you, I may one day. You know what I mean, smart-ass. I mean, how did he get a uniform?" He stood up and looked past me through the glass door. "Be honest. Do you think anyone here could do something like this? Get involved with crime and help this guy with the scar?"

I couldn't believe he was asking me for my opinion. I had to make sure it was good. No joking this time.

"I don't know everyone here. Everyone was at the scene, right? You had the entire department on task to help last night."

"Yeah..." He trailed off, nodding. He turned to face me. "Except Jenkinson. He was missing last night."

That's right! Lunatic Larry was 'sick' and Shane couldn't get a hold of him last night. I didn't think he was capable of something like that, though.

"I think a lot of bad things about that lunatic and I personally don't like him very much, but do you really think he's a part of all this?"

"I don't know."

"Are you going to talk to him about it?" I asked.

"No. I'm going to observe him. Very closely. I need you to remain silent about this. Whatever was discussed in this office remains here. Understood?"

I wondered if this meant I couldn't tell Kate. I couldn't betray Shane's trust like that. He would know it was me if she decided to publish the information. I had to find another way to impress her. Shane was, after all, taking me under his wing. I didn't think he'd expected to uncover everything he had, but it had been a very interesting experience following him around the last two days.

"I won't say anything. I promise," I told him.

He returned to his chair, leaned back slightly and stared at his computer. The photo of the man with the scar filled the screen.

"Adam," he said finally. "I think it's time we part ways. I'm going to head into the conference room and see what O'Brian and Jenkinson are up to. I think I need to oversee what's happening in there, and I don't think you would help the process, given your relationship with Jenkinson."

I understood. Shane had a lot on his plate right now. It wouldn't help if I interfered, as I knew I probably would.

I stood up as Shane did. He walked to the office door and opened it. O'Brian was passing by with two cups in his hands. "Want a cup of coffee? I have one for me and Larry," O'Brian said.

"I'll get my own, thanks," Shane said.

O'Brian walked away and entered the conference room.

Shane pointed to me. "If I find out any of this has gotten out, I'll know it was you. Please, don't speak about this."

"I know I'm kind of an idiot sometimes, but I promise I won't say anything," I said, trying to reassure him.

He left me and disappeared into the conference room. I headed to the front door, ready to head back home. I had a few more hours to kill before I started work with Chuck tonight.

As I walked outside, my phone buzzed in my pocket again. I took it out to see a text from Kate.

After processing everything last night, I need to know more. Will you be at the bar tonight?

Well, this was just great. I had information that might help, and I wanted to talk to Kate about it, and now I had to see her and try to not say anything. I really wanted to, though. I knew it would help—but I couldn't betray Shane.

I replied, *I'll be there working all night.*

The reply was a simple *OK.*

This was going to be an interesting night.

| 20 |

I ended up going home to shower and to research what had really been happening in Decker City. I seemed to come across the same things repeatedly. And *a lot* of it involved the vigilante. Now I could at least understand Shane's perspective a little. He was the one who had to clean up the vigilante's mess. I would be annoyed as well. But the Gray Hood was out there protecting people, and with all the crime happening in Decker City, maybe there had to be some negatives to counteract all the positivity he brought. If I tried the same thing, would I be able to bring that same positivity to Mapleton? Would the public get behind me like they had with the Gray Hood?

When I walked into The Stout House, Chuck was already behind the bar, wiping it down and polishing the glasses.

"Welcome to your first day, buddy." he said.

"Is it bad to say I'm dreading it already?" I asked. It wasn't as if I didn't want to be here. I just didn't want to be working right now. I wanted to be helping Shane and Kate.

"Come on, it's not bad. I'll even make it easier for you, since you may not know how to make a lot of drinks, if any at all. Just pour beer. I'll handle the mixed drinks. Sound easy?"

I shrugged my shoulders. "I guess so. Not really sure what I'm supposed to be doing anyway, but I'll figure it out."

"You'll be fine," he reassured me.

Throughout the evening, he taught me a few mixed drinks recipes and watched as I tried mixing them myself. I did alright, but I was tempted to try every one of them. I couldn't get drunk, but I enjoyed the different flavors. Chuck had me wiping up and making sure everything was kept clean and organized.

I talked to him about my time with Shane this morning, about visiting the doctor first and then going to see Devin and Lara at the hospital. He didn't know who they were, and I barely did either. But I kept my promise and didn't tell Chuck about what Shane and I had found at the police station, as much as I wanted to talk about it.

Around nine o'clock, Kate walked in. She came directly to the bar and sat down, then shook her head at me.

"I don't get you. Let me see your arm again," she said.

I reached over the bar and showed her my arm, which was free of cuts, bruises, and any other markings. She examined everything, feeling my arm all over where she had seen my cut yesterday. Satisfied, she let go and shook her head again.

"Okay. Start talking. How are you able to do it?" she asked.

I shrugged my shoulders. "I really don't know. I've always been able to do it as far back as I can remember. I don't get sick. I can't get drunk. Medicines do nothing for me. But getting hurt, it legitimately hurts. I feel pain."

"And it doesn't bother you?"

"It does. But I've become so used to it that I can easily tolerate the pain now. I know it goes away momentarily. It never lasts any more than a few seconds."

"I don't get it. I mean, I get what you're saying, but... you have powers. Super powers. Why aren't you helping the vigilante in Decker City? He could use someone like you. Well, maybe not anymore, with Mitchell out of the picture, but with this guy with the scar—I'm sure Decker City… hell, even Mapleton—could use someone like you."

"Are you kidding me? I *want* to do what he's doing! I've been reading nonstop about the Gray Hood and I just want to get out there and help."

"So why aren't you?"

"I can't. Shane won't let me."

"Who?"

"Sorry, Officer Cranston. He's one of the Mapleton police officers. The one I was riding around with when we met."

"And, what… is he your daddy or something? Why is he stopping you?"

"Well, you sure know how to make a guy feel good."

"You got tough skin. Actually, from what I've seen, *very* tough. I don't want to hear it. You're a big boy. We need people like you. Look at what the Gray Hood did in Decker City… *by himself.* The police weren't much of a help. He did a lot of what you read about, on his own. He tracked down Mitchell and put a stop to him. The police didn't do that. The vigilante did."

"I'm not him, though. How am I supposed to do what he did? He can move things without touching them. That's pretty freaking cool, and helpful. I can heal. How does that help?"

"The Gray Hood can steal guns from people by ripping them out of their hands. With you, the criminals can keep their guns. You just don't get hurt. You're like the Terminator."

"The what?" I asked.

"The killer cyborg from the future. Arnold Schwarzenegger," Kate said.

"Wait, the future? Now there's a super powered killer cyborg from the future too? I thought the guy with the scar is who we're after?"

"Adam," Chuck chimed in, "*The Terminator* is a movie."

"Ohh… you mean the one where the robot says 'Dead or alive, you're coming with me?'"

Kate smacked her head with her hand. "That's *Robocop*."

"Same thing. I don't watch TV," I said, waving my hands.

"It's a mov—Never mind." Kate shook her head and looked at Chuck. "Is he always this frustrating?"

"It's a talent of mine to put up with him," Chuck said.

"Hey!" I said. "I can take my super powered self away from here."

"Yeah? Where are you going to go?" Kate asked.

I looked around for a moment, then pointed to the left. "About ten feet over there."

A smirk appeared on Kate's face. "Of all the people I could have asked for information the other night, I had to find you…"

"And you won't find anyone quite like me either," I told her.

She nodded. "That, I agree with."

"Well, now that that's out of the way," Chuck said, "I believe Adam mentioned you guys had something to talk about. Hopefully, it doesn't involve more bickering."

The door of the bar opened and two guys came in.

"Hi guys. Welcome to The Stout House," Chuck greeted them.

Kate looked around, then turned back towards me. "Well, we're going to have to fast forward things. Like, right now. I was followed. Those guys are after me."

"Wait, what?" Chuck said.

"What did you do?" I asked.

The two guys noticed Kate at the bar, her back towards them, and they started power walking towards us.

"They're coming over here," I whispered.

"I need your help. Now." Kate stood up and faced the two men approaching her.

"Give it to us," the man on the right said, extending a hand.

It was time to step in and give Kate the help she needed. "I think you should probably buy the girl dinner first," I said.

"If you like to talk, I suggest you don't say another word. Or talking will be something you'll have a lot of trouble doing," the man on the left said. He was a little bigger than the other guy, but I'd taken on worse before. They both wore jeans and buttoned-down shirts. The guy on the left wore a black shirt and the other wore red. They both had buzz cuts.

I laughed. "I dare you."

This really pissed them off. The guy in the red shirt snapped his fingers and his partner reached across the bar and grabbed my shirt. It happened instantaneously, I couldn't even react. They must have practiced that move dozens of times, because it worked to perfection. I was pulled across the bar and tossed onto the floor. Kate yelled my name but was silenced as the guy in the black shirt pushed her against the bar and held her there.

"Let her go!" I yelled as I stood up.

"You sure you want those to be your last words?" said the man who'd thrown me to the floor.

People started getting up from their seats and rushing out of the bar. Obviously, two men coming in and attacking an employee and a girl at the bar wasn't a situation these patrons wanted to be a part of.

I looked up at the guy in front of me. "No. I actually wanted to ask if you were a failed athlete, because that throw was pathetic."

And then it began. He came storming towards me. I jumped up quickly and sidestepped him, pushing him into a table. He went sliding into it, catching himself but sending glasses and plates crashing to the floor.

I ran up to him and jumped on his back, then wrapped my arms around his neck, trying to choke him. He tried spinning, but that just made both of us dizzy. He collapsed with my arms still wrapped around his neck, but then threw his head back into my face. Pain instantly flowed from my nose. I thought he'd broken it.

He stood up and I followed suit. I shook off the pain and, suddenly, I could breathe through my nose again. My ability was coming in handy.

"Is that all you got?" I asked my attacker.

He came charging at me again, this time swinging with his right hand as he approached. I ducked, but he was quicker than me. He caught me with a quick hook to the side of my face. It connected, big time. It took me down, but only for a moment. I regained my strength and rolled away as he swung a chair down at me. It broke on impact with the floor, sending wooden splinters all over the place.

I grabbed one of the unbroken legs and jumped to my feet. I swung my new weapon at his side, landing a hit on his ribs. He clutched his side, and I took the opportunity to swing at his face, but he grabbed the chair leg in midair and kicked me in the stomach as I was caught off guard. I ended up letting go of the chair leg, and he swung it at my face. Unfortunately, he connected, and I fell down hard.

That hurt. A lot.

Things seemed kind of blurry. I overheard some voices. A girl was yelling.

Kate!

I regained my vision and the pain began to diminish. I jumped to my feet, and saw that both men had a hold of Kate and were attempting to walk her towards the door. Kate was putting up a good fight, though, flailing around and making things very difficult for them.

"Okay, guys, you're making me repeat myself. Let her go!" I yelled.

This caught their attention. The guy who had hit me with that chair leg seemed surprised that I was standing and ready to go again. He let go of Kate and came charging at me. He hadn't learned the first time, but I'd make sure he'd learn never to charge at someone again. I was holding the chair leg behind my back. As he came within a few feet of me, I swung. It connected with his head with a loud *smack*. He fell instantly.

The other man let go of Kate and started heading in my direction. "Umm... where's Chuck?" I asked.

"Probably picking glass out from his head," Kate said.

"What?"

The moron in the red shirt reached me, his arm pulled back. I ducked and then moved out of the way completely to avoid another one of those quick left hooks. I kicked him in the side of his knee. He grunted and fell onto his good knee.

"Do I have to do everything?" I asked. "Can someone call the police?"

The guy kneeling next to me pulled out a knife and stabbed me in my left side. I screamed in pain and went down.

"Adam!" Kate yelled.

The man ripped the knife from me and stood back up slowly, using the nearest table for support. I clutched at my side and waited. I knew it wouldn't be long now. I took a deep breath, and the pain started to go away. I pushed down on my wound and saw that it was almost fully healed. The man took a step towards Kate.

"Hey!" I yelled. "I prepared for knives." I stood up and leaped on top of my attacker. We both fell to the ground, but this time he was the one who was hurt. He tossed me off of him and I jumped to my feet.

I heard sirens. Not long now.

The man got back up slowly, and saw that his partner was moving again, too. He helped his partner stand up. "We have to go," he said as he put his arm around his neck and helped walk him to the door.

"And stay out!" I said, as the door closed behind them.

Chuck rose from behind the bar, holding onto his head. "Are you okay?" I asked.

"One of them smashed a glass on my head and pushed me down. I'll be alright. I called the police when I was on the floor," Chuck said.

"Thank you," Kate said.

The sirens grew closer. The police would be here shortly. I looked at Kate. "Start talking, now. What did you do? Why were they after you?"

"I stole something from them. Well, from the man with the scar, probably." She reached into her pocket and pulled out a flash drive.

"What's on it?" I asked.

"I don't know." Kate replied. "I just copied a bunch of stuff and ran off. They saw me but I got away. I didn't think they followed me, though."

"Well, you obviously took something they didn't want you to see," Chuck said. He grabbed a towel and held it to his head. When he removed it, there were droplets of blood scattered on the towel. "I'm going to have to clean this up. You two should probably go. I'll just tell the police there was a big brawl, and you all ran away once you heard the police."

"Thank you," Kate said again.

"Thanks, Chuck," I said. "Call me once the police are done here and I'll come by later and help you clean up."

The sirens were close now.

"Go," Chuck said, as he shooed us out the door.

| 21 |

"Are we going to meet your boyfriend?" I asked.

"You still feel pain, right?" Kate replied.

"Yes, why?"

She punched me in the arm. She had some strength to her. "Ouch," I said, rubbing my arm. "So, where are we going?"

"To your place."

"Why?" I asked.

"They probably know who I am at this point, so going to my place is out of the question. I'm pretty sure someone would be waiting for me there."

She was right. I'd seen that in movies before. The bad guys hide in the dark, waiting for an unsuspecting person to come walk in, maybe sitting in a chair facing the wall or hiding in a closet.

I turned around, hoping to not see a car following us.

"What are you looking for?" Kate asked.

"Making sure we're not being followed," I said. "And how do you know where I live?"

"I know a lot, and I can find information about almost anyone. I'm a reporter—I have my ways."

"Then why are you going in the complete opposite direction to my apartment?"

She looked in the rear-view mirror. "I'm making sure we aren't being followed, too. I'll drive around to check if any cars are copying our movements before we end up at your apartment."

I sat back in my seat. "Oh. Smart."

We drove around for about fifteen minutes before we finally reached my apartment. It would have taken less than five minutes if we hadn't driven in a circle.

Once we entered my apartment, I began moving things around, trying to tidy up as quickly as possible. "I… uh… haven't really been around much to clean. Been kinda busy." I used my arm to sweep trash off the counter right into the trash can below. On my kitchen table were dirty plates from who knew how long ago. I grabbed them and tossed them into the sink, was filling up as well. I turned on the hot water to soak them.

Kate shook her head. "This isn't as bad as the last guy I dated."

I cleaned up the last few items of trash off the kitchen table and headed for the trash can. "Really?"

"'Hoarder' would be the polite way of describing him."

A guess a few dirty things didn't seem so bad anymore. I hadn't been expecting company, especially Kate. I would have cleaned up beforehand if I'd known.

I gathered my laptop from my bedroom, came back into the kitchen, and turned on the computer. Kate handed me the flash drive, and I plugged it in. A folder instantly popped up and I clicked on it. Documents flooded the screen. PDF's, text documents, audio recordings, pictures, spreadsheets, and other files were scattered in no obvious order.

"Let's start with the first one," Kate said.

I clicked on the first file, a PDF. It was a picture of Mitchell Quinn. His name was on the top of the page, and underneath it had paragraphs of writing discussing who he was. It listed known whereabouts and his criminal record.

Kate told me to move on to the next file. It was another PDF, a man named Nathan Hobbes. He was clean shaven with a buzz cut. He wasn't smiling in his mug shot, if that's what it was. He looked like a military guy. I scrolled down to read the writing underneath his photo. The first section was headed *Known Family*. The only thing written was *Wife: deceased.*

"Let's move on—there's nothing here," Kate said.

"Hold on, I'm looking at it," I told her.

"Just close it!" she snapped.

"Do you know him?" I asked.

"Please, just move on. I'm telling you, there's nothing here. Trust me."

I had no reason not to trust her, but this seemed weird. I complied and closed the PDF, then clicked on the next one. It was a photo of the periodic table.

I looked at Kate. "Does this mean anything to you?"

She shook her head. "No idea."

I closed it and opened the next document, an audio recording. I hit the play button.

"You do this for me and I can make you a multimillionaire," a voice said.

"What do I have to do?" another voice said.

"That second voice sounds like Mitchell Quinn," Kate said.

"I'm going to have a team of guys working with you," said the first voice. "You're going to play the part of a multimillionaire entrepreneur. They won't suspect you. Especially after the funds I give you to dump into their city. They'll love you. My chemist is working on a new drug. Something that lets you manipulate brain functions and allows the individual to become basically a zombie. You can control them. They will listen to every word you say and do whatever you ask without hesitation. You tell someone to jump off a bridge, they'll do it. You tell them to walk down the street and shoot someone, they'll do it. We've been testing it, and so far we have had extremely positive results."

"What am I supposed to do with this drug, then?" Mitchell asked.

"There are criminals released from jail almost daily. There are people who are low on their luck and need money or drugs. It's not hard to find them. They'll be perfect. You have these guys run up the violence in Decker City and then you come in, dump a bunch of money into it after property values have fallen. We stop the drug distribution and slow some of the crime. You become the savior of the city. Market and property values rise again, money is made, and suddenly you're viewed as someone more than just a rich entrepreneur. Think of it this way: you come in and give the city and police money, and suddenly crime slows down. They look at you like you were the one who saved them. You become the hero."

"And all I really have to do is just be some front man for you? That's it?" Mitchell said.

"That's it. Just do whatever we ask of you and the city will be yours," the other voice said.

"That's easy. But what do I do if people ask questions about my criminal background, and how I turned into some rich business guy?"

"I don't care what you tell them. Make up some sob story. Pull on their heartstrings. They'll eat that shit up. Make them believe in you. It doesn't matter. But let us know first, so we can plant your back-story in case people check up on it, and they probably will. But as long as you follow our instructions, you'll have it all."

"I don't know what to tell you, Patrick. It's going to be a pleasure working with you," Mitchell said.

"That son of a bitch!" Kate exclaimed.

I was totally confused by this whole recording. I'd only come to know of Mitchell Quinn recently, because of everything what had happened in Decker City over the last few days. Dr. Kane had mentioned someone by the name Patrick earlier and that he saw him with the man with the scar. Other than that, I knew nothing about this guy.

"Who?" I asked, trying to get Kate to give up more information.

Kate reached over and hit the pause button on the keyboard. "Patrick Malloy. He was Mitchell's right-hand man. I mean, at least I thought he was."

"Sounds like it was the other way around," I said.

She hit the play button and resumed the recording.

"I'm going to make some phone calls once you leave, and get this in motion as soon as possible," Patrick said.

"Thanks," Mitchell said.

The sound of chairs skidding across the floor echoed in the recording. The squeak of a door suggested someone had left the room. The door slammed and then there was silence. There was still some time left in the clip, so I assumed there must be something else.

Suddenly, Patrick spoke again.

"Hey, he's on board."

Silence.

"Who's he talking to?" I asked.

"Shh!" Kate said.

The recording continued. "Yes, I know. It's taken care of."

Silence again.

"I told you, it's taken care of."

Silence.

"Yes. I'm working on it now. I think I have someone who we can trust, working their way into Mapleton's police department. We'll have officers from Decker City, Mapleton and Forest Hills on our payroll. We have enough to cover all sides."

Silence again.

"Understood. I'm going to call our guys to get everything started with Mitchell. I'll talk to you later."

The recording ended there.

What the hell did I just hear? Drugs? Money? People taking over a city? Police on their payroll? I knew Kate had a much better idea about it all, so I was hoping she would tell me.

"What was that about?" I asked her.

"Do you not follow any news at all?" she asked.

"Kind of. I mean, I've been mainly looking up what happened the other night and researching news about the vigilante. I don't know too much about Mitchell Quinn, except for him being that rich guy in Decker City, and now he's dead. Although, the rich part now seems like kind of a lie, right? And who exactly is this Patrick Malloy guy?"

Kate pulled out her phone and scrolled through her photos again. She swiped a bunch of times then handed me her phone. "This is Patrick Malloy."

I recognized him, instantly. "Oh—*that's* Patrick? I know him. He's the jerk who harassed me when I was delivering all my boxes to the entertainment center. But I'm more concerned about the police on their payroll. They mentioned Mapleton."

"I told you they were involved here," Kate said.

Now I was stuck. After hearing that recording and after finding out about the man with the scar in the police uniform, I had to say something. But if Shane knew I'd broken his promise, I'd be out of his little circle and in a whole lot of trouble with him. Something was going on and if Kate could help, I had to tell her.

"Okay, look. I need you to promise me what I'm about to tell you stays between us. No writing about it and no talking about it. Promise?"

Kate nodded. "Yeah, I promise."

I sighed. I was about to break Shane's promise. But I had a good reason. Keeping it to myself wouldn't get us anywhere. "On the recording, we heard about police officers being on their payroll. Well, Shane and I went through a bunch of the photos taken at the entertainment center after Mitchell was killed. We saw the man with the scar in one photo."

Kate looked stunned. "Are you serious? What was he doing? Where was he?"

"He was picking up a knife and bagging it."

"Why was he doing that?" she asked.

"I don't know. But the crazy thing is, he was wearing a police uniform."

"And that must be because there's someone in the police department who gave him access to one."

This was getting crazy. I hadn't expected to find myself involved in all of this. One day I was working at some retail crap job and the next I was in the middle of a major investigation into attacks on Decker City and whoever was behind it all. It was exciting, though. I wanted to go beat up bad guys, and I guessed that finding my way into this mess was going to get me my wish. Just tonight, I'd taken down two guys.

I continued scrolling down the icons and saw a folder within this folder. It was labeled *The Hood.*

"I wonder what this is?" I said sarcastically, clicking on the folder. More icons filled the screen, mainly pictures. I clicked on the first one to enlarge it. It was a picture of the vigilante, and looked like a screen capture from a security camera. I closed it and clicked on the next one. Same thing: another screen capture from a security camera. I scrolled further down, past the pictures, and found a PDF. It seemed to be information regarding the brain, a study done into telekinesis. I skimmed through it but then found my way to the last paragraph to get the gist of it. It stated that the study proved that telekinesis did not exist, and no one was capable of that kind of power. "It looks like these guys were investigating this vigilante and his ability."

"Open this one," Kate said, pointing to the screen.

It was another PDF. This one was about blood and DNA. It talked about molecules, cells, something about a genome. Science stuff, and all *way* over my head. Why did the man with the scar need this? And why was it stored in a folder with all of this stuff about the vigilante?

"This is crazy." Kate said.

"You understand this?" I asked.

"Kind of. From everything I'm seeing here, it looks like someone wants to replicate what the Gray Hood can do. They want to get his DNA somehow, study it, and use it to unlock the ability for themselves."

"I'm sorry, what? How did you gather all of that from this? You understand this science stuff?" I asked, completely stunned.

"Look, you get DNA from white blood cells." She pointed to the screen. "And I'm just gathering information from the articles referenced in this PDF. It's discussing DNA replication—that is, replicating what they find in the vigilante's DNA that could hold the key to unlocking the ability for others." She turned away from the computer to look at me. "Maybe other abilities. If someone found out about your ability, possibly yours, too? At least that's what I'm piecing together here. I'm a reporter, remember? I can do this pretty easily. It's my job."

"So you think the man with the scar was getting the blood on the knife in hope that it was the vigilante's blood?" I asked.

"That would be my assumption," Kate said. "But the police would know if the knife was missing. Someone that smart wouldn't just take it outright. That would cause people to look into missing evidence, which is something these guys probably don't want. My guess is he probably took a sample and returned the knife."

Kate was smart. She'd thought of these things way before any of it had even crossed my mind. I was still wrapping my head around the fact that the man with the scar was seen at the crime scene wearing a police uniform, and here was Kate already establishing what he was doing.

She reached across me and pulled the flash drive out of the computer. The files disappeared.

"Hey! What are you doing?" I asked.

"After what I've seen, I have to go. I have to go show this to someone," Kate said.

"Your boyfriend?" I said.

She clenched her first and swung it at my arm again. "Every time you say that, you get punched. Got it?"

It hurt, just like it did before. She'd even got the same spot. She was strong and accurate with her punches. "Yeah, I got it. Am I ever going to meet this guy?"

She placed the flash dive back in her pocket. "Doubt it. He wouldn't like you."

"You like me. Put in a good word for me."

"First of all, I don't like you. Second of all, you looking to date him or something? You want me to put in *a good word* for you?"

I rolled my eyes. "You know what I mean."

She picked up her keys off the table. "No, I don't." She smiled. "Please, tell me what you mean…"

"I meant—" I said.

"I don't care what you mean!" she interrupted. "I'm just kidding around. Look, I gotta go. There are some things on this drive that my partner needs to know about. And it can't wait," Kate said.

"Yeah, I guess I should go tell Shane what I found as well."

"Are you stupid?" Kate said.

"I believe that's a rhetorical question, and I'll allow you to answer that for me."

She shook her head. "Did you not hear that someone, possibly multiple officers at the police station, may be working for these guys? I know you look up to this Shane officer and you seem to trust him, but I don't know him and I *don't* trust him. What if *he's* the one working for the man with the scar? And Patrick?" She took a deep breath. "Look, there's a lot to work with here. You already know more than I think you should know, and I think you should keep it to yourself. Especially given what we heard."

"I trust Shane. I don't think he's working with anyone bad. I really don't think he would do that."

"And that's what they all say. 'He would never do something like that.' Until they turn out to be *that* person all along," Kate said.

"I'm serious. If there's one person who you can trust at that place, it's definitely Shane. I swear. I would bet everything I have on him."

Kate pondered this. "Look, if you think you can trust him and you're *that* sure about it, then fine. We may need his help. Especially if he can work on figuring out which officer has turned from the inside rather than us trying to do it from here. He'll have a better way of figuring that out."

"Okay, I'll get in touch with him tomorrow morning. I don't have his number and he's probably gone home by now. Plus, I have to go back and help Chuck with the cleanup."

"Do you want a ride back?" Kate asked.

"Nah, it's okay. It'll give me some time to think about all of this on my walk down there."

"Okay, well, I'm outta here, then. Thanks for your help tonight, and for protecting me from those guys. I owe you one," Kate said.

"How about a kiss?" I asked.

She rolled her eyes. "Bye, Adam." She opened the door and left my apartment.

I grabbed my keys and followed her out, but she was already gone. I walked down the stairs and made my way outside, heading back to Chuck's bar.

* * *

"Hey Adam," O'Brian said as I walked into the bar.

"Oh... hey there," I said. I hadn't expected to see him there. I looked around. "Is your hot-headed partner with you tonight?"

He shook his head. "Nope. Just me. He had to leave a few hours ago. He said he wasn't feeling well again."

"Oh, *not feeling well*," I said, making air quotes.

He shrugged his shoulders. "I don't know. I just do my job, whether he's here or not." He looked around at the mess the bar was in. "I thought maybe this was your handiwork again. I got here, and you were nowhere to be found and the owner tells me it wasn't you this time."

I nodded. "Yeah... uh, definitely wasn't me. I was home."

"Okay, well, looks like there's a lot to clean up here. I'm all done, so I'm going home. Have a good night, Adam."

"You too," I replied. O'Brian was easy to talk to, and much friendlier. The Lunatic was just a pain in my ass. I was glad he wasn't here right now. We probably would have had words again and gotten into another argument.

Could Lunatic Larry be the officer working with the man with the scar and Patrick Malloy? He'd apparently been *sick* lately.

No.

The thought immediately left my mind.

Jenkinson was a jerk, but he wasn't a traitor. He couldn't be. Could he?

"I thought I was supposed to call you after they left?" Chuck said.

"Yeah, well, Kate and I were done, and I just decided to come back over and help," I told him.

"Did you find anything on that flash drive?" he asked.

As we picked up the broken tables and chairs, I told him about everything we'd found. It was nice having someone on the outside to talk to. Chuck wasn't taking part in any of it, although he had found himself in the middle of it tonight.

About an hour later, we'd finished cleaning up. Chuck was excited to hear about what would happen tomorrow after I'd talked to Shane.

"See you tomorrow night?" Chuck asked.

"It's my job now, so yes, I'll be here," I replied.

"Hopefully not followed by another brawl, please. I can't keep having this happen."

"Hey!" I interjected. "It wasn't my fault this time."

He put his hands up in defense. "I know, I know. *This* time it wasn't you. But you're going down this path and just as those guys came after Kate, they may come after you. Especially after you scared them off tonight. They may know who you are now. Just be careful, okay?"

"I got this. I'm indestructible. Remember?"

"You may be indestructible," Chuck said. "But eventually, once people start figuring out what you can do, they will come after you. Maybe the same guys that came after Kate. Maybe different ones. Just be careful."

He cared. And maybe that's why he was my best friend. He was the only one who ever cared. All my life, I'd been thrown away because of my ability. Because I was different. I was called a monster.

Chuck was the only one who embraced it and cared enough to keep me close. I respected him for that. He was always there for me.

"I will. I'm..." I began.

"Indestructible. I know. Go home, Adam."

I nodded in agreement. I was getting a little tired, anyway. "See you later," I said and turned to the door. I couldn't wait to continue this investigation with Shane tomorrow.

| 22 |

"What do you mean Shane's not here?" I asked.

"It's his day off," the receptionist said.

"Day off? Police don't take days off," I said.

She looked at me in confusion. "It's a job. We don't work seven days a week. We have days off too, just like everyone else. We always make sure we have enough officers to cover all the shifts. Don't you have days off?"

"I do have days off. I work nights."

She closed her eyes for a moment and took a deep breath. "Sir, I can have you meet with another officer if that will help?"

"No thanks. I'll just come back tomorrow." I turned and walked out. There went the idea of working with Shane again today. I was eager to let him know what I'd found.

As I was walking down the stairs of the police station, O'Brian passed me in the other direction, holding two cups of coffee.

"Oh thanks," I said, trying to take a cup from his hand.

He pulled away. "I don't think so," he said.

"Why not? Where's my cup?"

"Do you work here? Are you my partner?" he asked.

"Sometimes I like to think so and no, definitely not," I responded.

"Then I won't be wasting my money on you," O'Brian said.

I was a little taken aback. I wasn't used to talking to him, let alone listening to his comebacks.

"I thought you were the nice one?" I asked.

He shrugged. "Maybe Jenkinson is rubbing off on me too much."

"Yeah, I'd stay away from him if I were you. The guy is kind of a jerk," I said.

"He constantly tells me to get him coffee. It's probably not the best for him if he's sick or something."

I threw my hands up. "I wouldn't know."

O'Brian said goodbye, turned and continued his walk up the stairs and inside the police station.

Strike one.

Shane was out, so I had to figure out what to do now. I thought back to Kate's flash drive and everything we'd discovered. There wasn't much I could do to try to figure out if someone at the Mapleton police was working with this Patrick guy. I needed Shane for that, so I had to move onto something else. I didn't know how to find Patrick either, so that was out. I didn't know where the man with the scar was. I didn't have the flash drive to keep searching for clues. Then I thought about the folder labeled *The Hood*. Shane was trying to figure out who this guy was. Maybe I might be able to help him. But how? The last idea came down to the science behind it all. Someone was researching the what the vigilante could do, hoping to steal a piece of the action. Maybe I could learn more about it myself—not from the internet, but from an actual doctor. And I'd just met one yesterday. Hopefully, Dr. Kane would know more about it.

I got a ride from an Uber to his house. The driver kept trying to talk to me the entire time. It reminded me when I was taken home by that officer after my first experience in Decker City. Couldn't he just leave me alone and let me play on my phone in peace?

Finally, I arrived at Dr. Kane's house, or office, whatever it was. In the lobby, an older woman sat in one of the few seats. I sat two seats from her. She had a magazine on her lap. It looked like she was doing a crossword puzzle. Her glasses dangled from a string around her neck. There must have been chimes on the string because every time she moved her head, I heard tiny bells ringing.

The office door opened and Dr. Kane came out with a patient.

"—and call me if anything changes, alright? Enjoy the rest of your day, Jake." Dr. Kane said. He patted his patient on the back and walked past him. "Good afternoon, Mrs. Warner. You can come—" He stopped suddenly as he noticed me. He pointed. "You're the police intern from yesterday."

"Yes... the intern." I'd completely forgotten about Shane's cover story. Luckily, I'd caught myself in time. "Do you have a minute?"

"Sure." He looked at his patient again. "Barbara, would you mind waiting for just a minute while I talk to..." He paused and looked at me. "What was your name again?"

"Adam."

"Yes, Adam." He turned back to his patient. "Would you give me a minute with Adam, please?"

She agreed and went back to her crossword puzzle. Dr. Kane waved me into his office then closed the door behind me and asked me to take a seat. I sat down and he took the chair next to me.

"What brings you in?" Dr. Kane asked.

"I've been working with the officer who was here yesterday, Officer Cranston, and we came across some information I wanted some help with," I told him.

"What can I do to help?" he asked.

"Shane... sorry—Officer Cranston and I are working on a case and he sent me here. We came across some information regarding DNA, blood work, and genomes." I was trying to sound smart, but I really wasn't sure what I was talking about, and I knew it may have come across as ignorance. "Anyway, there was something about DNA manipulation and since I didn't know what that was, I fig—*we* figured, since we just spoke to a doctor yesterday, we could come back and ask for your help."

Dr. Kane smiled. "I appreciate you guys asking for my help. Unfortunately, I'm a neurologist, and don't know too much about that stuff. You'll need to talk to a specialist in molecular genetics."

There were some big words in those sentences that I was going to have to remember to google when I walked out of here. Until then, I had to pretend I knew what he was talking about. "And where would I find one of those mol... cu..." I said, trying to sound out what he'd just said.

"Molecular genetics. Basically, you'll need to find a geneticist. And I hate to continue to be the bearer of bad news, but I wouldn't know where to find one. There isn't one at Decker City Hospital. I'm sure there must be geneticists in the city, but I don't know them. I'm sorry I can't help."

Well, this was strike out number two. I definitely needed a partner. I'd gotten so much done with Shane yesterday, and Kate and I had discovered a slew of information last night—but I was awful by myself.

"It's okay. I appreciate your time, though." Maybe it didn't have to be a complete strike out. Since this doctor had experience with the vigilante and his abilities, he may still have some useful information for me. I continued, "I have one more question."

"Go ahead," he said.

"You believe what this vigilante can do, right? Moving things without touching them?" I asked.

He nodded. "I do, yes. I've seen it."

"Do you know how it works? Like, where his powers come from? How he may have gotten them? Do other people have abilities like this?"

"That's a lot more than one question."

"Sorry, they all kind of fit together," I said.

He smiled. "Well, I'm not sure, since I haven't had the chance to meet this guy in the hood." Shane would have a field day with that comment, since he was certain the doctor knew who the vigilante was. "I couldn't really tell you how or why he has those abilities. I wish I knew. As for this pertaining to other people, I'd tell you that yes, other people can harness similar abilities. I've studied things like this in the past and I've seen some crazy things, like someone playing an instrument at professional levels after an accident, despite having no prior experience playing before. Trauma or accidents of some shape or form typically cause these phenomena."

"What about healing?" I asked.

"Healing? Like what the normal human body already naturally does?" he asked.

I had to think about that for a moment. I guessed I was so used to my almost instant ability that I'd forgotten that everyone else healed as well, just at a much slower rate than myself. I guessed I wasn't as special anymore since anyone can heal.

"Well, yeah, but at a much faster rate. Like, almost instantaneous," I told him.

He thought about it for a moment. "I'm not sure. Our bodies already have a regenerative ability. Our skin is highly regenerative. Some organs can regenerate as well. But this time frame usually takes days to weeks, sometimes months, and in some cases, even years. I haven't heard of instant regenerative abilities."

"Okay, but do you think it's possible? I mean, you have someone local running around moving things without touching them, right?" I said.

He was silent for a moment. "I mean, I guess it's possible after what I've seen. I don't know how it would actually work, but it sounds quite interesting. Why do you ask?"

"No reason," I lied. Part of me wanted to come clean to Dr. Kane about my ability. He seemed like a nice guy and had some experience dealing with these kinds of things. I just didn't know if I should keep letting my secret out like this. He may have been able to help me understand it, though. Maybe another time. I was here for this DNA manipulation stuff, which unfortunately, had led me to no answers.

"I'll let you get back to your appointment. I'm sorry for taking up your time so unexpectedly."

"It's no problem. I'm sorry I couldn't help more," he said.

We stood up and said our goodbyes. As I walked out, Dr. Kane called the waiting patient inside his office. I walked out of his house and pulled out my phone to call for another ride back to Mapleton.

* * *

During the ride back to my apartment, I googled geneticists in the surrounding area. These people seemed pretty hard to come by: I only found one, and she was about an hour away. Her name was Dr. Bethany Williams. I'd have to tell Shane about her, so we could drive out to visit her.

When I arrived home, I got changed and headed in the direction of Chuck's bar. I'd struck out at everything I'd attempted to do today, so might as well head into work early. I was sure Chuck had more training for me to do.

I'd barely made it to the end of my block when an object poked me in my lower back.

"Hey there," a voice said from behind me.

I turned slightly to see who it was. It was the two men who attacked Kate at the bar. "Oh, it's dumb and dumber from last night."

"One more word out of you and I'll shoot you right here. We have orders to bring you in," the one holding the gun said.

"But we also have no problem shooting you either," the other one said.

"Oh, so that's your gun against my back?" I sighed a breath of relief. "I was really hoping it wasn't something else."

He pressed the gun harder against my back. "Do you really want to test us?"

We were in broad daylight. Were they really going to shoot me right here in the middle of the street with people watching? I doubted it.

"Where are you taking me? Your mom's house?" I said. Again, I knew they wouldn't do anything.

"I guess he doesn't want to listen, does he?" The one guy said.

The one holding the gun responded, "I guess not. We don't need him anyway. It's the girl we're after."

We walked past a building, and then they shoved me down the alley hard enough for me to almost lose my balance. After stumbling, I regained myself and turned around. One guy was screwing on what looked like a silencer onto his gun. Was he really going to do this? No, they wouldn't. Silencers still made noise. He was just trying to intimidate me.

"Any last words?" the man with the gun said.

"Sure. After this is all done, would you guys like to grab a bite to eat? I'm starv—"

Pfft.

I didn't notice it at first since it was so quick, but he'd aimed his gun and shot me. I looked at my stomach and saw red soak through my shirt. Damn, I liked this shirt too. It was an old Metallica tour shirt. I wouldn't be able to replace it.

Then the pain kicked in, running rapidly through my mid-section. I lost my balance and fell to the ground, then rolled onto my back and stared up at the sky. I steadied my breathing trying to calm down. I knew I would be okay. At least I hoped so.

What a nice day it was. I hadn't noticed until now. Blue sky with very few clouds. I should probably look up more. Except now, the two men stood over me.

"You guys are blocking my view," I told them. I tried to wave my arm at them to get them to move, but it hurt too much. It was probably a half-assed wave. I winced in pain.

They looked at each other and the one holding the gun said, "You may be able to handle a knife wound, but you won't survive this." He aimed his gun at me again and pulled the trigger. I felt pain dart through my chest. And another hole in my shirt. I decided to hold my breath and play dead. Maybe they'd go away, and I didn't want them to keep shooting me.

I kept my eyes open and still so I could at least see what they were doing. The man holding the gun unscrewed the silencer and placed it back in his pocket. They looked around to make sure they were alone. He pulled back his jacket and placed his gun in a holster. They looked at me one more time and walked away.

"Now let's find the girl," I heard one of them say before their conversation became muffled and far away.

After a few seconds, when I figured they were far enough away, I took a deep breath, gasping for air. It felt nice to breathe again. The pain still lingered in my stomach, and my chest still hurt like hell. I sat up and lifted my shirt. I could see no mark from the first bullet, but my chest still looked like it was healing. It was always fun watching the skin close up like a zipper. Then the scarring just disappeared, as if someone had erased it. It was crazy how it worked, but I was sure these guys weren't expecting this. They'd be surprised to see me again. Although, if they thought they'd just killed me, they'd never suspect me of going after them.

I climbed back to my feet, but my chest still hurt. I knew I was healing, but the pain was still there, and it was slowing me down. This was something that would take some time getting used to.

Wait.

Getting shot was *not* something I wanted to get used to. I'd prefer to *avoid* getting shot.

I stretched, finally able to stand up straight. The pain seemed to have disappeared. I headed back towards the street to try to see where these the two guys had gone. I turned out of the alley, looking back and forth, but I couldn't see them. They must have gotten out of there in a hurry.

A woman walked by me. She had blonde hair and wore a light blue sun dress. She was cute.

"Hey," I said, smiling. She gave me a disturbing look and hurried away. What was that about?

And then I looked down. My shirt was covered in blood. She must have thought I'd just murdered someone. It was probably not the impression I needed to be giving right now. I needed to get back home and change. So much for going into work early.

I took my phone out of my pocket as I hurried along the street towards my apartment. Luckily, I was only a few buildings away, so it was a quick sprint. I pulled up Kate's contact information as I entered the building, and I hit dial. I took the stairs up to my apartment, taking two at a time. Kate answered on the second ring.

"Hello?"

"Kate, it's Adam." I walked into my apartment to make sure no one else could hear me. "I was just murdered," I told her.

There was a brief pause. "Would you care to repeat that? Because what I just heard was that you said you were murdered," she said.

"Who was murdered?" I heard a male voice on the other end say.

"Oh! Is that your boyfriend?" I asked.

"I owe you a punch. Now tell me, what happened?"

"Those two guys who came after you last night, they found me. They took me down an alley and shot me."

"Wait, what? They shot you?" she asked.

"Twice. I heard them say they were going after you next."

There was noise on the other end of the phone. It sounded like Kate was moving the phone around. "Pack this up. We need to go," I heard her say, but it was in the distance, as if she had pulled the phone away from her face to speak. Suddenly, her voice was loud and clear again. "Thanks for the heads up. We're going some-where safe."

"What should I do?" I asked. I wanted to help, considering those guys had just shot me and ruined one of my favorite shirts. I wanted to go after them and take them down, to figure out where they came from, who they were working for, and what this was all about.

"Nothing. Don't do anything," Kate told me. "Let us handle it."

"No, you can't let me sit this out. They just shot me. For all they know, they killed me. I want to get them back!"

"Go—I'll be right there," Kate said, holding the phone away from her face again. I heard a door shut, and then she sounded close to the phone again, but this time, she was speaking in a loud whisper. "Exactly. They think you're dead. If you go after them, they'll know something is off about you. They just shot you twice and you're magically okay again? That'll draw a lot of suspicion I don't think you're ready for just yet. Look, I can't say much more right now. Just continue with your day as if nothing happened. I'll contact you later."

"Wait, hold on!" There was no response. "Hello? Kate?" I looked at my phone and saw that she had hung up.

I threw my phone on the sofa. What was I supposed to do now? I wanted to go after these guys, but I had no way of finding them. I didn't know where Kate was or who she was with. Shane wasn't at work and I had no way to reach him. Funny thing was, Kate was right. It was my only option. I had to go to work. I had to continue my day as normal.

I jumped in the shower to wash myself off, and then I put on some new clothes. I felt so defeated and useless. I had this ability, and it was going to waste because no one needed me.

I walked outside and looked around to see if those guys happened to be waiting for me again. I was just being paranoid at this point. They didn't know I could heal, otherwise they wouldn't have just left me there in the alley.

I sighed as I made my way towards The Stout House.

| 23 |

The night at The Stout House was pretty uneventful. Chuck taught me some new drinks. I also worked the bar a little more by myself this time. His place had become the talk of the town. Something always seemed to be happening there, whether my fights outside or the one that had occurred last night. These things steered some people away, but others flocked to it, hoping to catch a glimpse of the action. In the grand scheme of things, it didn't really affect business all that much, according to Chuck. It may have attracted a unique kind of crowd, but business was business to him.

No one came in to cause a scene, either. Kate didn't come over and those guys who'd attacked us didn't come back. It wasn't like I'd been expecting them to. They thought they'd killed me. And Kate had gone into hiding to get away from those guys. It was an unusual kind of night at The Stout House. A quiet night. I was used to something always happening. This was different.

The next morning, I decided it was time to give Shane another chance. I got dressed and walked down to the police station. I had a lot to tell him after the last day and a half.

The same receptionist was sitting behind the counter. "Hi again," I said, smiling.

She looked up at me, and I noticed a slight sigh. She smiled politely anyway, and asked, "You looking for Officer Cranston?"

"Yup," I replied. "Is he here today?"

"Tell him I'm not here!" I heard a voice say from a distance. I looked around the corner and saw Shane walking behind a desk. He had papers in his hand and looked like he was busy.

"You can't say that when I can clearly see you," I said.

He stopped and faced me. "What do you want, Adam?"

"Can we talk in your office?" I asked.

He walked over to a cabinet to grab something I couldn't see. "I have to leave shortly. Just wait out there and I'll be out in a minute."

I turned and sat in one of the uncomfortable black leather chairs. I pulled out my phone, hoping to see a text from Kate. There was nothing. I wanted to reach out, but she'd said she would contact me later. I didn't want to seem like I was desperate to get a hold of her again, but I wanted to know what had happened to her.

I opened up Kate's previous text, contemplating if I should contact her. I kept closing it and opening it back up, not knowing what to do. Before I could decide, Shane came out of his office and said, "Let's go." He walked right by me and out the front door, not waiting for me. He liked to do that a lot.

I jumped out of my seat and caught the door just before it closed. I caught up with him halfway down the stairs. "Where are we going?" I asked.

"*We* aren't going anywhere. *I'm* going to investigate a homicide. You have two minutes to talk before I have to leave. Go."

"Okay. Hold on, wait. I have like a thousand questions to ask and you're catching me off guard here. If I only have two minutes, I have to concentrate and really think hard about what questions to ask, because it'll take you some time to respond properly and accurately. I want to ask about this homicide now that you've just said something about it, but I'd planned on asking other questions. You're throwing me off here. Okay, let me think for a second."

Shane looked at his watch. "You just wasted nearly twenty seconds telling me that."

"And you wasted five seconds to tell me that. That's time I could have used to ask you something. And I just wasted more time in my wasted response to your wasted question."

"You want to join me, don't you?" he asked.

"What? Why would you think that? How could you possibly think that from… Yes, please."

Shane shook his head. "Get in the car." He unlocked the doors of his police vehicle so we could get in.

"So what's this about a homicide?" I asked.

Shane started the ignition and kicked the vehicle into gear, then turned onto the street. "Someone was murdered on the border of Mapleton, about a mile from Decker City."

"Do you think it has anything to do with the current crime wave over there?" I asked.

"No idea," Shane said. "I would think after Mitchell Quinn was killed and most of his assailants were arrested, crime would have died down by now." He made a face and shrugged his shoulders. "I guess not…"

If only he knew what Kate and I had found out the other night, that Michell Quinn wasn't the mastermind. This was what I wanted to talk to Shane about, along with everything else we'd discovered on the flash drive, but once Shane started talking about the murder, I thought of the lack of response from Kate. Was she the victim? Had the two guys who shot me found her?

"Was it a guy or a girl?" I asked.

"What?" Shane replied.

"The person who was murdered. Was it a guy or a girl?"

"I don't know. All I know is there was a murder, and the location. I don't know what happened. Jenkinson is late to work again, so I have O'Brian going to pick him up. This should be their case, but I'm covering this morning so we can at least get started. They'll probably show up soon after I get there, making this trip pointless. Jenkinson is really walking on thin ice."

My heart sank. I desperately hoped it wasn't Kate. I knew those guys were after her. She couldn't handle them on her own. I hoped whoever she was with could handle himself and protect her, like I did the other night. I really wish she'd told me where she was going. I could have helped her.

Maybe she'd got away, and it was the guy she was with who was murdered. Maybe she was kidnapped, like that girl Lara I'd met the other day. I felt uneasy about this death now. I was anxious. I wanted to be at the scene now and get answers. I needed to know it wasn't Kate.

I reassured myself that it couldn't have been her. She was smart. She could handle herself. Those butterflies kept flapping around in the pit of my stomach. My heart was racing. My palms were beginning to sweat.

"How much longer until we get there?" I asked Shane.

He looked at the GPS on his computer screen. "About six minutes."

I stared out the window, hoping time would speed up. I tried distracting myself by looking at the lines on the road, the buildings we passed, the people wandering the streets. These people had no idea what was really going on behind the scenes. They had no idea what had happened and how dangerous things had become. And now I was back to thinking about death and hoping I wasn't going to find Kate's body.

"Are we there yet?" I asked, hoping I'd wasted those six minutes already.

"Are you serious? You just asked me how long literally thirty seconds ago."

I sighed.

"What's your rush? Something you want to tell me?" Shane asked.

"Not yet," I told him. "I just want to get there first." I tensed up, ready for Shane to start his interrogation.

"This goes against my better judgment and all my training, but okay." Shane continued driving and didn't pry. What was that about? I mean, I wasn't complaining, but that wasn't at all like him. I thought he would have questioned me until we got there and not gotten out of the car until he found answers. But he left me alone. Maybe he sensed my nervousness. Maybe he just didn't want to talk to me. Either way, I was grateful for the silence.

Finally, we arrived at the scene of the murder. There was yellow police tape blocking the parking lot. A police officer removed the tape and allowed Shane to drive through, then replaced the tape, blocking the scene.

Shane parked the car. I unbuckled my seatbelt and went for the door, but Shane held me back.

"I don't know what your rush is or what's so important about this, but I can't have you near the body," he said.

"Wait, what? I need—" I began.

He cut me off.

"What you need to do is stay back. You're not allowed near the body. You aren't trained to handle a crime scene. Not to be mean about it, but you'll probably contaminate it due to not knowing what you're doing. You can leave the vehicle, but you have to remain next to it."

"But I need to—"

He waved at me, cutting me off again.

"I will take pictures and notes. You can review them with me once I get back to the car. Jenkinson and O'Brian should be on their way and once they show up, I'll hand it over to them and we can review everything together. Okay?"

I didn't have a choice. I was grateful he was allowing me to help. I just had to wait a little longer. But it was hard to do that. I *needed* to know who was murdered. I had to know it wasn't Kate.

I agreed to Shane's terms, and he stepped out of the vehicle. I followed him out, then stood by the passenger-side door as he walked to the edge of the parking lot where the cement met the grass. A black tarp covered the body in the distance, so I couldn't see who it was. Shane met another officer who stood over the body. They gesticulated as they talked, pointing and waving. They both bent down, and the waiting officer lifted part of the tarp to look at the body. Shane took out his phone and took a few pictures. They moved the tarp lower, and Shane continued taking photos. A few seconds passed and the officer holding the black tarp replaced it, covering the body again.

Who was under there? Not knowing was killing me.

I pulled my phone out and opened up Kate's previous text. I started typing but was distracted by a car honking. I turned to see another police car approach the yellow police tape. An officer removed the tape and allowed the car to proceed through the barricade and pull up alongside Shane's car. It was Jenkinson and O'Brian. Jenkinson opened the passenger-side door and stepped out, then bent to reach back inside the car, grabbing a cup from the cup holder. O'Brian stepped out as well.

"What the hell are you doing here?" Jenkinson asked.

"Oh, hi Adam. Nice to see you. How are you?" I said. "I think we need to work on your politeness skills."

He took a sip of his drink and, with his free hand, gave me the finger.

"I don't know how you're drinking that. It's burning hot," O'Brian said.

Jenkinson looked back at O'Brian, "You're such a girl. Be a man and drink it hot like it's supposed to be. It's coffee, for Christ's sake."

"I don't think you should be drinking that, being sick and all..." I told him.

"Shut up," Jenkinson replied. He took another sip and walked away.

I nodded at O'Brian. "Well, isn't he pleasant today?"

"Tell me about it. I had to ride with him." O'Brian followed Jenkinson over to Shane and the body.

Shane seemed to have words with Jenkinson: he kept pointing at him and I could hear him yelling, though I couldn't understand what he was saying. Shane pointed at the body and his tone seemed to return to normal, because I couldn't hear him anymore. He waved his hands and walked towards the car. Finally, I'd get some answers.

As he approached the vehicle, I asked, "So? What happened? Who was under the tarp?"

All he said was, "Get back in the car."

Frustration filled inside me as all I wanted to know if it was Kate under that tarp. Shane had the answers, but wouldn't talk about it yet. I did as he asked, hoping he would start talking.

We both got back in the car and Shane started the engine. He reversed out of the parking lot and the guarding officer removed the yellow tape for us.

"I'm going to kill Jenkinson," Shane said.

No. He was not going to change the subject. I just needed to know, and I needed to know now!

"You said you'd tell me who was under that tarp when you got back to the car. You know how much I dislike Jenkinson, and I would love to contribute to the insults, but I need to know who was under that tarp!"

He clenched his jaw and shook his head. "Dammit, Adam, it was some guy named Bruce Smith. Does that help? Do you feel better now? Is your anxiety under control?"

The answer to every one of his questions was yes. I felt better. It was a relief knowing it wasn't Kate. But something was off with Shane.

"Whoa, what the hell is your problem?" I asked.

"My problem? I have to fill in for Jenkinson almost every day because he's 'sick' or whatever is going on with him. Probably just over-sleeping after a late night. I have a ton of work to do. I have you constantly on my case about everything going on around here and then suddenly you have this insane curiosity about this murder. I didn't ask earlier because you seemed extremely concerned. I wanted to see your reaction when I told you who it was, before I started asking you questions. And you didn't seem all that concerned. What's going on, Adam?"

Crap.

Now I felt bad.

Kinda.

Maybe I should have been more concerned about Shane, but I'd needed answers first.

"Okay, I rarely say this, but I'm sorry," I told him.

Shane quickly pulled the car over. He looked at me. "Wait, did you just apologize? All I had to do was freak out and you broke? Damn, you're weak. I thought you were stronger than that."

"I felt bad. I mean..." I actually didn't know what I meant. Was he just messing with me? If he was, he was good.

Shane smiled. "I can't believe it. You care."

He'd caught me off guard. "What? No. I mean..."

"You can't even finish a sentence. I can't believe there are feelings underneath that skin of yours."

He'd backed me into a corner. I didn't know what to say.

"And now I'm just embarrassing you." He started to laugh.

I had to fight back somehow. I had to change the topic. "I guess you don't want to know why I wanted to know about this murder so bad. It's okay, I don't have to tell you."

He kept laughing. "What? You can dish it but can't take it?"

I folded my arms. I was embarrassed, but I didn't want him to know that. All I managed to say was, "Shut up, Shane."

He calmed down and took out his phone, then tossed it onto my lap. "Here ya go, baby. I took those photos. You can check them out. And now you better start talking about what this is all about." He put the car into gear and pulled back onto the road.

I unfolded my arms and picked up the phone off my lap. I looked at the first photo on his phone and immediately pulled out my own phone. I brought up Kate's messages.

"Hey, you can't take pictures with your phone," Shane said.

"I'm not. Just give me a minute," I told him.

I deleted everything I had previously wrote and started writing something new.

Are you okay?

I hit send and hoped she would respond. I looked back at Shane's phone. The man lying on the ground had blood all over his shirt. His eyes were closed, but I recognized him immediately. How could I forget? He was the man who'd shot me yesterday. Had Kate and whoever she was with come across him? Had he found her? Did she kill him?

"Okay, so, a lot has happened since we last spoke," I told Shane. "*A lot.*"

I told him almost everything. Meeting up with Kate. The fight at the bar. The flash drive. The meeting with Dr. Kane. The two men attacking me. I left out the part where they'd shot me. I just told Shane I got away.

"There were two guys, though." I held up Shane's phone, displaying the photo. "This is just one of them. There's another one out there. They were at the bar together and they came after me together."

"We'll find the other guy, but first we have a lot to discuss. I know I'm going to regret this… but I'm going to need your help. You seem to have a way of getting yourself in the middle of things. I need you to find out where Kate is. I think it's time the three of us had a talk."

"I'm working on it. I just sent her a text. When you told me there was a homicide earlier, I thought it may have been her."

"Do you have any idea where she may be right now?" Shane asked.

"No. Last time we spoke, she didn't tell me where she was going and just said she would contact me." My phone chimed, startling me. It was a message from Kate. I held up my phone. "This is her now."

I'm fine. Had a bit of an issue, but it was taken care of. Are you okay?

I used my phone to take a picture of the screen on Shane's phone.

"Hey, I thought I told you no pictures," Shane said.

"Don't worry. I'm using it to get Kate's attention. You said you wanted to meet her, right?"

He shook his head.

I attached the picture to the text and wrote, *This issue?*

I sent the text and waited for a response. I was sure it would be immediate.

"What did she say?" Shane asked.

"Nothing yet," I said.

Would she even help us? I hoped so. After helping her out at the bar and everything we'd discovered on that flash drive, I would hope she would include me in this.

My phone chimed and vibrated in my hand.

"She says, 'One down. One to go. Care to lend a hand?'"

"So she's a murderer? And she's asking for your help in murdering the second guy?" Shane asked.

"Okay, hold on. I don't think she was the one who murdered him. She doesn't seem like she could do that," I told Shane. Truthfully, I didn't think she could have done that. It must have been that guy she was with.

"People can surprise you. Maybe she holds a secret you don't know about."

I guessed that was true in my case. Shane didn't know about my healing ability—a secret I'd kept from him.

"We need to find her," he said.

"Are you going to arrest her?" I asked.

"Let me handle that," he said.

"If you're going to arrest her, I won't meet up with her. You don't even know it was her."

"Stop defending her. Look, based on her text, she seems like a likely suspect. I'm a police officer and if she committed murder, I have to arrest her. I wouldn't be doing my job if I let this slide because the murdered guy was a bad guy, or because you're friendly with her. The law doesn't work that way. I need to know what happened first, and if talking to her helps me figure that out, then I need to talk to her. She may have acted in self-defense. The coroner will determine that in his report," Shane said. "But I still need to talk to her. Especially about this flash drive."

I stared at my phone, debating in my head how to reply. I had a bad feeling about Shane's plan, but if this was the only way I could see Kate, then I had to go through with it. Shane would be on my case and would probably follow me if I turned it down. He wasn't stupid. He knew I would just meet up with her another time. At least if I did it now, I would be a step further and hopefully help clear her name, as I was sure she didn't kill that guy.

I picked up my phone and replied, setting up a meeting in an hour. Hopefully, Shane would keep his word.

| 24 |

25 years ago

Martha and Steve brought their son to the doctor's office. A week ago, the doctor had set up a meeting with another family, having let them know about a boy up for adoption. The Price family had been trying to have children for years, and they were ecstatic about the opportunity to adopt. The boy was a year old, but that wasn't a concern for the Price's. All they wanted was a baby. They were made aware of the uniqueness of this baby boy, but that didn't matter to them. This was their dream, and one of their only opportunities at this point in time, so they jumped on it.

Dr. Peter Stone greeted Martha and Steve as they walked into his office.

"We are doing the right thing," Steve said, trying to reassure Martha.

"I know. It's the best for Adam." She turned to face her husband. "I just feel like I'm doing the wrong thing."

He put his arm around her. "I know. Me too. But we can't take care of him. We can't afford to. This family can give him the life he needs and deserves. They can love him and raise him better than we'd be able to. Isn't that what you ultimately want for him? A better life?"

Martha started to tear up. She did want a better life for Adam, but she wanted to provide it herself.

She slumped over in her chair as she sat down. Feelings of guilt rushed through her. She felt like a failure for not understanding what was happening to him. She was scared but knew she couldn't do anything about it. It broke her heart that it had come to this.

For months, Adam hadn't gotten sick, which would usually seem like a good thing. While examining him, his pediatrician had been a little concerned. Adam's blood work would always stump doctors. Everything was always perfect. This surprised Martha and Steve, but they had their concerns. Something had to be wrong. Children always got sick.

The doctors wanted to keep running tests on Adam, which in turn ran up Martha's and Steve's insurance costs. They couldn't afford to keep this up in the long term.

What had happened to Adam? What had made him like this?

Ever since Martha realized Adam could instantly heal himself, she had emotionally distanced herself from him. She just wanted a healthy and normal baby boy. She wasn't capable of handling Adam's uniqueness. She wanted to do what was best, and if another family could care and raise him better than she could, she felt Adam deserved that.

"Would you like to meet the family?" Dr. Stone asked.

Martha and Steve looked at each other. A moment passed before Steve said, "I think it's best if we didn't know. It would just make things more difficult for us."

"And Adam," Martha added.

"Yes, and Adam. A clean break would help our family move past this difficult decision and give Adam a fresh start," Steve said.

The doctor nodded. "I agree." He pulled papers from a folder, then slid them towards Martha and Steve. "I need you to review these and sign these when you're ready." He stood up. "I'll give you two a moment, and I'll go meet with the other family. I'll come back in a few minutes when you're finished."

| 25 |

Kate told me to meet her at the abandoned facility in Decker City, Mitchell Quinn's entertainment center. According to Kate, discussions were still ongoing about what to do with it, whether to continue moving forward and have some business or investor take it over, or to destroy it, given that it was now associated with such an evil person. In the meantime, there was nobody there, so she said it would be a good place to meet.

Shane pulled up with a few minutes to spare. "Where did she say we'd meet?" he asked.

"Behind the locked gate out front. She said you'd know how to get in," I told him.

He shook his head as he pulled out a small set of keys from his jacket pocket. "Let's go," he said as he stepped out of the car.

I followed him towards the locked gate, and Shane jingled his keys while searching for the right one. He moved them one by one, moving the discarded key behind the next key in line. "I think it's this one," he mumbled to himself as he stuck the key in the lock. It unlocked with a *click*. He placed the keys back in his jacket pocket, pushed open the gate, and gestured for me to move inside.

I stepped past him and proceeded through the gateway. Shane followed and closed the gate behind him, leaving it unlocked.

"You have a key to this place?" I asked.

He shook his head. "It's a skeleton key."

"Oh! I heard about these before," I said excitedly. "They open everything, right?"

"No. They only open a selection of things. This specific one opens municipal areas owned by the city, such as this property—and its gate surrounding it."

"Oh." I was disappointed. I'd seen these keys being used to open all locations. I was hoping to be able to use it for all kinds of things. TV and movies had lied to me again.

"Where are we meeting her?" he asked me.

"Right here is fine," Kate said, stepping out from behind the shrubs along the walkway.

Shane immediately put his hand to his gun, which was holstered on the right side of his hip.

"Shane," I whispered. He glanced at me and I shook my head. "No."

It must have been out of instinct he reached for his firearm, but I knew he wouldn't need it. Hopefully my reassurance would be enough.

Kate walked forward. "So, we're here now." She looked at Shane, then followed his hand to his gun. "You're not going to arrest me, are you?"

"That depends on how this conversation goes," Shane said.

Immediately, Kate responded, "Look, I didn't kill that guy. I mean, I was there when it happened, but I didn't do it."

"Who did?" Shane asked.

"Is it really that important?" I added.

"Adam, let me handle this," Shane said. "Kate, I need to know what happened. I know there's a lot going on right now and Adam seems to be in the middle of it all with you. He seems to trust you, but I don't. He's filled me in on the flash drive and the guy with the scar, but I need to know what else is going on. But first, I need to know what happened to the man who was murdered and who murdered him."

Kate nodded slowly. "Okay. I'll help. But I need your help in return. I also need to see this through. I can't help if you arrest me or prevent me from continuing this investigation. Do we have a deal?"

"I can't make any promises," Shane told her.

"Then I'm done here," Kate said, and started to walk away.

"Wait!" I yelled. Kate stopped in her tracks and turned around. "Shane, come on. We need her help. She's the one who discovered all this information I brought to you. Let her help," I pleaded.

I could see the frustration building within Shane. He shook his head slightly, his lips pursed, and he squinted at me. I could tell he was thinking of a way to say no. But he needed Kate's help, too. She had information he needed. He couldn't say no.

"Fine," he said finally, facing Kate. "She can help." He then turned and pointed at me. "Don't make me regret this."

"You won't," I told him.

Kate started the conversation. "The guy you found this morning, his name is Br—"

"Bruce Smith, we know," Shane interrupted.

She glared at him. "Yes, Bruce Smith. What you don't know is he attempted to kill me last night, he and his partner. The other guy you're going to be looking for, his name is Henry Quill. They are two hitmen working with the man with the scar."

"Scarface," I butted in.

They both looked at me.

I shrugged my shoulders. "What? Sounds better than 'the man with the scar,' right?"

They both ignored me.

Shane turned back towards Kate. "I guess these hitmen are not very good at their job."

"Ask Adam," Kate said. "They—"

I jumped in, interrupting her. "They attacked me at the bar. Remember, I told you about how they attacked Kate and me the other night?" I couldn't let Shane know they'd tried to murder me. He didn't know about my ability and I wanted to keep it that way, at least for now.

Shane looked confused. "Yeah? And that has what to do with this?"

I gave Kate a wide-eyed look. Hopefully she understood not to mention my ability again. "Uh, I guess nothing. Sorry, I'll shut up."

Kate continued. "Anyway, they attacked us, but then they came after me and my partner."

"Your boyfriend," I said.

Kate leaned forward and punched me twice. "One was for last night."

I rubbed my arm. "She just hit me. Are you going to allow that?" I asked Shane.

"You probably deserved it. I've seen you endure much worse. Don't be such a baby," he said.

Kate smiled, and gestured at Shane. "He's growing on me."

"I don't care what you think of me. I want you to continue your story. What happened to you and your partner? And who is this partner, by the way?"

Kate looked at me, then back at Shane. "I can't tell you who he is."

"You will tell me who he is. You promised your cooperation and if I'm not going to arrest you, I need to know *everything*," Shane said sternly.

Kate glared at him. "Look, you know how we reporters work. We don't give away our sources. I'd be betraying him. He's currently working a case to find this man with the scar and I can't let you get in the way."

Shane took a step closer to Kate to stare down at her. She returned the stare, standing her ground. "You have one last chance to tell me his name or I'll have to arrest you for obstruction of justice."

"You can't. Just because I won't tell you his name doesn't mean you can arrest me."

"Okay, fine. How about murder? You're a murder suspect. You admitted you were there." Shane pulled out his handcuffs and grabbed Kate's wrists.

"Wait!" I exclaimed. "This is escalating way too quickly. Let's all just calm down."

"Calm down?" Kate said. "How can I with this idiot harassing me?"

Shane clicked the handcuffs on one of her wrists, and grabbed her other one.

"Shane, stop," I said.

He stopped what he was doing, but still held onto Kate's other wrist.

I looked at Kate. "Just tell him. We won't get in his way of his investigation. We're just trying to get answers. We're all on the same team, remember?"

Kate considered my words. "I trust you, Adam. I don't trust him..."

"Feeling's mutual," Shane replied.

"Shane, let her help. Kate, please just tell him what he wants to know. I promise we will keep it between us. He just can't be left out in the dark. I trust Shane, and I'll make sure your partner's identity is safe with us."

"You will?" Shane asked.

"Shane, we need her help. Just please work together!" I pleaded.

They were both quiet.

"Please?" I asked again.

I hoped this would work. It was the only way we could get through this.

Kate finally spoke up. "This is because I trust you, Adam. His name is Nathan Hobbes."

Shane's head tilted slightly. "The DOC guy?"

"The what?" I asked.

Shane pulled out his keys and started unlocking Kate's handcuffs. "DOC, Department of Counterterrorism. Nathan is one of the top guys in that department." He stopped and turned to face me. "Sorry. *The* top guy. Trust me, you don't want to mess with him." He went back to unlocking Kate's handcuffs.

"I think I could handle myself," I said, feeling pretty confident given my ability.

Kate rubbed her right wrist where the handcuffs were locked on. "Adam, you wouldn't stand a chance. And if you break my promise, I'll make sure he comes after you and finds a way to put you down." She winked at me. I guess she understood my earlier hint about not mentioning my ability. But her last comment kind of worried me. I didn't know why, but it made a little nervous.

"She just threatened me," I told Shane.

"Again, you probably deserved it," he told me. He turned to Kate. "I have a lot of respect for Nathan. If he's involved in this mess somehow, he has my cooperation and I'll let you two be."

"What the hell just happened here? She mentions someone's name and you're okay with her now?" I said. "I mean, I'm glad we're finally on the same page, but I didn't expect that."

They ignored me, and Kate continued, "Those hitmen followed us and tried to attack us. Nathan took one out and the other one retreated. Nathan told me to find somewhere safe to go, and he followed the guy. I just crashed at a hotel."

"Do you know where he went?" Shane asked.

Kate shook her head. "He said he'd contact me. Haven't heard from him yet. My job was to figure out everything on this flash drive." She pulled the drive from her pocket. "I reviewed all of it, but there's a lot of information. I made a copy on my laptop. You can hold on to this one."

Shane reached out to accept it, but Kate quickly turned and handed it to me. Shane glared at her.

"I trust Adam. I don't trust you. Sorry," Kate said.

"Whatever," Shane said. "What's on the drive?"

"Everything you need to know. And I wouldn't take that to work with you. Pretty sure someone in your department is working against you."

"Do you know who?" he asked.

"No. I never found a name," she said.

Shane shook his head. "Alright, we're going to get going so I can review the information on the drive. Adam has your contact information, which he will pass on to me, right, Adam?" He glanced at me with an intimidating expression.

"Uh, yeah, sure," I said.

"Good." He turned back towards Kate. "We'll be in touch. In the meantime, once Nathan reaches out to you, please contact me. I want to know what's going on."

"Oh good. Since you want me to share information, it had better go both ways. You figure anything out, I want to know as well," Kate said. "We're a team now. And honestly, I don't think you can trust anyone else in this little circle here, anyway. Remember, you have someone working at the station on Scarface's payroll." Kate shook her head and looked at me. "Now you have me using that name."

"See? Easier isn't it?" I said.

She sighed. "I hate you so much sometimes."

"Aww, that's so sweet of you to say. I love you too."

"Come on, Adam. We're leaving. Stop flirting," Shane said.

"What? Me? No way." I pointed to Kate. "She said she hated me." Addressing Kate, I continued, "He plays a big brother role, you know, always looking out for me and trying to protect me. Sometimes he just misinterprets certain things because he doesn't have what you and I have. We—" I was suddenly tugged away by my ear. "Ouch, ouch, ouch."

Shane dragged me away. "Say goodbye Adam."

I waved at Kate. "Goodbye, Adam!"

She smiled and wave back.

Shane let go of my ear as we approached the gate. I rubbed it. "Was that really necessary?"

"I'm pretty sure your girlfriend got a kick out of it." He waved me through the gate so he could lock it. "Come on."

"She's not my girlfriend," I told him as he closed the gate and locked it. "Wait—Kate's still in there. How is she getting out?"

"Not my problem. She got in without us, she can get out."

I followed him to his police car. When we got in, he extended an open hand. "Flash drive, please."

I reached into my pocket and handed it to him. He took it and placed it in the USB port at the side of his mobile computer.

"Who's this Nathan guy you were crushing over back there?" I asked.

Shane stared at the screen as the flash drive was loaded. "He's someone you don't want to mess with. A real badass."

"Care to elaborate?"

He turned towards me. "He used to be a military guy. Did a few tours overseas. Decided to leave once he got married. He was recruited by the Department of Counterterrorism. He worked around the country, preventing terrorist attacks which you probably never even heard about."

"Okay, thanks for giving me his resume, but I asked what makes him such a badass, as you claim he is?"

"Remember hearing about the building bombing in Shallow Falls?"

I nodded.

"Terrorists were trying to take down the building. Because of Nathan, only one bomb ended up going off, instead of all ten. Only reason that one did is because it malfunctioned. He alone took down all the terrorists inside that building. He snuck in through the sewer systems and crawled up through a ventilation system. Then he took everyone out, one by one."

"Don't you guys usually work in teams for stuff like that?" I asked.

"He works alone. And as I explained, he gets the job done, *by himself*. They call him the Lone Wolf."

A folder icon finally popped up on the computer screen. Shane reached for his mouse and clicked on it. "There are a few stories about him, just like the one I told you. And they all end the same way. Nathan gets the job done. *Alone*."

Just as before, folders and files flooded the screen. It all looked familiar.

"If he's the guy who works alone, why is Kate able to work with him?" I asked.

Shane shook his head. "No one really knows about Nathan. He keeps to himself. Stays out of sight. Like I said, he works alone—and a lot of the stuff he's done, you've never heard about. If Kate knows him somehow, there's obviously some way she's able to help him. I don't know what that is just yet, but I intend to find out."

Shane examined the icons on the screen. "Is this what you were talking about earlier?"

I nodded. "I only looked through a few things. Kate took it after a few minutes."

Shane turned to face me. "Who's this Scarface guy?"

I shrugged my shoulders. "I don't know. I know Kate's looking for him with that Nathan guy. From what I saw on that flash drive, he's probably behind all the violence that happened in Decker City."

"I thought the DC police determined it was Mitchell Quinn?"

"Once you take a look through the flash drive, you'll see they're wrong."

Shane's eyes wandered around the car. He was clearly in thought. He let out a deep breath and turned back towards the computer monitor. He finally said, "Show me where to find this information. If you're correct, we're going to have a lot more work to do."

Shane and I spent at least an hour clicking through the files on the drive. He was particularly interested in the ones relating to the Gray Hood. There were videos and photos of him which seemed to have come from security cameras, but they never showed his face. Every time Shane watched the vigilante move something without touching it, he just shook his head and mumbled under his breath.

He did find something, though. The name Patrick Malloy kept popping up in documents, bank statements, and signed statements with Mitchell Quinn. Plus, Shane said he was one of the guys at the warehouse he had seen being wheeled out on a stretcher the other night. He was obviously involved, especially since we had that recording between him and Mitchell Quinn. When Shane heard that, he understood that Mitchell wasn't the key guy, and the Decker City police had been wrong. Patrick wasn't Mitchell's assistant; Patrick was *above* Mitchell.

Shane told me it was time to pay Patrick a visit at the hospital. And that's exactly where we were heading.

* * *

Once we arrived, he said, "Same routine as before. I do the talking."

I agreed and we got out of the car. We walked up to the receptionist's desk and Shane flashed his badge. "We're here to speak with Patrick Malloy. Can you tell me where he is?"

"Certainly, Officer..." The lady behind the counter squinted to read his badge. "...Cranston. I need to call the officer upstairs to check in first."

"I understand," Shane said.

She picked up the phone and dialed. "May I ask what your business is with Mr. Malloy?"

"We're just here to ask him a few questions, that's all," Shane responded.

She nodded and held the phone to her ear, waiting for someone to pick up. "Hello, this is Barbara, down at reception. I have an Officer Cranston here to speak with Mr. Malloy." She paused for a moment, then said, "Okay, will do." She hung up and looked at us. "You guys can head on up. Floor five, room 502. You'll see an officer outside the door. He'll let you inside."

"Thank you," Shane said. We walked towards the elevators and headed up.

The doors opened on the fifth floor, and we were greeted by the waiting officer. He shook Shane's hand and told him he'd wait outside while we talked to Patrick, but we only had a couple of minutes. Shane agreed, and the officer unlocked the door and let us in.

We walked into a fairly dark room. A TV hung in the corner, opposite Patrick's bed. Other than the bed and IV drips, the room was empty. Patrick lay motionless, handcuffed to the bed. He looked familiar. His face was bandaged up, but I remembered him from when I dropped off boxes to the Discount Pavilion's store in Mitchell Quinn's entertainment center.

"Hey Patrick, wake up," Shane said. Patrick didn't move. Shane walked closer and pushed his shoulder. "Wake up."

Patrick's eyes squinted as he began to move around. He opened his eyes slowly, one at a time. He looked at Shane, then at me, and back at Shane again. "Who are you?" he asked.

"My name is Officer Cranston. This is my trainee. We're here to ask you a couple of questions."

Patrick smiled. "Go to hell." He closed his eyes and turned his head to the side.

"I think you're going to want to listen to what we have to say," Shane told Patrick.

With his eyes still closed and facing away from us, Patrick said, "I don't know you. I don't care about you. And I really don't care about your questions."

Shane proceeded anyway. "We know you're not Mitchell Quinn's assistant. He actually worked for you."

Patrick's eyes opened.

"See," Shane said. "I told you you'd want to listen."

"I only opened my eyes because I'm curious how you would come up with such a crazy idea like that?" Patrick said, turning to face him.

"See, I'm pretty sure you're trying to bait me into telling you how I know the truth. But I'm not going to tell you. I want it to eat at you. I want you to dwell on it. I want you to think of all the ways I might have found out. Maybe someone betrayed you. Maybe we found evidence that you didn't hide very well. But I know you were behind a lot of what happened in Decker City, and not Mitchell Quinn, as we were all led to believe. But I need you to start talking and tell me everything you know—otherwise, you're going to jail for a *long* time."

Patrick laughed. "You're funny, Officer Cranston. Why would I talk to you, anyway? Jail doesn't scare me. I probably won't be making it there, anyway."

Shane squinted. "What do you mean by that?"

Patrick stared right at Shane. "I'm not going to tell you. I want it to *eat* at you. I want you to *dwell* on it," he said mockingly.

I could tell Shane was holding back. I saw his hand curl into a fist. I knew he wouldn't do anything, but I could see he wanted to.

Patrick smiled at Shane. "Now, if you don't mind, I would like to get back to sleep, since you so rudely woke me up. It was very nice talking to you, Officer Cranston. I hope we meet again under different circumstances." He turned away and closed his eyes again.

Shane stared at him in silence.

I spoke up finally. "What do we do now?" I whispered to Shane.

He continued to stare at Patrick. "We leave. Come on." He turned and headed for the door. When he knocked on it, the officer waiting outside unlocked it and let us out. He shut the door and locked it behind us.

"All good?" he asked.

"All good," Shane replied.

We headed for the elevator. Once we stepped in and the door shut, Shane finally said, "What a dick. I just wanted to punch him."

"I could tell," I said. "What do we do now?"

"I need to head over to the Decker City police department and talk to them about their plans for Patrick. I need to know what they know about him and when they'll be moving him."

"You mean *we*, right?" I reminded him.

The elevator doors opened. Shane sighed and walked off. "Fine. *We*."

* * *

We pulled out of the parking lot and onto the street. Shane was quiet and seemed tense after his brief conversation with Patrick. I had to break the tension somehow.

"So, Patrick, huh? Kind of a character, am I right?" I said.

"Not now, Adam. I've dealt with a lot of criminals before. He was the first who gave me the impression that he wasn't scared. At all. He seemed comfortable being where he was."

"Couldn't that have just been the drugs they're giving him?"

Shane shook his head. "He's on a very light dosage. Not enough to make him loopy, just enough to numb the pain a little. He seemed like he was in complete control, even handcuffed to that hospital bed. It was just… weird."

I agreed. Patrick had seemed very comfortable. He didn't fight back. He just shrugged Shane off and went back to sleep like nothing had happened.

Shane continued, "Patrick definitely perked up when I said I knew he was in charge of Mitchell Quinn. But it was almost like he didn't care that I knew." He glanced at me. "What do you think?"

"You're asking me? I'm just as clueless as you."

"You're right. I'm sorry. I'm just thinking out loud," he said.

"It's okay. The guy was definitely a creep. He—"

Shane interrupted me. "Look out!"

Immediately, there was a loud *crack* and the car lurched forward. I was thrown into the dash.

"What the hell was that?" I yelled.

Shane floored the gas. "Someone rammed us. Hold on!"

The car lurched forward again with another *crack* of metal on metal from behind us. This time, the car skidded a little to the right. Shane gripped the wheel and pulled it back and accelerated quickly.

"Who is doing that?" I asked, turning around in my seat to look behind us.

"I don't know. Probably someone who followed us after talking with Patrick," Shane said.

Suddenly, I heard a gunshot from behind. Instinctively, Shane and I both ducked. There was another gunshot, then another. I ducked each time. The fifth shot took out the rear window, glass shattering all over the back seat. I peeked above my seat and saw the passenger of the black SUV hanging out the window, holding a handgun.

I faced forward again. "Can't you do something?" I yelled at Shane.

"What do you think I'm trying to do?" he shouted.

I turned around again and saw that a black SUV was pulling up on the passenger side. "Shane, speed up!"

"I'm trying!"

The car pulled up until it was side by side with us. The driver of the black SUV pulled out a gun, aimed it at us and fired twice before having to pull around another car. Then he pulled side by side with us again.

"You missed!" I yelled at him.

"Adam, shut up!" Shane scolded.

The driver took aim and shot two more times. He hit the passenger door. I saw the markings on the inside door frame, which thankfully hadn't penetrated the metal.

Suddenly, the passenger window shattered from another bullet. Glass fell all over my lap. I shook my shirt and kicked my legs to toss the glass off of me.

Shane pulled the car to the left to avoid oncoming traffic, then quickly turned left. Horns blared from vehicles as we passed them.

The black SUV sped through the intersection and then slammed on the breaks. I heard the screeching of its tires as we turned down the street.

"Adam, open the glove compartment," Shane told me.

I opened it to reveal a handgun.

He glanced at me. "Take it."

I reached for it and picked it up. It felt heavy in my hands. I expected it to be lighter. I had never held a gun before. I examined it in my hand, turning it in all directions.

"Safety is off. Pull back the slide and fire it next time they approach us." I gripped the top of the gun to pull back, but it was harder than I'd imagined. I'd assumed it would just pulled back instantly with no force.

Shane must have seen me struggling. "Stop being such a pansy. Pull the damn thing back. They're coming!"

Shane swerved around a vehicle while I attempted to ready my weapon. The black SUV had finally caught up to us.

"Hey, could we talk about this first?" I yelled, as they drove next to us again.

The passenger leaned above the vehicle and shot as us again. I ducked quickly behind the door frame. He hit the hood of the vehicle and my door again.

"Damn it, Adam! Fire the weapon!" Shane exclaimed.

I peeked up and fired a shot blindly. The recoil took me off guard, throwing my hands backwards.

"Again!" Shane screamed.

I pointed and fired again. The driver of the black SUV pulled away, but not before one of my four shots took out the driver's side mirror.

"Did you see that? I got the mirror!" I shouted, proud of myself.

"I don't care about his mirror. Take the driver out. Or the vehicle."

I aimed at the vehicle, but an 18-wheeler drove between us. Once we passed it, I took aim again, but before I took a shot, the passenger of the SUV clambered back out of the window, leaning over the roof. He was holding an automatic weapon. "Uh… Shane?"

"Fire, Adam!"

I unloaded the rest of the magazine just before the guy began firing. I, of course, missed all my shots. The moment he started firing at us, Shane yelled, "Hold on!" He rammed the car into the driver's side of the SUV. I ducked down as the sides of the vehicles scraped together, sparks flying and pieces of metal came peeling off the cars.

I peeked out the window and saw the passenger drop his weapon onto the street. Shane tossed me another magazine, and then swerved again to avoid rear-ending another vehicle. He made another quick left, trying to lose the SUV. I turned in my seat to see it side-swipe another vehicle while trying to make the turn.

"Left side of the gun, next to the trigger, there's a release button," Shane said. I turned the gun and pushed the button. The magazine dropped out of the gun instantly. "Good! Now slam the next one in." I placed the magazine inside the gun and used my palm to slam it into place. "Now pull back the slide and fire!"

The black SUV pulled up next to us and I opened fire again. This time I aimed lower, going for their tires. It took me three shots to take out the tire on the driver's side. It popped and pieces of black rubber burst into the street. The black SUV was now driving on the rim. Sparks littered its underside.

"I got it! I got it!" I yelled.

Shane looked in the rear-view mirror. "We may have another problem."

"What?" I asked.

"Another car is catching up on us. Looks like we have more company." He glanced at the car next to us, sparks all around it. He looked in the rear-view mirror again. "Hold on!"

He slammed our vehicle into the SUV next to us. It skidded towards the right, but the driver regained control fairly quickly. Shane slammed into it again. This time, he did what he set out to do. The vehicle lost control due to its missing tire and slammed into a parked car on the side of the road.

I watched as it came to a complete stop.

"Yes!" I exclaimed.

"Don't cheer just yet. Here comes their backup," Shane said. He turned right quickly and the vehicle, a blue sedan, followed suit. Shane sped around two cars as he tried to outrun the other vehicle, but it still remained behind us. He turned left, and the other car followed. The passenger began shooting at us.

"What are you waiting for? Return fire!" Shane said.

I stuck my head out of the window, then fired the handgun at the vehicle behind us. One of the six shots penetrated their front windshield. I was an awful shot. I made myself a mental note to learn how to fire a gun.

The passenger opened fire again. One shot took out the passenger mirror next to me. I felt a tug on my shirt and then was pulled into the car.

"Don't stay out there like that. You'll get shot. Fire and get behind cover."

"Got it."

Shane spun the car left again to turn down a different street. I turned to see that the blue car was still following us. Pikes River, which separated Decker City and Mapleton, was now on our right. A guardrail was the only thing between us and the depths of water below us.

The other vehicle was gaining on us. It tapped the rear of our car, making the steering wheel spin slightly in Shane's grip. He gained control and sped on.

"Shoot at them!" Shane yelled.

I put my head out of the passenger window again and turned, then fired once before the other vehicle rammed into the rear corner of our car. I lost my balance and dropped the gun onto the road.

"Dammit!"

"What?" Shane asked.

"I dropped the gun!" The second I finished my sentence, I heard gunshots again. Sharp, piercing pain flooded my right shoulder.

They'd shot me. I flinched and screamed in pain, more so because it had taken me by surprise. I made my way slowly back inside the car.

"Are you shot?" Shane exclaimed, trying to control the vehicle.

I couldn't let him know what had just happened. The pain was vanishing anyway. I could play it off somehow. "No, I—" was all I managed to say before a loud *pop* came from the driver's side.

"They blew the front tire. Hold on!" Shane said.

He swerved the car to the left. He hit the blue sedan, but because of the blown tire, there was little strength behind it. The other car started pushing us to the right. Shane was screaming as he used all his strength to turn the car away from the guardrail. He slammed on the brakes, but that only made the car spin out and smash into the railing next to us. My head and shoulder connected with the side of the car, almost making me forget about the gunshot pain moments ago.

I shook off the momentary headache and spun around. Luckily, the railing prevented the vehicle from falling over the edge into the river. Unfortunately, we were dangling over the edge, the driver's side tire entirely over it.

"Are you okay?" Shane asked.

"Yeah, I'm fine," I told him. This was the first moment I had to breathe. I tried to control the adrenaline still flowing through me.

Our car shook as the blue sedan smashed into our car, pushing us closer to the edge. We moved slowly, closer and closer to the edge as the other car attempted to push our vehicle into the river below.

Shane unbuckled his seat belt and reached for a gun under his seat, then turned and opened fire through the blown-out rear window. Bullet holes lit up the front windshield of the other car, which was pushing us. Blood exploded inside the car. He got them! But we were still moving over the edge.

"Oh, shit! Get out!" Shane shouted.

He opened his car door and jumped into the water below. I just managed to open my door as the car slipped over the edge. I felt like I was floating for a moment. I watched as the water came rushing towards me. I took in a deep breath, not knowing if it'd be my last, as I anticipated going under water,

The vehicle hit the water, and my head slammed onto the dashboard. I was dizzy for a moment. Water started filling up inside the car, which was beginning to submerge. I had to get out. I reached for the door and pulled myself out.

"Adam! Look out!"

I didn't even have time to fully comprehend what Shane had said. I looked up and saw the blue sedan come falling down on top of me.

| **27** |

Darkness.

"Adam…"

A distant voice. Muffled. Where did that come from? Where was I? What was happening?

Pain.

Wetness.

The car!

"Adam!" The voice again, louder this time.

I opened my eyes wide. I was lying down with Shane kneeling beside me. He let out a huge sigh of relief.

"Oh good, you're okay," he said.

I groaned. "Can't get rid of me that easily." I sat up slowly.

"How the hell did you survive a car falling on top of you?" Shane asked.

What was I supposed to say? *I have superpowers and can heal from almost everything.* I couldn't let him know what I could do. He hated the Gray Hood. I didn't want him to show that kind of hatred towards me, too.

"I don't remember," I said. Well, it was actually partially true. I remembered the car falling down on me, but nothing after that. I continued on with my lie. "I know I went back to the car for protection when you called my name. I don't really remember too much after that. Something hit me and must have knocked me out."

"I'm just glad you're okay," he said.

"Aww, you care."

He nodded. "Thanks Adam. You know how to ruin it." He groaned and stood up. He pulled his phone out of his pocket and tapped the screen. It lit up. "Good, at least this thing still works." He tapped icons on his screen and began making a phone call.

What the hell had I just experienced? A car chase. A shootout with criminals. Car crashes. For a brief moment, I felt like the Gray Hood. Didn't he just go through this the other night? All of this was exciting! Deadly, but exciting. It was what I wanted to experience by working with Shane. I couldn't believe what I had just gone through. I wondered if the Gray Hood would have survived in the same situation.

Shane hung up the phone and put it back in his pocket. "The DCPD will be here momentarily. They already know about the car chase and shootout." The sirens in the distance gave credence to his statement.

I sat up, but Shane held me down. "I don't know how you survived that, but I need you to stay there until the paramedics check on you."

I pushed his hand away and stood up. "I'm fine. See?" I got to my feet and waved my arms around. "All good."

Flashing lights became visible as the police car and ambulance turned onto the street and headed in our direction. Soon, three vehicles arrived, and officers and paramedics jumped out of their vehicles, heading for us. Shane immediately told them to check on me. I just went along with it. I knew I was okay, but I still had to play the part.

I accompanied the paramedics to their vehicle while Shane walked away with one of the officers. I sat on the wheel well of the ambulance while they checked on me. Even when I told them I was fine, they continued with their exam.

Shane walked over to the water and pointed. I ignored the examiners and watched. Shane had a look of surprise on his face. Suddenly, his lips curled and his eyes widened. His hands curled into fists. I could hear him yelling. Profanities were definitely in his vocabulary. He reached towards the officer with his palm out. The officer reached in his pocket and handed him keys, and then Shane walked purposefully towards the police car and got in.

"Whoa, wait a second," I said out loud, to no one in particular. I pushed the paramedics aside and ran after the police car, waving my hands furiously, trying to get Shane's attention. "Shane! Hold on! Wait!"

The car briefly began to move forward, but stopped. I caught up to it and knocked on the passenger door. I heard the *click* of the door unlocking, then opened it, and climbed inside.

"What the hell, Shane? Leaving without me?"

"Shut the door. Let's go," he said. I closed the door, and he immediately sped off.

"What was that all about?" I asked.

Shane was fuming. He was breathing heavily. "I'm pissed. That's why. Those guys who chased us almost killed us. And do you know why?"

I hadn't even considered that yet. I was still getting over everything that had just happened.

Shane answered his own question. "Because of that son-of-a-bitch, Patrick."

"He's handcuffed to a bed. How could he have done this?" I asked.

"Who else knew we talked to him?" Shane asked me.

The question floated around my mind for a moment. I didn't think anyone knew we'd talked to Patrick. We didn't tell anyone we were going to see him. I had no idea how to answer Shane's question.

Finally, I said, "I don't know."

"The officer that let us in the room," Shane told me.

"Yeah? So?"

"DCPD doesn't *have* an officer protecting the room. What I just found out was that the doctors were in charge of the room. They cleared the surrounding rooms, and that entire area was off limits to anyone but doctors and law enforcement. Patrick is handcuffed to the bed, and the door is locked. They felt that was enough protection and had the officers leave."

"So who did we see outside his room, then?" I asked.

"I don't know. But I'm assuming he was the one who called in the attack on us."

* * *

When we arrived at the hospital, Shane didn't even bother parking correctly. He just pulled right up to the front entrance and got out.

I followed him as he stormed inside the front entrance and headed directly for the elevator. I had to keep at a slow jog to keep up with him.

"Uh, Shane, you okay?" I asked when we got inside. He looked like he was going to murder Patrick.

"I'm fine," he said.

"Tell that to the pulsating vein in your head."

He ignored me. As usual.

The doors to the fifth floor opened. He walked out of the elevator and over to Patrick's door. The so-called officer wasn't here now. Shane looked around in all directions, looking for any sign of him.

A nurse walked by. "Excuse me," he said. "Where is the officer who was here earlier?"

"He left a few minutes ago," the nurse replied.

Shane's face was tight with anger. He sighed heavily and reached for the handle of Patrick's room, but it was locked. He twisted it harder, as if he was trying to break it.

"Shane, calm down," I told him. "Let's get a key."

"I don't have time for that." He took a step back and kicked the door. It flew open and slammed against the wall. The nurse standing by us looked on in disbelief. I hesitated, but Shane walked directly into Patrick's room. I had to follow him and make sure he didn't do anything to Patrick. Before I entered, I saw a doctor staring at me and making a phone call. Whatever Shane was planning, he'd better do it fast. I followed him into the room.

The noise must have startled Patrick: he was wide eyed and sitting up in his bed.

"Surprised to see me?" Shane asked.

Patrick took a breath and seemed to relax. "Why would I be surprised to see you?" He looked Shane up and down. "You look a little wet. Did you swim here?"

"Cut the crap! You almost had us killed."

"Now, how could I have done such a thing? I'm handcuffed to the bed and locked in this room, remember?"

"The officer outside this room was working for you. You had him do it for you. Where did he go?"

He shrugged his shoulders. "I don't know. Shouldn't you know where your officers are?"

Shane took a step closer to him. "If you don't start talking, I'm going to—"

"What?" Patrick interrupted him. "What *are* you going to do, Officer Cranston? Attack me? Helpless, innocent me? I'm handcuffed to a bed. I'm sure it wouldn't look good, assaulting an unarmed suspect, would it? So why don't you take your little ol' trainee and prance on outta here."

"Hey…" I said, not liking the mockery.

Patrick looked at me. "Oh, the trainee speaks. I suggest you talk to your superior and tell him he needs to walk away before he gets himself in trouble." He looked back at Shane and smiled.

I said, "Hey, we're not done here. Turn that ugly, bruised face this way."

He looked at me. "And he has a mouth on him. Interesting."

"Of course I have a mouth on me. How else would I breathe, eat, and speak?" I looked at Shane and shrugged my shoulders. "This guy, right? Doesn't know how mouths work." I turned to Patrick again. "Oh, sorry about the breathing comment. I didn't mean to offend you. Must be hard to breathe out of that broken nose of yours."

Patrick smirked. "I like you. What's your name?"

"Ollie."

"What's your last name, Ollie?" Patrick asked.

"Tabooger."

"Nice to meet you, Ollie Tabooger."

I smiled. I think I heard Shane chuckle. Patrick's face went from smiling like he was in control to serious. I didn't think he enjoyed being fooled.

"Aren't you funny," he said. "I wouldn't try that again."

Shane stepped in again. "What is so important that you tried to have us killed?"

Patrick looked at Shane. "I'm sorry, Officer Cranston, but I still don't know what you're talking about."

Footsteps came rushing from the hallway. Three officers approached the door and drew their guns on Shane and me. "Don't move!" they yelled.

Patrick smiled again. "I guess we'll have to continue this conversation at a later time."

As the officers approached Shane, he put his hands up. One officer took his right hand and shoved it behind his back, cuffed it and grabbed his left to do the same. Another officer placed his hand on my shoulder and pushed me up against the wall.

"Hey!" I shouted.

"Adam, just shut up and don't resist. We'll be fine," Shane said.

The officer handcuffed me and walked me out of the room. The third officer shut the door behind us and stood guard while the other two officers walked us to the elevator.

| 28 |

Shane and I sat in an interrogation room. We sat on one side of a table, facing a mirror. We were the good guys. Why were we in here? It made no sense. Patrick was a criminal, and for some reason, we were the ones in trouble and stuck in this room. I knew someone was on the other side of this mirror watching us, talking about us.

Shane had been almost silent throughout the entire trip here. The officers took us to the Decker City police department and left us in this interrogation room. I wondered if they treated everyone like this, just stuck them in here and forgot about them. We'd probably only been in here for less than five minutes, but it felt like hours.

The door finally opened, and an officer walked in. "Hello there. My name is William Conway. I'm the police chief in Decker City." He carried a folder underneath his arm.

Shane stood up. "I know who you are, sir. Nice to meet you." He stuck his hand out for a friendly handshake.

The chief dropped the folder on the table and accepted his hand. "Officer Cranston. I'm surprised to see you here. I read about you, and this is out of character for you. Based on your record, I wouldn't expect to be having a conversation like this with you." He gestured to a seat. "Please, sit down." Shane complied.

The chief opened the folder. "You broke a door at a hospital and threatened a suspect in our custody."

"Let me add," Shane said, "I never threatened him."

Conway stared at Shane.

"Sorry, sir," Shane added.

"Thank you. As I was saying, Patrick Malloy is a suspect in *our* custody. He's in a secure location and poses no threat. Why did you feel the need to damage city property and interrogate *my* suspect without authorization?"

"Sir, he tried to have us killed," Shane responded.

Conway nodded. "Yes, I heard about what happened. I'm glad you two survived that awful ordeal. But it still gives you no right to storm into his room and interrogate him. We have procedures for these kinds of things. He is in *our* custody, not Mapleton's. There is a chain of command for a reason. You simply cannot bypass that because of a vendetta or with the aim of retaliation."

"Sir, we have reason to believe he's behind all of the violence that has happened in Decker City. Well, him and someone else," Shane said.

"And do you have evidence of these claims?" Conway asked.

Shane slumped in his seat. "Damn it," he muttered under his breath. We had a flash drive with all the evidence in my vehicle."

Conway nodded. "Which is conveniently at the bottom of the river, correct?"

"Yes, sir."

Conway exhaled loudly. "Without proper evidence, I cannot allow your investigation into my suspect to continue. We are prosecuting Patrick tomorrow afternoon. He will be moved to the county jail."

"May I please assist with the transport of the suspect?" Shane asked eagerly.

"Request denied. After what happened earlier, I want to make sure you and him are nowhere near each other."

"But sir—"

"That's final, Officer Cranston. Is that understood?"

Shane pondered his next move in silence. I could sense the anger in him building. His jaw was clenched and his breathing became heavy.

"Officer Cranston?" Conway said.

"Yes, sir," Shane responded finally.

"I will be contacting your superior about your actions today. I will be requesting that you face some form of disciplinary action. And as for your friend here," Conway said, pointing at me, "I *strongly* encourage you to keep citizens out of your investigations. You are both dismissed."

Shane stood up and gave a simple nod to the police chief. I stood too, and made the same gesture, feeling awkward about it. I didn't know this guy. Why was I nodding to him?

Shane opened the door and walked out and I followed him.

"Now what?" I asked Shane as we walked out of the police station.

He took out his phone and dialed. "We're getting a ride back to Mapleton."

* * *

"Heard you guys had a fun afternoon," Jenkinson said.

We climbed into the back seat of Jenkinson's and O'Brian's police car. I felt like a criminal back here, although it was something I was kind of used to, considering the many rides I'd had with Shane or these guys to the police station. But lately I had been getting used to riding up front. I didn't like being back here anymore.

"You guys okay?" O'Brian asked.

"Yeah, we're fine," Shane responded.

"I heard you attacked a suspect in police custody?" Jenkinson asked.

"I heard you can't manage to show up to work," I replied to Jenkinson.

"Why are you even here?" he said.

"I'm doing your job for you."

"You're lucky there's a partition between us, otherwise I'd climb back there and kick your ass," Jenkinson said from the front passenger seat.

"Would you two stop!" Shane exclaimed.

"He started it," I said.

Shane glared at me. He was serious. I respected him, so I would at least listen to him, especially after everything we'd been through today. He'd gotten us through a lot. I needed him on my side. I couldn't piss him off now.

"Take us back to the station, O'Brian," Shane said.

"Got it, boss," O'Brian replied.

We drove in silence the rest of the way back to the Mapleton police department.

* * *

When we arrived at the station, the sun was just beginning to set. O'Brian parked the car, and we all exited the vehicle, still silent. Shane led the way inside the police station, and I followed him, with Jenkinson and O'Brian bringing up the rear. Inside, Shane stormed past everyone and walked directly into his office. I followed him inside and sat in the chair across from his desk. Shane paced back and forth behind it. Jenkinson and O'Brian stood by the doorway inside the room.

"Anything you need us to do, sir?" O'Brian asked.

Shane shook his head. "Just get me your reports, and have them to me before you leave."

"Got it," O'Brian replied. He nodded to Jenkinson, and they both walked out of Shane's office.

"Shut the door," Shane told me.

I jumped up and closed the door, then sat back down quickly, anticipating Shane's plan.

"Can you get another copy of that flash drive?"

"Probably. I just need to contact Kate."

"Good. Get that to me ASAP. I need to show that evidence to Conway so we can interrogate Patrick and prosecute him for the right crimes." He looked at his computer screen. "We only have maybe thirteen hours."

"I'll try to get it. And what are you going to do?" I asked.

Shane sat in his seat and reclined backwards. "I have a lot of paperwork to do tonight. I have a car chase to write about. I have at least two deaths to report. I think I'm going to be here for a while."

"I'm sorry, Shane. Is there anything I can do to help?"

"Just got me a copy of that evidence from Kate."

"Okay. I'll get it. And just so you know, thank you for today."

Shane shrugged. "Thank you for what? We were almost killed."

"It was exciting. Thrilling. Dangerous, but eventful. So thank you for giving me something entertaining to do with my life." Today had literally been one of the most eventful days ever. A few days ago, the most exciting thing had been my daily fight nights at The Stout House. Lately, this crime fighting lifestyle had been way more exciting and entertaining.

"I'm not sure if that truly requires a 'you're welcome' but... I guess, you're welcome?" Shane said.

I left his office and walked out of the police station. I felt alive. I wondered if this is how the Gray Hood felt after his crime fighting sprees.

I needed to find Kate and get another copy of that flash drive. I pulled out my phone and made the call.

| **29** |

I called Kate repeatedly. There was no answer. What the hell was she doing? This was going to take longer than I expected.

I walked all the way to The Stout House to hang out with Chuck. There was nothing more I could do. I didn't know where Kate was, and I had no idea how to get a hold of her. My only job was to get another copy of the flash drive, and I was already struggling. My confidence felt a little weakened. I was on limited time.

When I walked into the bar, Chuck greeted me.

"Hey, Adam."

I sat with my elbows on the bar and rested my cheek against my hand. "Oh man, what a day I've had."

He smiled. "You sound like every other drunk that comes in and sits in that seat."

"Yeah, well, I bet my day tops all of theirs."

"Oh yeah?" Chuck said. He turned, poured a beer and handed it to me. "Let's hear all about it."

"Well, someone put a hit on me."

"You mean like someone tried to kill you?" Chuck asked.

I nodded. I took a sip of my beer. "That was me in all that action that occurred in Decker City today."

"Hold on, you mean the shootout and the car chase?" Chuck said, stunned.

"Yup. I had a car fall on top of me."

"What!"

"Well, I mean that was after they pushed our car into the river."

Chuck put his hands up. "Okay, slow down. I don't know too much about what happened today. I just saw a headline pop up on my phone earlier. I didn't have time to read the story. Tell me what happened."

I sat and told Chuck what happened during the meeting with Patrick and how he'd sent people to kill us. I filled him in on the car chase, about how I fired a gun at the bad guys and how Shane had shot two guys, which led to our car being pushed into the river, and their car falling on me.

He just shook his head. "I don't get it, man. You're living the life of an action hero. What you've been going through lately is just incredible."

I shrugged my shoulders. "I'm just doing what anyone would do."

"Oh, stop being so modest. You know damn well that not every-one would jump at the situation you found yourself in."

He made a good point. I was only half joking, but Chuck made me think about it for a moment. Given my ability, I knew I'd be okay if I got hurt. At least, I hoped that was the case. Anyway, it gave me more confidence in my actions; being able to jump into dangerous situations without considering the consequences was a bonus. I could heal from my wounds. What could go wrong?

I took another gulp of my beer and pulled out my phone.

"Expecting a phone call?" Chuck asked.

I nodded. "Kind of. I'm waiting for Kate to get back to me. I called her like twenty times. She isn't returning my calls."

"You gotta stop harassing that girl. If she doesn't like you, move on. You'll find someone else."

I looked up at him. "What? No. She gave me that flash drive with all that information she stole from Scarface."

"Who?" Chuck asked.

"The guy she stole all that information from."

Chuck had a confused look on his face.

"The man with the scar? The guy she spoke about the other day?" I told him.

"Oh, yeah!" he said.

"Oh, so you remember him when I say 'man with the scar' but 'Scarface' is foreign to you?"

"I didn't know who you were talking about?"

"It's his nickname! His evil villain name!"

"Let me guess, you came up with it?" Chuck asked.

"Yeah! Come on… it's good, right?" I responded.

"Does it really matter?" Chuck said.

No one was accepting this name. Shane and Kate had ignored me. Chuck didn't care. What was wrong with coming up with a shorter name for a villain that *actually* made sense?

"You all suck." I picked up my glass and took another gulp of beer. I finished the drink and slammed it back down on the table. "*Anyway*, I'm waiting for Kate to return my call because the flash drive she gave me is damaged. It was in Shane's car, which ended up at the bottom of the river."

"Oh, that sucks. And she has a copy, I hope?" he asked.

I nodded. "I'm trying to get a copy over to Shane so he can give it to the police chief in Decker City before they transport Patrick over to jail."

"But if he's going to jail, why does it matter if you get that flash drive to the police chief before he's moved?" Chuck asked.

"Shane said he needs to question Patrick. There's evidence on that drive that implicates him in everything that happened in Decker City over the last few months. Pretty sure he needs to go to a maximum-security prison rather than just a county jail. This evidence will allow Shane to continue his investigation and prove Patrick was more than just some assistant."

Chuck agreed, but was distracted by a customer who needed a refill. I pulled out my phone again and called Kate. It rang. And rang. I got her voicemail again. I hung up and tried texting her, telling her to call me ASAP. I kept the phone in my hand, waiting for something—anything—from her. Even a simple text would have done. I was getting anxious.

Chuck walked over. "Still nothing?"

"Nothing." I stood up. "Look, I'll let you get back to work."

Chuck put his hands up. "Don't be silly. You aren't interrupting anything. Hey, look, why don't you just help me for the rest of the night? Make a couple bucks. I know it's your night off, but what else are you going to do?"

I thought about it for a moment. I couldn't do anything relating to the investigation without getting in touch with Kate first.

"Alright, I'll hang around and help. But if Kate calls or texts me, I'm outta here!"

"Deal."

* * *

I finished work at 2:45 am, and I still hadn't heard from Kate. I tried calling her one more time. There was no answer. I decided to just go home and get a few hours of sleep. There was nothing else left to do.

I was really starting to worry at this point. I only had a few hours left to get in touch with her, get the information from the flash drive, and deliver it to Shane, *then* make our way to Decker City in time.

I hoped nothing had happened to Kate. It wasn't like her to not respond. Did the other hitman get her? Were there people chasing her and shooting at her like they had Shane and me? As I walked home, I scanned news headlines on my phone but saw nothing other than the car chase and shootout I experienced earlier today.

I got home, took a quick shower, and got into bed.

* * *

Sunlight shone through the window of my small bedroom. I cracked open my eyes, trying to adjust to the light. I reached for my phone from the charger on the nightstand, but it wasn't there. I reached all over the nightstand with my hand but felt nothing. I opened my eyes and sat up quickly. My phone was missing. My heart skipped a beat as nervousness flooded my body. Was this what people meant when they said they had butterflies in their stomach?

Where had I put my phone? Had Kate called, and I'd missed it because I'd misplaced my phone?

I turned and saw it lying on the bed next to me. I must have fallen asleep with it in my hand, waiting for Kate to call or text me back.

I tapped the screen, but there were no notifications, no missed calls or texts.

My eyes widened, and I immediately woke up fully. "Crap!" I muttered out loud. It was after nine o'clock. I rubbed my eyes and swung my legs out of bed, stood up, and started searching for clothes to wear.

I got dressed quickly and headed out of my apartment. I dreaded confronting Shane and telling him I had nothing. I tried calling Kate again. It rang and rang. Then, just like the last thirty times, it went to voicemail. Why wasn't she returning my calls?

I started walking to the police station, but I took my time. Maybe Kate would call on my way there. The longer I took, the more time I had.

I didn't want to disappoint Shane. I didn't want to let him down. It wasn't all my fault. I couldn't get a hold of Kate. I didn't know where she was. It wasn't my fault that I couldn't get the information in time. I did everything I could. My phone records would clearly prove that.

I arrived at the police station. I stood at the bottom of the steps and stared at the front door. I felt like such a failure walking in there.

I pulled out my phone one last time. Still nothing from Kate. I sighed and slid it back into my pocket. It was time to get it over with.

I walked inside and was greeted by the receptionist. "May I help you?"

"I'm here to see Shane Cranston," I told her.

"Hold on one moment. Let me see if he's available," she replied. She picked up the phone and placed a phone call. I knew he was available, but she was just doing her job.

She hung up the phone and said, "He'll be right out."

Seconds later, Shane came rushing to the lobby. "Adam, great! Come to my office."

Of course he was excited. This was going to be difficult for me.

I followed him through the department and into his office. He shut the door behind me. Before I could even sit, he said, "Were you able to get it?"

I sighed. "No."

His excitement turned to frustration. In an angry tone, he said, "What do you mean, *no*?"

"I called her all night! I texted her! She didn't respond. What else was I supposed to do?"

"You had to get that information by any means necessary!" he exclaimed.

"Then you tell me how. She wasn't answering me. I don't know where she is. How was I supposed to get it?"

He rubbed his eyes and sighed. "I'm sorry, Adam. I'm tired. I've been here all night. I haven't slept. I'm just… tired. And angry. But you tried." He took a deep breath and relaxed visibly. "Thank you for trying."

At that moment, my phone rang. Both Shane and I looked at each other and in a hurry I struggled to reach into my pocket. I finally pulled the phone out and saw Kate's name on the screen.

I showed him the phone. "It's her!"

"Idiot! Answer it!" he yelled.

I swiped the screen to answer the call. "Kate?"

"No time to talk!" she said. "Listen carefully. Something big is happening—"

I tried to interrupt her. "Wait, wait. Hold on. I'm with Shane. Let me put you on speaker."

"There's going to be an attack in Decker City!" she exclaimed. "A helicopter just took off and they're going after Patrick."

Shane and I looked at each other, and he leaned towards the phone. "Who's going after Patrick?"

Kate either hadn't heard him, or she ignored him. "You have to stop them! We're too far away. They're planning to break him out of police custody. You have—"

She was cut off. The phone screen had turned black. I picked it up and started prodding at the screen. "Hello? Kate?" Nothing was working. I hit the power button and a battery icon popped up. "Damn it! The phone is dead!"

"What's her number? I'll call her back," Shane said.

"I don't know. I didn't memorize it," I told him.

"You were supposed to give me her contact information!" Shane looked around his office for a moment, then jumped out of his chair. "Forget it. We have to go to Decker City. Now!"

Shane and I raced to his vehicle. We sped out of the parking lot and onto the streets like a bat out of hell. He put his lights and sirens on and swerved in and out of traffic.

Shane called the Decker City police department. The ring sounding over the Bluetooth speaker echoed around the interior of the car.

After one ring, somebody answered, "DCPD, what's your emergency?"

"This is Officer Shane Cranston from the Mapleton police department. I need to speak with William Conway, immediately!"

"May I place you on hold briefly?" she asked.

"Ma'am, I know you're just doing your job, but this is an emergency. I need to speak with him right away," Shane said.

"I understand, sir. Please hold."

Shane shook his head. "I don't have a good feeling about this."

I didn't respond. I had the same feeling. The feeling you get in the pit of your stomach when you just *know* something is going to go wrong.

The woman came back on the line. "I'm sorry sir, but he's not available right now. May I leave a message for him?"

"Ma'am, I know for a fact he's available. He's in the process of getting ready to transport a suspect. I believe there's going to be an attack on his transport. Someone is planning an escape for the suspect. I suggest you do everything necessary to get him on this line, immediately."

There was a brief pause. For a moment I thought she'd hung up on Shane, until I heard her say, "Please hold."

Shane swerved to avoid hitting a car. "Bunch of idiots on the road. Don't they see the flashing lights and hear the sirens?"

"That's why I don't drive anymore. I can't stand stupid drivers," I said.

Shane glanced over at me. "Oh, yeah… *that's* why. It has nothing to do with the fact that you were car-jacked and don't have a car anymore? Huh?"

"Irrelevant," I said, waving away the notion.

"Conway here," a voice on the speaker echoed. "Cranston? What do you want?"

"Sir, I believe there's going to be an attempt to rescue Patrick Malloy from your custody," Shane told him.

"And where is this information coming from? Do you have proof of this?" Conway asked.

"No sir. But—"

"Then I don't need you interfering. He's already in the process of being transported, anyway. I also told you yesterday not to come to me without evidence. Is that clear?"

"But sir—"

"Goodbye, Cranston."

"Wait!" Shane yelled. There was no response. Conway had hung up.

"Damn it!" He slammed his hand against the steering wheel. Then he let out a loud sigh and floored the vehicle. We sped up quickly, racing down the street, continuing to weave in and out of traffic.

"What's the plan now?" I asked.

"Stop the transport somehow. I don't know. I haven't gotten that far ahead yet," Shane said.

A loud rumble came from overhead. Shane and I both looked through the windows and the windshield, trying to see where it was coming from. A low-flying helicopter came flying over us and raced towards the downtown section of the city. It was low enough that I could see four pairs of legs dangling out of the helicopter.

"That's not good," I said, pointing to it.

"No, definitely not good," Shane agreed. He crossed the bridge heading into Decker City and turned onto Broad Street. Now we had an unobstructed view of the helicopter. It was very far ahead of us, but we could at least see it.

Shane picked up his phone and redialed the DCPD again.

The same woman answered after the first ring. "DCPD, what's your emergency?"

"Don't hang up! I need to speak with Conway. *Now!*" Shane yelled.

"Sir, they advised me not to take your calls."

"It's an emergency!"

"I understand, but I have orders to hang up if you call again. I'm sorry, sir."

"There's a low-flying helicopter in Decker City's airspace! It's going to attack the transport holding a criminal in your custody. Do you want that on your conscience, knowing you could have done something?" Shane asked.

"I'm sorry, sir. I have orders I must follow. Goodbye."

The car speaker clicked as the line went dead.

"She hung up on me? Are you serious?"

"What's wrong with these people?" I asked.

"They're crazy. We have to—"

An explosion underneath the helicopter distracted him. A ball of fire floated up from the ground.

"That's not good," Shane said.

"Wow," was all I managed to say. The fireball was huge. I'd never seen anything like that before.

Shane swerved in and out of traffic like a maniac. He didn't seem to care anymore. Clearly, the goal was just to reach our destination.

The fireball turned to smoke, billowing out from below. As we got closer, I realized the helicopter was hovering in one place. Now we could see what had caused the explosion. A quick streak of smoke left the helicopter, heading downward. Another explosion followed. Fire filled the sky again, followed by black and gray smoke. This was getting bad. Really, *really* bad.

Debris covered the streets as we got closer. People were screaming and running in all directions to escape the destruction. Shane had almost hit someone as they darted across the street.

Suddenly, four black ropes dropped from the helicopter. Four men slid down and then moved out of sight once they touched the ground. Shane couldn't get there fast enough.

If only Conway had listened to Shane, this could have been avoided.

We were still a few blocks away. The black ropes still dangled as if someone down below was holding a giant balloon.

The mass of smoke grew larger. We turned down another street and then I could finally see the transport vehicle in the distance and the destruction that lay in its wake. The vehicle looked as if a small school bus had been transformed into a miniature, mobile jail cell, with barred windows. The four guys from the helicopter had completed destroyed the two police vehicles in front of the transport. Both of them were on fire. Two officers were taking cover behind a third vehicle and opening fire on the men firing back at them with automatic weapons. As we approached, the noise of crackling fire, coupled with the helicopter hovering above us, was extraordinary loud. How could anyone hear down here?

Shane slammed on his brakes. Immediately, bullets hit his car, riding up the hood and onto the windshield. He ducked instinctively and opened his door, using it for protection.

"Adam, stay behind the car and don't move. Understand?"

I nodded.

Shane took out his gun and moved forward to the vehicle in front of him. Did he really expect me to stay back and do nothing? I leaned up to look over my hiding spot and a bullet came whizzing past me. Okay, *that* was close. Maybe staying put was a good option.

No.

I couldn't just sit here and do nothing. I knew I could heal from bullets, but it wasn't like I enjoyed being shot in the first place. It hurt. I kind of wanted to avoid it as much as possible.

I leaned forward for a moment to get a feel for my surroundings. Shane was in front of me with two other officers opening fire at the four men with automatic weapons. They looked like military guys. They had on camo attire with black vests. They wore black helmets with some kind of goggles over their eyes.

Bullets were flying all over the place. One of the windows above the officers shattered, and glass sprinkled over them. The officers didn't stand a chance here.

In front of Shane and the two officers was one of the destroyed cars. In front of the men with automatic weapons was another burning car. In between the two destroyed and burning cars was the transport vehicle.

Another bullet whizzed past me, making me duck back behind the door. This was a war zone. I looked to my left and there was a shotgun positioned between the front seats. I didn't know how to use it, but I figured I could use it to help in some way. I reached inside the vehicle and tried to remove it, but it was stuck. What was it stuck on? How could I get it out of here?

More bullets flew by me with a few hitting the police car. I ducked in fear and lost my balance. I fell inside the vehicle, and on top of the gun, knocking it out of its protective holding. I crawled backwards out of the passenger side of the car, dragging the gun with me. I had seen people work this kind of gun in a couple of movies. I grabbed the slide underneath the barrel and cocked it back and forth. I felt so cool holding this weapon. Now it was time to fight back!

I peeked above the door and saw that the officers were back under cover. They weren't firing. Had they run out of bullets? That couldn't be a good thing. Bullets kept flying from the other side, then became less frequent and eventually stopped.

Without the gunfire, the ruble of the helicopter suddenly seemed louder than it was.

I heard yelling from the military men but I couldn't understand what they were saying. I saw them leave their position, one by one, in a very coordinated maneuver.

This was my time. I jumped up from behind the car and charged forward.

I ran past Shane and the other two officers. Shane tried to reach out for me but reacted too late. "Adam! No!" he yelled.

I didn't listen. I fired blindly towards these military guys. I knew I couldn't die from their gun shots. This would give Shane and the other officers time to regroup and do whatever they had to. They were better trained than my dumbass, running blindly into danger.

When I fired the shotgun, it had a kick to it that I wasn't expecting. I almost lost my balance.

I positioned the stock into my shoulder this time and fired again. I cocked the gun again and fired a third time. The first guy in the group went down. I had hit one!

My excitement didn't last long. I heard gunfire, then my leg gave out and I fell hard on the ground, dropping the weapon. I used my momentum to roll forward, coming to a stop between the police car and the transport van. I hadn't made it far. Pain made it difficult to stand back up again. My leg hadn't quite healed yet. I knelt on the ground and reached for the shotgun. I held the weapon in front of me. I aimed it, but there was no one there. Where had they gone?

"Adam, lookout!" I heard Shane scream.

I looked around to see Shane and the officers running away. A whizzing sound came from above me. I looked up and a streak of smoke came flying out of the helicopter. There was a man standing in on the side of the helicopter holding a rocket launcher. With the split second I had, I recognized him from Kate's photo. He wasn't just any man. It was Scarface!

The rocket zoomed past me and exploded into the police car behind me. The blast threw me into the transport vehicle, hitting it with my back and then slamming into the ground.

I couldn't breathe. I couldn't see. I couldn't move. What happened?

The darkness consumed me.

Crackling noises.

Someone screaming.

The helicopter rotor whirled loudly above me, sounding like machine-gun fire.

My breathing recovered. Slowly. Everything still hurt. But there was another feeling.

I was warm.

No.

Not warm.

Hot.

Finally, I could open my eyes. Pain overwhelmed my entire body. I groaned as I tried to move. I turned my head slightly and my shirt was on fire. I've never dealt with fire before. Fear took over, leading to multiple questions. Would I heal from fire? I'd recovered from cuts, bullet holes, and minor knife wounds, but the fire was burning large areas of my skin.

Intense heat consumed most of my upper body. I rolled onto my back and finally got motion back in my arms so that I was able to raise them and quickly remove my shirt. I looked down at the burn marks on my chest, watching as the pain faded and the markings slowly faded back to my natural light skin color. The charred blackness disappeared completely. I could heal from fire too.

My body felt somewhat better now. The pain was disappearing. The fear faded away. I felt more confident with every dangerous situation I found myself in.

I leaned forward and crawled towards the shotgun. I reached out for it with my right hand.

A foot came down on top of it.

"Ouch," I said. "Excuse me, but you're on my hand."

"Yes, I know."

I looked up and Patrick was staring down at me. "Hello, Adam."

"Oh, it's the ugly-faced, broken-nose guy," I told him. "Could you please remove your foot? I would like to grab my self-defense tool, if you don't mind."

Patrick chuckled. "You're funny."

"You know what's funny? The fact you step on someone's hand without so much as an apology. I mean, who does that? I was even polite and said please, and here you are, still on my hand. Completely disrespectful, if you ask me."

"I wasn't asking you," he said, and removed his foot.

I made a fist and then stretched my fingers out again. "About time. Thank—"

Pain flooded the left side of my face. Patrick's foot had swept across it, taking me off guard. I fell forward. I reached up to hold my cheek. I squinted and shook off the pain.

I sat up and leaned back against the tire of the transport van. Patrick bent down to pick up the shotgun.

"Well, that was unnecessary," I told him, still holding my face, opening and closing my jaw.

He cocked the shotgun, aimed it at me, and said, "I'm sorry. It's nothing personal."

He pulled the trigger.

Nothing happened.

He cocked the gun again and pulled the trigger.

Again, it only clicked.

He tossed the shotgun away. "You're a lucky guy, Adam."

"Not as lucky as I was last night with your mom. She and I had a great time."

"Ah, mom jokes. How juvenile."

"We have to go!" one military man said, tapping him on his shoulder.

Patrick nodded, then looked at me. "Until we meet again," he said, then turned and followed the men towards the ropes dangling from the helicopter. I watched as they strapped their harnesses onto the ropes. A ladder fell from the opening above and rolled out below. The helicopter came closer to the ground. The three men attached their injured fourth onto one of the ropes before clipping themselves in. Patrick began climbing the ladder as the helicopter climbed higher into the sky. He waved as they picked up speed, leaving behind a scene of absolute devastation.

I climbed to my feet slowly, shaking off the lingering pain. Surprisingly, I felt fine. This adventure was really testing my ability.

I heard Shane screaming my name. "Adam! Adam!" He burst through the smoke between the two police cars on fire with his arm covering his face.

"I'm over here!" I yelled back.

He ran over to me and asked, "Are you okay?"

I nodded. "I'm fine."

We stood there for a moment, watching the helicopter fly away in the distance.

Shane cocked his head to one side and said, "Where's your shirt?"

I pointed to the ground. "Probably in a pile of dust. It was on fire so I had to take it off."

He shook his head and smacked me on the arm. "What were you thinking, running into the firefight like that? You could have gotten yourself killed!"

If he only knew...

I rubbed my arm. "I'm alright. I can take care of myself," I told him.

"No! That was extremely dangerous and careless!" he shouted at me. He wasn't wrong. I didn't really know what I was doing. It was definitely dangerous and careless. But I didn't care. I hurt one of them and I had at least tried to stop the attack. I wouldn't have been able to live with myself if I'd just hidden behind the car like a coward.

"Fine. Whatever you say. But we can't argue about this now. Patrick is the enemy, not me. And he just got away."

"You're right." Shane let out a breath of relief. "Let me check on everyone else. Hopefully, someone will have a phone charger for you. We need to get in touch with Kate."

| 31 |

Officers flooded the scene. Paramedics were all over the place, and firetrucks lined both sides of the streets, spraying water over anything with a flame. I'd never expected to see this level of destruction. Three vehicles had been hit with rockets from a rocket launcher. Casing shells lined the streets. Bullet holes littered the surrounding vehicles.

I sat in a police car, charging my phone. I'd only plugged it in a moment ago, so it would be a few minutes before it would have enough power to boot up.

Shane was walking around talking with other officers. One officer gave me a DCPD T-shirt to wear.

Another police car showed up. This one had Mapleton logos on its side. Another one followed it. O'Brian and Jenkinson stepped out of the two separate cars. Shane walked over to them and they started talking.

A noise dinged in my hand. My phone was on. Finally!

I opened it up and was met with a ton of notifications, of missed calls, all from Kate. Texts messages began popping up, too. As I scrolled through them, I got the impression they were pretty angry messages. I went to return her call, but a commotion outside distracted me. Shane was yelling at someone.

I stepped outside of the car, looked through the crowd of people, and saw Shane was arguing with the police chief. Conway was giving it right back to him, too.

I started heading towards them.

"If you'd listened to me, those officers would be alive and Patrick would still be in your custody!" Shane told Conway.

"If you hadn't shown up and caused a scene, maybe our officers would have been able to handle the situation without your friend charging into the line of fire and going all Rambo on those guys!" Conway screamed back.

"If it wasn't for him, we'd probably all be dead! We were out of ammo. He distracted them. He helped us!"

Was Shane defending me?

"He caused another rocket to be launched in *my* city! More destruction. More taxpayer dollars to clean up this mess."

"You're unbelievable! Can't you just admit that you were wrong? We were right. We had information about this, and you ignored it. This is on your hands." Shane turned and walked away.

"Get back here, Cranston!" Conway shouted.

Shane ignored him and walked to the driver's side of one of the Mapleton police cars. I hurried over to him.

"Get in," he told me. I hopped in the car as Jenkinson and O'Brian approached the driver's side window. "You two, I need to know where that chopper went. Do whatever it takes to find it. Understand?"

"Yes, sir," they said in unison. They walked back to the remaining Mapleton vehicle.

Conway started walking towards us, but Shane put the car in drive and peeled off, swerving around him. I looked in the rearview mirror to see him mouthing something and throwing his hands up in the air.

"Jackass," Shane muttered. "I can't believe him. He let this happen, and he's not taking responsibility for it."

I didn't know what to say, so I just let Shane vent.

"Absolutely ridiculous. Lives were lost today because of his poor judgment. More lives could have been lost as well, if it weren't for you. Don't get me wrong, you were definitely reckless, but it saved our lives. Thank you."

Again, I was speechless. Still, I figured it wouldn't hurt to acknowledge the polite gesture.

"You're welcome," I said finally.

Shane reached over and punched me in the arm. "Ouch. What the hell was that for? Why does everyone keep hitting me?"

"For being a moron. You don't *ever* just go running into gunfire blindly like that. Are you crazy?"

"Yes, I most certainly am crazy," I told him.

"I'm serious, Adam. You could have gotten yourself killed. Do you have a death wish, or something? You're lucky to be alive right now."

I felt this would be an opportune time to tell him about how I kind of couldn't die, at least not as far I was aware. But I just didn't know how he'd react. I was enjoying being a part of this whole adventure and investigation. I didn't want to ruin it by coming out to him that I was some kind of super freak with super healing abilities. Although, maybe he'd actually be on board with it.

I pushed that thought out of my mind. He was so against the notion of superpowers and believed the Gray Hood was a fake. He had it out for him. There was no way he would be okay with me. It was best to keep this a secret from him, for now. Maybe one day I'd be able to tell him.

"I know. I'll be more careful next time." It was what he wanted to hear, regardless of whether or not it was honest.

I grabbed my phone and unplugged it from the charger.

"Is it charged?" Shane asked.

"Charged enough to make a phone call," I said. I found Kate's contact details and hit the dial button. This would not be a pleasant phone call.

On the third ring, she picked up. "What the hell is wrong with you?"

I'd expected that.

"My phone died. I'm sorry. This was the first moment I had to call you back," I told her.

"What happened? Were you able to stop Patrick in time?"

Another disappointing conversation awaited me. "Turn on the news. Maybe you'll see the aftermath."

"So you weren't able to stop him?" she asked.

"Well, see, I was at least able to chat with him. But then he kicked me in the face and got away."

Shane turned in his seat and looked at me. "He what?"

I could hear Kate sigh into the phone. "He got away?"

I nodded, even though she couldn't see me. "Yeah."

The phone line went silent. Shane wasn't speaking either. Kate finally said, "Crap. Alright. I'll call you back."

"Wait!" I yelled into the phone quickly.

"What?"

"I need another copy of the flash drive. We kind of left it at the bottom of the river."

"Wait, you what? You know what, never mind. I'll drop by your apartment later tonight."

"Okay, thanks."

She hung up, and I plugged my phone back in and stuffed it in the cup holder.

"What did she say?" Shane asked.

"She's getting me another copy. Said she'll drop it off at my place later tonight."

"Sounds like we have a lot of time, then." Shane said.

I wasn't sure what he was getting at, but I played along anyway. "Yeah, I guess so. Why do you say that?"

"Good. We have some errands to run."

"Where are we going?" I asked.

"I remember that on the flash drive there was something about DNA manipulation. They looked to be developing some kind of experiment to change people's DNA. We need to figure out what that's about, and if they can really do something like that," Shane said.

It jogged my memory. Dr. Kane had mentioned a geneticist when I'd spoken to him. He'd told me to find someone in Decker City.

Shane continued, "I did some research last night, or this morning. I don't know. It's all kind of running together at this point. But I found someone who may help us. Her name is Bethany Williams."

And he beat me to finding this geneticist in Decker City. Good thing Shane was always thinking ahead. He always had a plan.

"I assume that's where we're going now?" I asked.

"We're currently in Decker City, so that's exactly where we're going now," he said.

| 32 |

We pulled up to a tall building. It seemed kind of odd for a geneticist to be located inside what appeared to be a bunch of business offices. People in suits were walking in and out of the revolving doors.

"Here?" I asked.

Shane pulled out his phone and then looked at the giant numbers on the building, displaying the address. "That's what the GPS says." He looked back at his phone. "Suite 702. Guess we're going to the seventh floor."

He opened the door and stepped outside. I felt awkward walking around in my DCPD shirt, but it fit the cover story of me being a trainee.

We passed many business professionals dressed in their suits and headed for the revolving doors. Inside, a giant fountain was stationed right in the middle of the lobby. It was at least two stories tall, with a circular waterfall, and a giant globe revolving above the fountain. The open lobby stretched at least four or five stories high. This was a classy building.

We were watched by curious eyes as we walked through the lobby towards the elevators. Shane reached out to push the button. Four elevators stood in front of us.

I pointed to the one on the far right. "I pick this one." I went over and stood in front of it.

"What?" Shane asked.

"Oh, come on. You never did this as a kid? Waited for an elevator and picked which one would be the one to arrive first?"

"And this is why I tell you to leave the talking to me," he replied. "You're such a child." He didn't move from his spot.

The elevator dinged, and the doors in front of Shane opened. He turned towards me and said, "I win." He smiled and stepped forward into the elevator.

I hurried over and stepped inside.

When the doors opened on the seventh floor, we followed the wall plaque that read *Suites 700–721*, with an arrow pointing left. Of course, it was at the end of the hall. We walked up to the glass door where "Dr. Bethany Williams, Geneticist" was written in black lettering. Shane pulled the door open and walked inside.

Three long tables filled the giant, white room: one on the right-hand side, one in the middle, and one on the left. The one on the right was full of papers, folders, and books. The middle table had equipment all over it. I could only identify beakers and a couple of high-tech looking microscopes. Everything else looked completely foreign to me. The table on the left had liquids in various beakers and cups. Hoses attached everything together somehow. It looked like a mess.

A woman at the back corner of the far-left table had her back towards us. She wore a white lab coat with her black hair pulled back in a ponytail.

"Excuse me," Shane said. "Dr. Bethany Williams?"

"Oh my God!" The woman jumped and spun around, holding her chest. "You scared me."

Shane let out a small chuckle. "I'm sorry, ma'am. I didn't mean to startle you."

The woman took a deep breath and relaxed. "It's okay. Yes, I'm Dr. Williams. What can I help you with?"

"My name is Officer Cranston, and this is my trainee, Adam. We're here—"

"Oh no—is Michael okay?" she interrupted, placing her hands over her mouth as if expecting terrible news.

"Michael?" Shane repeated. He glanced at me for a moment, then returned his attention to the doctor. "Who's Michael?"

She removed her hands from her mouth. "He's my partner here. Michael Rason. He hasn't come to work in two days. Well, today is day three. I called the police yesterday when I didn't hear from him. I've been trying to call him, too, but his phone keeps going right to voicemail."

"Have you tried to stop by his home?" Shane asked.

"I did last night. I knocked over and over. I rang his doorbell multiple times. No answer."

"If you provide me with his address, we can check it out ourselves after we leave here," Shane said.

"That would be great! Thank you! I'm just really worried about him."

"I understand, and we'll do what we can to figure out what's going on. You said you called the police. What did they tell you?"

"That they'll look into it. I understand they're busy with the whole Mitchell Quinn investigation, but they seemed to have just ignored me."

Shane nodded. "I understand, ma'am. After we leave here, we'll go look into his residence for you."

"Thank you." The doctor's eyes had a hint of water building up in them and her lips had started to shake. She shook off the moment of sadness, then took a deep breath. "I'm sorry. I interrupted you earlier. What can I help you with?"

"It's okay. We're part of an investigation, and we've stumbled across something regarding DNA manipulation. What can you tell me about it?"

She laughed. "That's a very broad and open-ended question. What do you want to know? Anything specific?"

Shane looked at me again. Was he expecting an answer from me? I shrugged my shoulders. I knew nothing about this. I guess he didn't either. I decided to cover for him while he thought of something intelligent to say.

"Is there a way to genetically enhance your DNA? Change it? Fix it?" I'd surprised myself. It actually sounded like a good question.

"Well, yes, and no. You can't just change your DNA like *that*." She snapped her fingers to emphasize her point. "But we are coming up with ways to enhance plant-based DNA. For example, we can genetically engineer plant DNA to become resistant to specific insects or pesticides."

"What about humans?" Shane asked.

"Engineering human DNA is essentially frowned upon all over. We have the technology and the capabilities to study it, but its been kind of banned. Well, not exactly banned, but it's kind of an unwritten rule—you don't mess with human DNA."

"Are there any advantages to studying it and using it on humans?" he asked.

"Oh, of course! We could potentially figure out specific chains and genetic structures that could lead to certain diseases and remove them from our biology, essentially eliminating those specific diseases and cancers."

"Well, that sounds promising," I said.

"Exactly! But what about the cons?" the doctor said. "Imagine everyone walking around genetically engineered. No diseases. No cancers. Maybe people enhance specific things about themselves. Suddenly, everyone is perfect. We don't even know what the long-term effects would be. Hell, we don't even know what the short-term side effects would be. How would that affect childbirth? What kind of DNA would that reproduce? We just don't know and I think there's just a consensus that we don't want to find out. At least not right now."

"Sounds like a lot to digest," Shane said,

The doctor smiled. "Sorry. Forgive me for going off on a tangent."

"It's okay. Now, what if criminals could use this?" Shane asked.

"Use what? DNA engineering?"

Shane nodded.

"Well, we just don't know what that would mean. I mean, we certainly don't want criminals running around genetically engineered. We already have enough violence happening around here. We don't need anything worse. And we already have someone in a hood with… let's call them *advanced skills.*"

I glanced at Shane, who rolled his eyes.

The doctor continued, "I'm not sure how he can do what he does, but I would love to find out. I'm sure others are as well."

"So, yes or no question, doctor," Shane said. "Is it possible to genetically engineer or manipulate the DNA of a human?"

She shrugged her shoulders. "It's more complicated than that. There are a lot of variables that—"

Shane interrupted her. "Yes or no, doc."

She pondered this, looking at me and then back at Shane. "Well, yes, theoretically it's possible, but like I said, it's more complicated than just a yes or no answer."

"You just answered yes right now, so it can't be that compli-cated," Shane replied irritably.

"Shane," I butted in, trying to calm him down. He was usually polite to people during an interview, but I figured exhaustion must have been settling in.

He faced me and seemed to understand immediately. "I'm sorry ma'am. It's been a long day. I appreciate your time and your help."

A smile appeared on her face. "It's okay. I understand. I know you guys have a lot to deal with, especially after that shootout earlier," she said, mentioning the explosions and Patrick escaping.

"Yes, it's been hard on a lot of us," Shane said. "I'll let you get back to work. We're going to go check out Michael's place of residence for you."

"Oh, thank you so much! I really appreciate it." She rushed over to the crowded table full of papers. She moved some folders around and picked up a business card. She wrote an address on the back of the card and handed it to Shane. "Here's his address." She flipped the card to the front. "This is my contact information. Please let me know if you find out anything."

Shane took the card and placed it in his pocket. "I will. Thank you again for your time."

He turned and headed for the door. I followed.

"To the partner's house?" I asked.

"To the partner's house," Shane replied.

* * *

After a twenty-minute car ride, we arrived at Michael's house. It was a small, single-story house. It didn't look like the best of neighborhoods.

Shane typed his name into his dashboard monitor and the missing persons report popped up.

"It looks like she called yesterday and reported him missing." He continued skimming through the document, then made a huffing noise. "Unbelievable. They didn't even check his address. She was right. They kind of ignored it."

"That's messed up," I said.

We got out of the car and walked to the door. Shane walked up the two steps to the front door and pushed the doorbell. We waited for a few seconds. He reached out and pushed it again. We continued to wait. No answer. No noise.

I opened the screen door and started knocking. "Heelllooooooo?" I said.

Shane grabbed my hand. "Stop that."

"What? He's not answering," I told him.

He shook his head and reached for the doorknob, trying to turn it. It didn't budge. He stepped away from the front door and looked up at the house, then hopped down onto the grass, and began walking around the house, peeking into the windows.

"See anything?" I asked.

"No," he said. The blinds were all shut. We made our way to the back of the house and checked the back door. Shane reached out and found that this one was locked, too.

"What do we do now?" I asked.

Shane put a hand on my chest. "Step back."

I stepped backwards. "Why?"

Shane charged the door. It cracked on the hinges, but didn't break. He stepped back and charged again. A bigger crack appeared. Then he gave it a giant kick.

"What are you doing?" I said. The door looked like it was hanging on splinters.

"We're going inside," Shane responded.

"But isn't this breaking and entering?" I asked.

"Not if we found it like this." He turned and winked at me.

"We can just break things and claim we found it that way?"

"Well, no. You know how it is: do as I say, not as I do. Don't do what I'm doing."

"Too late!" I yelled and stormed towards the door. The moment I stepped on the back porch, the vibration must have knocked the last splinter loose, and the door came falling down. I plowed through an empty space where the door had been and fell flat on the door, which was lying on the floor. It knocked the wind out of me. I groaned as I turned over onto my back.

Shane walked through the doorway, laughing. "You're an idiot." He continued to laugh as he stepped over me and began his search of the house.

I regained my breath and pushed myself onto my feet. "Thanks for the help."

Shane didn't reply. He started looking around the kitchen.

"What are we looking for?"

"Anything out of the ordinary," he said. He glanced around the kitchen again, then walked into the hallway. I chased after him.

"What would you consider out of the ordinary?" I asked.

Shane tilted his head back in frustration. "Adam, anything that looks out of place. You'll know it when you see it." He had an angry tone about him now. I could tell he was tired.

He took out his gun and held it by his side. He flipped on the light switch and slowly made his way down the hallway and into the first room. He opened the door and found a bathroom. I peeked over his shoulder to see.

Empty.

Shane closed the door and moved to the next room on the right. He walked slowly, and quietly. I followed his lead.

He turned the handle and opened the door to a bedroom. It must have been the master bedroom. There was a large bed positioned in the middle of the room, its headboard against the wall. Shane walked into the room and checked under the bed and in the closets. I looked around the room, checking for anything out of the ordinary, like Shane had asked.

Again, empty.

Shane moved past me, walked back out into the hallway and opened the door opposite the master bedroom. It was an office with an L-shaped desk against the wall. A computer monitor dangled from the desk, held up only by its power cord. A small desk lamp had been left on. Papers were scattered around the room.

"Is this what we're looking for?" I asked.

Shane nodded. "Looks like something happened in here." He holstered his gun and started his search. "Look for anything that could lead to a conclusion about what happened here."

I looked around. "Like what?" I asked.

"Blood. Something he left behind as a clue. Anything that you think may not belong to this Michael guy."

I started looking. There was no blood. His bookshelf was still intact. Nothing else seemed to be missing. The office just looked like a mess.

I leaned over and started picking papers off the floor. Equations filled one sheet from top to bottom. I had no idea what I was looking at. After I'd collected the papers, I tapped them on the desk to make a nice, organized pile, and then placed it on the desk. I pulled up the dangling monitor and put it back in its rightful place. Then I sat down at the desk and pressed the power button on the computer tower underneath the desk. The computer came to life, out of sleep mode.

A video appeared on the screen, showing the vigilante. Everyone was into this guy, except Shane. It looked like the same video my old boss had showed me, the footage from the convenience store. I minimized the internet browser, but there were no other windows or tabs open. This was a lost cause. There was nothing here.

"Find anything?" I asked Shane.

He sighed. "No. Nothing. You?"

"Just a video of the Gray Hood on his computer," I told him.

A noise came from Shane's pocket. He grabbed his phone and answered the call. "Go ahead, O'Brian."

There was a pause while he listened. I continued looking around, but still found nothing. I picked up a pen and twirled it between my fingers.

"You found the helicopter? Where?"

This piqued my interest. I stared at Shane, watching his eyes grow wider.

"Great! I'll meet you there." He hung up and put the phone back in his pocket.

"Let's go!" Shane said, heading for the doorway. "We have a location!"

| 33 |

Shane sped down the highway towards Forest Hills, a good forty minutes away from where we were. He told me O'Brian was meeting us there. Being that far away, it seemed unlikely we'd find anyone there by the time we showed up. But it was, at least, worth a shot.

O'Brian had told Shane the helicopter was at an abandoned piece of farmland not far off the highway.

Shane turned off the highway and followed the road around a bend, at which point the surrounding area became rural. We were in farm country. Corn stalks littered the land on either side of the road. We kept driving until we reached a junction and had to turn right or left. Following his GPS, Shane turned left.

Once we hit the next bend, I saw the helicopter sitting in an empty field next to a barn. There was a car parked out front. Its lights flashed twice as we approached. Once we got closer, I realized it was another police car.

Shane pulled up next to it. O'Brian was standing beside the driver's side of his car. Shane got out and asked, "Where's Jenkinson?"

"He said he didn't feel well again. I dropped him off at his house," O'Brian said. Shane's face flushed red. He was pissed. "On a more positive note," O'Brian continued, noticing Shane's expression, "I got a tip immediately after I dropped him off and came out here to check it out. Called you on my way."

Why was Jenkinson constantly disappearing? I hoped Shane was keeping an eye on him like he said he would.

"Thanks for letting me know. Good work, O'Brian," Shane said. "Where'd the tip come from?"

"Someone called about a helicopter flying too low near their property. Called in to report it," O'Brian said.

They walked towards the helicopter while I stood a few steps back, staring at it. It was hard to believe this piece of machinery had been hovering above me just hours ago while Scarface fired a rocket towards me and assisted in Patrick's escape from custody.

Shane went to the passenger side and opened the door, then climbed inside, using his flashlight to peek around. O'Brian did the same on the pilot's side. He slid open the back door and held his flashlight, shining it from left to right. He climbed inside and started looking around. I watched lights flickering and swinging around through the windshield.

I walked over to the passenger side to talk to Shane. "Find anything?"

He was trying to pull things apart, looking for any evidence. "No," he said. He leaned back in the passenger seat. "You see anything, O'Brian?"

"Nothing," O'Brian said.

Shane shook his head. "I'm not seeing anything. I mean, they even cleaned up any trace of that guy Adam injured. There's no blood anywhere."

I peeked inside. "Can't you get fingerprints or something?" I asked.

"How would that help us? We already know who was in here and who we're looking for."

I agreed, but I didn't speak up about it. Shane was usually right. I opened the sliding door on the passenger side and jumped inside the helicopter. I sat there, swinging my feet over the edge while O'Brian and Shane continued to look around.

"There's nothing here," O'Brian concluded. "It's been cleaned out."

Shane sighed. "Yeah, I agree." He slumped in the seat and put his hands over his face. He sat like that for a moment, then slid his fingers through his hair and placed his hands back on his lap. "Alright, it's going to get dark soon. Do we have any idea where they went from here?"

I'm not sure who he was asking, but I assumed it wasn't me.

O'Brian spoke up. "I don't know."

Shane shook his head and said, "Then there's nothing left here to do. Let's pack it up."

I leaped out of the side of the helicopter and onto the grass. Shane and O'Brian climbed out and we made our way back to our vehicles.

"O'Brian, reach out to the neighbors. See if they saw any vehicles leaving this area. See if anyone has any information for us," Shane said.

"On it!" O'Brian said eagerly. "What are you going to do?"

"I'm going home to close my eyes for a few hours. I will literally collapse soon if I don't get some sleep. I've been awake for about..." he looked at his watch, "...thirty-five hours."

"Damn, okay. Go home. I got this. I'll call you if I get anything," O'Brian said.

"Thanks," Shane replied.

I followed him to his car.

"I need some sleep," he said. "I'll drop you off at home. Go meet with Kate and get me that information. Anything major happens in the meantime, I don't care what, call me. Got it?"

"Got it," I said.

***

Shane dropped me off at my apartment and drove away. As much as I wanted to figure something out tonight, I knew he needed to sleep. I didn't want to bother him.

I walked up to my apartment and sat on my sofa. I grabbed the remote and turned on the TV. The only story covered on the news was the attack in Decker City today. It was only now, watching the videos, that I realized the full extent of the destruction. Buildings had been damaged. Roads were barricaded. Tow trucks were towing away what was left of the charred and bullet filled vehicles.

A shot of the fire trucks putting out the car fires appeared on the screen. This was insane. I couldn't believe I'd been a part of that. I couldn't believe it had happened.

Then a thought occurred to me.

Where was the vigilante during all of this? If he was supposed to be the hero of Decker City, shouldn't he have turned up to assist? Where was he?

I sat and watched the news for the next hour, making myself dinner in the meantime. Kate finally arrived and I let her in. She walked in with a duffel bag.

"What's that for?" I asked.

She dumped the bag on the floor next to my kitchen chair. "Just some stuff."

I leaned over to peek inside the bag. She slapped my hands away. "My stuff. Back off."

"Overnight stuff?" I asked, winking.

She punched me.

I rubbed my shoulder. "Right in the joint. You sure pack a punch."

She smiled. "I'm tougher than you think." She reached into the front pocket of her bag and pulled out a flash drive. She zipped up her bag and handed the it to me. "Try not to lose this one too."

"Yeah, yeah." I told her, taking the flash drive and putting it in my pocket.

She looked around my apartment. "Can I use your bathroom?"

"I don't know? Can you?" I replied. It was one of the few things I remembered from a teacher I'd once had at school.

She rolled her eyes. "You're such an idiot. *May* I?"

I smiled. "You certainly may." I pointed down the hall. "That way. The door on the left."

She walked past me and slapped me on the head.

"Oww!" I said.

"Oh, you're such a baby. You heal from everything. You'll be fine."

"Yes, I heal. But that doesn't mean I don't feel pain."

"Deal with it!" she exclaimed as she walked down the hall towards the bathroom.

I glanced down at her bag. I really wanted to know what was in there. A small peek wouldn't hurt, right?

I bent down and pulled the zipper, opening the bag and stuck my hand inside. I pulled out white gloves with had black lines across them. I didn't know what these were. I stuffed them back inside and looked around some more. I pulled out a white jacket. It looked pretty cool. It had some kind of belt attached to it. I shoved it back in the bag, but in doing so, I pushed on something hard. I moved the jacket aside and grabbed the hard object, and pulled it out of the bag. It looked like some kind of helmet.

No. Maybe goggles? More like a headset.

There were no eye-holes to look out of. It looked like there was just a black visor that blocked your vision. There were three circles on the front, positioned like a triangle, too far apart to see out of. They looked miniature lenses on a camera. And why would there be three?

I walked into the light of my living room to get a better look at it. The top was covered in a black mesh that sat on your head. It looked like it covered your eyes and nose but left your mouth exposed. What was this thing? What did Kate need it for?

Suddenly, the bathroom door opened. I was too far away from the bag to have her see me put this thing back. I didn't want her to know I had been looking through her stuff, so I shoved it under a pillow on my sofa.

She walked out of the hallway and into my kitchen. She reached down and picked up her bag. She looked at it weirdly.

"Did you touch my stuff?" she asked.

I did my best poker face. "No."

She looked at me, then back at her duffel bag. She zippered up its top. Damn it, I'd forgot to zipper it up. She must know I was lying.

"I have to go," she said. "If you find out anything, let me know."

I nodded. "I will."

She turned to the door, then reached for the handle and opened it, but stood motionless. She turned and looked at me. "Be careful."

"I'm indestructible. What can go wrong?" I said.

She rolled her eyes again. "No, you have a death wish. Goodbye, Adam."

That's the second time someone told me that. Did I have a death wish?

Kate walked out of my apartment and closed the door. I jumped over the sofa and raced to the door and locked it. I looked back at the pillow which hid that weird-looking face mask. I pushed myself away from the door, lifted up the pillow, then picked up the headset. I turned it around in my hands, trying to examine it. It seemed oddly heavy.

I held it over my head and brought it down slowly, fitting it on my head. Darkness consumed my vision, but only for a moment. Something hissed, and the straps tightened around my head.

What was happening?

I reached to pull it off, but suddenly I could see. I didn't understand it. A second ago, I had a black face-plate over my eyes and now it looked like I had nothing in front of me. I could see everything. I reached out and placed my hands in front of my face. I felt the face mask still there.

This was weird.

"Hello. Cybermodel A.D. 101 booting up. Please wait," a female voice said.

It caught me off guard. I spun around in circles.

"Who's that?" I asked, but found no one.

Did this mask just talk to me? I reached up and started trying to pull it off my head. It was on there pretty tight. I couldn't lift it up. I felt around the sides for an off switch, or some way to get it off of me.

"Welcome. What is your name?" the voice said. It sounded like another human was speaking to me. It didn't sound mechanical or robotic.

I paused for a moment, not knowing what to do. A mysterious voice was talking to me. Was it a part of this headset? Why was it asking for my name?

"Umm… Adam." I stammered.

"Name accepted. Umm Adam."

"No! No! Wait. Just Adam. No umm."

"Welcome to the future, Umm Adam," the voice said.

Damn it.

"Change name!" I yelled.

"Would you like a tutorial of your new headset?" the female voice said.

"No! I want to change my name!"

"You wish to skip the tutorial? It is highly recommended you take the tutorial because once you skip it I cannot—"

I interrupted it. "Change. My. Name!" I demanded. And then I wished I hadn't.

"Understood. You wish to change your name. Tutorial has been canceled and deleted."

"Wait, what?"

"Welcome. What is your name?"

Crap. I'd screwed this up already. "Adam."

"Welcome to the future, Adam."

There we go. That sounded better. I guessed I'd have to figure this thing out myself. I couldn't believe I deleted the tutorial. I probably could have used that. I was sure I could figure this thing out. It couldn't be that hard.

I could hear the movement of those lenses outside the headset. They sounded like they were moving in and out, adjusting themselves. What was it doing? Was this thing dangerous? And what was Kate doing with this headset anyway?

"I wonder where Kate got this?" I mumbled out loud.

"Who's Kate?" the female voice said.

I spun around quickly, startled by the voice. "You can hear me? You listen to everything I say?" I asked it.

"Yes, I listen to everything. You can talk to me and I'll respond as best I can," the voice said.

"What are you?"

"I'm an advanced augmented reality headset. My name is Cyber-model A.D. 101. But you can change my name if that doesn't fit your need."

"Yeah, I'm definitely not calling you that. Umm... how about Brittany? No! Wait! Jen! No! Umm... Belle. Yeah, Belle. Wait! No. I got it. Your name shall be... *Dun Dun Dunnnn—*"

"My name has been changed to Dun Dun Dunnnn."

"No! I was emphasizing the change. Ugh, never mind. Change your name to Skye. I like the name Skye."

"Understood. My name has now been changed to Skye. You can now call me Skye," the voice said.

"Nice! Okay, Skye, what can you do?"

"I believe all the answers you are looking for can be found in the tutorial which you canceled and deleted."

"Oh good, Skye's a smart-ass," I said.

"Technically, I'm an advanced aug—"

"I was joking!" I interrupted.

"Joking. To make jokes. Talk humorously or flippantly. I do not believe those fit your definition of what you claim was *joking*."

I shook my head. Just someone... err, some*thing* else to give me crap now. "We're going to get along very well, aren't we, Skye?" I said.

"I look forward to a very exciting and entertaining future with you, Adam," Skye replied.

At least she was nice and respectful. A bit of a smart-ass too, but I could deal with that. I could get the hang of this, but I still wanted to know what else this thing could do.

"You have an incoming phone call from Kate Phillips. Would you like me to answer it?" Skye said.

"You connect to my phone? That's awesome," I said. "Wait, how did you do that already?" I shook my head, ignoring my own question. "Never mind. Yes, answer it." I spoke too soon. I was too excited to try something out on this headset that I completely forgot to think about why Kate would call me.

Then I realized why. I was wearing it. She knew I'd taken it and she was calling to get it back.

"Hello, Adam. Enjoying a new toy?" Kate asked.

"What new toy? What are you talking about?" I asked. I started fiddling around at the sides of the headset, trying to find a way to take it off.

"Don't play dumb with me. I know you went through my bag and took the headset. I'm coming back to get it!"

"I don't know what you're talking about," I said again. My fingers came across something on the strap behind my head. I pushed it and the straps instantly came loose. I grabbed both sides of the device and lifted it off my head.

"Connection with Kate has ended," Skye said.

I ran around the sofa and stuffed the headset behind the pillow again. It hadn't been long since she'd left. She was probably still close.

I decided not to be here when she got back. I opened the door and raced out of my apartment. Once I made it outside, I looked around. Kate was nowhere in sight.

I decided to head to Chuck's bar to hang out with him. At least if she turned up there, I wouldn't have the headset with me.

| 34 |

"I have had one hell of a day!" I said, walking into the bar.

Chuck looked over at me. "Sounds like every day of yours lately. Come on over and let's hear it."

I jumped onto one of the bar seats and told him all about Patrick Malloy escaping from police custody.

"Again with this? You were a part of that shootout with the helicopter?" he asked.

I nodded. "Yeah. It was pretty intense. What you won't hear about on TV was that I was shot in the leg. The third explosion blew me into the transport vehicle and probably broke my back. And that idiot Patrick tried to kill me by using my shotgun against me."

"Since when do you shoot guns? And since when do you have a shotgun?" Chuck asked.

"It was Shane's, I think. I found it in his vehicle. Anyway, when Patrick fired the gun, it was out of bullets."

"Shells," Chuck corrected me.

"Huh?" I asked.

"Shotgun ammo is called shells, not bullets."

I waved my hands. "Whatever. Shells. Bullets. Either way, the gun was empty, and he ran away."

"Flew away," Chuck corrected me again. "He got away in a helicopter."

"Okay—I already had one smart ass give me crap tonight. I don't need a second."

"What do you mean?" he asked.

"I took this piece of technology from Kate earlier. It's some kind of headset. I'm not really sure exactly what it is. But she was giving me crap earlier," I told Chuck.

He looked confused. "Kate was?"

"No, the headset. It talks to me."

Chuck nodded. "Okay, Adam. Whatever you say. I think you've been on this adventure with Shane for far too long. Maybe it's time we got you back to real life?"

"I'm serious, Chuck. Her name is Skye. Well, it's actually Cyber-something 101. I forget. But I changed her name."

"Uh-huh. And what does this *headset* do? Is it like Alexa or Google Glass?" Chuck asked.

"I don't really know. Kate called me—oh! It connects to my phone. I know that much!"

"Dude, you need a break. This police and vigilante stuff, your ability, all of this violence you've found yourself in today, and yesterday… it's all getting out of control."

"I'm serious, though. I'm not making it up. Look, I'll go get it and prove it to you" I told Chuck. I figured Kate would have already gone to my apartment and left by now, seeing as I wasn't there.

I spun around in my seat and hopped off. I was already in full motion when I accidentally stepped into someone. I moved backward quickly, apologetic—until I saw who was in front of me.

"Hello again, Adam," Patrick said.

"Oh, it's you. If I would have known it was you, I would have run you over and then tea-bagged you."

"Again with the juvenile jokes," he muttered. "I believe we have some unfinished business."

"With you?" I looked around but saw he was alone. "Look, I'm sorry, but I don't fight disabled people. Seems pretty—" My throat closed up after Patrick shot forward and made a chopping motion at my neck. I instinctively grabbed my neck but then he then kicked out my knee. I heard a crack. I was pretty sure he'd broken it.

I fell down on the floor, gasping for air and holding my knee. I heard people around the bar scream. I felt the vibrations of footsteps as some people went running for the door.

Patrick reached behind his back, pulled out a gun and aimed it at me.

"To be honest," he began, "doing this kind of thing bothers me. I like you. But you're in the way. Don't worry, I'll make it painless." He pulled back the hammer and aimed.

A gunshot went off.

Patrick ducked. A glass broke behind him. I looked up at the bar and saw that Chuck was holding a gun, aimed at Patrick.

"Drop the weapon and leave," he said. "The police are already on their way."

Patrick was completely calm. He kept the gun trained on me and spoke to Chuck. "I'm going to forgive your terrible aim and warn you not to do that again. This has nothing to do with you, so I suggest you leave before you become a part of this. And I don't think you want that."

"What makes you think I missed?" Chuck said.

A smile appeared on Patrick's face. Was he enjoying this? He didn't take his eyes off Chuck, though he still had his gun trained on me.

"Chuck, just leave," I told him. "Don't make things worse. I got this."

"Yeah, Chuck. He's *got this*," Patrick said, mocking me.

Chuck looked at me lying on the floor, not taking his aim off Patrick. "Adam, I—"

Patrick swung his gun up towards Chuck so fluidly, it was as if he had trained for a moment like this. Chuck didn't even notice until the bullet struck him in the chest.

"No!" I yelled.

Chuck fell back into the rack of glasses behind him and slumped to the floor as glass shattered all around him.

I kicked my leg out and knocked the gun from Patrick's hands. It fell a few feet from him. I jumped up and rammed into him with my shoulder. As we crashed into a table, he plunged his elbows into my back, forcing my grip to release. I rolled away and jumped to my feet. He climbed back to his feet as well, only a little slower.

"You shouldn't have done that," Patrick said.

"You shot my friend. I'll do whatever I want!" I yelled. I charged at him again.

He side-stepped me and threw me into one of the chairs that had been positioned by the table we had just destroyed. I knocked the chair over and broke it, then I grabbed one of the legs, jumped to my feet and swung behind me. Patrick leapt backwards. I swung a second time. He avoided the attack again. I swung a third time. This time, he caught the leg in midair. He yanked it towards him and lifted his knee into my stomach, pushing all the air out of my lungs.

It weakened me for a moment. Patrick pulled the chair leg up and it struck me in the chin. I instantly dropped to one knee, holding my chin. I looked up for a split second, only to see Patrick swinging the chair leg at my face. Pain overwhelmed me.

You know how cartoon characters see stars when they get hit in the head? Well, I definitely saw stars.

I fell to the ground and hoped my ability would speed up at this moment. Blood dripped into my eyes. I tried to shake off the pain and confusion, but the healing wasn't quick enough. Patrick walked over and picked me up by my shirt. He tossed me on a chair, which skidded backwards under my weight.

"*You people.* You think you're doing the right thing by fighting back. But you just don't get it. You can't win," he said. He walked over to pick up his gun, and then returned to me.

I could feel the healing finally taking effect. I could see straight. The stars had disappeared. The pain was diminishing.

"Well, that's certainly interesting," Patrick said, looking at me in confusion. He squinted as he leaned closer to my head. He backed up and took a bunch of napkins from a table, then wiped my head down.

Shit.

He had just watched me heal. He knew what I could do.

"That certainly explains a lot about you," he said. "No wonder you survived that explosion earlier, with no injury to show from it."

I heard the faint sound of sirens in the distance. Patrick's head perked up as he noticed them too. He leaned close to me again, pointing the gun at my head.

"How are you able to do that?" he whispered.

"Well, once upon a time, there was a baby named Adam. Fast forward twenty-six years when he told a guy holding a gun to his head to *go to hell.*"

The sirens became louder. Patrick turned his head to listen. He sighed and turned back towards me.

"Looks like you're saved again. We need to talk further about this healing thing of yours. But in the meantime, I don't want you following me once I leave." He pulled the gun down to point at my right knee and pulled the trigger. Twice.

"Oww! Dammit!" I yelled, clutching my knee.

"Well, at least I know you can feel pain," he said.

I fell off the chair in agony. Patrick stood up and placed the gun behind his back, then walked towards the exit.

"Bye, Adam," Patrick said, then he stepped outside.

The sirens were growing closer. I started crawling towards the bar. I needed to check on Chuck. I prayed he was okay.

I pulled myself up using a bar stool. The pain had started to disappear. It was only a matter of time now. Hopefully, I'd be okay before the police came.

I got to my feet, limping on my right leg. I leaned over the top of the bar to see Chuck lying on the ground, covered in broken glass.

"Chuck!"

No answer.

"Chuck! He's gone! Answer me!"

Still no answer.

Pain meant nothing anymore. I used my remaining strength to pull myself over the bar. Glass cracked under my shoes as I landed. I leaned down to brush the glass off of Chuck, then sighed with relief as I saw his chest moving up and down.

"Chuck, it's going to be alright. Help is on the way." I picked up one of the clean towels from the shelf behind me and pressed down on Chuck's wound. I sat in silence. Sadness washed over me as I listened to the sirens approach. How could I have let this happen to Chuck? He was my best friend. He didn't have an ability like I did. He needed to stay out of this. I had to keep him safe.

I felt my eyes tear up. I couldn't lose him. I had no one else. Patrick would pay for this!

The police cars came skidding to a stop outside the front door, then I heard car doors open and voices directly outside. Finally, the front door opened and four police officers came charging in, guns drawn.

"Over here!" I waved to them from down behind the bar.

The officers peeked over and immediately holstered their weapons. One by one, rushed around over the bar and started tending to Chuck's gunshot wound. Hopefully, he would be in good hands now.

| 35 |

21 years ago...

Adam was riding his bike on a warm summer day. His new adoptive parents, David and Andrea Parker, had just removed his training wheels and, so far, Adam was riding like a champ.

David had the video camera out and was recording his son's achievement. They were so proud of him. For weeks, they had been loosening the wheels, little by little, giving Adam more chances to balance himself without the training wheels being planted on the ground.

Andrea ran around the driveway with him at first, following closely behind. But once she saw Adam riding without her hands guiding him, she backed away and let him ride on his own. They cheered for Adam when he rode down the driveway on his own for the first time.

"Go Adam!" David shouted.

A smile appeared on Adam's face, but he was too busy concentrating to look up and acknowledge them. He rode the bike up and down the driveway, circling at each end and doing it again and again.

Andrea waved as Adam passed by. For the first time, Adam took his eyes off the driveway, and suddenly his balance started to waver. His hands vibrated upon the handlebars as he tried to balance himself. He lost control as his front tire spun to the right and made him flip over the handlebar. The bike tumbled forward as well, landing on top of him.

"Oh my God!" Andrea exclaimed.

She rushed over to him and tossed the bike off of her crying child. David instantly turned the camera off, placed it on the ground and ran over to assist.

As Andrea picked Adam up, she saw blood running down his arm. It wasn't until David ran over and pointed that she saw that Adam's fingers were bent backwards, obviously broken.

"Take him to the bathroom. I'll get the medical supplies," David ordered.

"What about his fingers?" Andrea said, freaking out.

"We'll take him to the hospital. Let's clean him up first and then we'll go," David told her.

They both ran into the house. Andrea went towards the downstairs bathroom, holding Adam, and David ran towards the stairs, as the medical supplies were upstairs in their master bathroom.

In the bathroom, Andrea turned on the light with her free hand, then reached down and turned on the cold water. She grabbed the hand towel and soaked it under the running water, then sat on the closed toilet seat, holding her crying son in her lap. At this point, he had calmed down. She was thankful for that.

"Shhhh," she whispered. "It'll be okay."

She rubbed his head with the cold towel. She moved the towel onto his arm to dab at the scratches carefully, making sure not to hurt Adam.

"Mommy, look," he said.

He was watching his fingers as they pulled back to their normal position, readjusting themselves.

Andrea looked on in shock. "Honey, what are you doing?" she asked, panicking. Her eyes widened in alarm.

"Nothing," Adam replied. Satisfied that he was all better, he said, "Can I go back out and play again?"

She looked at him, completely frozen in shock. A chill flowed through her. Adam's fingers had magically healed. They weren't broken anymore. He could bend them and was ready to go back out and play, as if nothing had happened.

She looked at his arm and saw that the scrapes were gone. They had disappeared, too.

How was Adam doing this?

Adam pushed himself off his mother's lap and walked out of the bathroom. Moments later, David came pounding through the hallway and saw Adam heading for the door to go back outside.

"Adam, buddy, please come back to the bathroom. We have to take care of you. You're hurt," he said.

"No, Daddy. I'm fine. I want to go back outside and play," Adam said.

"Andrea? Is he okay?" David asked.

No answer came.

Adam opened the door and walked outside. David threw his hands up in confusion. He swore he had just watched his son break his fingers, and receive scratches all along his arm, only moments ago.

He walked into the bathroom and saw Andrea sitting on the toilet seat. She was staring at the wall, breathing heavily. He got down on one knee next to her.

"Honey, what's wrong?" he asked.

She continued staring, not moving.

"Are you okay?" he asked again.

Finally, she spoke.

"Adam is the devil."

| 36 |

When we arrived at the hospital, I went with Chuck to his room. The doctors had to stitch him up and give him an IV with antibiotics and painkillers. Luckily, there was no surgery needed. The bullet had passed through, missing any major arteries or organs.

Chuck had remained tough throughout all of it. The doctors were going to do some tests to determine if he had a concussion. When he was shot, he'd fallen back and slammed his head on the bar, and then again on the ground. He had a pretty nice lump on his head. There was nothing broken, thankfully, but he was definitely going to be in some pain for a while.

I sat in a chair next to Chuck's bed. The TV was on. I wanted to say something, but nothing came to mind. Unusual for me.

I felt horrible. He was here because of me. He was shot because of me. He almost died because of me. It was all my fault. I almost lost my best friend.

"You don't have to stay here, you know?" Chuck said, finally breaking the silence.

"I know. But I want to," I told him.

"Thanks, Adam."

Another moment of silence passed until I finally found the courage to talk. "Look, Chuck. I'm sorry. This is all my fault. If I hadn't got so involved with Shane and using my ability, none of this would have happened."

He huffed and shook his head slightly. "Don't even try that crap with me. Pretty sure *I* was the one who encouraged you. You're out there doing the best you can. I know you didn't mean for any of this to happen."

I felt a little relieved knowing he didn't lay the blame on me. But it didn't change the fact he was sitting in a hospital bed, healing from a gunshot wound.

"*You* didn't pull the trigger. It wasn't *you* who shot me. Patrick did. He's why I'm lying in this hospital bed. Not you."

"I know," I agreed. "But I still feel bad."

"From what the doctors have told me, I'll be fine. Stop worrying. Don't you have a bad guy to catch, or something?"

"I do. I called Shane on our way over here. He told me to wake him up if anything important happened. I believe Patrick attacking me at the bar and shooting you would classify as *something impor-tant*," I said, making air quotes.

The door opened.

"Speak of the devil—" I said.

Shane nodded to me and looked at Chuck. "How are you feeling?"

"I'll be alright," Chuck said. "Not much damage, luckily. And I probably have a concussion."

"You're lucky that's all that happened," Shane replied.

"Well, I'm lucky to have someone like Adam around to pro-tect me."

Shane turned to me. He gave me a hard pat on the back. "Yeah. He's a good kid to have around."

"I mean, guys—come on." I waved my hand, fanning my face. "You're making me blush with all these compliments. I feel so loved."

Shane looked back at Chuck. "Does he do this often?"

Chuck nodded.

Shane smacked me in the back of the head.

"Ouch! You know, I'm getting hit by a lot of people lately. I don't like it."

"Maybe there's a reason for it," Shane replied.

The door opened again, and a doctor came in.

"Chuck Bassman?" she asked.

"That would be me," Chuck said, raising his arm slightly.

"My name is Dr. Alison Davis. I'll be taking you to get your MRI."

I leaned over and whispered to Chuck, "She's cute. You should ask her out."

"Pretty sure you're loud enough for the entire room to hear you," he whispered back.

Alison smiled, clearly having heard our conversation. Her blond hair was pulled back in a ponytail and she had bright green eyes, which must have been contacts. No one's eyes were *that* green.

Shane and I stepped out of the way as she adjusted Chuck's bed and IV bags, and got ready to move him.

"You guys don't have to wait for me, I'll be fine," Chuck said. "I'll probably just try to sleep after the MRI."

"We have some things to do anyway, so we'll leave you alone," Shane said.

"We do?" I asked, looking at Shane. I turned back to Chuck, "I guess we do." I shrugged my shoulders.

Alison swung Chuck's bed around and started pushing it through the doorway.

"He's single," I said.

Chuck stuck his middle finger up as he turned the corner, and then he was out of sight.

"Come on," Shane said. "We have some work to do. And I have some waking up to do."

I followed him out of the room. "Where are we going?"

"I'm taking you back to my place while I shower and get something to eat. You woke me up after three hours of sleep. I'm tired. And hungry."

"Shouldn't we go after Patrick?"

Shane paused in doorway. "Do you know where he is?"

I hesitated. "Umm, no."

"Then how do you expect us to go after him?"

"I guess that thought didn't occur to me."

Shane nodded and walked out. "That's what I thought. Now let's go."

* * *

Shane opened his front door and welcomed me inside his apartment.

"Nice place," I said. I sat down on his couch.

"Just make yourself at home. I'm going to take a shower and try to feel more awake," Shane said. He pointed to the right. "Kitchen is over there. If you're hungry or thirsty, just help yourself."

"Thanks."

He walked down the hallway, then closed what I presumed was his bedroom door. I turned on the TV and cycled through a few channels before I settled on some late-night cartoons.

Once the commercials came on, I rested my head back and closed my eyes for a moment. A quick tap came on my shoulder, making me jump.

"Wake up, sleepy head," Shane said.

"Wow, you showered quickly," I replied.

He cocked his head to one side. "I showered almost five hours ago. You've been asleep."

"Wait, what?" I got to my feet and pulled out my phone from my pocket. It was 6:39.

Something fell on the floor out of my pocket. I reached down and picked it up.

"Oh, Shane. Here's the flash drive you asked for."

He glared at me. "You mean to tell me you had a copy this whole time?"

"I forgot."

"How could you forget something *this* important?"

"For starters, my best friend was shot. I kind of had other things in my mind."

Shane took a breath. "You're right. Okay." He took the flash drive from my hand. I'm going to copy this onto my computer. I can't risk it getting lost or damaged. I made some coffee in the kitchen if you want some."

I thanked him and then he took off down the hallway again. In the kitchen, I made a cup of coffee. I took my mug and headed to the room through which Shane had gone.

I pushed open the door and found him sitting at an L-shaped desk littered with papers. A computer monitor sat in front of him. An icon indicated the transfer was in progress.

I moved towards the desk and peeked at the papers to his left. There was an article about the vigilante in Decker City. I placed it to my left and another article laid underneath, followed by yet another article, all about the vigilante. Was Shane keeping track of the him?

On a post-it note on the wall, were written three names.

Andrew Kane, Devin Shephard, and Lara Scarlett—the three people we'd spoken to about the vigilante.

"What's all this?" I asked.

"What?" Shane said, rotating around in his chair. His tone became more aggressive. "Hey, what are you doing in here? Get out!"

"I didn't know you were this obsessed with this guy," I said, holding up one of the articles.

Shane stood up and snatched the paper from my hand. He placed it back on the table and pointed to the door. "Out. Now."

I put my hands up in surrender. "Alright, I'm leaving."

I took a sip of my coffee, turned, and headed for the door. Shane's computer *dinged*. I turned to see Shane pull the flash drive from the computer's USB drive. He stuck it in his pocket and headed towards me, pointing to the door.

"Out."

I stepped out of his office. He followed and closed the door behind him. He slid past me and moved to the kitchen to filled up a travel mug with coffee.

"Come on, Adam."

"Where are we going?" I asked.

"To the station. Morning shift begins at eight. I want to get there early and start reviewing the information on this flash drive."

I nodded. "Sounds good." I stood by his office door and took a gulp from my mug.

"So… come on. Why are you just standing there?" Shane asked.

"I didn't know if you had some kind of ritual for saying goodbye to the shrine of the Decker City magic man in there."

"Remember how you mentioned getting hit a lot? Well, this is one of those times where I would really like to hit you."

"Hey, I'm not the one with pictures all over my office of another guy. Just sayin'…"

Shane closed his eyes and took a deep breath. When he opened his eyes, he said, "Are you coming or not?"

"Yeah, yeah. I'm coming."

| **37** |

"That's a nice collection you had back there," I said. Shane hadn't spoken about it at all, but I was curious. Was he tracking the vigilante? Had he figured out who it was?

Shane stared out the windshield, not saying a word.

"Ah, the silent treatment. Okay. Well, I gather you secretly admire the guy. Or maybe he's a she, which is why you had Lara's name on your note. She was the girl from the hospital, right? She was cute. Do you have a crush on her? Is *that* why you're following the vigilante? Do you think the vigilante is a girl? Is it Lara? I don't think it was the doctor. He seemed too old. I saw this video once, and he seemed to move like a younger guy. Oh, sorry. Or a younger *girl*. So I think that rules out the doctor. How do you think they got their ability?"

"Do you ever just stop?" he snapped.

"Unfortunately, no."

"Look, I'm trying to investigate the guy in the hood. I feel like I'm the only one who's taking it seriously."

"So you think it's a guy. I guess that rules out my previous statement about it being Lara."

"I honestly don't know, Adam. That's why I'm looking into it. We can't have someone running around taking the law into their own hands."

"Why not?" I asked.

"For the obvious reason—it's illegal. But also, let's say someone else gets the crazy idea they can pretend to do what this guy in the hood can do. There are many people who look up to this guy. They call him a hero. They could get themselves hurt or killed. Are you okay with a child thinking he or she could go stop a criminal by sticking their hand out and pretending to move them somehow?"

"Well, when you put it that way—no, not really."

"Exactly. We can't have people out here doing that. And I plan to put a stop to it."

He couldn't possibly think children would *actually* take to the streets and stop crime, pretending to be like the vigilante in Decker City. Could he?

We came to a red light, and the car stopped. Shane turned to face me.

"And that goes for you too," he said, pointing at me. "Don't think I've forgotten about our conversation and how we got here in the first place."

"Okay, *Dad*. I get it. You want me to stay out of trouble and be a good boy."

The car began moving again, and Shane faced ahead. "Shut up, Adam. I worry about you. I don't want you to get yourself into trouble."

"You mean all the trouble that you had to arrest me from?"

"Exactly. And currently, you're doing some good to make up for it. I just don't want you to continue with what we're doing when I'm not around."

I decided to remain quiet. A rarity, but I did it because I knew arguing with Shane wouldn't change his mind. It didn't change it earlier and it wouldn't change now. Maybe if he knew of my ability, that would that change his mind?

The sun was just beginning to rise. An orange and yellow glow filled the sky in front of us. It looked like it was going to be a nice day.

We arrived at the police station moments later. Shane opened the door to his office and we both walked inside. He sat at his desk and stuck the flash drive into his computer. A folder popped up, and he clicked on it.

"There has to be something on here that will give us some kind of clue as to where Patrick and that guy with the scar are hiding."

"Scarface," I reminded him.

He shook his head and started clicking through the icons on the screen. He clicked on the folder about the vigilante in Decker City.

"I don't think this will help us find Patrick," I said.

"You never know," Shane responded.

He started printing out documents, photos, articles on DNA manipulation, and other news articles. He stapled each set of papers as they came out from the printer, then stacked them neatly together on his desk.

He closed the folder related to the vigilante and opened one up labeled *Plan B*.

"What's that?" I asked.

"I'm opening this for the first time. If I knew, I'd tell you."

The first document in the folder was an Excel file. Shane opened it up, and a spreadsheet full of numbers filled the screen. I stared blankly at it. It just looked like random numbers in boxes. Shane closed it and moved on.

The next file was a PDF. It had a blue background and white lines scribbled all over it.

"Is that a blueprint?" I asked.

Shane nodded and continued scrolling through the document. "I can't tell what is is, though. There's no name on it." He continued scrolling through the document. "It looks like a building of some kind. But whether it's here in Mapleton, or Forest Hills, or Decker City, or anywhere else, I have no idea."

Shane continued scrolling, but after reaching the last page, he simply closed the document. He clicked on the next document, another PDF. This one I recognized immediately.

"That's a bomb," I said.

"Yes, it is," Shane responded.

There was a clock of some kind, attached to a device, held together by plastic and wires, which was planted on top of a small barrel. Underneath the diagram were instructions on how to put together this explosive device.

"This is crazy. Are they going to blow up something?" I asked.

Shane closed the file. "It looks like it."

"And what's *Plan B*?"

"You're asking me like I know the answer. Again, I'm seeing this for the first time."

Shane glanced at the clock on his wall.

"It's 7:57. I need to go do roll call. Stay here. I'll be back." He was about to walk out, when he turned and said, "And don't touch the computer."

I saluted him as he walked out, shutting the door behind him.

I waited until he was out of sight. Did he expect me to just sit here and twiddle my thumbs while I waited for him? How long would he be, anyway?

I wasn't going to wait for him. I walked around the desk and sat in Shane's chair. I looked at the screen, then backed out of the folder. A canvas of folders and documents stared back at me.

I clicked on the first one and a photo of Mitchell Quinn popped up. I remembered this from when Kate and I looked through the flash drive previously. I closed it and opened the next one. The photo of Nathan Hobbes filled the screen. He was the military guy Kate was working with. I needed to continue with this document. Why had Kate been so quick to close it? What didn't she want me to know about?

The first thing written underneath the photo was that his wife was deceased. Did Kate know what happened? Did she not want me to know? Why did it matter, anyway?

Underneath, were listed names of some kind. *Operation Killer. Operation New Moon.* Were these the names of assignments or conflicts he fought? What was all of this? Who was this guy?

There was no explanation of these names—they were just listed, one by one, fourteen in total. I scrolled down to a picture of a demolished building. Under that was a picture of what looked like Nathan lying on a hospital bed, badly wounded. His left arm was completely bandaged up. Under the photo were the words *Operation Fire & Storm.*

I scrolled to the next page. There was a picture of a metallic arm lying on a table. It looked like a human arm, only robotic. It was kind of cool-looking, actually.

A blurred movement outside Shane's office caught my attention. Shane was storming down the hallway. I stood up quickly and moved back to my seat. Had he seen me?

When Shane opened the door and his face was flushed with rage. His eyes were squinted, and his jaw was clenched. I could see the vein on his forehead pushing to the surface. I jumped ahead and just apologized.

"Shane, I'm sorry. I only used it for a minute," I told him.

His eyes met mine. "What? No. I knew you'd use the computer."

"You did?"

"Do you ever listen? Come on, I'm not that stupid. No. I'm pissed because Jenkinson is not here again. But this time, he didn't even call out. He just didn't show up."

"Did you try calling him?"

He smacked his forehead. "Call him! Why didn't *I* think of that?"

"Are you being sarcastic?" I asked.

He glared at me.

"Okay, sarcasm. Got it."

"O'Brian called him when we were in there, and I called him too." Shane sat at his desk and picked up his phone. He hit two numbers and waited.

"Stacy, hi. It's Shane. Can you please pull all forms with Jenkinson's name on it over the last ten days?" He paused, listening, then said, "Thank you."

He hung up the phone and stood up. "Adam, come on. We're leaving."

"Where are we going?" I asked.

"We're checking out Larry's apartment. It's not like him to not show up like this without even calling one of us. He's been flaky over the last few days. Something is going on."

Shane walked into a conference room and pointed to O'Brian.

"Get Liz and meet us at Jenkinson's place. Adam and I are heading there now. I want you guys right behind us."

O'Brian stood up. "Got it."

"Who's Liz?" I asked.

"She's our tech expert. Anything involving a computer, she's a pro. Also, she's a skilled lock picker. If I want to get into Larry's apartment, she's my key."

We walked through the front door and headed down the steps towards Shane's vehicle.

"Why couldn't you just kick the door down like we did before?"

"If there's something going on, I'd prefer to be stealthy about it."

Was Jenkinson really up to something suspicious? I still had a hard time thinking he could be the mole, but it made sense since he'd been dodging work a lot lately. He had been leaving early due to "sickness." I wondered if he was really sick, or was he hiding something?

We headed towards Jenkinson's apartment. We'd barely made it a mile before Shane's phone started ringing through the car's speakers. He answered it.

"Shane, it's Stacy."

"What do you have for me?" Shane asked.

"For starters, over the last week, Larry has left early every shift but one. The one was because he called out. He's always called in to request that he leave early. And over the last two years, since he started, he has only missed two days of work—which he called out for. One of them being a few days ago."

"Okay," Shane replied. "Anything else?"

"He checked out some evidence from case number 072495. A notebook and a photo."

Shane shook his head. "Anything else?"

"Honestly, I don't know what I'm looking for here. You asked me to pull this stuff, but it's all just random to me."

"Anything out of the ordinary. Anything that makes little sense to you. It doesn't have to be something big."

I heard papers rattling. We sped through traffic and approached a red light. Shane flipped on his flashing lights and we blew through it.

"He ordered a new uniform three weeks ago," Stacy said finally.

Shane looked at me, wide-eyed. "That's it," he said. "That's where that other uniform came from. The night Mitchell Quinn was killed in Decker City, was Jenkinson working?"

I heard papers rustling again. "That was the day he called out sick."

Shane nodded. "Stacy, thank you. Put everything you found on Jenkinson on my desk for me."

He hung up and continued speeding through traffic.

"So, what are you thinking?" I asked.

"I didn't think Jenkinson was capable of this. I watched him, knowing there was a mole in our office. I let my feelings get the best of me."

"You didn't know," I tried reassuring him.

"I did know," Shane said, smacking the steering wheel with his hand. "I don't think I wanted to admit someone on my team was betraying us. But, I'll tell you this—Jenkinson better not be home, because if he is, he's about to get his ass kicked."

| **38** |

Shane turned off the lights as he approached Jenkinson's apartment complex. He drove around the corner and pulled into a parking spot. The apartments looked like small, two-story town houses.

"Is this his place?" I asked.

Shane turned off the engine. "No. He's about five houses down. I didn't want to park right out front." He pulled out his phone and called Jenkinson again, then held the phone to his ear and waited. A few seconds passed before he tapped the phone and shoved it back in his pocket.

"Still not answering?"

"Nope." He stepped out of the car.

"So, what are you going to do?" I asked, following him outside.

"Liz and O'Brian should be here any minute. In the meantime, I'm going to go scope his place out," Shane said, moving along the sidewalk towards Jenkinson's apartment.

I followed him as he walked up to Jenkinson's front door. He looked through the window on his left, then returned to the door. He knocked three times.

"Jenkinson, it's me. Open up," Shane said,

Silence.

Shane waited, then knocked again.

"Open up, Larry," he repeated.

Nothing.

"Maybe he's not home," I suggested.

He turned and pointed to the vehicle to our left. "That's his car." Shane turned and knocked again, harder this time.

A car pulled up and parked next to Shane's car, and a female officer stepped out. It must have been Liz. Her brown hair was pulled back in a ponytail. She took off her aviator sunglasses and placed them on top of her head, then reached into the backseat for a small bag. She joined us at the front door.

Shane introduced us. "Officer McKenzie, this is Adam. Adam, Officer McKenzie."

We said hi to one another, then I asked Shane, "I thought you told me her name was Liz?"

"It is. But you will address her as Officer McKenzie," Shane told me.

"It's fine, Adam. You can call me whatever you want," the officer said.

"I can? *Anything?*"

"Adam," Shane said.

"Sorry," I replied.

Liz pulled out a small, thin tool from her bag, along with something that looked like a drill. She held it to the door knob.

"How long will this take?" Shane asked.

"Depends on how long you keep interrupting me. Maybe a minute."

"Oh, burn!" I said to Shane. He glared at me again. "You want to hit me again, don't you?"

He nodded.

We both watched as Liz worked her magic. Finally, the lock *clicked,* and she slowly turned the knob to crack open the door.

Shane unclipped his holster and pulled out his gun. Liz placed her lock-picking tools back in her bag, and pulled out her own gun. Shane pushed open the door slowly and peeked inside.

"Wait," I said, throwing them both off guard.

Shane turned around and said, "What?"

I looked back at the vehicle Liz drove here. "Where's O'Brian?"

Shane did a double take. He looked at Liz. "Yeah, where's O'Brian?"

She shrugged her shoulders. "What do you mean? He told me to meet you here. So I left. He said nothing about coming along."

Shane shook his head. "Whatever. I'll deal with it later. We're inside already. Let's go."

He stepped inside, looked around the entrance and then whispered, "Clear," before he moved forward. Liz followed him. I brought up the rear, unfortunately unarmed. Not that it would have mattered, anyway, but I would just be nice to feel a part of the team and have a weapon.

We entered the den and made our way into the kitchen. Shane pointed to the bathroom door. Liz crossed the room and opened it. She looked inside, then stepped out seconds later, making a thumbs-up signal. Shane nodded, and led the way towards the staircase, pointing his gun upwards.

When Shane reached the top of the stairs, he peeked to the right and left. Then he turned to Liz, then pointed left. She nodded, and they went their separate ways.

It was so impressive, how they moved so silently and understood each other. I'd never known Shane could do that. I so badly wanted to ask a question or just get some insight into what they were doing, but I stayed silent, hoping not to get in their way.

Shane approached a door on his right. He reached for the doorknob and opened it to reveal a closet full of bath towels and toilet paper. He moved to the next door.

Liz had reached the door at the other end of the hallway. She and Shane made eye contact, and Shane stuck up his hand to count to three.

One.

Two.

Three.

They opened their respective doors simultaneously and entered the rooms. I followed Shane, who swung from side to side, looking all around. The room we had entered looked like an office. A table was positioned under the window, with a computer monitor on it. A few books were piled next to it.

Shane walked to the closet doors and opened them. They were empty. He closed them and looked beneath the reclining chair stationed in the corner of the room. There was nothing there.

"Cranston!" Liz yelled. "I found him!"

Shane was out of the room immediately. I pursued him down the hall, but he was fast. He was already in the other room by the time I made it to the hallway.

The bathroom door was open and I could overhear the two of them talking.

"He has a pulse," Officer McKenzie said.

"Do you have keys for these?" Shane asked.

I walked into the bathroom to see a pool of blood by the toilet. Jenkinson was lying on his stomach, his head surrounded by blood. His arms were wrapped around the toilet, handcuffed together.

"Is he okay?" I asked, suddenly concerned for the lunatic. I didn't like the guy, but I didn't want to see him like this, lying in his own pool of his own blood.

Liz handed Shane a key, and he reached behind the toilet and uncuffed him. He pulled Jenkinson's arms to his side and rolled him onto his back. He reached a towel from the rack and started wiping away the blood.

"McKenzie, call the paramedics," Shane commanded.

Liz took her phone out of her pocket and walked out of the bathroom.

"Is he okay?" I repeated.

"I don't know." Shane said, gently wiping the blood off Jenkinson's face and head. "He's unconscious. I don't know what happened, or how long he's been like this. And right now, I'm trying to find the wound where the blood is coming from." He made a gasping noise. "Found it." He put the towel on the back of Jenkinson's head and applied pressure.

Shane looked up at me. "Adam, find me another towel. Also, look for hydrogen peroxide or any kind of antiseptic."

I nodded and started looking around the bathroom. I opened up the cabinet above the sink, but saw only basic necessities: deodorant, toothpaste, cologne, floss. I shut the cabinet and left the bathroom, passing Liz as she was finishing up on the phone.

"Five minutes out!" she shouted to Shane.

I continued along the hallway and opened the closet door. I picked up a clean towel and ran back into the bathroom, and handed it to Shane. He thanked me, placed the bloodied towel on the floor beside him, and wrapped the clean one around Jenkinson's head.

"I found nothing else you asked for. I'm sorry," I told Shane.

"It's fine. The paramedics are on their way," he said. "McKenzie, go check for any clues about what might have happened."

She nodded and walked out of the bathroom.

I looked at Jenkinson as Shane held his head in his arms.

I began to wonder who could be responsible for injuring Jenkinson. Did Patrick or Scarface come here and attack him? How involved was he and what did he do to find himself in this position?

Shane and I remained silent for about a minute before I finally spoke. "Who do you think did this?"

He shook his head. "We'll find out once he wakes up."

Liz made her way back to the bathroom doorway. "I found drips of blood in the bedroom opposite the bathroom, so whoever did this, they did it right here," she said, pointing directly outside the door. "The suspect must have dragged him here, handcuffed him, then left. There are no signs of a struggle."

Shane nodded.

The door downstairs opened. "Hello? Paramedics!"

"Up here!" Liz yelled. She hurried out to go meet them.

Shane patted Jenkinson on the shoulder. "Help is here. You're going to be okay. And then you're going to start talking."

* * *

The paramedics loaded Jenkinson onto a stretcher and into the ambulance. They shut the doors and drove away.

I stood with Shane, watching them drive away. Hopefully, Jenkinson would wake up soon so we could find out who did that to him. I had a feeling it was Patrick. It seemed like something he'd do. But why, though? What did Jenkinson do?

"Alright, let's head back to the station. There's not much more we can do here," Shane said. "McKenzie, I'll see you back there. Thanks for your help here."

"Not a problem," she replied. "Bye, Adam."

"See ya," I said.

She got into her vehicle and drove away.

Shane entered inside Jenkinson's home again.

"What are you doing? I thought we were leaving?" I asked.

"We will. I want to search his home first. If he's been working with Patrick and the man with the scar, I want to know what he's been up to."

We went back upstairs into Jenkinson's office and started searching around. Shane sat in the chair in front of the computer and turned it on. I looked through some loose papers but nothing seemed of relevance.

"His computer needs a password. Any ideas?" Shane asked me.

"How about 'Larry sucks.' All uppercase," I said.

I heard Shane type for a moment before he stopped. He swung the swivel chair to face me. "Seriously, Adam."

"Sorry," I said.

Shane swung back to face the computer and started typing. He shook his head after putting in his first attempt of a password. I heard him type again.

"Anything?" I asked.

"Hold on," he said. I heard him type again. "Damn."

"Still nothing?"

"No."

"Try password." Shane turned to look at me. "What? It's a commonly used password."

He went back to typing.

"Didn't work," he said.

"Okay, this goes against all my better judgments, but try qwerty123."

Shane typed it into the password box and hit 'enter.' The computer booted up.

He turned again in his chair to face me. "How did you know that?"

"I didn't. It's… umm… my password too."

Shane smirked. "Good to know."

"I can't believe he'd use the same password as me. What an idiot."

"An idiot for having the same password as you or for being dumb enough to use one of the most commonly used passwords?"

I thought about it for a moment. "Let's go with the first one."

He rolled his eyes, spun back around and opened up an internet browser.

"What are you looking for?" I asked.

"I'm going through his browser history. Maybe there's something here," Shane said.

He scrolled through the history but shortly became dissatisfied. He huffed, and closed the browser.

"What about his email?" I asked.

Shane moved the mouse and clicked on the email icon at the bottom of the screen. A screen popped up, displaying all of Jenkinson's emails. I noticed a bunch from O'Brian, a few from Shane and some officers from the police department, but nothing that would raise any red flags.

Shane closed his email and started opening random files and folders on his computer, clearly determined to find something.

"I'm going to check his bedroom," I told Shane.

I left the office and made my way into Jenkinson's bedroom. I went to his night stand and opened the top drawer. A book laid alone in the drawer. I took it and opened it. A bookmark dropped to the floor. I picked it up and placed them both back in the drawer, pretending I didn't just lose his place in his book.

I moved onto the bottom drawer and found a container of change. I pushed it aside but found nothing else.

I wandered around Jenkinson's room for a few minutes but didn't seem to find anything.

I heard Shane's phone ring from down the hall.

"Hello?" he said.

I left the bedroom and made my way back to Shane.

"He's awake?" I heard Shane say. "Yes, I want to talk to him. Put him on the phone."

I moved closer to the door to eavesdrop on the call.

"Jenkinson, I'm having the paramedics take you to the hospital to treat your wound but I'm placing you under arrest."

A pause.

"Uh-huh… *Sure it was.*"

Another pause.

"Wait, what?"

What was Jenkinson saying? The one time Shane didn't have his phone on speaker was the one call I wanted to listen in on.

"Are you positive?"

What was happening? What was he saying?

"Alright. You better not be lying to me."

He hung up the phone and turned to see me peeking outside the office door.

"Adam. We need to leave."

"What did he tell you?"

He shook his head. His jaw was clenched. His hands were balled into fists. At first, I thought he was going to attack me. But I knew I'd done nothing wrong. All the same, I definitely didn't want to be in the way of whoever was the problem.

"He told me it was O'Brian."

| 39 |

Shane floored it out of the parking lot, then swung his vehicle around the bend at such high speed that I expected the car to flip. He flew onto the main road without acknowledging the traffic. Horns blared from all directions as he sped off towards the police station.

He pulled his phone from his pocket and tossed it to me. "Call McKenzie. I need to let her know what's going on."

I opened his list of contacts and tapped on Liz McKenzie's name. The phone started ringing through the speakers in the car.

"Officer McKenzie speaking."

"It's Shane. Listen—Jenkinson said it was O'Brian."

"What?" she asked.

"I just got off the phone with Jenkinson. He's awake. He told me O'Brian attacked him. How far away are you from the station?"

"I'm actually pulling up—wait. O'Brian is walking out of the station now. Hold on."

"Liz, I need you to keep him there until I get back."

"Hey, O'Brian. Do you have a minute?" I heard Liz say.

The response sounded a little distant. I heard O'Brian say he had to go.

Suddenly, there were more voices in the distant. It sounded like people were yelling.

Gunfire erupted on the other end of the phone. Five gunshots, maybe six. They came so fast.

"Liz!" Shane shouted. "Liz!"

I heard rustling on the other end of the line before she finally spoke again. "He shot me."

"Shit." Shane's face scrunched and he shook his head. "How bad?"

"I'll be fine. He got me in the leg. I can't walk. He ran off. I can't see where he went."

"Okay, just hold on. We're a few minutes away. Where are the other officers?"

"Someone just came over. Hold on—"

She started calling out to someone. Multiple voices came from the speakers.

"Liz, what's going on?" Shane asked.

"Seth and Damian are here," she replied.

"Hi, Shane," they said in unison.

"O'Brian shot Campbell inside the station," a voice said. "They're attending to him now. Doesn't look good though."

"Dammit. Alright, thanks, Seth. What else happened?"

A different voice spoke up. This must have been Damian. "We don't know. We heard a single gunshot. That's when we found Campbell on the floor, bleeding out from a chest wound. He was unresponsive. I went looking for who shot him and that's when we heard the gunshots outside. We came out and found McKenzie here."

Shane swerved out of the way of another vehicle, making me drop the phone. I reached down to pick it up.

"Anyone see where O'Brian went?" Shane asked.

The response was negative.

"Guys—bring McKenzie to the hospital," Shane said. "Get her some help. Let the paramedics handle Campbell. I'll be there shortly to sort this out."

They said their goodbyes and hung up.

I wanted to help somehow, but I knew if I spoke up he'd just release his anger out on me. I had a way of annoying him at these sorts of times; better to just keep my mouth shut.

Minutes later, Shane pulled up to the police station. Liz's vehicle was gone. They must have taken her car to the hospital.

Shane parked and we got out of the car.

"What's the plan now?" I asked.

He jogged up the stairs to the station's entrance. "The plan is to figure out where O'Brian went. And then deal with him."

"Deal with him how?" I asked.

"Deal with him by arresting his ass. Do you think I'm going to kill him?"

I shrugged. "I don't know. I was just asking. You seem pretty pissed."

He opened the doors and walked inside, where we were greeted by a confused and broken police station. A woman had her face in her hands, crying. Another officer had his arm wrapped around her, consoling her. One officer paced around the receptionist's desk. I couldn't even imagine what must be going through everyone's head right now. One of their own had just betrayed them. O'Brian had shot two people and assaulted his partner.

I watched as paramedics wheeled out a covered body on a stretcher. He had *killed* someone.

Shane pointed to the white sheet. "Campbell?" he asked the paramedic.

He nodded.

This was an absolute kick in the gut. There was a grudge to be settled. If attacking Jenkinson hadn't pissed off Shane and the rest of the officers enough, murdering one of their own definitely put O'Brian in their crosshairs.

The station was quiet until Shane spoke.

"Guys," he began. "I know we just lost Officer Campbell moments ago. McKenzie was injured outside as well. She's on her way to the hospital. She'll be fine. Jenkinson will be fine as well. Now is not the time to stop working. We need to find O'Brian and bring him to justice for his crimes. Let's get to work!"

People started moving with a purpose. Voices became audible. Shane's pep talk seemed to have worked. The station became operational again.

"Follow me," Shane said.

We walked into a room with multiple screens on one wall. Views from all around the station flickered on each screen. Shane sat in a chair in front of the monitors.

"Security cameras," I said, looking at all the screens.

"Yes. I want to see what happened. What was O'Brian doing? Why did he shoot Campbell? Where did he go?"

I pulled out another chair and sat next to him. The top-left screen displayed a menu. Shane clicked on the *Playback* icon, which brought up a different menu which displayed a time and boxes with numbers in them.

"What's that?" I asked.

"These numbers represent the cameras. They start at the front of the building and move towards the back. The lower numbers are in front. We're looking for something towards the back, where Campbell was. We have thirteen cameras, so let's start with number ten."

He pulled up a view of a jail cell.

"Nope. Not that one."

He tried number eleven, which brought up a view of the entrance to the evidence shelves, where people were cleaning up the result of what had happened between O'Brian and Campbell.

"This is the one. Now I need to rewind it."

Shane rewound the footage a few minutes. We watched O'Brian come back into the frame and shoot Campbell, all in reverse. Shane kept rewinding and we saw O'Brian rifling through the boxes of evidence. Shane set the video to play.

"What are you doing?" he mumbled to himself.

We watched as O'Brian look around and started examining boxes, his finger tapping on each box as he passed. He reached for a box and took it off the shelf. He went through its contents and grabbed something in contained in a plastic bag.

Shane paused the video, then rewound it a few frames and zoomed in.

"What is that?" I asked.

"I don't know." Shane said. "But we can figure it out pretty easily."

"How?"

Using his phone, Shane took a picture of the screen, then stood up "There's a list of contents of each box. We need to find which box it was. Then, we need to get the identification number and find the list associated with that box, then crosscheck all the items to see what's missing."

I followed Shane to the evidence room. He picked up a binder off the table at the entrance and walked to the area where O'Brian had been standing. He double checked the picture on his phone to make sure he was in the right spot.

He looked at the first box and checked the numbers, then flipped the binder open and scrolled through its pages.

"How do you know which one he took from?"

"I think it's this one," he said, while searching through the binder. "Or maybe this one." He flipped the page and tapped it. "Yup. Definitely this one."

"How do you know?"

Shane showed me the page in the binder. Next to the identification number was labeled *Mitchell Quinn Investigation*.

"Hold this," Shane said, handing me the binder. He took the box off the shelf and placed it on the floor. "How many items are associated with this box?"

I glanced at the number at the top. "Eleven."

Shane handed me a pencil, and I started crossing items off one by one as Shane pulled them out of the box.

"Why do we have this stuff, anyway? Shouldn't the Decker City police have this?" I asked.

"They asked us to assist in the investigation. We were labeling everything and logging it. They just haven't come to pick up anything yet, and I sure as hell ain't bringing their stuff to them, only to have to deal with Conway. At least, not yet."

"Fair enough."

Shane pulled out the last item, and I crossed it off the list. "Okay, what are we missing?"

I ran my index finger down the page until I found the missing item.

"It's the knife."

Shane's eyes squinted. "Why the knife?" He reached for the binder and I handed it to him.

He mumbled to himself as he read. "Why take a knife from the crime scene?"

"We saw Scarface with the knife in those photos."

"Yeah, I remember. But when I went through all the evidence with Jenkinson and O'Brian, the knife was there. Why take it now?"

"Fingerprints?" I asked.

"It belonged to Mitchell. At least we think. We checked for fingerprints and it only had Mitchell's on it. So that's not it."

Then my conversation with Kate hit me.

"The blood!" I exclaimed.

Shane looked up at me. "What?"

"The blood. It has the vigilante's blood on it. Kate said something about these guys collecting DNA to figure out what the vigilante can do."

"And you're just telling me this now?"

"Again, it never came up. And I didn't know you even had this stuff here anymore."

Shane shook his head and stood up. He walked out of the evidence room.

"So what's O'Brian doing with this knife?" he asked as we walked along the hallway.

"I don't know. I think it has something to do with understanding the vigilante's DNA and trying to replicate it somehow."

Shane gave a deep sigh. "This is too much for me. When did it get this complicated with bad guys? Just a few days ago, it was as simple as arresting someone for an outstanding warrant or a *bar fight*." He glared at me.

"I was just trying to prepare you for all of this," I said.

He stopped outside the security office. "You know, all of this began when *you* started following me around. I'm going to venture a guess that a lot of this is *your* fault." He opened the door and walked back inside.

"Yeah, well..." I paused. He was kind of right. Shane may not have been as deep as he was if I hadn't been around. Although, O'Brian was undercover, so Shane may have gotten involved eventually. He was a smart guy. He would have figured it out. Maybe I'd just sped up the process.

"Nothing to say?" Shane asked.

"No, I was just thinking that if it weren't for me, you wouldn't have figured this all out as quickly as you did. So, I believe a 'thank you' would be in order right about now."

Shane sat at the computer again and pulled up the view from a camera at the front of the building. "I'll thank you after it's over. For now, we have work to do." He pointed to the screen. "Look—there's O'Brian." Shane switched to another camera once he left the frame, then another before O'Brian finally popped up again. "There. He got into one of our vehicles. We can track him."

Shane jumped up and headed out of the room. We reached the lobby and he spoke with Stacy at the front desk.

"Stacy, I need you to get everyone to head to the location of vehicle number 804. O'Brian took it and Adam and I are going to follow it now."

"Got it," she said and started typing quickly. As we reached the exit, she started making her announcement.

Shane and I ran down the steps and headed to his personal vehicle. Once inside, he pulled up the GPS on his phone. He located O'Brian's car and started to drive.

| 40 |

"Where are you going, O'Brian?" Shane mumbled to himself.

"Where is he?" I asked.

"He's heading north. Back towards where we came from when we found the helicopter in that field."

"They've been out there this whole time?"

"Again, you ask me questions you think I know the answers to. I don't know if they've been out there the whole time. It would make sense, since I asked O'Brian to canvass the area—which he probably didn't do. Son of a bitch kept Jenkinson out of action so he could move around freely." Shane slammed his hand on the steering wheel. "I should have seen it."

"You didn't know," I reassured him.

"That's the thing, I didn't know, and it was right under my nose. Makes me wonder what else I don't know about."

I couldn't provide any comfort, because I hadn't known either. I'd joked about having a mole in the station, but I hadn't expected it to be true. I'd just wanted to see some action. I'd gotten my wish.

I couldn't begin to understand how Shane felt. He had one officer murdered, minutes ago. Another one had been shot. Another attacked, bloodied, and left tied up in his own home. And the source of it all was an officer who'd betrayed Shane and everyone else at the Mapleton police station.

"I have another question. Don't worry," I said, putting my hands up, "this one I'm positive you have the answer to."

"Go ahead."

"Why are we in your car and not one of the police cars?"

Shane smirked and held up his phone. "I'm tracking O'Brian, right?"

"Yeah, and?"

"*And* all the vehicles can track one another. We can see where all of our vehicles are at all times. So if I can track him, he can track me."

"Oh, that makes sense. Does he know this?" I asked.

Shane nodded. "Absolutely, he does. Which makes me wonder— why not take his own vehicle? It would have taken us longer to track that down. Why did he make it easy for us?"

"Maybe he was in a rush and just took a vehicle?"

Shane shook his head. "He'd be smarter than that. I mean, he outsmarted us this whole time."

"You think he wanted us to follow him?"

Shane took one hand off the steering wheel and pointed at me. "Bingo."

I thought about it for a moment.

"If you can track him, he can track you. But since you're taking your own car, he can't. You want to surprise him and beat him at his own game," I said.

Shane smiled. "Adam, I'm impressed. You're learning."

"Yeah, but I still don't know *why* he wants us to follow him."

"And that's the million-dollar question. Which is why we are ahead of the entire force, closing in on his location. I want us to surprise him and catch him off-guard."

I was glad to have Shane around during this adventure. I had learned a lot, and I wouldn't have gotten far without him.

We drove for another twenty minutes before we found ourselves surrounded by fields again. Shane pulled to the side of the road.

"What are we doing?" I asked.

"Preparing," he said, and got out of the car.

I opened my car door and followed him to the trunk. He opened it and drew back the carpeted floor, revealing three guns—two handguns and a rifle along with multiple magazines. He grabbed one of the handguns and two magazines.

"Here," he said as he handed them to me. "Do you know how to use this?"

"Have you forgotten about the other day?" I reminded him, thinking about how he'd given me his gun while Patrick's goons chased us down, firing at our vehicle.

Shane nodded. "That's right. How could I forget? Anyway, this is for your protection. *Do not* just fire blindly."

"Don't worry. I'll make sure my eyes are open."

Shane shook his head, then reached into the trunk and pulled out the other handgun. He loaded it, stuck it in his pants, and then took out the rifle.

"What kind of gun is that?" I asked.

"An M4 carbine. It's a semi-automatic rifle." He picked loaded the gun, then placed the rest of the magazines into his vest pockets. "Let's go. Not much further now."

We got back in the car, and Shane tossed his weapon in the back seat. As he drove, he kept glancing down at the phone. I peeked at it every now and then. A few dots were behind us, which must have been the rest of the police force. O'Brian's dot was very close to us. It seemed like we'd be on top of it at any moment.

In the distance was a clearing. Beyond it I saw a long, one-story house, or maybe it was a barn. I thought barns were red? This was yellow with a brown roof. Two smaller buildings were to its left.

Shane slowed down to a stop, and stared out the windshield. He looked at his phone and then back at the building in front of us.

"He's in there," he said, pointing out the windshield.

"So let's go get him," I said, opening the door.

Shane pulled me back. "Stop it. He knows we're coming. Maybe not you and me at this very moment, but he can see the police are on their way. He knows he only has moments left. Whatever he's planning, he's a step ahead. And most likely, he's not alone."

I shut the door. "So what do we do, then?"

Shane reached in the back seat for his rifle. "Open the glove compartment, Adam."

I popped it open to find a lens that looked like one part of a pair of binoculars.

"This?" I asked.

Shane turned, rifle in hand. "Yes, that. Thank you." He took it from me and attached it to his weapon, then looked through it.

He moved it around, aiming at different objects outside the car. "I don't see anyone on the roofs or outside. They must all be inside," Shane said, then lowered his weapon. "Look, this is going to be dangerous. I need you to listen to everything I say. Do not be a lone wolf here, okay? We need to work together."

I wouldn't have known what else to do. I wasn't ready to go in guns blazing. I didn't want to get bullets unloaded at me. One bullet hurt. I didn't need more than that. Shane's plan was more along the lines of what I wanted to do—sneak in, find O'Brian, and arrest him. It sounded easy, but I knew it couldn't be *that* easy. Shane said this was likely a setup. If O'Brian was with anyone else, they were probably waiting for us. Was Patrick here too? Scarface? There was only one way to find out.

"Got it," I said. "You need my help. You can't do this without me. I'm the only one who you can count on to help you find O'Brian and bring his ass to justice."

"Oh my God, that's not what I said. I said—you know, never mind. Let's just go." He stepped outside, took a deep breath and started heading towards the building.

We entered what looked like a corn field and crept lower as we jogged forward. The stalks were fairly short so there wasn't much to use for cover, so keeping low was our only option.

Shane peeked in his scope every few seconds. He said nothing, so I assumed he still didn't see anyone. I was starting to wonder if anyone was even here.

We made our way to the side of the building and pressed our backs against the wall. Shane looked back and forth multiple times. He pulled out his phone and looked at it, then placed it back in his pocket.

He pointed to his left. "That's where we're heading. Are you ready?"

I wasn't sure if I was or not. My heart was racing. My stomach was all in knots. I had found myself in plenty of dangerous situations lately, but this was at least one I kind of prepared myself for. Everything else, I'd been just thrown into. This time I was on the attack—at least I hoped I was. I knew I couldn't die from bullet wounds, but Shane could. Was I concerned about Shane? Was that the reason I was so nervous?

My hands were sweaty. That wouldn't not make for a good grip on my gun. I wiped them on my pants before I pulled my gun from my pocket, and held it close to me.

"I'm ready," I said.

| 41 |

Shane and I crept around the side of the building, making our way to the front. He peeked around the corner, then waved for me to follow.

There was an opening close to us, big enough to fit a car through—or a tractor, given that it was a barn. Shane crept towards the opening and peeked inside, then held up a fist, which I assumed meant *stop*. I wasn't sure, but I stayed put anyway.

"Okay. I saw O'Brian's police cruiser in there. There's a handful of other people too, maybe eight to ten? I'm not sure."

"Did you see O'Brian?" I asked.

"Oh yeah. I saw that red-headed bastard."

"What now?"

"Well, there are at least two people we're nearby. I'm going to try and take them down and we can move in. Remember, they think we're further away, so we'll take them by surprise. We may be able to work our way in before the rest of the force joins us. It'll work to our advantage."

"I'm following your lead, so lead the way," I said.

"Once I get in there, I want you to head for the police car. It's literally right across from the entrance. Use the car as cover."

I nodded.

Shane flipped the safety on his weapon and swung it into the entrance. That was my cue to get ready and run. I stood up and ran behind Shane, sliding in front of the police car. I watched as Shane snuck around the side of the barn, using the bales of hay as cover. A guy in a hat, dangling an assault rifle stood just feet away from Shane. I watched as he snuck up behind him, using the butt of his gun on his head and pulling him to the ground out of sight.

A few seconds passed before Shane leaned out from cover. We made eye contact before he turned and continued into the depths of the barn. Did he expect me to just stay here and wait for him? Why hadn't he told me what I was supposed to do after reached this car?

I decided to leave cover and start working my way into the barn as well. I crept towards a fencing area and jumped over. I ducked and made sure I was in cover. There were trays that looked to be used for food and water, positioned along the fence. For a moment, I wondered what kind of animals used to be here.

I suddenly heard footsteps walking towards me. I peeked through the cracks of wood and watched someone pass by. I held my breath, hoping they wouldn't hear me. I heard the rusty sound of a gate swinging open next to me. I turned toward the noise and saw someone step in. I had to act fast, otherwise, I'd ruin Shane's plan.

I jumped to my feet and wrapped my arms around his neck. I threw myself onto his back and we fell to the ground. My gun fell from my hand and bounced a few feet away.

I clutched my arms tighter around his neck, trying to prevent him from screaming. Wait, I didn't want to kill this man. I was choking him. What was my next move here?

I didn't have to think long as a sharp pain ran through my thigh. I winced and glanced at a knife sticking out of my leg.

My grip weakened around the man's neck and he threw me off him. He coughed, trying to catch his breath, and then leaned in for his attack. I reached for my gun and swung as hard as I could, connecting with his cheek. He tumbled over and was still. His chest resembled breathing so I figured he was unconscious.

I wrapped my hand around the knife in my leg and pulled. It came out, but it was painful. I bit down hard on my lip to avoid screaming in pain.

A gun shot distracted me from the pain in my leg. I peeked over the wooden fence and saw someone aiming towards where Shane had been.

"Shane!" I exclaimed. It probably wasn't the smartest move but there was nothing I could do about it now.

The man holding the gun turned towards me and fired. Bullets flew in my direction, breaking apart the wood behind me. Just as the pain in my leg had gone away, a throbbing pain shot through my shoulder.

"Dammit," I shouted to myself.

I rolled to the side, out of the way of gun-fire, then climbed to my feet and ran back towards the police car. I jumped over the fence and dove behind the car. A bullet whizzed past me, shattering the red light above the police car. The hard plastic fell across the hood of the vehicle and slid down onto me. I brushed it off quickly and looked around for an escape.

I saw Shane peek out from cover, aiming his gun at my attacker. He fired four quick shots and the guy fell to the ground.

I heard voices and the sound of people scattering in the distance. More gun-fire erupted from inside the building, firing in our direction. My instinct was to duck. I guess the element of surprise was officially over.

I looked over at Shane, who was using the wall as cover. He pointed to me and pulled out his handgun, gesturing at it. Then he pointed at the back of the building. I understood.

Holding my gun close to my face, I stood up, spun around quickly, and fired. I didn't know where I was firing, so I guess my promise to not fire blindly was already broken. After firing four shots, I ducked back down and then Shane fired his weapon again. He spun around, planting his back against the wall as the other guys returned fire. I ducked as bullets flew overhead, penetrating the metal and glass above me. I glanced at Shane who had crouched, ready to move. How could he be so calm?

The gunfire slowed and then stopped. There was a voice from the distance.

"Cranston, is that you?"

I looked at Shane, who was looking at me.

"Yeah. It's me, O'Brian. Give yourself up," Shane responded.

"Not likely," O'Brian said, and then opened fire again.

Shane took out his handgun and fired blindly towards the people shooting as us. I leaned to my right and returned fire as well. On my fourth shot, I saw someone drop. Had I hit someone? Or was that Shane? I wasn't a great shot. I was doing the best I could, so if I'd managed to hit someone, I chalked that up as a victory.

Shane switched back to his rifle, stood up and began firing, as he made his way to the police car. He ducked down next to me.

"You okay?" he asked.

I nodded.

"Good. Keep firing. There's some machinery over there," he said, pointing to my left. It was a large, green tractor of some kind. It had a giant circular blade in the front. "I'm going to work my way over there and try to sneak up on them. Cover me."

I didn't exactly know what he meant, but I went along with it. I stood up and opened fire. Shane ran as I fired into the distance. He made it to cover, and I ducked back down quickly as they returned fire instantly. My hand touched something wet on the ground.

What was that?

I held my wet hand up to my nose. It smelled like gasoline. I looked underneath the car and saw a puddle forming.

I turned and watched Shane move discreetly towards the guys shooting at us. They kept firing at me until Shane crouched and aimed his rifle. He fired three times and ducked. Had he hit someone?

I looked above the car but a sudden pain hit me in the arm and knocked me backwards. Luckily, Shane was too far away to see what had happened.

I sat up and leaned back against the police car. I wanted to know which jackass shot me so I could shoot him back. I waited until the pain subsided, stood up and fired into the depths of the building. Unfortunately, I only got off two shots before I was out of ammo.

I looked over the police car and noticed O'Brian in the distance. He was standing on top of a white van, and tossed something in my direction.

"Adam, watch out!" I heard Shane yell.

An object bounced off the police car and rolled in front of me. It was a grenade. I leapt to my feet and ran for cover outside the barn, but the grenade had already exploded, creating a fireball from the exposed gasoline. The force propelled me forward, and I fell flat on my face.

Everything went blurry. My vision moved from side to side, but I remained still. I felt sore. I let out an enormous sigh and rolled over. The police car was destroyed and on fire. I saw people scurrying around in the barn.

Then I heard the sirens. I looked in the distance and saw six police cars heading towards me. Backup had finally arrived.

The pain had disappeared, and it was time for a little payback. I climbed to my feet and I loaded the extra magazine Shane gave me into my handgun. I charged into the building, firing at anyone and anything I saw in front of me. I probably should have known better, though. Within seconds, pain shot through my hand, making me drop my gun.

"Dammit!" I screamed.

It was as if I'd learned nothing after charging into gun-fire during the helicopter incident. Maybe I did have a death wish as Shane suggested earlier.

I grabbed my hand and ducked behind a metal crate. Blood gushed from the bullet wound in my hand. The gun lay about five feet away. I went to reach it with my other hand, but a volley of bullets made me think better of it.

Suddenly, the front entrance of the building lit up. Police cars swerved and parked in all different directions, then officers started opening their car doors and returned fire. Bullets flew all over the place in both directions.

I ducked to avoid the bullets coming from all sides. I wasn't as nervous anymore, more so paranoid about being shot again. I didn't want to deal with the pain anymore. I felt like I couldn't duck down far enough to stay out of the line of sight.

The police moved in. I looked above my cover and watched as the remaining people with O'Brian had started retreating. Were they running away?

During this ordeal, I had lost sight of Shane. I thought he'd said no lone wolf behavior?

"Are you okay?" an officer asked me.

"Yeah, I'm good," I responded. "Any idea where Shane is?"

"Not a clue. Stay down while we handle this," he replied.

Yeah, *they'd* handle this. Not like Shane and I hadn't figured out all the details to get to this point. Where was Shane, anyway?

I picked up my gun, tucked it in my pants, and followed the officers as they made their way through the building. They stayed quiet as they maneuvered around. I looked all around for Shane, but didn't see him anywhere. Had he been shot? Was he dead?

I followed the officers through a room at the far end of the barn. One officer opened the door as two others stormed inside. A metal hatch was embedded into the ground. One by one, the police officers filed into the room and looked at one another. A female officer stepped forward, reached down and lifted the metal door. The rest of them had their guns pointed at the opening. No one fired.

"Let's go," she said.

The officers climbed down into the hole. Nine officers went down, leaving me and two others above ground.

A gunshot startled me. I glanced to my left to see the officer standing next to me fall to the ground. I pulled out my gun, but then another quick shot left the other officer dead as well.

I stood motionless as Patrick appeared at the entrance of the room. O'Brian came running in and kicked the metal door so that it slammed shut. He pulled a padlock from his pocket, wound it through the hole, and locked it in place.

Within seconds, I heard banging from underground. Voices yelled to be let out. I looked at Patrick and he was smiling.

"It's certainly nice to see you again, Adam," he said.

"Yeah, well, it's really *not* nice to see you," I said. "Honestly—and can I be honest with you?"

"I encourage honesty," he replied.

"Good. As long as we're speaking the truth then—I have this gun in my hand, and I would love to shoot you with it. Would you mind staying still while I did that? I'm not that good of a shot and would prefer to hit someone standing still rather than moving."

Patrick chuckled. "Always with the jokes." He pulled a gun from a holster I hadn't even noticed. This guy was quick. He pointed it outside the room. "You see, Adam, I have my gun trained on someone who you care about. If you pull your trigger, I'll pull mine."

I took a step to my left and saw that the back doors of the white van were held opened by O'Brian. I leaned a little further and saw a body lying in the back.

"Is that Shane?" I asked.

"The one and only," O'Brian said.

"I need you to come with me," Patrick asked.

"And if I don't?"

"Then I'll just put a bullet in your unconscious friend over there," Patrick replied.

I could heal from bullets, and Patrick knew this too. But Shane couldn't heal, and I didn't want to risk anything happening to him.

I could stop both of them. Unfortunately, it would come at the cost of Shane's life. I couldn't risk that. I had to do what Patrick wanted, at least for now.

I dropped my gun.

"There you go," Patrick said.

O'Brian entered the room and shoved me towards the door past two armed guards.

"Watch that room," Patrick said to them. "I don't want any of those officers getting out of that hole. Understood?"

They both nodded.

O'Brian placed his hand on my head and shoved me into the back of the van. I fell next to Shane, who was tied up and unconscious on the floor.

O'Brian hopped into the van and closed the door. He grabbed my hands and tied them behind my back. Shane's life was in my hands, which were now tied behind my back. I had to do what they asked of me.

Patrick got in the driver's seat and started the engine. O'Brian placed a cover over my head. Shane was unconscious. The Mapleton police were trapped underground. I took back my comments about the lame setup. Patrick and O'Brian had succeeded.

"Where are you taking us?" I asked.

Patrick's voice was muffled by the cover I was wearing. "I'm taking you to someone who really wants to meet you."

Sitting in the back of a moving van, tied up with a cover over my head, was very uncomfortable. There were no seats or seatbelts. I moved around frequently. Adjusting myself and making sure I didn't roll over while tied up proved to be an arduous task.

I couldn't see anything, which threw my sense of direction completely off. After many turns, I could no longer tell which direction we were headed. Part of me wished I was in Shane's shoes right now. He was still unconscious.

"Who's this mystery person you're taking me to meet?" I asked.

No one responded.

"Hello?"

Still, no one answered me.

"I know you guys are there. I can hear the whistling coming from ugly face's broken nose up front. And O'Brian, your red hair is so bright, I can see it through this thing on my head."

"Shut up," O'Brian said.

"Make me," I replied.

I heard him take out his gun.

"Stop," Patrick interrupted.

Had Patrick not told O'Brian about my ability?

"Put the gun away. He needs to meet *him* first. Then, I don't care what you do with him," Patrick told O'Brian.

I heard him put the gun back in his holster. "You're lucky he was here to stop me," O'Brian said to me.

"No, I'm just lucky you didn't pull something else out."

The back of my head slammed into the wall of the van from the momentum of his unexpected punch, and pain engulfed the left side of my face. I slid down to the metal floor.

"Ouch," I said, trying to wiggle my way back to a sitting position. I guess I should have expected that. I was grateful it wasn't a bullet. I was tired of experiencing bullet wounds.

I turned my head to the front of the van, or at least what I thought was the front. "Patrick, can you teach O'Brian how to punch good? No, wait. Punch well. Right?"

I turned back to face O'Brian. "Is it well? Punch well?"

"Can I please just shoot him?" O'Brian asked.

"No, but if he keeps it up, you can put a bullet in Cranston. We don't necessarily need him," Patrick responded.

"Got it," I said. "We'll just leave it at *to punch well.* All good now." I leaned back against the wall of the van and shut up. I didn't want to put Shane in any danger, especially if they claimed they didn't need him.

Wait.

Did that mean they were only after me?

Then I understood. The DNA manipulation. Patrick knowing what I could do. They wanted to know how my ability worked. Well, lucky for them, so did I. But I didn't want to find out like this.

A few minutes later, the van stopped. The front door opened and Patrick got out—I thought it was him; I still couldn't see. The back door opened a moment later and O'Brian grabbed my left arm and raised me to a standing position. He walked me to the edge of the van and helped me down to the ground.

"You guys are so sweet. Thanks for helping this disabled soul out of the van. Can you take this thing off my head now?" I asked.

The bag was whisked off my head.

"I think you took some hairs along with that," I said, wincing.

My eyes adjusted to the new light. I was in another barn, standing in a mixture of grass, dirt, and hay. I looked around but didn't see any animals.

"What's with you guys and farms?" I asked.

They ignored me and guided me to a chair in the center of the barn. Patrick and O'Brian then returned to the van, pulled Shane to its edge, and then Patrick picked him up and tossed him over his shoulder. O'Brian grabbed another chair from against the wall and placed it a few feet from me. Patrick sat Shane in the chair and placed his hands behind it. O'Brian reached behind to tie them up.

Shane's eyes opened slowly as he came to. He looked around the barn with curious eyes, looking in all directions. He started to tug at his arms, then realized they were tied to the chair.

"Where are we?" Shane asked.

O'Brian stepped in front of him. "Hi, Shane," he said with a wave.

Shane fought against his restraints, but he couldn't escape.

"This is an abandoned barn. Well, it is now. The people who previously owned it are, shall we say, permanently unavailable," O'Brian said.

"You killed them?" Shane asked.

Patrick spoke up. "I did."

Shane turned his head slightly to look at Patrick, but continued to speak to O'Brian.

"Why'd you do this?"

"Easy—money. Patrick offered me a lot of money. Then he offered me a new identity after I completed my assignment. I can start over somewhere else as someone new, and I'll never have to work again."

"And what was your assignment?" I asked.

O'Brian turned back to me, but addressed both Shane and I. "Originally, it was just to feed Patrick information. Then, when you guys started investigating him, it was to keep you away from him."

"You sent those guys after us from the hospital?" Shane asked him.

O'Brian nodded. "I did. I had to. It was my job."

"Your job was to be a police officer and to serve and protect!"

"I *was* a police officer. And I *did* serve and protect. Just not the same people *you* serve and protect."

"You're an asshole," Shane said.

"I'm aware of that," O'Brian replied, "but a rich one. And I'm sorry about Jenkinson. I really am. I liked him. I didn't want to hurt him."

"Okay, enough of this," Patrick interjected. "He's here."

A black car pulled up outside the barn doors, next to the white van. A driver wearing a suit got out of the driver's seat, then walked to the rear door and opened it. A man dressed in a bomber jacket and black cargo pants stepped out. His jacket had four large, button-like pieces sticking out on each shoulder. His hair was slicked back, almost in dreads. His black beard covered most of his face, but when he stepped closer, I noticed it.

I turned to Shane and whispered, "It's Scarface."

He approached, nodded, then looked at me and Shane. He pointed at me.

"This the one?" he said, asking Patrick.

"That's him," Patrick replied.

Scarface looked me up and down.

"You checking me out?" I asked. "I'm sorry, but I don't swing that way. I have a girlfriend. Well, kind of. I mean—I like her. I think she likes me too."

Scarface looked back at Patrick.

"I told you he's got a mouth on him," Patrick said.

Scarface's black shirt was half tucked in; a gun peeked out from the side of his pants. He was thin, and the T-shirt fit snugly against his body. I could see he was fit, and appeared strong and intimidating. He wasn't someone you'd want to cross, but I didn't mind. I wasn't scared of him.

Scarface swung a fist at me. The next thing I knew, O'Brian and Patrick were placing me back in my chair. Did he just knock me out? How long was I out for?

I shook my head as I tried to comprehend what had just happened. The pain he'd caused was barely noticeable now, but it was there. I couldn't have been out for long.

"Do all you guys punch someone when you get annoyed? Didn't you learn in school how to talk about your problems using words and not violence?" I said.

"Would you like me to knock you out again?" Scarface said, leaning close to me.

"Not really. I'd like to see where all this is going. I kind of don't enjoy being left in the dark." I looked around. "Nothing? Really? You guys don't understand puns?"

They ignored me.

"The joke doesn't work if I have to explain it," I said.

"Let's get started," Scarface said. "Mr. O'Brian, go retrieve Michael from the vehicle for me."

O'Brian headed towards the vehicle, and Scarface faced me.

"How do you do what you do?" he asked.

I leaned a little closer to him and whispered, "You're going to have to be more specific. I have many talents."

Scarface smiled at me. "No worries. I don't need you to talk for this next part, anyway."

I heard a car door shut and then O'Brian walked back with a gun pointing at someone holding a briefcase. The black car had that brought Scarface and this other man now drove off.

Patrick dragged a folding table next to me and opened it up. O'Brian brought Michael over and he placed the briefcase on the table.

"Wait," Shane said. "Are you Michael Rason?"

Michael opened the briefcase and looked at O'Brian. He then nodded at Shane. "Do I know you?"

"Your partner, Bethany, was worried about you. She said you were abducted," Shane said, looking at O'Brian standing behind Michael. "Which I guess was true."

"Is she okay?" Michael asked.

O'Brian pushed his gun against Michael's back. "She will be if you continue to do as we ask. Don't make us go to your lab and hurt her."

Michael nodded and began taking out the contents of his brief-case. They were medical supplies; a few needles and some tubes.

"What are you doing?" I asked.

"I have to take some of your blood," Michael responded.

"Oh. Okay. Because that's normal, right?"

"I just do what I'm told," he said.

"What's all this for?" Shane spoke up.

O'Brian pointed his gun at Shane. "None of your business. One more word out of your mouth and I'll put a bullet in it."

Shane fell silent.

Patrick untied my arms and placed my left arm on the table. "Don't try anything. Otherwise, O'Brian will kill him."

Scarface watched as Michael stuck the needle in my arm. It was attached to a hose that led to a vial, which began to fill up with blood. He got another one ready and replaced the first when it was full.

Scarface pulled his phone from his pocket and tapped the screen. He appeared to type something and then put the phone away.

Michael filled four vials of blood, then took the needle out of my arm. He packed everything up and closed the briefcase.

"I'm sorry," he said.

"That will be all, Michael. No further need to talk to the boy," Scarface said.

"Boy? Seriously?" I responded.

"If you're going to act like a boy with your childish jokes, I'll treat you like one," he said.

"You're just mad because you don't get my jokes."

He waved me away. "Patrick, my ride will be here momentarily. I'll be taking Michael outside with me. Make sure you handle everything here before you leave."

"Yes, sir," Patrick replied.

"Adam, it was a pleasure to meet you. I'm sorry we won't be seeing much of each other anytime soon," Scarface said.

"This seems like a one-sided transaction. A little unfair if you ask me," I said.

"No one asked you," O'Brian said.

"And no one was talking to you," I told him. Now it was as if I was arguing with Jenkinson all over again. What was happening here?

I looked back at Scarface. "So, what do I get out of this?"

He smiled. "You get to die. That's what you get out of this."

"Again, seems a little unfair," I said, trying to remain calm. I didn't want to die. *Could* I even die? Over the last few days, I'd taken a couple of bullets, and been injured pretty badly, and I'd been fine.

It scared me to think about death.

A rumbling sound came from outside. Was that a helicopter?

"Well, my ride is here. Gentlemen—" Scarface said, nodding. He put his hand on Michael's back and gestured for him to turn and walk towards the entrance of the barn.

A helicopter landed just outside the entrance, pushing hay and dirt inside the barn.

Scarface assisted Michael into the helicopter first, then he climbed inside. Immediately, it took off.

"Nice guy," I said.

"Shut up," O'Brian replied. "Can I kill him now?"

Patrick smiled. "I'm sorry I can't stick around to watch this, but I need to go. I have two other annoying pests I need to take care of."

Two others? Was he talking about Kate and Nathan? I needed to warn them. But I had to get out of this predicament first.

Patrick headed outside, towards the van.

"A little rude, Patrick. You say I'm going to die and won't even say goodbye to me?" I yelled at him.

He opened the driver's side door, "I'm sorry. Where are my manners? Adam, goodbye." He waved and got inside, then started the engine and drove away. It was now just me, Shane, and O'Brian, who still had the gun trained on Shane.

"Just like old times, huh?" I said. "Well, I mean, we're missing the lunatic and I can't say I've ever seen you holding a gun at Shane, but still."

"Yeah. About this gun—" O'Brian said, then swung his arm around to aim the weapon at me. "I'm sorry, Adam. Nothing personal."

"Says the guy pointing a gun at me," I said. "And why do people keep saying 'nothing personal'? It's *clearly* personal."

"No, stop!" Shane yelled.

"Okay, what the hell, Shane?" O'Brian said. "Why do you care so much about what happens to this idiot? I mean, you've always been looking out for him—every time we arrested him, *you* let him go. You even brought him with you while you investigated this whole thing. I don't get it. It's the one thing that's been bothering me. Why?"

Shane stared at me, then back at O'Brian. "Because I look out for people in need of—"

"Cut the crap. You don't treat everyone like this. Only him. Why?" O'Brian started yelling. He got closer to Shane and held the gun under his chin. "Why?"

Shane kept his eyes on O'Brian. It was true that he had always given me preferential treatment, but I'd never thought much of it. I thought he treated everyone that way. Now the question started to linger in my mind. Why was I different? Why did he help me out so much? What was so special about me?

O'Brian pushed the gun harder into his chin. "Tell me why."

Shane pursed his lips. He was holding something back.

"Tell me!" O'Brian yelled in his face.

"He's my brother!"

My heart dropped out of my chest. What did he just say?

"What?" O'Brian asked.

"Yeah, what?" I asked.

"Adam is my younger brother," Shane said. "My parents gave him up for adoption when he was a baby."

O'Brian lowered his gun slightly. He seemed to be in shock, just as I was.

Shane was my brother? How long had he known? When did he find out? And why was I just finding out about this now?

O'Brian looked at me and then back at Shane. He shook his head. "I can't believe it. How is this possible? You never mentioned having a sibling before."

Shane shrugged his shoulders. "It's true."

I was speechless. I couldn't put together any words to say to either Shane or O'Brian. I couldn't believe that after all these years, after all the homes, all the different families, I'd finally found someone to call my own flesh and blood. My brother.

Immediately, I began to question it. Shane was a good liar. Was he really my brother? Or was he just playing O'Brian?

O'Brian pulled the gun away from Shane's chin and aimed it back at me.

"Well, after a delightful trip down memory lane," he said, "it's time to finish what we started. Sorry, Shane. I gotta do it."

"No!" Shane shouted.

O'Brian aimed. And fired.

| **43** |

Blackness.

Silence.

Was I dead?

I couldn't move. I had no feeling in any part of my body. I couldn't hear. I couldn't see. Was this what it was like to die?

Suddenly, pain flooded my head. It felt like the worst headache I'd ever had. The pain wrapped around my entire head and stemmed down my neck. What was happening to me?

Muffled noises.

I could hear again. I couldn't make anything out, only mumbled voices. It sounded like I was underwater.

The pain subsided. I was lying down. I wiggled my fingertips.

I opened my eyes slightly. The light hurt my eyes. It was as if someone decided to shine a bright light in my face after suddenly coming out of a dark room. I squinted until they adjusted.

Abruptly, I had the intense urge to breathe.

I sat up and took a huge breath.

"What the f—" a voice said, before it was cut off by a gun going off in my face.

| 44 |

Blackness. Again.

Silence. Again.

What the hell was happening to me?

Pain pierced through my head again and shot down my neck. Was O'Brian shooting me in the head?

The feeling started to return throughout my body. The headache started to feel like pins and needles, when blood rushed back to an area of the body. I had the sudden urge to breathe again.

My eyes shot open. O'Brian knelt over me, staring at me and holding a gun to my head. Instantly, I reached up and grabbed his hands, shoving them above my head. When he fired his weapon instinctively, he missed. The loud shot next to my ears sent a ringing noise throughout my skull.

"Stop doing that!" I yelled.

"What the hell are you?" he exclaimed.

"I have a brother that calls me Deathwish. Let's go with that."

I head-butted him in the face, knocking him backwards. He dropped his grip on the gun as he fell, holding his nose. I quickly stood up and kicked the gun away from him.

He kicked me in the knee, which made me fall to the ground. He stood back up and kicked me again, this time in the chest. I curled up in the fetal position to try and block his kicks. After a few attempts, he stopped and reached down to grab my hair. He pulled me to my feet, but I threw a quick punch to his face.

He released his grip on my hair and covered his face again. He removed one hand, and I saw his nose starting to bleed.

"Oh, look at that. You have a broken nose to match the ugly-faced moron who just left," I told O'Brian.

I looked at Shane and pointed to O'Brian. "Right? Doesn't he?"

A mischievous smirk appeared across my face. I couldn't help it. I enjoyed breaking O'Brian's nose, especially after he had shot me in the head—twice. I never wanted to feel that headache again. Worst headache ever.

"Adam, look out!" Shane alerted me.

I turned to see O'Brian charging at me. He thrust his shoulder into me and I went flying backwards into the chair I'd previously sat on. I stumbled into it, breaking the metal frame. I fell onto the ground, bringing the broken chair with me.

O'Brian started looking around for the gun. I picked up the chair, got to my feet, and swung it at him, hitting his back. He arched forward and fell to the ground. I hit him one more time for good measure before dropping the it. I started to move towards Shane to untie him, but took just one step before O'Brian reached out and held onto my foot. I looked down. He had little strength—what was he doing? I didn't expect O'Brian to have *this* much fight in him. I tugged my foot away.

"Let go of me, you bottom feeder."

I got my foot free and kicked him in the face. I was pretty sure he'd be feeling that for a while.

I made my way to Shane and untied him. He stood up and stared at me. I stared back.

"I have no words for what I just witnessed," Shane said.

"I know, right? I kicked O'Brian's ass!" I told him.

"No—I mean, how the hell can you do what you do?" he asked.

"Oh, no. No, no, no. We aren't starting with that first. You're telling me about this whole brother thing," I said.

I noticed movement on the floor. O'Brian had lifted his arm, still holding the gun. He pointed it at Shane.

"No!" I exclaimed as I pushed Shane out of the way.

O'Brian fired and shot me in the chest. I fell backwards into the chair Shane had been sitting on. The chair fell back, and I landed on the floor.

Shane pulled out his handgun and fired three shots into O'Brian. I watched his arm fall to the ground, and the gun tumble from his hand. Shane kicked the gun away and came over to me. He knelt and put his hand on my chest wound.

"Ouch," I said. "Major ouch."

"Lie still. Don't move," Shane said.

I shook my head. "Give me a break. You saw me come back from a headshot. Wait, scratch that. Two headshots. This is nothing."

I took a deep breath. Even that hurt.

"Adam, he shot you in the chest."

"Were you not listening? Minutes ago, I was shot in the head, twice!"

The pain was diminishing. I could feel the healing taking its effect. It still hurt like hell.

Shane lifted his hand off of my wound and looked at the blood on his hand.

"Adam, you're bleeding."

I waved it off. "Have you learned nothing over the last few minutes? Do you see any marks on my head?"

Shane's eyes gazed to my forehead. He shook his head.

"Exactly." I reached up towards him. "Now, help me up, please."

Shane stood up and reached down to take my hand, then pulled me to my feet. I brushed the dirt and hay from my shirt.

"I'm seriously concerned you have some kind of a death wish," he told me.

"Yeah, yeah…" I waved it off. "You told me that before."

Shane took his phone from his pocket and started dialing.

"Who are you calling?" I asked.

"Seth. He took Liz to the hospital. He wasn't part of the team that was stuck in that hole. Maybe he can get some help to those guys—Hey Seth, it's Cranston." He paused. "You're there already?" He continued listening. "Wait, Jenkinson is there with you? How? Is he okay?"

How did Jenkinson get there? I thought he was in an ambulance somewhere.

Shane continued, "Alright, well, we got O'Brian. He's dead. The others got away. One escaped in a white van and the other took off in a helicopter. We don't have any transportation here, so can someone come get us?"

I wondered how long we'd have to stay here before someone came for us? For once, on my journey with Shane, we had to stay put. We had to wait. It would give me a moment to relax.

"Okay. Thanks," Shane said and hung up. "Someone will be here in about twenty minutes to pick us up."

Shane sat down on the hay and backed himself against the side of the barn. He leaned against it and sighed. I sat down next to him.

"You owe me an explanation," I said, pointing at him. "What's this *brother* stuff and why didn't you ever tell me?"

"Doesn't feel good when someone doesn't tell you something, does it?" Shane said, smirking.

"Okay, okay. I get it. I'm sorry I forgot to tell you things before. But this is kind of major. Start talking!"

He nodded.

"I was four when I first learned about it. I would sneak out of my bedroom at night and listen to my parents talking downstairs. I heard them speak about giving you away. At that time, I didn't know what it meant. I thought they were talking about me. I was so scared. I remember crying every night, thinking my parents didn't want me and they were going to throw me away."

"Wow, way to have such a negative spin on that."

"I was *four*. I didn't know any better. Anyway, one day my parents picked me up from daycare and I remember not seeing you in the car with me. Your car seat was missing too. My parents said you had to leave for a while and they didn't know when you'd come back. I didn't realize until I was much older that another family had adopted you. No one ever told me why. It was always kept quiet.

"Anyway, it made me want to track you down somehow. But I didn't know how. I started getting into investigating things that went missing or stolen at school. It became something I fixated on. I guess since I couldn't find you, I'd find other things to fill that void. Friends were always asking me to help them track down things that had been stolen. I went to college and majored in criminal justice, then became a police officer. I thought, maybe I would be closer to finding you if I had all the resources on my side. My parents didn't tell me anything, so I had no information to start with. They told me they didn't know where you were."

"Well, technically, they were right," I told him.

"How so?"

I told him how I had multiple families growing up. I'd been in and out of different foster homes. Families gave me up left and right. I'd never had a steady home for longer than a few years. It was depressing for a while, but eventually I just got used to it.

"I didn't know that," Shane said. "That must have been hard for you."

"It was. But I got over it." I sighed, thinking about my childhood and all the painful memories of being pushed away by family after family. It was awful feeling like no one wanted me.

"When did you realize we were related?" I asked.

He smiled. "Remember when you claimed you weren't hurt when you first came on that ride-along?"

I nodded.

"Well, I didn't believe you. Something didn't seem right. I got the sample of blood I found at the scene and ran a DNA test on it. I tested it against the guy I arrested to make sure it wasn't his."

"You mean *we* arrested," I reminded him.

He rolled his eyes. "*Anyway*, it didn't come back as a match, so I knew it must have been yours. But it resembled someone else's DNA in the system—mine. That's when I knew I had found you."

"That was so long ago, though. Why didn't you say something then?"

"It wasn't *that* long ago. And samples like that take a few days to come back. I literally just got an email with the results yesterday."

"And you waited until you had a gun pointed at you to tell me? You couldn't have said something sooner?"

"Do you remember anything we've been through over the last few days?"

"Touché."

"Also, I didn't know how to bring it up. It's not like you ever really mentioned your history. We, at the station, all knew a little bit about it, after having you arrested multiple times, but I never really thought much of it. I took a liking to you because you seemed like someone who needed direction. Someone who needed help." He looked around the barn and let out a chuckle. "Looks like you found what you were looking for. You found your action and ex-citement, your car chases and big explosions. And—" Shane looked around the barn, then whispered to me, "—finding out who the deep cover mole was."

I smiled as he reminded me of the conversation that had led us on this journey.

"I did. It was exciting to hunt down criminals and work with you. Sure, maybe I got myself into trouble on more than one occasion, but it was all worth it."

Technically, our investigation wasn't over. Patrick and Scarface got away. Michael was their hostage. How were we going to find them now?

"Oh, crap!" I exclaimed.

"What?" Shane asked.

"When Scarface was leaving, he said he had two issues to take care of. I think he meant Kate and Nathan." I took my phone out and called Kate.

"Why do you think that?" he asked, leaning his head against the wall and closing his eyes.

"Oh, look at you. The one with all the answers finally has a question of his own."

Shane kept his eyes close but stuck up his middle finger.

"Appropriate. Anyway, Patrick said *two* issues to take care of. What other *two* do you think he would have been talking about?"

"Sounds like we have a detective in training over here," Shane said.

On the second ring, Kate picked up.

"Adam, I can't talk right now."

"Kate, listen. We were just kidnapped by Patrick and Scarface. We got away, but they did too. They mentioned coming after you next."

"Was there a doctor there too?"

"Yeah, why?"

"Did the doctor leave with the man with the scar?"

"Scarface," I reminded her.

"Adam—yes or no?"

"Yeah, why? How do you know there was a doctor here too?"

"I placed a tracking device inside his briefcase. We've been trying to follow him. We lost the signal a while ago but it just came back. If he's with *Scarface*, then we can find him."

"Wait, how did you do that? Do you know where they're going?"

"Don't worry about it. Adam, I gotta go. We'll talk later."

"Wait, Kate! Where are they going?"

Silence.

"Hello?" I took the phone away from my ear and looked at the screen.

"She hung up on me." I hit her number again and called her back.

"Dammit." I tried her number again.

"What?" Shane asked, opening his eyes slightly.

"It's going right to voicemail. She must have turned her phone off—Yup, voicemail again." I put the phone back in my pocket.

Shane fully opened his eyes and repositioned himself to a sitting position after sliding down the wall slightly.

"So tell me about this healing trick of yours," he said.

I told him everything. It was a huge relief being able to tell him what I could do. I'd been knocked out, stabbed, blown up and shot, and I'd healed from it all. I was feeling pretty confident. Maybe I couldn't fight like the vigilante from Decker City, but I could heal. And that may prove to be a better ability than moving things without touching them.

Shane took it all fairly well. He didn't argue with me. He didn't call me names. He didn't threaten to turn me in. Maybe now that he knew we were related, it made it easier for him. Also, I wasn't running around taking the law into my own hands like the Gray Hood was doing. Shane and I worked side by side.

A few minutes later, a vehicle pulled up in front of the barn. Shane leaned forward to see. The front door opened and Jenkinson stepped out. He had a white bandage wrapped around his head.

"Tick-tock," Jenkinson said, tapping his wrist. "We're on the clock. We got work to do. Let's go."

Shane and I stood up and made our way to the car.

"Surprised to see me?" Jenkinson asked.

"Kind of," Shane said. The last time we spoke, you may have had a concussion, and you were on your way to the hospital. Why are you even here right now?"

"I'll be fine. I never made it to the hospital. Once I heard about what happened at the station, I *had* to get back. There was no way I was going to let O'Brian get away with what he did." He turned around in his seat to look at us. "He didn't get away, did he?"

"Seth didn't tell you?" Shane said.

Jenkinson faced the road. "No? He only told me to come pick you guys up."

"He's dead," I told him.

"What? Don't tell me this little twerp killed him," Jenkinson said.

"No. I killed him," Shane said. "But if it wasn't for Adam, O'Brian would have killed me."

Jenkinson sighed. "This doesn't mean I have to be nice to him, does it?"

"I'll take that as a thank you," I said.

"No, wait, hold on. I did no such thing. I'd never thank that moron in the back seat. How is he even still allowed to tail you around like a little puppy dog?"

"Stop, both of you. Geez, I sound like your parents. Jenkinson, we're taking Adam home. Then you and I have an appointment in Decker City with the chief of police."

"Wait, why can't I come too?"

"Because, this is between me and Conway." Shane reached in his pocket, pulled out the flash drive, and held it up.

| 45 |

The next morning, I laid in bed thinking about how I'd found my brother. I didn't even know I had a brother until he told me. Unfortunately, the news had come at gunpoint. I never imagined discovering any relatives *that* way. I wondered if he would have told me if O'Brian hadn't had a gun to his head.

I shook off the idea. Of course he would have told me.

I had someone I could call family now—my brother. Although, we didn't discuss our parents much. I'd have to get more answers from Shane later.

Shane called an hour later and told me he was on his way to pick me up. We were going to visit Chuck in the hospital and he had a surprise for me. I had no idea what it was, but I liked surprises, so I agreed.

When he showed up, I got in his car, and we headed for the hospital.

"How's Chuck doing?" Shane asked.

"I talked to him last night. He said they'll be releasing him tomorrow," I told Shane.

"That's great news. He must be doing well, then."

"He is. He said he's just bored and wants to get back to the bar. It's been closed since he was shot."

"That sucks. But he's got you to help him out and get it back open again."

"Yeah, I guess."

I was hoping to continue working with Shane, but it seemed I was destined to go back to work at the bar. Maybe I could convince him later.

"Alright," I said eagerly, "you have to tell me what happened with Conway yesterday. What did he do? What did you do?"

He chuckled. "Well, I certainly gave him hell. We yelled at each other. I told him he's a moron and some other profanities I didn't think he appreciated. I'm pretty sure I'll get some sort of punishment for what I did, but it was worth it to prove him wrong. I threw the flash drive at him and then walked out of the station."

"Pretty sure I expected a little more than that," I told him.

He shrugged. "Can't help you. That's all that happened. He's probably looking through the information on the drive right now and feeling pretty stupid."

I laughed. "I would love to have seen the look on his face when he realized the mistakes."

Shane nodded. "Me too. So, have you tried calling Kate again? Can you reach her?"

"I've tried many times. Straight to voicemail." I pulled out my phone, hit her number and put it on speaker. Once the voicemail kicked in, I hung up. "See? Doesn't even ring."

"Well, if you ever find out where she is, you know that you're calling me immediately, right?"

I agreed.

Shane then explained how Jenkinson made his way to the barn yesterday and took out the two guards on his own and freed the rest of the officers. Shane said he was like John McClane, taking out the enemies by himself. It surprised me to hear that Jenkinson was the one who rescued everyone. He must have used all that aggression he had built up towards O'Brian on those guys. Come to think of it, maybe it was all his hatred towards me. Either way, it impressed me.

We drove up to the hospital, and Shane parked his car. We headed inside to Chuck's room.

"Hey guys," Chuck said, as we entered the room.

"Hi, Chuck," I said. Shane waved and said hello.

"So, all is well with the world now? No more car chases or fiery explosions to tell me about?" Chuck asked.

"Nope. It's been pretty calm around here since Patrick and Scarface got away," I said.

"Still no idea where they are?" Chuck asked.

"No. Waiting for Kate to get back to me, but her phone is off."

"You're a police officer—" Chuck said, turning his attention to Shane.

"Thanks for noticing," Shane replied.

Chuck smiled. "Not what I meant. Can't you just track them somehow? I mean, I'm sure you can figure something out, right?"

"I have feelers out there, but I really don't have any clues or leads currently. I kind of need one of those to head in a specific direction. And our best lead isn't answering her phone, so at this point, we're back at square one. We'll be going through some evidence we gathered yesterday and hopefully we'll find something."

"Fair enough. Hopefully you find something."

"I hope so," Shane said.

"Hey, would you mind if I talked to Adam alone?" Chuck asked.

Shane nodded. "Sure. I'll wait outside. I'm glad you're feeling better." He waved and left the room.

"Adam, I wanted to talk to you about the bar," Chuck said.

"What about it?" I asked.

He reached over to the table next to him, grunting in the process. He still seemed in a lot of pain.

In his hand was a set of keys. "Here." He tossed them to me. "These are the keys to the bar. I want you to clean it up while I'm gone and get it ready to open back up."

"Aren't you getting out of here tomorrow? Wait—what do you mean *while you're gone?*"

"Adam, I was shot in the chest. I'm still in a lot of pain. I can't move like I used to. At least not right now. I can't go back to work, as much as I want to. I want you to run the bar while I'm gone."

"What? Me?"

I'd never had that kind of responsibility before. This would be like it was my bar. I didn't know how to run a bar. I'd need to order inventory, serve people food and drinks, handle payroll. I couldn't do this. What was Chuck thinking, putting me in charge of his bar?

"Yes, you, Adam. You can do it. And I'm only a phone call away if you need me. I don't know how long I'll be out, but I need your help. And I don't want it to be temporarily while I'm away. I want to make you my partner."

"I don't have any money to be a partner."

"Stop it, Adam. You just ran around the city fighting crime for the last few days. You put yourself in harm's way countless times. You helped Shane stop O'Brian." He pointed at me. "*You* did that. And if you can handle everything you just went through, you can handle running a business. Sure, it's clearly two different things, one *hopefully* being less violent. I've seen you grow since as you've embraced your ability and been working with Shane. You need to work. Here it is. Don't argue with me about it. Just accept it and be grateful you've got a friend like me who has your back."

I smirked. "Someone is a little full of themselves, aren't they?"

"Shut up, Adam, and just say you'll do it."

"You'll do it."

"You know what I mean. Tell me you'll take the job."

I couldn't say no to Chuck. He'd been there for me for so long. And even after everything I'd gotten myself into by leading Patrick to the bar and Chuck getting shot, he'd still stuck by my side. He was a good friend. He had my back and it was time to have his. I had to do this for him. I *would* do it for him.

"Alright, I'll do it. But expect a lot of phone calls, because I know nothing about running a bar."

Chuck smiled. "Thanks, Adam. And don't worry, I'll help you every step of the way."

I approached him and patted his shoulder gently. "Thanks, man. I appreciate it."

We talked for a while longer before parting ways. I met Shane outside and we headed to the car.

"Everything alright in there?" he asked.

I held up the keys. "He gave me the keys to his bar."

"Hopefully not to drink him out of business."

"No, smart-ass. He wants me to help him run it while he's out."

"That's awesome. Congratulations."

Shane seemed genuinely excited for me. Until now, the only person to show any kind of positive emotion towards me was Chuck. It felt good being as close to Shane as I was now. I had found my brother. I couldn't get much closer than this. Although, we had a lot of catching up to do.

As we drove away from the hospital, I asked, "So where are we going?"

"I told you it was a surprise," he said.

We reminisced about our different childhoods, our time in school, our hobbies, the trouble we both got into when we were kids. It made me realize I'd missed a lot during my childhood. I would have loved to have had a brother growing up. Instead, I was basically given roommates. There was no relationship with the families I stayed with. I was just a troubled child with an ability no one understood. But everything I had been through had led me here. My brother had found me and I found a piece of my true family.

We pulled up to a house, and Shane turned off the engine. I looked around in confusion.

"Where are we?" I asked, looking out the passenger window.

"Home," he said. "You were probably too young to remember, but this is the house I was raised in. You spent a brief time here as a baby."

I was taken aback. I had no memory of this place, but I felt comfort finally knowing where I had come from, and knowing this was the house my brother lived in. I couldn't believe any of this was happening. All my life, I had had no idea about my past. All I knew were my foster families. And all of them abandoned me. I didn't know if I had any blood siblings. I didn't know who my actual parents were. After everything I had gone through as a child, I'd just assumed I'd never figure it out.

"What are we doing here now?" I asked, still staring out the window.

"Taking you to meet Mom and Dad," Shane said. He opened the car door and stepped outside.

"Wait, what?" I opened the door and jumped out. "They're here? In there?" I said, pointing to the house.

"Yup. Come on, let's go," Shane said, waving me on to follow him.

I followed him up to the house. My heart raced and my stomach was in knots. I was about to meet my parents. I couldn't tell if I was more scared of this than the dangerous incidents I found myself involved in over the last few days.

For the longest time, I didn't really care to find my parents or meet them. They'd abandoned me just like everyone else. But being here now, having my brother with me, changed everything.

"Hold on, wait a second," I told Shane as we approached the front door. "Do they know about me? Do they know you've brought me here?"

He nodded. "They do. And they're just as excited and nervous as you are. They know about your ability and they know you're about to walk through that door and back into their lives any moment now."

I took a deep breath and exhaled. I was about to meet my parents. Honestly, as nervous as I was, I couldn't wait to meet them.

"Ready?" Shane asked.

"Ready," I told him.

Shane put his keys in the lock, unlocked the front door, and stepped inside. I stared at the open door for a moment. A thousand thoughts quickly raced through my head, but only one made sense. It was time to meet my parents.

I walked inside and shut the door behind me.

Epilogue

One Week Later

Shane sat alone in his apartment, staring at the pictures on his office desk. He began placing them on his wall, connecting all the articles, all the little post-it notes, every piece of information.

He took a step back and stared at the web of pictures and information. He had a theory, and it was the only one that made sense. All his investigating and documenting had led him to the answer he was looking for.

He grabbed his gun and secured it in the holster on his hip. He placed his police badge in his pocket and then picked up his backpack full of supplies—just in case. It contained extra magazines for his handgun, a GoPro camera for surveillance, a face mask, a water bottle and a medical supply kit. He threw the backpack over his shoulder and, with one last look at the wall, left his office and closed the door.

At the front door of his apartment, he took one last look around, making sure he had everything he needed.

He murmured to himself, rattling off everything he needed. Once he was done, he nodded, opened the door, and left his apartment.

Shane reached his car and tossed the backpack onto the passenger seat—nobody would sit there, anyway.

He drove in silence, wanting to be alone with his thoughts. How would he handle this situation? What if he became violent if he saw

Shane? What if who Shane was after, threatened him? What if he wasn't there when Shane showed up?

All questions he needed to have answered before he arrived. Shane just didn't know if he had the answers to them yet. He hoped he'd come up with something on the drive over.

He passed Chuck's bar. It reminded him he needed to call Adam later. He hoped Adam's first day had gone well.

Just days ago, their family had become complete again. Adam had met his mom and dad for the first time since the adoption. It was a joyful reunion. Shane was glad to have finally found his brother. He was even more proud to have brought him back to his mom and dad.

His parents had eventually grown to regret their decision to give Adam away, but they had to stand by it. How could a parent give up their son for adoption only to turn around and ask for the child back? Maybe it had happened before. It wasn't up to Shane to figure that out now. It was all in the past. What mattered now was that they were a family again.

Shane reached the bridge where Patrick had first escaped. They had repaired a lot of the damage in a short amount of time. It wasn't all done, but it was close.

He looked at his GPS, which told him he had six more minutes to drive. He was almost there, and he hadn't come up with any answers to any of his questions. At this point, he was as prepared as he could be. He'd just wing it from here.

The GPS brought him into a neighborhood. He entered the first street. The houses were big and far apart from one another. This was a pleasant neighborhood.

He turned right, and at the third house he came to a stop out front. He sat there, staring out the window.

Was he home? he thought.

Shane got out of his car, swung his backpack over his shoulder, and began to walk down the sidewalk, still staring at the house. He made it to the driveway and approached the front.

He peeked inside the first window. Inside looked like a dining room. There was a large, rectangle table in the center of the room with six chairs surrounding it. He saw no one inside.

He made his way to the front door and looked through the little glass window to one side of it. He could see an empty hallway which led into what looked like a kitchen with a small round table with two chairs on either side. There was a counter to the left of the table, and behind it was a sliding door, which must have led to a backyard.

He jiggled the doorknob. It was locked. Shane assumed it would be, but he had to check anyway. He turned towards the street to make sure no one was watching him. Satisfied, he continued his search.

He stepped off the walkway and onto the grass at the side of the house. As he passed another window, he looked inside.

It was a living room. There was a sofa, a fireplace and a television. There were some photographs on the wall, but he couldn't quite see them to recognize anyone in them. He backed away from the window and moved on.

The house appeared empty. Shane was beginning to think no one was home. He thought about calling Officer McKenzie and asking her to help him break in, but then thought better of it. This investigation was completely off the books. No one knew what he was doing. No one knew he was even here. This was something he was doing on his own.

Shane made his way to the rear of the house, where there was a small patio with a shed. The yard appeared as if it had just been installed, with lines showing where the patches of grass had been lined up.

Why would someone redo their yard like this? Did all the grass die? Was something buried here? Maybe some*one*?

Shane didn't have time to dig up the yard. He took out his phone, took a picture, and then moved on.

He walked to the patio and checked to see if the door was open. Of course, it was locked. He peeked inside, but all he saw was a reverse image of the interior he'd seen when he looked through the front of the house.

Next, he made his way to what looked like a shed. It seemed a little bigger than a shed, though. He placed his hand on the cold metal frame, then brought it back to his side.

Who has a metal shed? he thought.

It almost looked like a bomb shelter—a sophisticated one at that. Maybe it *was* a bomb shelter. A bomb had just gone off recently, after all.

Beside the door was a touchpad. Shane touched it and the screen flickered to life to display a keypad.

Who has a metal shed and locks it with this kind of security?

He thought about trying a combination, but he didn't know what would happen if he input the incorrect numbers. Would nothing happen? Would an alarm go off?

He took his phone out again and took a picture of the keypad, then continued on his way.

Returning to the driveway, he approached the garage doors, and tried to lift them up. They were locked.

Shane huffed, feeling disappointed that he had found nothing. He decided to head back to his car and simply watch the house from further along the street. Maybe he would see something. Maybe he would get a better idea about this guy.

As he walked down the driveway, he felt the ground rumble.

What is that? An earthquake?

He knelt on the ground, feeling it with his hand. It felt like the chugging of a motor. Something was moving underground.

Suddenly, part of the yard shifted. Shane unclipped his holster and took out his gun. He held it in both hands by his side as he crept towards the source of the movement. As he walked closer, he saw the ground drop away. A dark hole appeared before him.

What is going on here?

Shane walked closer, keeping his gun ready by his side. An engine noise stopped him in his tracks.

Is there a car in that hole? What's down there? Is he down there?

The engine revved several times. It got louder. And louder.

Then a motorcycle appeared suddenly in front of Shane. It just popped out of the black hole in the yard, then skidded to a stop.

It was a black motorcycle. The person riding it wore a dark jacket with a silver hood over his head. Shane couldn't see his face, but he knew who he was. Instantly, he lifted his gun and aimed. His heart was racing. Adrenaline was pumping through his body. All of his research and time spent investigating every little detail had finally paid off. The web of information he'd created on his wall had led him to exactly where he needed to be. Shane was proud of himself. He'd tracked down the vigilante down and figured out exactly who he was.

Shane held up the gun. "Police, don't move!"

He aimed it directly at the vigilante. Shane had him right where he wanted him.

He stared at the stranger, trying to see beyond the silver hood.

For a moment, they both froze.

Shane was the first to speak.

"Hello, Devin."